The Wedding Girls

Kate Thompson is a journalist with twenty years' experience as a writer for the broadsheets and women's weekly magazines. She is now freelance, and as well as writing for newspapers she's also a seasoned ghostwriter. *The Wedding Girls* is her third novel, following the *Sunday Times* bestseller *Secrets of the Singer Girls* and *Secrets of the Sewing Bee*.

Praise for *Secrets of the Singer Girls* and *Secrets of the Sewing Bee:*

'I've re-discovered my passion for reading.
It feels as though I'm catching up on lost time!'
Anita Dobson, actress

'We love this nostalgic read with friendship at its heart'
Take a Break magazine

'Hair-raising and gripping'
Daily Mail

D0231315

The Wedding Girls

Kate Thompson

PAN BOOKS

First published in 2017 by Pan
an imprint of Pan Macmillan
20 New Wharf Road, London N1 9RR
Associated companies throughout the world
www.panmacmillan.com

ISBN 978-1-5098-2223-2

1 3 5 7 9 8 6 4 2

A CIP catalogue record for this book is available from the British Library.

Typeset by Palimpsest Book Production Limited, Falkirk, Stirlingshire
Printed and bound by CPI Group (UK) Ltd, Croydon, CR0 4YY

Visit www.panmacmillan.com to read more about all our books
and to buy them. You will also find features, author interviews and
news of any author events, and you can sign up for e-newsletters
so that you're always first to hear about our new releases.

To Mum and Dad,
for planting the kernel of an idea for this story
and for their unstinting love and support.

Married when the year is new,
he'll be loving, kind and true.

When February birds do mate,
you wed nor dread your fate.

If you wed when March winds blow,
joy and sorrow both you'll know.

Marry in April when you can,
joy for maiden and for man.

Marry in the month of May,
and you'll surely rue the day.

Marry when June roses grow,
over land and sea you'll go.

Those who in July do wed,
must labour for their daily bread.

Whoever wed in August be,
many a change is sure to see.

Marry in September's shine,
your living will be rich and fine.

If in October you do marry,
love will come but riches tarry.

If you wed in bleak November,
only joys will come, remember.

When December snows fall fast,
marry and true love will last.

Prologue

St Margaret's Church, Westminster, London

A fine frost covered the churchyard in a glittering blanket of silver as the first flecks of snow began to drift from an ivory sky.

To some, January might have been a queer month in which to tie the knot, but to Kitty Moloney it was perfect.

Married when the year is new, he'll be loving, kind and true, or so went the old rhyme. The bride, Miss Nancy Beaton, would enter the church, but she would emerge, quite transformed, as Lady Smiley, wife of Sir Hugh Smiley, a Grenadier Guards officer and baronet. There was something irresistibly romantic about starting the New Year with a new name, especially one as grand as that, Kitty thought.

Stamping her frozen feet on the flagstones to keep out the cold, she tried her hardest to nudge her way to the front of the crowd for a better view, but it was impossible. Everyone loved a wedding, and no one could resist the sight of a bride, especially a well-known society one such as Nancy.

Kitty was hemmed in on all sides by stout matrons in damp wool coats, all clamouring for the best spot from which to view the bride enter the church.

A whiskered constable was holding back the crowds, a disapproving figure in black, his cloak spread wide like a bat, with the Palace of Westminster arching up into the skies over his helmet.

'Mind yourself, girlie,' tutted the woman in front; a dress-maker, judging by the sketchbook and pencil in her hand. 'Us hoi polloi gotta keep a respectable distance.'

Kitty felt foolish. Her gaze slid down and a flush of pink washed over her pale cheeks. What was she even doing here? She was just a girl from the wrong side of town, a shabby fourteen-year-old in cardboard-patched boots and her big sister's hand-me-downs. And then she remembered. She *was* somebody. In five days' time, she was to start an appren-ticeship under the tutelage of wedding dressmaker Gladys Tingle at her Bethnal Green workshop.

Gladys's voice when she had hired Kitty while she was still at school, not two and twenty days previous, rang through her mind as clear as a bell in the chilly churchyard.

'If a wedding marks the first day of the rest of your life, then the story starts with the dress. Immerse yourself in wedding gowns, my girl, leave no stitch unturned, 'cause it's the society sorts from up West that the girls from the East End wanna look like. It's pictures of their wedding gowns in the *Daily Sketch* they'll be bringing in for us to copy!'

After a brusque examination of Kitty's hands and nails, Gladys had dismissed her with orders to start at 9 a.m. prompt the first Monday morning after the new school term began.

A sudden burst of handclapping and the distant thud of horses' hooves brought Kitty back from her wonderings.

'I say! There she is,' called out an excited voice. 'God bless you, Nancy!'

Applause and cheers rang out and the crowd stirred into life. The dressmaker gasped and dropped her pencil. A small space opened up in the crowd as she bent to retrieve it. Seizing her chance, Kitty wriggled through the sea of stockinged legs and found herself at the very front.

She opened her eyes wide, then wider still and just like that, her grumbling tummy and frozen feet were forgotten. For gliding down the flagstones on the arm of her father was the bride, and what a marvellous bride was she!

Nancy emerged dreamlike from the snow, a tiny ethereal vision in a long sweep of buttery silk, its diaphanous overskirt shimmering with silver embroidery and hundreds of tiny pearls. In her pale fingers she clutched a spray of chalk-white flowers.

Kitty gazed in wonderment, for Nancy looked like no other woman she had ever seen: a perfect china shepherdess, her brown eyes large and liquid, her lips full and rosy. Atop her gleaming curls, tiny white flowers and a dusting of snow. In her wake, two pageboys in white satin breeches and tails, holding the train as if it were made of glass. In the swirling snow, looking like they had stepped straight from the pages of a children's fairy tale, they drew a collective sigh from the crowd of admiring matrons.

And then came the bridesmaids: tall, slender and serene in white tulle and taffeta. Kitty counted seven – no, wait, eight of them – and oh, how dreamy, how utterly dreamy. As they slid past like a bevy of swans, she realized they were all connected by a long continuous garland, smothered in snowdrops, which looped from one maid to the next like a maypole. Everywhere Kitty looked there was light, snow-white blossom: encircling slender waists and trailing over shoulders.

Kitty felt her heart turn over. It was a performance, a thrilling, spectacular show with a Snow Queen its star. She sighed deeply. If the walk to the church door could be *this* glamorous, Kitty could only guess how heavenly the interior of the church must look. How dashing the groom, how regal the guests, to what impossible height the ceiling must soar.

The bride was drawing closer now, so close Kitty could almost reach out and touch the hem of her ermine-trimmed gown. Instead, she gazed up at her with shining eyes and realized she was holding her breath.

Please look at me, Kitty from Bethnal Green. Notice me.

But the Snow Queen bride passed on by, poised and unreadable, leaving in her wake a scented trail of allure.

Kitty sagged and scuffed the toe of her boot on the ground. Who was she fooling? Girls like Nancy were born to glide on marble floors bedecked with roses. Girls like her were consigned to watch them from the damp darkness of the crowd, anonymous and unseen.

But as the bride reached the church porch, something magical happened. She turned. Flickered those large dark eyes over the crowd and settled on Kitty. A whisper of a smile, the flash of a diamond as she raised her hand. And then she was gone, stepping into the church, off to meet her glittering future, leaving Kitty as pale and faint as the January sky. Nothing could ever come close to the lavish, romantic dream Kitty had witnessed.

As the crowd dispersed and she reluctantly began the long walk back to the narrow streets of the East End, Kitty made a vow in her secret heart. She wouldn't just be the wedding seamstress. One day, *she* would be the bride.

One

Valentine's Day

From out of the reddish gloom of the darkroom emerged a spellbinding image. Stella held her breath, as she always did, for there was a curious alchemy to this moment, as if her breath alone might disturb this delicate part of the process.

The surface of the clear liquid rippled as Herbie gently lifted the print from the processing tank with a pair of tongs.

'Here's our bonny bride,' the photographer smiled, relieved, as he lifted the image up and placed it in the drying cabinet, as proudly as if he were a physician who had just helped to deliver an infant into the world.

'Say, Herbie! She's a pocketbook Venus!' Stella breathed, transfixed, as she gazed at the image. Stella must have looked at hundreds, if not thousands, of photographs of brides over the years, but there was something captivating about this one. She had known eighteen–year–old milliner Doris Simpson was a beauty from the moment she and her beau

7

had first stepped into the photographic studio all those months ago, but seeing her now, smiling adoringly up at the face of her new husband, she was the very image of radiance.

Stella had never seen such spirit etched on the face of a new bride. It had been a wild and blustery day yesterday when Stella and Herbie had stood shivering on the steps outside Christ Church on the Isle of Dogs, to photograph the newlyweds. The wind whipping off the docks had sent the bride's veil billowing around her face as a shower of green leaves spiralled down from the trees above and cascaded over the couple like confetti.

It had been a simple wedding, the bride clutching a tiny bouquet of red carnations and maidenhair fern, her green eyes sparkling under a headdress of orange blossom, attended by two skittish bridesmaids in apricot satin. There had only been time for a few photographs on the church steps, none of the usual elaborate family formations Herbie would have preferred, before the wedding party retired to the bride's mother's for a buffet and a knees-up. Stella knew the married couple didn't have two ha'pennies to rub together and had opted for the most basic wedding photography album their slender means would permit.

Doris's new husband was whispering something in her ear, his hand snaked around her twenty-two-inch waist drawing her close, and her head was thrown back in laughter. Hope and love were transformative. Stella knew that this day was the birth of their future life together.

'Gladdens your heart, don't it?' she grinned, unable to tear her eyes from the picture. 'I hope they choose to frame this one.'

'I dare say they will,' sighed Herbie. 'You'd think a bride

might want . . .' His voice trailed off, frustrated, as he stroked the ends of his small neat moustache in the hope it might conjure up the right words.

'. . . more formal pictorialism in a studio. A bride that beautiful – just think, Stella. I could have made her look like Ginger Rogers with the right lighting . . .'

With that, he gazed around his basement darkroom. To anyone else, the small room below the earth would be an oppressive place; icy-cold, dank and heavy with the cloying odour of chemicals. But to Herbie, it was his sanctuary. Glass-stoppered bottles of ammonia, ethyl, potassium cyanide, red prussiate of potash crystals and silver nitrate sat up on high, next to pots bulging with scalpels and paintbrushes. Racks of mounts and frames were neatly stacked according to size, and sitting in pride of place were three processing dishes.

It still seemed astonishing to Stella that through the application of chemicals – developer, stopper, fixer and washes – images could emerge. There was a physicality to it that never failed to thrill her.

'Hark at me, eh, Stella love?' Herbie smiled sadly. 'Whatever do I sound like? A real old fuddy-duddy.'

'Not at all, boss, but I know money's tight for the Simpsons. She'd have loved the full choral and floral, but they're saving every last penny. They're moving out to Dagenham soon as the ink's dry on the wedding certificate.'

'Really?' he exclaimed. 'Why this sudden exodus from the East End? Indoor plumbing will never replace the spirit of these streets. Mind you, I never was much good at change.'

His eyes flickered to a framed portrait of King Edward

VIII, just weeks into his reign, following the sudden death of his father.

'Out with the old and in with the new. I hear His Majesty's stepping out with a married woman. An American, would you believe? At it like a fiddler's elbow, according to Gladys next door.'

Tutting, he straightened the portrait and rubbed an imaginary smudge from the corner of the glass.

'I don't much care who's warming his bed sheets as long as he shows his face in the East End like his father did; cruised right through Stepney, he did, in an open landau. God rest his soul.'

Stella felt her heart go out to the elderly widower. Herbie Taylor, photographer – or in his words, commercial photographic artist – was the doyen of studio portraiture in Bethnal Green. The Jewish in neighbouring Whitechapel had Boris Bennett, and Poplar had William Whiffin. Bethnal Green had Herbie Taylor & Sons Photographic Portraiture, a longstanding family business, based proudly at number 224 Green Street, London E2.

In its day, there had been a Herbie Taylor & Sons on every major thoroughfare in all the East End districts, from Poplar to Shoreditch, five studios in all; there had even been talk of opening one up West! Herbie was a part of the fabric of the East End community, and there wasn't a family in Bethnal Green whose life he hadn't documented from the other side of his lens; from christenings to coming-of-age portraits, weddings and processions, to beauty queen contests and even last year's Silver Jubilee celebrations. But big East End weddings, photographed in his studio upstairs, were what Herbie loved best, and he poured his heart and soul into making every bride look the very best she could.

Herbie had photographed all the Cockney great and good, from costermongers to corset makers, local dignitaries to boxers. No matter that most of the families in this neighbourhood were so poor that Herbie's portraits more often as not covered a nasty patch of damp, or that people saved for years to afford it. To have a 'Herbie' on your wall was a badge of honour for the proud working-class folk of Bethnal Green.

Stella had felt blessed when Herbie had taken her on as a fourteen-year-old apprentice, straight from school in 1933, just as the Depression had crept in and taken a savage bite out of his business. She had watched helplessly as Herbie's fortunes had trickled away, and with it, most of his staff. One by one, the stores had closed, leaving only this one, his flagship shop on Green Street. Herbie had been forced to give up his grand house by Victoria Park and move into the stuffy attic rooms above the studio, but Stella suspected they didn't get much use. Her boss worked from eight in the morning until past midnight, six days a week, as if driven by a motor. Herbie was a good old-fashioned grafter, but deep down, she suspected he also worked to forget. Stella was seventeen, Herbie nearing sixty, so it had never seemed respectful to ask the widower what had happened to his wife and son all those years ago, but it didn't stop her wondering.

'Penny for 'em,' Herbie said as he shrugged off the brown coat he wore to protect his suit when developing photographs. Stella had never seen Herbie dressed in anything other than an immaculately cut dark suit, with sharp creases on the trousers. Only his slender fingertips, permanently stained a deep purply-black from the silver nitrate chemicals used in processing, revealed his profession.

'Nothing, boss,' she replied, stifling a yawn with the back of her wrist. They had been hard at work now for hours, developing glass-plate negatives from yesterday's wedding, as well as some official portraits of the unveiling of the newly refurbished People's Palace up at Mile End.

'Why don't you get off early, love?' Herbie remarked. 'We've got a big floral and choral number tomorrow, so we'll need to have our wits about us. If Winnie's finished clearing up upstairs, tell her to knock off an' all.'

Her boss fished about inside his waistcoat pocket and produced two brown packages.

'Extra half a crown in there for you both, but don't tell my bookkeeper,' he winked. That was half their problem, Stella mused. The loss of his other studios wasn't entirely down to the Depression. Goodness only knew how many half-crowns were handed out like this, how many jobs never quite settled in full.

'Herbie . . .' she protested, but her boss silenced her with a firm hand on her shoulder.

'I'll hear no more of it.'

'Thanks, boss,' she said fondly. 'Winnie and me are off to the baths and then the pictures to take in that new flick with Humphrey Bogart, so this'll come in handy. We'll see you bright and early.'

'That's my girl,' he replied, tweaking her chin, but as he did so his elbow dislodged some photographs stacked neatly on the side and they slid across the linoleum floor.

Stella bent down to retrieve them, but Herbie's voice, full of alarm, cut through the stillness of the darkroom.

'I'll get 'em, love.'

But it was too late. Stella stared, stunned, at the images in her hand, and shivered in the cold of the unheated darkroom.

Row upon row of men and women lying in hospital beds, all ages, their faces torn and scratched, torsos covered in ugly, dark bruises and limbs swaddled in bandages.

'Not for the eyes of a young lady,' said Herbie, deftly removing them from her hand. 'The police inspector's a friend, he asked me to go up to Bethnal Green Hospital and photograph these crime victims and tint their bruises purple, for their official records. Reckons they've had a flood of street muggings, but I can take a shrewd guess at who the perpetrators are.'

He sighed deeply. 'Never mind penal servitude, they want eighteen strokes with a cat-o'-nine-tails.'

'A street gang, you mean?'

'Something like that,' he muttered darkly.

Stella was taken aback at the brutality displayed in the photographs. Gangs were nothing new in East London, the Depression had been the perfect breeding ground for crime, but they never targeted innocent passers-by on the street, and certainly never women. She felt an uneasy sensation prickle up her backbone. Bethnal Green had always been such a safe place, but lately . . .

'Let me do it,' she insisted, squashing down her fears.

'You'll do no such thing, your mother'd skin me alive,' Herbie tutted. 'I don't even like doing it myself but, well, money's money these days and I can't turn down commissions, even if they are a bit grisly.'

'Well, only if you're sure . . .' Stella said.

'Quite sure,' he soothed. 'Now be on your way, a young

girl like you oughtn't be wasting her Friday night stuck down in a basement darkroom with an old relic like me.'

Stella lingered at the door, and smiled sadly at Herbie. She knew he would be down there for hours yet, drying, flattening, trimming, glazing and mounting Doris Simpson's wedding photos, so they would be ready to present to her tomorrow before she left for her honeymoon.

'Don't work too hard, Herbie. Even "old relics" need their rest,' she teased. 'I'm sure Doris shan't mind waiting a day or two. Which reminds me, has her father been in and settled the account yet?'

Herbie pushed the police photographs to one side and picked up the photo of Doris, captured at her happiest.

'All in good time, Stella,' he said vaguely, his kindly brown eyes shining. 'Besides, a little praise is of far more value.'

Pity praise didn't pay the rates, Stella thought.

'Very well,' she said instead, 'but please don't work too late.'

'What else am I going to do?' he shrugged. 'I've got no one waiting at home, have I? Cheerio, love. God bless.'

With that, he turned his attentions back to his beloved negatives and the darkness of the room seemed to swallow him whole.

*

Winnie glanced up from over the top of her cloth as she suspended her polishing of the studio's glass shopfront.

'Work on a ship, do you, Winnie Docker?' rang out a shrill voice. 'Come on, duckie, it's a window, not a bleedin' porthole! Get in them corners.'

Gladys winked to show she was teasing and, puffing like a steam train, the stout elderly lady settled down on her haunches and began to whiten the step of her shop so vigorously, her round little body wobbled like a jelly.

Winnie chuckled to herself. Gladys Tingle's cleaning was legendary in Green Street, no one could mark out their turf with a hearthstone quite like her. Of all the many shops that lined this busy thoroughfare, Gladys's small bridal gown workshop at number 226 shone the brightest. Her magnificent frontage put the other traders to shame. Tubby Jacobs, who ran the tobacconist a few doors along, had given up trying, but the old maid opposite, Miss Sugarman, who owned a milliner's, was in a state of perpetual one-upmanship with the wedding dress seamstress. Sure enough, not two seconds after Gladys had started to attack her front step, the milliner was out with her birch broom and pail, matching her ferocious cleaning efforts stroke for stroke.

This was one of the many reasons Winnie loved working in this popular Bethnal Green artery, which stretched half a mile long, linking Bethnal Green to Bow in the East, and the City of London in the West.

The banter was good-natured, though. There was a close affinity between Herbie, Gladys, Miss Sugarman and all the other tailors, milliners, corsetieres, haberdashers, hosiers, linen-drapers and dress-makers who operated their businesses from Green Street, and it was customary for business to flow between traders. In fact, a bride-to-be could just about get everything she needed from this vibrant, bustling street, from bouquets to rings and everything else besides.

Green Street was where every housewife in the vicinity

came to do her shopping in the stores and market stalls, but the daily task of buying bread was about so much more. Winnie never tired of the noise of their high-pitched chatter, mingling with the clattering of horses' hooves on the sooty cobbles, the rumble of handcarts and the background hum of trams.

Thanks to the shared plight of poverty, for the most part, everyone rubbed along quite nicely. Take Miss Sugarman over the way. Winnie had grown up running errands for her on the Sabbath and lighting her fires when her religion forbade it and, in return, Winnie would come home with a nice piece of fruit or a roll of pastry. Yiddish or Cockney, it didn't matter what tongue you spoke, as long as your first language was respect.

Winnie took in a deep breath of the choking air and sighed happily. Green Street might be situated in the heart of a great stinking, sprawling metropolis, but it had all the close-knit community of a village high street where your struggles were shared by all. She knew it was parochial to admit it, but Green Street was *her* street, *her* family, which Winnie reflected was just as well, given the state of her real family. She jumped as the door to number 222a, on the other side of Herbie's studio, slammed shut and a smartly dressed man emerged into the gathering dusk, lifting his trilby to Winnie and Gladys.

'Evening, ladies,' said the man, his toothbrush moustache twitching slightly.

Winnie's heart sank and she realized that if Green Street was a family, then the new occupants of number 222a were definitely the black sheep. A heavy cloud of fear had settled over the street when they had moved in last year, and already the much-predicted trouble had begun.

'Good evening, Mr MacNab,' Winnie replied politely. She loathed saying anything to the man, but her mother had brought her up not to be saucy to her elders. Gladys, on the other hand, had no such compunction and, glaring in his direction, she spat hard into the gutter, before angrily continuing her scrubbing.

The stranger's dark eyes stared back at them, fathomless beneath the brim of his trilby.

Why did she have to go and do that? Winnie felt her heart begin to thump and she shifted uncomfortably on the kerb-side.

'Goodnight,' he said crisply, as he turned abruptly and strode up the street.

'Yeah, goodnight and pleasant dreams to you an' all,' muttered Gladys, once he was out of earshot. 'Hope you get run over in 'em.'

They were saved from any further conversation on the awkward encounter when a steam hooter from the docks let out a hoarse shriek. Six o'clock.

The door to Herbie's studio opened and Stella poked her head out, her unruly pale blonde curls tucked under her trademark cheese-cutter flat cap. Winnie had to laugh. With her boyish physique and rakish grin, her friend Stella certainly cut an androgynous figure, not that she gave two hoots what other people thought of her.

'Oh, there you are, Win. Guv'nor says we can knock off and he's popped a bit extra in our pay packet, so let's get a wriggle on . . . Ooh hello, Glad, didn't see you down there. How you doing?'

'Hello, love. Mustn't grumble, all parts bearing an equal strain,' the older woman replied with a deep sigh of martyrdom. 'I expect you'll be wanting to take your Kitty with you.'

'If she's finished her work,' Stella replied with a hopeful grin.

'Yeah, I can let her knock off. She could do with letting her hair down, bless her. She's had a busy week finishing off all the last bits on that wedding for tomorrow; six brides-maids, the lady's got attending her. We've done our bit now. It's over to you tomorrow.'

'Oh, Herbie'll be ready,' Stella assured her. 'Once he's finished in the darkroom, I know he'll be up in that studio half the night preparing it.'

'I dare say,' sighed Gladys, hauling herself to her feet and dusting down her crossover apron. 'I'll fetch him up a bowl of soup. It ain't right, a widower living up there and fending for himself.' She looked back at her workshop door, just as Kitty emerged.

Kitty Moloney, Stella Smee and Winnie Docker were as different as oranges and apples, but inseparable since their school days in Bethnal Green. The trio had been brought up in the same buildings not five minutes' walk from Green Street, and even after Winnie had moved to Cable Street in neighbouring Stepney, the friendship had remained intact. In fact, it had been Stella who had persuaded Herbie to give Winnie a job as a receptionist, and with Kitty working right next door as an apprentice dressmaker under Gladys Tingle, the girls got to see each other every day.

'Look at'cha all,' sighed Gladys, folding her arms over

her ample bosom and standing back to admire the trio of friends. 'My beautiful Wedding Girls.'

Winnie chuckled and shook her head at Gladys's nickname for them. It was true, they did spend their days transforming women into beautiful brides but, ever the pragmatist, Winnie couldn't help but feel the biggest illusion was their own lives. The glamour and romance they created was in stark contrast to their fractured homes.

Winnie shook away the cloud of memories and forced a smile. What had happened in the past ought to remain there. Right now, it was a Friday evening, there was a wage packet burning a hole in her pocket and the prospect of a night with Humphrey Bogart ahead.

'Come on then, girls, time for a quick wash down at York Hall Baths then we can catch that new flick up at the bug 'ole.'

Kitty's pretty face fell as she untied her headscarf. 'I don't know, Win. I think me dad needs me back at home.'

'Aww, come on, Kitty,' urged Stella. 'I'm sure old Mrs Flood from next door will look in on him. Go on, it is Friday. You gotta let your hair down sometimes.'

Kitty shook her head and her long wavy auburn hair tumbled about her face. She really was the prettiest thing, Winnie reflected. A heart-shaped face framed eyes as bright and blue as forget-me-nots. Not only that, but she had a smashing figure with legs up to her armpits, a naturally indented waist and small rounded breasts. With her curves and child-bearing hips, Winnie felt like a galumphing great carthorse in comparison. Treacle, her boyfriend, was forever telling her she had a cracking figure, but what did he know? She felt a smidgen of guilt that she was spending Valentine's

Day with the girls and not him, but she had always been straight with him about where her loyalty lay. Friends first. Men second.

'Please, Kitty,' she pleaded. 'I threw Treacle over so I could spend the evening with you.'

'Very well, I'll come to the baths, but then I'll head home after that as Dad'll only fret,' Kitty replied. 'He's been going downhill fast since we lost Mum.'

'How are things at home?' Winnie asked cautiously. She and Stella both worried about Kitty since her mother had passed the previous year. Both of Kitty's older sisters worked in service, so the burden of caring for her frail father had fallen to her. Most nights Kitty scurried straight home after her shift to see to his tea, then help wash and get him to bed.

'Well, he gets muddled at times,' Kitty confessed.

'Don't we all, ducks. I forget to put me teeth in most mornings,' Gladys remarked. 'Teeth like stars, me.'

'How so, Gladys?' Kitty asked, puzzled.

'They come out at night,' Gladys replied with a great hoot of laughter. 'Now go on, you girls go and have some fun – and don't worry about your father, Kitty. Once I've taken Herbie's tea up, I'll drop some round to him and check he's comfy. Now, before you go, have you all got your hat pins?'

'Why?' Kitty asked.

'It's the pictures on a Friday night. There's bound to be some mucky men about.'

'Oh honestly, Glad,' Stella laughed. 'It's Bethnal Green, not Soho!'

'Safety first. Now go on, shoo,' grinned Gladys, untying her apron and sweeping the girls off down the street.

Giggling, the friends held their arms up in surrender before turning and walking in the direction of the baths.

Winnie threaded her arms through Kitty's and Stella's, and relished the feel of the fresh evening air tingling on her cheeks. The sun was like a red ball sinking in the misty, grey sky, burnishing the soot-coated shopfronts in a fiery glow. Market stalls covered with cheerful red rhubarb and oranges glowed under the hissing naphtha flares and braziers being lit as darkness descended along Green Street.

The air was soupy with smells: overripe fruit, manure, meat, asphalt and spices. You could buy anything at this time of the day, as the traders tried to get rid of their perishables. Winnie never tired of the sight of it all; Indians selling silk scarves by candlelight straight from the kerbside, patent medicine sellers pushing cures for all from glass bottles, a little old lady selling nothing but grated horse-radish and soused herring from a stool, and even pornography from a paper envelope, if you knew the right side street to duck down.

Dodging the flow of human traffic and the odd auto-mobile, Winnie got a sudden whiff of something warm and sweet in her nostrils and spied an Indian Toffee man straight off the boat, selling his wares by the ounce from a rolled-up paper cone.

'I'm famished,' she announced. 'Once we've washed the week away, who wants to go for some pease pudding and saveloy before the picture starts?'

'Sounds good,' Stella agreed, 'but I reckon someone might have other plans for you.' She nodded in the direction of the Salmon and Ball public house, at the junction of Green Street and Cambridge Heath Road.

Winnie squinted her eyes into the smoky evening air and spotted her boyfriend, Treacle, standing outside the pub with an air of quiet triumph, clutching a white bundle in his hands.

'Oh, blimey,' she groaned. 'I told him I don't want anything to do with all that Valentine's Day malarkey. It's a load of old guff.'

'Don't give him a hard time, Win,' Kitty scolded. 'I think it's ever so romantic.'

As they drew near and Treacle spotted them, his grin stretched wider over his handsome face. Standing at over six feet tall, with intense brown glittering eyes, nineteen-year-old stevedore Treacle was a man confident of his place in the world, and that place was either unloading cargo at East India Docks or by Winnie's side. When he wasn't there, he was usually to be found knee-deep in mud and slime, scouring the silted banks of the Thames foreshore. 'Mudlarking' Treacle called it. Winnie had a few other choice names for it.

Treacle's real name was Michael Brody; as was the case with so many East End nicknames, no one, least of all him, seemed to be too sure where 'Treacle' had come from.

''Ere, what's the big idea?' Winnie called out. 'I told you I was spending tonight with Kitty and Stella.'

'I know, Win, but I couldn't help myself,' Treacle grinned sheepishly. 'Be my Valentine?'

His eyes shone as he carefully unfolded a grubby handkerchief and offered it to her.

The girls all craned their necks to take a look.

'What is it, Treacle?' asked Stella.

'Looks like a load of old muck to me,' Winnie remarked.

'Not muck,' Treacle said as he wiped down the objects with a mud-stained finger. 'Magic!'

As he rubbed the surface, the objects revealed themselves.

'That's a bit of Bellarmine jug,' he said excitedly, 'that there is Tudor pottery, and look! A complete clay pipe! But this . . . this is what I wanted to give to you for Valentine's, Win.'

'What, that?' Winnie asked, prodding a smaller object buried at the bottom.

'No, not that – that's a horse's tooth.'

Winnie whipped her hand away. 'Urgh! Now I'll definitely need to get down the baths.'

'This,' he breathed, presenting her with a crooked silver coin, engraved with two entwined initials. 'It's Georgian, been buried for centuries in the mud. Do you know, Thames mud has no oxygen so it preserves whatever it conceals?'

'You don't say?' quipped Winnie.

Treacle pressed the coin into her hand, his fingertips warm against the flesh of her palm. He smelt of oil and his strong jawline was smeared with grime.

'Look, Win, it's even pierced so it could be worn round the neck. They were given as lovers' tokens on Valentine's Day, back then, and well, now I'd like it to have its final resting place with you . . .' Treacle faltered, '. . . as a token of my love . . .'

'Thank you, Treacle,' Winnie mumbled, unsure what to say next.

'It's a rare find,' he went on, eyes glowing intensely. 'Like you.'

'Oh, Treacle,' Kitty sighed. 'That's so much more romantic than a card! Have you got a brother?'

Winnie was grateful for the interruption, as they all burst out laughing.

'Before I go and clean myself up,' Treacle said, taking Winnie's hand in his and folding her palm safely over the coin, 'when can I see you next? Tomorrow?'

'I'm working in the day. Remember, I told you we're photographing a big wedding?' she replied, glancing up at the clock face on the church opposite. 'Look here, we really must get going, or we'll miss the start of the picture.'

'The evening then?' Treacle went on, jokingly getting down on bended knee on the cobbles.

'Get up, you silly sod,' she giggled, shaking her head. 'Tomorrow evening, then. Mum's taking my sisters away for a little holiday. So we'll have the place to ourselves.'

'I'm holding you to that,' he said. 'Don't be throwing me over neither, 'cause I've got something important to ask you and it shan't keep.'

Treacle smiled enigmatically and then he was gone, bounding up the dark street, his long legs easily outpacing the rest of the pedestrians as he dodged past the newspaper sellers and street hawkers.

Winnie could feel the girls' eyes burning holes into her cheeks.

'Don't start,' she began.

'As I live and breathe, he's only going to propose to you, Winnie Docker!' Kitty gushed, clutching her elbow. 'Oh, you lucky devil. You'll be the talk of the tenements!'

'You're being a bit previous, ain't yer, Kitty?' Winnie warned. 'Even if he were to ask for my hand in marriage, what would we live on? Fresh air? We need money, not ancient artefacts to survive. As sweet as this is,' she said, holding up Treacle's love token, 'it ain't gonna satisfy the rent collector.'

'Yeah, believe it or not, marriage ain't the summit of all women's ambitions,' Stella interjected.

'Hark at Phileas Fogg here,' Kitty teased.

Winnie laughed. Tomboy Stella made no secret of her ambition to travel the world. Even as a child growing up in their tenements, she'd sensed that Stella would never be satisfied with the narrow East End streets and her horizons stretched further than the bells of Bow.

'Maybe Winnie'd like to carry on working, see something of the world before she saddles herself with a load of kids and a demanding husband,' Stella protested, fishing a Craven A from under her cap and lighting it. 'After all, what's wrong with women working? During the war, my mum actually had a job in the print. They had equal rights of a sort and now she's housebound again, a slave to the washtub.'

'Oh, here we go,' groaned Kitty, rolling her eyes. 'Marriage is a great institution, Stell.'

'Yeah, but in the words of Mae West, I ain't ready for an institution. I want to be like my heroines,' Stella insisted, drawing heavily on her cigarette and blowing a long stream of blue smoke into the air, 'women like Emmeline Pankhurst, Amy Johnson . . .'

'That's all well and good, but look around you,' Kitty urged. 'The streets are filled with spinsters, thanks to the war. Do you really want to end up as an ageing aunt?'

'If it means I get to keep my freedom and see something

of the world,' Stella insisted bluntly. 'I'd sooner wear a saddle than a solitaire!'

'You better not let Herbie or Gladys hear you talk like that,' Kitty warned.

'All right, keep your wig on, girls! Look, even if Treacle were to propose – which he's not,' Winnie said diplomatically, 'you know I don't believe in marriage. Look at my mum, what did it do for her?'

The girls fell silent.

'Do you honestly believe a piece of paper can hold a man's love?' Winnie went on, her eyes boring into Kitty's.

'Treacle is not your father, Winnie,' Kitty whispered.

From nowhere, Winnie felt hot tears prick her eyes.

'Come on,' Stella said, mashing out her cigarette on the kerb. 'Enough of this talk. Bloody Valentine's Day, I ask you! Let's get going. My feet are killing me and I'm dying for a hot bath.'

As they walked, the number of people on the streets seemed to grow. So absorbed had they been in their conversation, the girls had scarcely noticed the gathering crowds, or the traffic grinding to a halt. Suddenly a surge of people crowded around the busy intersection, blocking their path.

In alarm, Winnie spotted men laying out soapboxes outside the pub and thrusting leaflets into the hands of passers-by. Three black loudspeaker vans were parked at strategic points nearby. Two police omnibuses screeched to a halt and uniformed officers clutching whistles and truncheons disgorged onto the street, forming a wide circle – with the girls trapped inside.

'Oh, bleedin' hell, how did we get ourselves caught up

with this lousy mob?' Winnie muttered, threading her arms protectively through Stella's and Kitty's.

In a heartbeat, the atmosphere on the streets grew electric and Winnie felt the crowd stiffen.

'Brace yourself. They're coming!' yelled a man in a baggy blue serge suit standing next to her.

'What's happening?' Kitty panicked. Her fingers gripped tight onto Winnie's arm. 'Oh, I knew I ought to have gone home to Dad.'

'Listen,' Stella blurted.

It was the sound of feet. Faint to begin with, then growing ever stronger. Hundreds of pairs of jackboots ringing on the cobbles. Then came the deep and rhythmic boom, boom, boom of a drum, beating so loudly, it drew Winnie out by the roots. The roar from the crowd rose up like a wave: shouts, jeers, hoots and hisses filling the evening air.

And then she saw them, looking like an army marching into battle. Column after column of young men and women, all dressed identically in pristine black uniforms and peaked black caps, goose-stepping up Green Street.

'Blackshirts,' murmured Stella.

'Quick, let's get out of here,' Winnie urged, eyeing the crowds as they poured from the side streets.

'How?' asked Stella. 'We're packed in like sardines.'

Stella was right, they were crushed up against a solid wall of bodies. Escape was impossible, and Winnie felt her heart sink.

'Bloody rabble . . . Smashed my mum's windows, they did,' spat the man the other side of her. 'And look, here comes one of their crowned leaders. Might have known, no show without Punch!'

Winnie rose up on her tiptoes and, over the heads of the crowd, she saw a black van pull to a halt next to the other loudspeaker vans. There was a brief loaded silence and an eerie reverberation of the speakers then, quite suddenly, a man appeared on the roof of the van, like a villain coming up through a pantomime trap. Winnie stared, transfixed.

Framed by the setting sun, he cut an impressive figure, dressed in a military-cut jacket and riding breeches, his belt and buckles gleaming, and wearing a brassard of white and blue, shot through with a streak of forked lightning.

A spotlight bathed his face in light, showing off a deep scar that zigzagged across his right cheek, from his earlobe to the corner of his mouth. Winnie shivered, but despite her unease, she was forced to concede that there was something quite magnetic about his face.

'William Joyce, in the heart of the East End,' muttered the blue-suited man, fists clenching into balls.

'Who is he?' Stella gaped.

'He's Oswald Mosley's right-hand man and a more poisonous fascist you'd be hard pressed to meet,' the stranger spat with vitriol. 'This is a bad day for democracy.'

Joyce raised his arm in fascist salute and hundreds of black-shirted arms clustered around the vans answered his salute, and even, to Winnie's horror, a shop owner she recognized from Green Street.

'Long live the blackshirts,' cried his followers. Winnie glanced behind her and spotted cameramen and reporters clinging to the railings outside the church taking photos and scribbling shorthand notes.

'Wouldn't fancy coming across him on my own on a dark night,' Winnie grimaced.

'You've got to admit, he knows how to hold a crowd,' Kitty remarked, wriggling slightly to free her shoulder.

Winnie bristled with anger.

'Look at him,' she spat, irritated that their plans for the evening had been scuppered. 'Acts like all the lights of Piccadilly shine out his arse.'

'Ever so smartly turned out though, ain't he?' Kitty murmured.

Trust gentle Kitty to try to see the good even in a rotten fascist. 'You can't tell a sausage by its skin, Kitty,' Winnie said. 'Trust me, I know this lot are gonna bring trouble.'

Only Stella remained silent, glaring at the fascist speaker with a queer expression on her face, her arm rigid against Winnie's.

'You all right, Stell?' Winnie asked.

'Yeah,' she muttered. 'Look who's standing next to him.'

Winnie squinted her eyes and picked out the face of their neighbour on Green Street, Mr MacNab, proudly flanking his leader on the roof of the van. If he had been affronted by Gladys's frosty reception earlier, he certainly didn't show it now, his arm raised in salute to his superior.

Winnie felt a jolt of shock. Not that she should be surprised. Ever since the shop next door to Herbie's studio had changed from the London Unemployed Association to the darker association of the Bethnal Green branch of the British Union of Fascists, she had known it would only be a matter of time before they had a visit from one of their top brass.

Mr MacNab was the area's local District Leader and insisted on weekly marches and outlandish open-air meetings, all designed to inflame tensions and stir up trouble in the neighbourhood. Up until now, they had all ignored it, but it looked as if that was going to be harder to do from here on.

William Joyce's magnified voice cut through the crowd.

'Men and women of Bethnal Green, you are entitled to live as human beings and not as companions of every type of vermin that gather where filth and squalor are rampant . . .'

His powerful speaking voice was mesmeric yet sinister, and the crowd stirred, volatile and tense. The twin spectres of mass unemployment and poverty loomed like a vast dark cloud over the East End. Winnie could feel the threat of violence pulsing in the air. She watched, agog, as Joyce continued with his forceful oratory.

'It's time to reclaim our territories.' Warming to his theme, he threw his arm aloft against the blood-red sunset. 'Jews are Oriental sub-men . . . an incredible species of sub-humanity.'

Winnie's mouth dropped open in shock as a roar of indignation rose from the crowd.

'Sub-humanity?' said Kitty, confused.

'What is this rubbish?' Winnie gasped.

'Oh, you wait, lovey, it'll get worse,' piped up a woman standing nearby. 'Bleedin' rabble-rouser.'

'Get out of here!' roared an enraged voice from behind Winnie. 'Before you goose-step us straight into another war.'

'We don't care for your opinions!' yelled another angry heckler. 'Shove off and leave our manor in peace.'

With that, he took off his shoe and hurled it in the direction of the van.

Some things in life are inevitable. As Winnie watched the shoe sail through the air in a perfect arc, she knew that single action would be enough to spark all-out chaos. It struck Mr MacNab square on the nose. It was as if a switch had been flicked and pandemonium broke out around them. Black arms shot out and wrenched the hecklers to the ground.

Kitty screamed as the sickening crunch of cracking jawbones filled the air. Herds of black-shirted men piled into the crowd, sending people crashing like skittles, and fists flew.

Everything seemed to go into slow motion as Winnie saw Stella's cap knocked to the ground. Kitty's mouth was frozen open in a scream.

A thud hit her in the back with such force, Winnie felt the breath leave her body as she hurtled to the floor. The shouts and shrilling of police whistles was deafening as she crawled through the scrummage of stamping boots.

'Winnie, where are you?' screamed Stella's voice from somewhere up above.

'Help,' she whimpered. The terrible thought dawned on her that she could be trampled to death down here.

Suddenly, a strong pair of arms reached down, hooked under her armpits and plucked her to safety. The crowd was a blur of writhing, flailing bodies and, frantically, she tried to suck in oxygen.

'It's all right, Win, close your eyes, breathe!' ordered a deep male voice and, weak as a lamb, she allowed her head to slump against his chest. She felt the man's body bump and rock as the crowd surged around him, but he stood his ground.

'You're going to be all right,' Treacle soothed, clutching her trembling body close to his chest.

'Treacle! Where did you come from?'

'When I saw the march coming I knew I had to come back and get you. I had a hell of a job getting through that crowd, mind. I managed to get Kitty and Stella over to the church steps.'

Winnie allowed him to guide her through the chaos towards the safety of the church. The brawling and bedlam continued and, to her alarm, she spotted the heckler being bundled into the back of a Black Maria by two officers. A second later, a crash rocked the van, and a blood-curdling scream rang out from the inside. Over it all, Joyce continued to speak, undeterred by the violence breaking out beneath him.

'My coin!' Winnie cried, skidding to a halt and patting her coat. 'It's not in my pocket no more, it must've been knocked out when I fell. Oh, Treacle, I'm sorry.'

'Don't worry about that, Win,' Treacle replied. 'You're safe. That's all that matters. Now come on. Quickly. I want to get you all home.'

Two

By the time Treacle had escorted first Winnie, then Stella and Kitty home, darkness had bled in over the chimney pots of Bethnal Green.

Kitty paused at the bottom of the stairwell and turned to Treacle.

'What a night! You get off and see Stella to her door. I'll be fine from here.'

His face, lit by the glow of a gas-jet, melted into concern. 'You sure, Kitty? I promised Win I'd see you right to your door.'

'Honestly, Treacle,' she said, smothering a yawn.

'Very well, night-night sweetheart, mind how you go.'

'Night-night darlin',' Stella said, popping a kiss on her cheek. 'Sleep tight.'

'I will,' Kitty replied gratefully.

As she walked alone in the flickering darkness, the quiet after the earlier crowds was deafening, save for a lone dog barking in the empty courtyard outside. Kitty paused and watched Treacle disappear up the stairwell after Stella, his broad shoulders hunched against the cutting wind. What she wouldn't give to know the love of a decent man like that; Winnie didn't know how lucky she was to have his heart. She would gratefully take his crooked penny any day. How she hoped her dear friend wouldn't throw someone so precious over, just because of what had gone before.

Then another thought cut through her swirling mind. How could she ever bring a fella like Treacle back to her home? Kitty was too embarrassed to have Treacle see her to her door, much less a suitor!

She glanced around her neighbourhood and felt the familiar shame engulf her.

Kitty and Stella's buildings were situated on a grimy byway sandwiched next to a railway viaduct. The brick facade was blackened by smoke and smuts from passing steam trains, which rattled the bedknobs as they thundered past. At the end of the street, an industrial factory chimney pumped out clouds of noxious vapours into a thickening yellow smog.

Stella joked she and her mum lived in luxury as they had a larger flat two floors up with four whole rooms between them. Kitty and her elderly father had to make do with two tiny rooms at ground level.

The wall outside their landing had a perpetual dirty tidemark about hip level where local men were in the habit of standing as they smoked their pipes, and the mortar below was crumbling with kick marks. The toilet was on the landing and shared with four other families. The sour smell of it stung Kitty's eyelids as she walked past. Its broken door hung on one hinge, creaking and banging in the cold wind.

Thank goodness for the old widow Mrs Flood, their neighbour and the local matriarch, known to all as simply 'Auntie'. It was Auntie who insisted they all have a twice-yearly smoke-out to control the bugs, she who hounded the tenant landlords to come and make repairs. More importantly, *her* strict values which encouraged everyone to keep their standards up and their heads held high. 'That woman's got curtains round her keyhole,' so the affectionate saying went. Not that anyone dared say it to her face, mind you.

Mrs Flood was not a woman to be trifled with, as her six sons knew all too well. But despite her formidable personality, she was kindness itself. Kitty was forever coming home to find her windows cleaned, a warm loaf wrapped in a tea towel on the side and her father's chamber pot emptied.

Just then, Mrs Flood's door swung open and Kitty found herself face to face with the lady herself.

Kitty smiled as she gazed fondly up at her neighbour. Auntie was always dressed in a black, ankle-skimming dress and black button-down boots and was never seen without her trademark black hat, complete with a black feather stuck defiantly on the top. She carried herself bolt upright and cut a striking, proud figure amongst the gloom of the tenements.

'Hello, Auntie,' Kitty said, greeting the older woman warmly. 'You ought to have seen the trouble outside the Salmon and Ball this evening, it didn't half . . .'

'Never mind about that,' she said, lowering her voice and gently pulling Kitty into her doorway.

'Your Gladys popped around earlier with some soup for your dad, but the door was wedged shut. So together we forced it, and well, I'm sorry, love, but your dad was taken ill, he'd gone over by the doorway.'

'Oh no, where is he? Hospital? Oh, why wasn't I here?' Kitty cried. 'I must go to him.'

'Get a hold of yourself, my girl,' Mrs Flood ordered, gripping her firmly by the shoulders. 'He's all right. I sent my boy to fetch Dr Garfinkle. Doctor's in there with him now. I just wanted to warn you.'

'Thanks, Auntie,' Kitty cried.

Hastening through the front door, she made her way into the small room she shared with her father, tripping on a piece of ripped lino at the door.

On the other side of the worn muslin curtain that separated his side from hers, she could make out her father lying on his back, asleep. A gas lamp hissed softly in the corner, casting an ominous black shadow over his face.

'Oh, Doctor, whatever's the matter?' she asked, touching her father's forehead. It felt icy cold and clammy to the touch.

The doctor looked up.

'Miss Moloney,' he said gently. 'Don't be alarmed. Your father has bronchial trouble. Mrs Flood has already been in here to oversee me and rubbed linseed oil and camphor on his chest.' He grinned ruefully. 'I fear she doesn't trust my medication.'

'Don't worry. I'll see he takes his medicine, sir,' Kitty reassured him, inwardly dreading the fee. Her father had not long recovered from a nasty bout of influenza, the cost of which she was still paying off with the chemist.

'For now, just continue with Mrs Flood's chest rubs, plenty of nourishing food and keep him warm. I'm afraid to say, Miss Moloney, any medication will be like putting a sticking plaster over a gaping wound,' the doctor said gravely. He lowered his voice.

'Kitty, I've known your father a long while and I have nothing but the utmost respect for him, but the fact is, I fear his mind is now as frail as his body. Earlier, when I arrived, he had no notion of who I was. In fact, he seemed to think I was my predecessor, Dr Barker, who treated him as a young man. In my opinion, he is showing signs of senility.'

She stared at him, not understanding.

'Losing his faculties,' he added.

'But that's impossible . . .' Kitty blurted before pulling herself up. 'Sorry, sir. I don't mean to be rude, but well, he's only just turned sixty!'

'My dear, I'm not stating it as fact,' he said soothingly. 'He has suffered a run of illness and that could be temporarily blunting his mental faculties, but the signs are not promising. Your father is getting old, Kitty.'

Kitty couldn't summon the words to reply, simply staring at her father's face, his jaw slackened in sleep, a thin spittle of drool escaping the side of his mouth.

'One thing I am certain of is that these conditions are responsible for his ailing physical health.' He swept a despairing arm around the dilapidated room.

'I keep it as nice as I can, Doctor,' Kitty cried, biting down hard on her lip to stop the exhausted tears that were threatening to bubble over.

'I cast no aspersions on you, my dear,' he insisted. 'These buildings are a disgrace, they aren't fit for human habitation. The walls are sodden with damp, which is why your father has such a weak chest, and you could sorely use electricity.'

'And you want to see the state of the privy outside,' Kitty

muttered. 'It's a disgrace. And the washing facilities on the roof are broken again. I've complained, we all have, but they don't listen. Not even to Auntie.'

'These slums need condemning,' said the doctor, rising wearily to his feet and scrubbing at his face, 'but in any case, there might come a time when you will need to consider admitting your father to an infirmary. There's one right here in Bethnal Green.'

'No,' said Kitty sharply, waiting a beat before going on. 'Sorry, but no. No, my father stops here with me.'

'But you can't possibly be expected to care for him all by yourself, my dear,' he replied. 'Your sisters are rarely here, you work all day . . .'

'But I'm not caring for him by myself, Doctor,' Kitty protested. 'Auntie's right next door, Gladys comes in, and once he's back on his feet . . .'

'Please, Kitty,' urged the doctor, 'you might think you are caring for him, but your love can't cure your father, nor keep him well.'

Kitty steepled her hands over her face, the tips of her fingers pressing into the corners of her eyes to abate the stinging weariness, but when she removed them her eyes burned with indignation.

'I will never put my father in an infirmary. His place is here. With me.'

'Even if his home is crumbling down around his ears?' the doctor replied, gesturing to the gloomy rooms.

Kitty's voice flattened. 'Yes.'

She reached into her pocket for Dr Garfinkle's half-crown from her wages, a simple enough gesture, but one that would see them short.

'Please. Don't worry yourself, my dear,' he said, closing her palm over the coin. 'I'll see myself out and I'll return. On my time.'

'You're so kind, Doctor,' Kitty replied gratefully, fighting the urge to break down at his act of compassion.

Once he had left, Kitty stroked her father's forehead and bent down to kiss him.

At the touch of her kiss, his eyes flickered open and he scanned the room, before his gaze came to rest on his youngest daughter's face.

The strong ruddy complexion that once belonged to a vibrant market trader had all but vanished; in its place, a weary, befuddled old man. Kitty wanted to cry out at the indignity of ageing. Her mother's death and losing his market pitch in the space of a year had stripped away his dignity and spirit. But losing his mind? No, he was a little forgetful, but couldn't everyone be at times?

'Hello, Dad,' she smiled bravely. 'You gave me a right fright then. Can I fetch you a cocoa?'

'Hello, love,' he said, patting her hand with cold, trembling fingers. 'You're a good girl, but don't trouble yourself. I think your mum's making me one. Where you been, then? Out climbing trees with your sisters? Mother'll tear a strip off you if you've ripped your dress again.' He chuckled with mirth, but his laughter quickly dissolved into a convulsive cough.

'No, Dad,' Kitty said softly, propping him up and gently rubbing his back until the coughing fit had passed. 'I work now, making wedding gowns, remember?'

His eyes scrambled wildly in his head, and confusion and fear flooded his cheeks.

'Yes, yes, course . . . course, sorry, love, I'm getting meself a bit muddled.'

'Just rest, Dad,' she soothed, tucking the coverlet under his chin. 'I'll fetch you that drink.'

She had no sooner reached the doorway when his rasping voice called her back.

'Please don't send me away to no workhouse, Kitty. I've never been in one in me life. Go in there and I'll never come out,' he muttered in a moment of lucidity.

'No one's sending you away, Dad,' she said firmly. 'Besides, the workhouses have all closed. Remember? The County Council took them over six years ago, they're infirmaries now.'

'Same difference,' he said petulantly.

*

An hour later, the Veronal the doctor had given her father to ensure a decent night's sleep had done the trick, and Kitty could finally get herself ready for bed. Fighting down a yawn, she felt for the pins in her hair and tugged them free. She was so exhausted every movement felt like wading through treacle. Shedding her blouse, skirt, her stays and stockings – so darned and patched they were more cotton than silk these days – Kitty pulled a nightgown over her head. Usually, she took care to brush her hair, one hundred strokes, but tonight it was as much as she could manage to clean her teeth and rub a little Vaseline into her cheeks before wearily pulling the eiderdown over herself.

But once settled, sleep did not come. Kitty lay in her bed, listening to the soft and laboured rasp of her father's breath from the other side of the flimsy material divide. A dull ache of despair spread over her own chest.

The makeshift curtain protected their modesty, but it did little to alleviate the noise. A steam train thundered past outside, causing a sudden vacuum of wind to rattle in through the small cracked windowpane and a shower of dust mites to drift down from the ceiling.

The back bedroom overlooked a fire escape and a small yard, where passers-by slung their rubbish. The breeze brought with it the sour odour of dog wee and vegetable putrescence, stiffening Kitty's resolve that one day, somehow, she and her father would escape this place. She would find a way to a better life for them both. She had to. Her father's very being depended on it.

Three

Saturday dawned bright and gin clear, crystalline sunshine bouncing off the cobbles. The skies over the East End were a crisp blue, and was that a hint of spring Stella could smell stirring in the breeze? Outside, the market traders were in fine fettle as they set their stalls and barrows up for a busy day's trading.

'Morning, pal, how's your luck?' Stella cried to a fruit seller known only as 'Big Mickey'.

'All the better for seeing you, beautiful!' he grinned, glancing up from the tower of fruit he was stacking. 'Lovely apple for the prettiest girl on Green Street, only need a banana and we got us a party,' he winked, tossing her a polished red apple, which she caught with the flick of a wrist.

'Behave, yer saucy sod,' she shot back with a grin. Stella loved the good-natured banter of the market and the promise of a new day on Green Street.

Inside Herbie's studio, it was a hive of activity. Winnie was already there on her hands and knees, vigorously polishing the parquet reception floor with a tub of Mansion Polish.

'Can't see my face yet,' Stella teased, leaning over her friend's shoulder.

'Shut your cakehole,' Winnie warned, reaching up and playfully twanging Stella's garter belt.

'I'm only pulling yer leg, Win,' Stella grinned, handing Winnie her red apple as a peace offering, 'but you know you'll have Gladys in here, checking up on you.'

'More like checking up on Herbie,' Winnie puffed, getting to her feet. 'She can't keep away, she's so sweet on him. I do wish he'd start courting again, he's been on his own too long.'

'He can't,' Stella remarked, patting her blonde curls and smoothing down her smart cream blouse, 'he's married to this place. Talking of which, is he in yet?'

'You have to ask?' Winnie replied. She gestured upstairs, and Stella bounded up the stairs two at a time. She passed the first floor with its neat changing room, dotted with vases of lily of the valley, and storeroom, and kept on going up the next flight.

Herbie had insisted the studio be situated on the second floor to make the most of the natural light. He had customized the building when he had taken it over in his business's heyday, and this vast room, which dominated most of the floor, had huge windows on one side through which a stream of morning sunshine poured in.

Stella felt her heart rate steady as she breathed in the studio's clean white elegance.

A sitter could take their pick of any number of lavish hand-painted backdrops on wheels to pose against. Herbie might have been taking photos since he was tall enough to peek through a glass focusing screen, but to Stella's pleasure, she found her boss respected her opinion. He still insisted on his formal props – such as a lace antimacassar on high-backed chairs, dark velvet drapes and heavy ferns – but gradually, Stella was introducing a more elegant, feminine look that better reflected the 1930s, rather than the rigid conventionality of the Victorian age in which Herbie had trained.

Over the years, the pair had been engaged in a gentle battle of wills as Stella attempted to drag Herbie into the Art Deco era. For every fussy aspidistra plant he insisted on buying as a backdrop, Stella would create a simple white archway or lightweight wooden blocks, which could be arranged to look like steps, or draped with silver lamé.

Little by little, she was getting her way, one prop at a time. Herbie's trailing spray of lilies on a mock Doric column had been replaced with an Art Deco lamp; silver lamé was finally winning the day over green velvet. Simple, fresh and uncluttered was the look she – and most of the young brides in the East End – craved these days.

Her heroes were pioneering photographers like Boris Bennett, who blazed a brightly coloured trail of neon glamour over in neighbouring Whitechapel. The procession of brides queuing outside his studio and the uniformed commissionaire employed to greet them, were testament to his success and vision in the poorer quarters. And further to the West, Cecil Beaton photographed a dizzying array of society starlets in his Bond Street studio. Stella had lost count of the number of times East End brides-to-be came in clutching a copy of the *Daily Sketch*, demanding to be photographed like their favourite actress or It Girl.

Glamour. Escapism. Hope. That's what their wedding day gave these proud East End girls, and the photograph was a precious memento to cherish when they returned to the factories.

There was, however, one small thing that traditionalist Herbie couldn't bring himself to do away with. Placed in each corner of the studio were glass bowls filled with water to bounce extra light around the room, a throwback to when the dwelling was used by the old French Huguenot silk weavers.

The East End had come a long way since then and, thanks to the bright lights, mirrors, archways and white drapes, at times Stella fancied – or rather dreamed – she was onboard an ocean liner sailing to Manhattan, not slap bang in the over-congested heart of the East End.

Stella's mind flickered back to the ugly fracas at the march the previous evening and she shuddered.

'Morning, my dear,' rang out Herbie's peppy greeting. 'I heard there was some trouble outside the Salmon and Ball last night.' She glanced up to see Herbie fiddling with a large carbon arc lamp. He loved his lamps – used to produce a great beam of light and angled depending on whether he wanted directional or sultry lighting – almost as much as he adored his beloved wooden Kodak plate camera.

The photographer, well turned-out in a tailored suit, bustled over to Stella as bright and breezy as a summer washday and planted a kiss on her cheek.

'I say! You're very chipper today,' she beamed.

'That I am, my dear. Nothing like a big wedding to set my spirits soaring.'

Stella suspected it was more to do with the fact that they were saved from the chill of photographing outside, and back in the comfort and warmth of Herbie's beloved studio. She knew the strain of lugging wooden boxes, heavy plate cameras, the tripods, brass lenses, filters and a flashgun to churches around the East End was taking its toll. At sixty, Herbie wasn't getting any younger, but in the studio, he was king.

'So was it that mob from next door?' Herbie jerked his head to the wall that connected his studio to the British Union of Fascists' offices. Stella nodded and instinctively lowered her voice.

'Yes, boss. Spewing their usual rot, with a bit of Jew-bashing thrown in for good measure.'

Herbie frowned. 'Why can't they just let decent folk be? Anyway, let's not dwell on that, we've a busy day ahead of us, Stella. The bride, groom and their entourage are arriving at one o'clock for portraits between the ceremony and reception, and we must be ready and waiting. I've asked Winnie to have reception gleaming for their arrival . . .'

As Herbie rattled off the details of the rest of the day, Stella forced herself to forget last night and pay attention. No cheap wedding clubs here; the bride and groom had ordered the full set with ten framed photos and an album at sixteen guineas, and the business could sorely use the money. No detail could be left to chance and nothing could go wrong. Hell hath no fury like a woman scorned, but a bride whose wedding pictures weren't pin-sharp and perfect was a far scarier proposition. This wedding had to go off like a dream.

*

Next door at number 226 Green Street, in Gladys Tingle's small wedding dress workshop, Kitty flopped down on a chair and stretched luxuriously. Gladys was at the home of the bride-to-be, overseeing the dressing and making sure everything was just so, and had left Kitty in charge of her precious business.

This small room was the epicentre of the fifty-five-year-old lady's world and it was meticulously ordered. Gladys was legendary round these parts for her invisible stitches, and the finish and quality of her work. There must have been dozens of other similar workshops churning out gowns in the East End, but only one other local dressmaker, Hetty Dipple, could come close to matching her immaculate standards. Both had their signature finish, for Hetty a strand of her hair sewn into the seam and for Gladys, a tiny silk label bearing her name stitched in blue cotton to the underside of the seam allowance.

Gladys approached her workshop like a surgeon might his operating theatre. Scrupulous about cleanliness, she insisted Kitty wear her hair tied back with a headscarf to stop it getting caught in the sewing machine wheel, and absolutely no lipstick.

The room was lined on two sides with a long wooden workbench, and covered in the tools of their trade: two Singer sewing machines, an overlocker, an Irish machine and a steam iron. The bench was dotted with tins filled with hundreds of needles of all shapes and sizes. Dominating the centre of the room was a huge cutting table. The shelves over their heads were groaning with boxes of seed pearls, crystals, sequins, buttons, fasteners, ribbons of all colours, appliqué, cottons, metallic thread and beaded trimmings by the metre.

From pearls and pincushions, pinking shears to press studs, it was a veritable Aladdin's cave of sewing treasures.

The far corner housed a rack with bolts of fabric pushed

in, containing delicate silks, satins, voile, chiffon, lamé and lace, frothy organzas and heavy velvets. Not that it mattered if they ran out; there were half a dozen haberdasheries and linen drapers within a stone's throw. Overseeing everything were two dressmaker's mannequins for pinning and adjusting the gowns on. Not that they needed them, mind. Kitty rarely made a dress for anyone without a sylph-like waist of twenty-two inches and a bust measuring thirty inches.

Her pale blue eyes suddenly stung with tiredness. What a week! Gladys's voice echoed through her mind.

'*Clean that neckline out, my girl, unpick it . . . seam's not straight . . .*'

Still, Gladys wasn't here now, and for one glorious moment, she could do nothing but relish the feel of stretching out her limbs. Kitty had been hunched over her workbench for so long, her body felt as twisted as a pretzel. She had to admit that all their hard work had paid off. The bride would look a picture. Her gown was entirely hand-stitched so as to get the lightest touch and most invisible seams. Oh, it was a dream, one of the loveliest dresses she had ever helped to create. Bias cut, ivory satin with an angel-skin lace appliqué over parchment satin train. The bride had even requested her grandmother's wedding ring be sewn into the hem of the train. East End women were a superstitious lot, and sewing sentimental keepsakes somewhere into the wedding gown was commonplace.

Kitty had spent countless hours sewing tiny lace-covered buttons up the back of the dress, not to mention the back-breaking work that had her hunched over a tambour frame so she could hand-embroider hundreds of minuscule crystal beads onto the veil. Just as well Kitty shared her boss's perfectionist nature and nimble fingers. For the past month, neither had dared take a break, sewing long into the evening by the light of a small hissing gas lamp. She swore even the clouds were starting to look like they were made from chiffon!

Kitty adored her job, for she was a hopeless romantic. She might live in a slum, but that didn't mean she couldn't reach for the stars, did it? With every tiny stitch she sewed, the longing to one day be a bride herself, and not just the wedding seamstress, intensified. The vow she had made outside Nancy Beaton's thrilling wedding three years ago was still so vivid in her mind's eye. Kicking off her shoes, she slid her stockinged feet over the brown waxed paper Gladys insisted cover the workshop floor to protect the delicate materials, and allowed her thoughts to wander back to that snow-flecked churchyard.

What must it feel like to be swathed head to toe in shimmering silk and smothered in pearls? To be attended to by eight flower-festooned bridesmaids? To float down the aisle on the arm of her father . . . *Her father.* And just like that, the bubble burst. The poor wretched man was at home alone, in that horrible dank room. The promise she had made last night to somehow escape came hurtling back and she squeezed her eyes tightly shut.

Who was she fooling? She would need to sew a thousand wedding dresses before she could think about moving them somewhere bigger, or better yet, out of the East End altogether, to a house with indoor plumbing, and a garden for her father to sit out in.

The awful realization hit Kitty that her skill with a needle and thread was all that was saving them from destitution, never mind getting hitched in a lavish wedding!

A cough startled her and Kitty's eyes snapped open.

'I'm sorry to interrupt you, miss,' said an elderly man, hovering awkwardly by the door. He removed his cap, eyeing the curves of the mannequin nervously. 'I'm looking for Mrs Tingle.'

'I'm sorry, sir, but you've missed her. She's out on a job,' Kitty replied, quickly placing her feet back in her shoes.

'In that case, miss, would you be so kind as to hand her this, this . . .' The gentleman paused, stumbling for words. '. . . well, I suppose I can only describe it as a gift.'

Kitty gazed, intrigued, as he lifted a sewing machine case onto the workbench.

'It's my wife's Singer,' he explained. 'I'd like Mrs Tingle to have it.'

'That's a very generous gift, sir,' Kitty gushed. 'Are you quite sure your wife shan't mind?'

'Sorry, my dear, I'm not making myself clear. My wife's passed.'

'Oh . . . oh, I'm so sorry, sir,' Kitty mumbled.

'Mrs Tingle made my wife's wedding dress many moons ago. I was lost for words when I watched her walk into my arms that day . . .' The widower's eyes brimmed over with love and grief as he stumbled on, his voice splintering: '. . . she had never looked so beautiful to me.

'When my wife realized her time was coming to an end, she asked me to make sure her machine was bequeathed to Mrs Tingle – her way of saying thank you. I rather think she thought her needlework would never quite match Mrs

Tingle's, but she was a good little seamstress in her own way. A good wife too . . . I'm lost without her.'

The stranger's eyes suddenly filled with tears and he looked desperate to escape.

'Oh, look, I've got muddy footprints all over your paper,' he blustered, backing up to the door so fast, he collided with a mannequin.

'Wait, sir,' Kitty called, leaping to her feet. 'Before you go, who shall I say called?'

'Just tell her a grateful customer,' he replied. The bell over the door tinkled as he retreated into Green Street as fast as he had come.

'Poor man,' Kitty murmured out loud. He had been so grief-stricken, he hadn't known whether he was coming or going. She turned her attention back to the machine. It really was a beauty. Gladys would be pleased with such a generous gift. Ornate gold lettering and the most exquisite lotus flower unfurled over the base. Kitty allowed her fingers to trace the flower's trailing blossom until they reached the wooden base and it was there she felt a catch. How strange. She had never come across a machine like this before. Her breath caught in her throat as she lifted the catch and a wooden drawer concealed within the base sprung open. A secret compartment!

Feeling more clandestine by the moment, she reached into the tiny drawer and her fingers met a cool strip of paper. Puzzled, she lifted it out and realized to her astonishment she was holding a letter. She knew she ought not to read it, really she oughtn't to. She kept on telling herself that, even as she unfolded the paper and gently flattened it out over the workbench.

Kitty read out loud, in the vaguest hope it might make what she was doing feel less furtive.

Dear Harry,

Isn't it awful how it is only being forced to contemplate my own mortality that has forced me to put pen to paper to you after all these years.

I am deeply ashamed that I have allowed matters to come to this.

A good mother ought not have reacted the way that I did and now it is too late to repair the damage my lack of understanding has inflicted. I have let you down, but please, my darling Harry, know this. I implore you to feel no guilt.

You always were the best of sons. Cheeky, headstrong, impulsive . . . And I see now that it was these attributes, rather than any sense of malice, which led you down the road you travelled.

After you joined the Merchant Navy, I went to the docks many times with the intention of telling you just that, but each time my courage deserted me.

I hope you can find it in your heart to speak my name with tenderness. I beg of you too, do not grieve for me after I am gone. Know that one day, you and I will be

*reunited in a better place, where I will be the mother to
you there that I should have been to you in this life.*

*This is a queer letter to write, because I know that if
you are reading it, I will be dead, but know this,
Harry: wherever you are, whoever you have become,
I love you. I have never stopped loving you, son.*

*May God protect and give you strength, as he does for
me now as I write this.*

Your devoted mother,

Agnes

Kitty stood quite still for a time as she digested the contents
of the letter. Guilt tore through her and folding the letter
as hastily as she dared, Kitty dashed to the door and
wrenched it open.

Frantically, she scanned the long busy street for an elderly
gentleman with a cap, but it was market day and the street
was densely packed.

'Curses,' she muttered. A tap on the shoulder made her
jump.

'What you standing there for, you daft little article?'
screeched a voice.

'Gladys,' Kitty said flatly.

'Well who were you expecting? His Majesty himself?' she
tutted. 'Now stop your dawdling, I'd said we'd nip over to
Herbie's. That man never eats and I want to take him over
some dinner before the bridal party arrives.'

'Oh, it's just that . . . er . . . um . . . I . . .' Kitty stammered.

'You talking to me or chewing a brick, girl?' Gladys scolded. 'Come on now. Sharp's the word!'

Gladys stared at her expectantly, before hustling her back inside.

When she had found her voice, Kitty filled her in on the gentleman's visit and watched as Gladys admired the Singer and fired questions at her. Guilt stopped her from telling her boss about the letter that had lain undiscovered in the secret compartment. As it was, Gladys was mightily ticked off that she hadn't got a name or address for the gentleman so that she could write and thank him. She would have a fit on the mat if she discovered Kitty had read a letter not meant for her eyes. Feeling wretched, Kitty quietly slipped the letter away inside her coat pocket. She would work out what to do about tracking the mysterious Harry down later.

*

Green Street stopped still for the spectacle of the wedding of Miss Beatrice May, a comptometer operator from Bow, to Mr Jimmy Stern, a sergeant in the Tower Hamlets Rifles. The bride's father was big in hosiery and clearly not short of a bob or two. He had certainly spared no expense, and when the wedding party emerged from their chauffeur-driven cream Daimler outside Herbie's studio, the market traders and shop girls cheered and clapped so loudly, Winnie half wondered whether their new King himself hadn't come to the East End.

As the bride and groom made their way, beaming with

joy and still flecked with confetti, up the stairs to the studio, they made a dashing couple. Kitty and Gladys had done a marvellous job with the bride's gown, and she looked as ravishing as a matinee movie star. Rumour had it, Beatrice had once worked as a Tiller girl and, watching her sashay past now, her beauty luminous, Winnie could believe it.

And the flowers . . . my, oh my! She had never seen such lavish displays. The bride carried an enormous wraparound wreath of silver-sprayed arum lilies emerging from a forest of maidenhair fern. The never-ending stream of bridal attendants who followed in the newlyweds' wake, from a lady-in-waiting down to tottering chubby-cheeked flower girls, each clutched baskets brimming over with tulips. Even the bride and groom's mothers proudly wore a spray of orchids each, pinned next to their fox-fur stoles. They passed by her reception desk in a great chattering wave of fragrant excitement, like heavy-crested birds showing off their plumage.

Winnie's head was spinning at the scent and the hubbub of excited chatter, when the bride's father sidled over to her.

'I'll settle up the bill on my way out,' he said under his breath.

'Of course, Mr May, I'll prepare your docket,' she smiled. 'Congratulations. It's a beautiful wedding.'

'It ought to be, it's costing me enough,' he muttered, dabbing at his florid brow with a handkerchief. 'That's why I've teamed it with mine and the wife's wedding anniversary. Save the cost of two parties.'

'Really? How long have you and Mrs May been married?' she enquired politely.

'Eighteen years – you get less for murder,' he tutted, before puffing his way up the stairs after the bridal party. 'I'd do anything for a quiet wife – I mean, life.'

Inside the studio, Herbie and Stella were in their element, arranging the bridal party around a sweeping backdrop of a sylvan glade and a forgotten grotto.

The bride's dress, not to mention the glittering rock on her finger, looked ostentatious enough to Winnie, but Herbie insisted on deftly arranging a spare length of tulle around the hem of her skirts to create an illusion of even greater grandeur, a trick he'd borrowed from Boris Bennett. Stella scattered orange blossom around their feet and a great arc of light was beamed over the whole ensemble. It was as if a Hollywood picture had burst into life right here in Bethnal Green.

Just a few feet away on the street outside, all was a cacophony of noise as housewives bantered over the price of fish, and carts and delivery boys on bikes rattled through the smoke. But here in the sanctuary of Herbie Taylor & Sons Photographic Portraiture studio, real life was suspended.

'I feel like I'm on a film set,' said Beatrice breathily, as she clutched her new husband's arm.

'Why, how perceptive you are, madam,' Herbie smiled, 'for surely all weddings are a performance and the portrait, the grand finale.'

'In that case, mind you get rid of my lumpy bits when you come to retouch the photos.'

'I would, if you had any,' Herbie chuckled. 'You look a million dollars,' he smiled reassuringly. 'As do you, sir,' he said with deference to the groom, whilst gently tilting his chin up and simultaneously smoothing the lapel on his suit.

'And you must be the bride's elder sister?' Herbie enquired when he reached the mother of the bride. 'Might I take your stole? It's a stunning piece, almost as handsome as you.'

'Get away with you, sir,' she cackled, her colour high as she handed Herbie her fox-fur and allowed him to escort her to her spot. It was daft really, nothing more than music hall sauce, but it did the job. The compliment peeled ten years off the family matriarch as she stood proudly to the left of the bride with her head held high.

Winnie exchanged a look with Stella and smiled. Herbie was a master at this game. Thanks to his quiet air of authority, the wedding party eventually settled down. Even the bride's cynical father was beaming with pride, and the smallest bridesmaids were sitting cross-legged, staring rapt at Herbie.

The groom only had eyes for his new bride though, gazing at her with a beatific smile. But it was the bride who looked the most ecstatic, a look of such dreamy love emblazoned on her face, even Winnie felt a lump in her throat.

Then she thought of her mother and her throat tightened further. A spike of pain stabbed at Winnie's heart. What good had marriage done Jeannie Docker? It was all smoke and mirrors anyway, wasn't it? Marriage was the biggest fraud out, as fake as the cardboard-and-paste painted grotto the bride and groom were posing in front of.

Chances were the bridal party would all go back to the bride's mother's terrace for a buffet of sausage rolls and a knees-up. The bride's father might have made good, but you couldn't make a silk purse out of a sow's ear, she thought bitterly.

She glanced to her right at Kitty, whose pale blue eyes glittered with tears. To Kitty, this was a portrait of hope. Unending love. To Winnie, it was all top show, like wearing a housecoat at home and heels outside, as temporary as the interchangeable backdrops. Wisely, Winnie kept her counsel and, reaching over, she squeezed Kitty's arm supportively.

Herbie did a last-minute whirl around the room, making tiny adjustments; tapping slouching shoulders and gently straightening backs, before positioning himself behind his trusty camera.

'Right, Jimmy, I know your wife's face is far more attractive than mine, but if you could be so good as to look at me,' he joked.

A ripple of nervous laughter rang round the room. The laborious work of setting up the shoot was done. Herbie slotted the plate-holder into the back of the chunky wooden camera and positioned his finger over the shutter release. At the very last moment he took out a fine camel-haired brush and gently brushed any lingering dust off the lens.

'Don't want anything to detract from such a beautiful portrait,' he smiled. 'Now, backs straight, look straight into my lens, eyes open, smile. Hold it and . . .'

The smashing of glass was followed by a high-pitched scream.

'Hell's fire,' gasped the bride's father.

'What the blazes?' screamed the groom's mother, frantically scooping the children into her dress skirts. Tiny slivers of glass and slashed petals were scattered over the bridal party.

Beatrice stood stock-still in the chaos, staring, dumb-struck, at her dress. It was soaked through and the silver spray from her wreath of lilies was slowly staining the bodice.

It took all of a moment for Winnie to see what had happened. A brick had smashed through the large window and straight into the glass bowl of water in the corner, showering the bridal party. She pelted to the window just in time to see Tubby the tobacconist on the street outside, red-faced with rage, pumping his fist up the street at the miscreants.

'Come back here again and I'll wring your bloody necks,' he hollered after the black-shirted men as they tore up the street, dodging the market stalls. In mounting dismay, Winnie's eyes were drawn up the length of Green Street. Every Jewish trader's window had been smashed, or their shopfronts ransacked. It was bedlam. A barrel of gherkins outside the grocer's was upended and pickles were rolling into the gutter. Lazarus' fried-fish shop floor was spattered with batter and glass. Old Miss Sugarman opposite was sobbing on the step of her milliner's, her prized window display reduced to a mangle of feathers and straw. It was Shabbos, so the Jewish traders had been inside, quietly observing their religious festival.

Feeling a crawling dread, Winnie turned around. The bride wept in her mother's arms. 'My dress . . . it's ruined,' she sobbed, inconsolable.

Kitty, Gladys and Stella dashed around like cats on hot bricks, attempting to clear up the glass and mop up the water. Herbie stood frozen to the spot as he surveyed the scene, and Winnie's heart went out to him. She had never seen her boss look quite so shaken. Herbie was a man who prided himself on his reputation, good name and innate professionalism. This would be a bitter blow.

Half an hour later, the damage had been repaired and the bridal party cleaned up and pacified, though Winnie feared the damage to Herbie would run far deeper. He drew Winnie to one side.

'It goes without saying that there'll be no bill for today and we must arrange for flowers to be sent to every member of the bridal party.'

Winnie nodded and followed him, still apologizing profusely, down the stairs, past the reception desk and the uneaten sandwich which Gladys had brought him, past the unpaid bill and into the street outside.

'There'll be murders when I get my hands on them bleedin' blackshirts,' Gladys scowled, after the wedding car slid away from the kerb. 'I'm boiling. Who the hell do they think they are, terrorizing innocent folk? This is a peaceful neighbourhood.'

'Calm yourself, Gladys,' Herbie cautioned. 'Ignore it, or we play straight into their hands. Let's leave it to the constabulary to sort.'

'A fat lot of good they'll be,' she snorted. 'I'm off to help Miss Sugarman clean up.' Winnie knew Gladys didn't place much faith in the police, preferring the old East End way of sorting things without outside interference.

Herbie sighed as he watched the indefatigable seamstress bustle across the road.

'Winnie, you get off home, love,' he said wearily. 'Stella and I will see if there's anything salvageable on those negatives.'

Herbie suddenly looked every one of his sixty years.

'Come on, boss,' said Stella. 'Let's get inside and I'll make you a cup of tea, or perhaps something a bit stronger.'

*

Winnie walked the thirty-minute route back to her home in Cable Street with a heavy step, still dismayed at the shocking turn of events.

The brutality at last night's march and now this . . . Violence and fear lingered on every street corner. Until now, Mosley had been nothing but an irritant, spinning the line that Jews were thieves and bad landlords, but recently he had changed the name of his political party to the British Union of Fascists and National Socialists and his rhetoric echoed that of the other fascist they seemed to be hearing so much about, Hitler.

A cold fist tightened round Winnie's heart. She had heard it muttered on the street that another war was brewing. And look how the first had damn nearly destroyed her family!

As she trudged the length of the sooty street, her eyes chanced upon some graffiti daubed on the high wall in white paint: *Kill all Jews.*

Underneath it, a couple of blackshirts were handing out a free fascist periodical, *The East End Patriot.*

Winnie shuddered and hastened her step, shaking her head as one attempted to thrust a copy into her hand. Admittedly, she didn't know much about politics, but coming off the back of the Depression, with poverty and unemployment still rife, she knew that despair and anger were flourishing. There would be some desperate enough to believe this claptrap! The half a crown and new pair of boots Mosley was handing out struck a powerful chord when your pockets were empty and your shoes patched with cardboard.

A large black boot blocked her path and, startled, she looked up.

'You sure I can't interest you in this, miss?' said the tall blond blackshirt, standing so close, she could see the pimple by his nose and smell the meat pie he had just devoured. 'You might learn something.'

He leaned in even closer. 'After all, when the day of reckoning comes, you need to ensure you're on the right side.'

'If it's all the same to you, no thanks,' she said tartly. She was aware of their gazes burning into her back as she turned and fled to the end of the deserted street. Only once she had joined a busy thoroughfare did her heart rate start to slow.

Biting down hard on her lip, she felt her unease give way to fury. How dare they try to intimidate her like that? The anger coursing through her stirred other emotions. A fear so strong it was almost visceral resonated deep within. Using every ounce of her control, she quashed the fear. That was all in the past!

The smell of cooking onions and garlic sausage greeted her as she rounded the corner of Cable Street. Dusk was gathering over the crooked chimney pots.

The long and notorious street, which carved its way through the East End, linking the City to the docks, looked a little forbidding in the smoky half-light. It had taken some getting used to when Winnie, her mother and three younger sisters had moved to this neighbourhood from Bethnal Green over a year ago. The street was so narrow, you could shake hands with the person coming out the shop opposite. When the thick, consumptive fog rolled in off the nearby docks, it was suffocating.

At ground level, every building was either a workshop or a store, and the rooms above teemed with poor families, housing the Jewish on the west side and the Irish on the east, with a smattering of seamen's boarding houses for good measure. The tenement housing was densely packed, the narrow spaces between flapping with laundry.

The street had started out as a rope-walk, where workers would twist giant lengths of hemp rope into cables for sailing ships. Nowadays the hemp industry was rumoured to have made way for brothels and opium dens – which was utter poppycock so far as Winnie was concerned. In her time on the street she had seen nothing but decent working-class folk trying to get by.

Two doors up from Winnie's lodgings, a woman supported a paralysed husband and six nippers by making shirts at eight pence a dozen. Opposite was a poor widow with a family of little ones who survived by sewing on buttons for a tailor.

Winnie spotted two of the widow's children playing marbles on the kerbside and waved cheerily before pushing open the small door to the side of the rag merchant's and making her way up the scuffed linoleum stairs.

'Mum?' she called out cautiously as she let herself into their three-room dwelling. 'You still here? Herbie let me knock off early.'

A part of her longed to be greeted with silence.

'In here, love,' a voice called back.

Jeannie Docker was sitting in the middle of what passed for living quarters, surrounded by luggage and Winnie's three younger sisters. The light coming from one small window was partially obliterated by a sign from the shop beneath inviting people to *Bring Your Rags Here*. Jeannie was once a handsome woman, but life had worn her down and she, like the room she was sitting in, was a little threadbare and tea-stained.

'I oughtn't to go, love, it ain't right,' she said, twisting the frayed hem of her skirt between her fingers. Winnie's mother used to have beautiful hands, slender and soft as velvet. Now they were as worn down as the rest of her. Dry and livid red from the endless washing she took in for other women. Between that and the charring she did in the city at the crack of dawn and the dinnertime cafe job she worked, those hands were barely still.

'Mum, you deserve a rest,' Winnie insisted. 'So do the girls.'

Since their father had left and they had moved to Cable Street, Jeannie and Winnie had not stopped working, but they both knew why. Never again had either of them wanted to feel the raw humiliation of eviction, the harsh scrutiny of the welfare board or the shame of receiving relief. A month of surviving on grocery parcels and bread tickets had been enough to convince Winnie that hard graft was their only salvation.

'What if your father returns, comes looking for us and finds us gone?' Jeannie asked worriedly.

'He ain't coming home, Mum,' Winnie replied patiently, tugging off her gloves and moving to the small fire to warm her hands. 'He went off to find a job in Dagenham and never came home. And when you come back from holiday, I'm gonna take you down the Town Hall so we can look into what we need to do to go about getting a divorce. It's been a whole year now!'

'Winnie, love, I married him for better, for worse—'

'—but not for good!' Winnie insisted. 'He's a lousy swine who abandoned his own family. Remember?'

Winnie walked over and dropped a kiss on the top of her three younger sisters' heads; Sylvie, fifteen, Betty, twelve, and Bertha, rising ten. It was a source of constant regret that she hadn't been able to shield them from all the horror. They, like she, had been forced to grow up too soon.

'Now then, Mum,' she said, forcing a bright smile. 'There's a bus leaving from outside St John's church in half an hour, and I want you lot on it.'

Thanks to hers and Jeannie's joint incomes, they had managed to scrape by enough to replace the wireless that had been sold in order to claim relief, and pay 3d a week into the church's Country Holiday Fund.

'A week in Suffolk will make everything feel brighter, trust me.'

'Oh please, Mum,' Sylvie implored, her quick eyes gleaming. 'Rumour has it there's a moon in the countryside.'

Pure love stretched Winnie's smile further. Her Sylvie always was as bright as a button. She loved her little sisters with a protective love that bordered on motherly.

'Very well,' Jeannie sighed, standing up and reaching for her case. 'But only if you're sure you can manage on your own, Winnie. You must remember to cover my washing, and

I promised the tailor at number 18 I'd sew on all them buttons by Wednesday, and—'

'Just go, Mum,' Winnie insisted, opening the door.

Jeannie touched her eldest daughter's cheek, her eyes baggy with exhaustion.

'I found this pinned to the outhouse door. You're a good girl.'

She held up the note that Winnie had left that morning next to the neatly torn squares of newspaper nailed to the toilet door.

It's easy enough to be pleasant when life goes along with a song, but the man worthwhile is the man who can smile when everything goes wrong.

The note was one of dozens that Winnie had left dotted about the place over the past year, in the vainest of hopes they would lift her mother's spirits and keep her frazzled nerves at bay. That and the packet of Shadphos brain sparklers she had bought from the chemist and popped in her mother's case earlier!

'I know what you're trying to do, love,' Jeannie whispered, pressing the note back into Winnie's hands, 'but there's a part of me that will always love him. You don't know how he suffered . . .'

'Ta-ta, Mum,' Winnie replied, kissing her cheek and ignoring her comment. She had heard that argument one time too many. 'Make sure you and the girls have a smashing time. And you girls stay out of trouble – no scaring the cows, you hear,' she chuckled, ruffling each girl's head in turn as they passed.

Her mother turned to leave but Winnie gently pulled her back.

'We're on our feet again now, Mum. You're finally free.'

The door closed. Winnie waited until she could hear their footsteps retreating down Cable Street before she sank down, shattered, onto a chair by the fire. Mothering her own mother and sisters could be exhausting. She longed to sleep, but Treacle was due over.

Rising wearily, Winnie checked her reflection in the looking glass over the mantel and pinched her wan cheeks to try to put some colour back in.

Treacle was a good man, and he deserved to be greeted by something a bit brighter than this. Reaching into the kitchen drawer, Winnie pulled out a comb and some grips. A bit of sugar and water to set her wave and she'd be looking herself again.

Nestled next to the comb were a number of Treacle's gifts, which he had dredged from the riverbanks and proudly presented to her. Everything from old coins to bits of pottery and even an ancient clay pipe lay loose in the drawer. Winnie felt a sudden flash of guilt at losing the love token he had given her yesterday, before they got caught up in the march. Shaking her head at her carelessness, she slammed the drawer shut and hurriedly set about fixing her hair. She had no sooner finished when a sharp crack at the window at the back of the room startled her. Setting down her comb, Winnie squinted out through the window that overlooked the backyard. Nothing untoward there. A jumble of red-tiled rooftops, an old lady with a chenille hair net covering her grey hair passing in and out of the smokehouse yard next door preparing a sawdust fire. The last of her mother's washing, left out to dry, swayed gently in the evening breeze.

'Psst, down here,' came a voice, and Treacle emerged from behind the flapping forest of linen.

'What on earth are you doing down there?' Winnie gaped, pulling up the sash and squinting into the brackish air, sweet with the scent of smoking kippers and coal fires.

'Come down,' he said, breathlessly.

'What? I'm not coming down there. I've just done me hair. It'll end up stinking of fish.'

'In that case, I'm coming up,' he said with a mischievous grin.

'Have you taken leave of your senses?' she laughed.

Winnie shook her head in amazement as Treacle used the dividing brick wall between hers and the smokehouse as a springboard to leap up. Effortlessly, his tall, athletic body shinned up the side of the building and, with the help of an old piece of lead piping, he wedged himself right under Winnie's window ledge.

Resting her chin in her hands on the ledge, she laughed. 'You're barmy, you are, Treacle!'

'Barmy for you,' he grinned, his eyes dancing with excitement. 'Is your mum still here?'

'No, she's gone, so you could have taken the stairs, Romeo. Now come in, before someone sees you.'

'Not before you give me a kiss,' he said teasingly.

It was tempting. Treacle looked so handsome in his dark suit, starched white shirt and braces, his jet-black hair slicked back from his face. Even a tiny razor nick on his jaw by his right ear didn't detract from his dashing good looks.

'What, and set all the neighbours' tongues wagging?' she scolded, reaching out and gently dabbing at the nick.

'Give a fella a break, would ya?' Treacle laughed. 'I'm hanging four floors up here.'

Giggling, Winnie leaned down and brushed her lips against his. The kiss felt nice, his lips so tender and warm on hers. And he smelt so good; of lemon-scented pomade and Sunlight soap. Involuntarily, her eyes flickered shut as the sensation travelled down to the soles of her feet. When she opened them again, there was a small velvet-covered box on the windowsill.

'Marry me, Winnie Docker?'

Treacle gazed back at her hopefully, and her heart thumped.

'Oh, Treacle . . .' she began.

'I swear I bought it,' he blurted. 'From an actual shop. I didn't dredge it from the Thames.'

The pigeons in next door's loft cooed into the inky blue dusk, urging her to answer.

'Just come inside, would you?' she said eventually, shaking her head.

Treacle looked crushed as he replaced the box inside his suit jacket pocket and hauled himself through the open window.

Once he was safely inside and the window closed, she led him to the worn couch.

'Sit beside me,' she said shakily, patting the cushion next to her.

'Is it because we're young?' he asked, running his hand through his Brylcreemed hair and sitting down heavily. 'I'm nineteen, but I'm a man now. I've got savings. The foreman reckons I've got prospects . . .

'Feel my heart,' he urged, taking her hand and placing it over his chest. 'It's galloping because this is all I've ever wanted. I've dreamed of this from the very first moment I laid eyes on you, sweeping the street outside Herbie's, giving that Mickey on the market some lip. I knew you were a strong woman. So strong, in fact, you stole my heart clean away.'

The aching tenderness in his voice twisted Winnie's insides into a tight knot.

He really did love her.

'Oh, Treacle,' she replied, pulling her hand back. 'It's nothing to do with your age . . . or your wage, for that matter.'

'Then what is it?' he asked despairingly. 'I'm not your dad, Winnie. I don't even know the half of it, but I know he was a wrong 'un. I shan't *ever* leave you. And your mum and sisters, they could come and live with us too. I want something better for you all than this place.'

Determined, he took her hand back in his.

'I'm not taking no for an answer unless you give me a good reason. We're perfect for each other.'

He lifted her hand and brushed her knuckles with his soft lips, his brown eyes devouring her.

'You have my heart, Winnie,' he whispered. 'Be mine?'

'I care for you,' she replied, 'truly I do, but I belong to no man.'

'That's not an answer,' he cried in frustration. 'I don't want to own you. I just want to love you. Am I not good enough, is that it?'

'Of course you are . . . it's . . . it's not that. Look, I can't go into it without betraying my mum, but when a marriage fails, well, these things have a sort of circularity to them.'

'What do you mean?' he asked, puzzled.

'Look, my old man's done a runner. Last we heard, he'd gone to Dagenham to try and get a job in a pharmaceuticals factory out there and one of them new-build homes in the suburbs for us all, and he never come home!

'Maybe there's a taint on my family. I see happily married brides, day in, day out. They look so full of hope for the future, and then I think of my mum and what happened . . .' Winnie's voice trailed off and she felt so consumed with guilt. 'Marriage just ain't for me and that's the end of it,' she said smartly to lock down the tears that were threatening their way to the surface. 'I do want to be with you, but I'll understand if you want to go elsewhere, find a nice wife. You deserve better than me.'

Treacle shook his head and exhaled slowly.

'I can't pretend to understand, Winnie, but hear this: I ain't going nowhere. My place is here. With *you*.'

The warmth of the fire had wilted the sugar solution on Winnie's wave and a lock of her dark hair fell over one eye. She felt a sudden scorch of vulnerability.

Treacle pushed back the strand of hair and gazed at her with unknowing, innocent eyes.

'I'll never give up on us.'

Four

Monday morning, 8 a.m., and Stella was already hard at work hand-colouring the only image Herbie had managed to salvage from Beatrice and Jimmy's disastrous wedding shoot two days before.

Outside, she could hear the faint cracking of glass as borough workmen swept up the remains of the debris from Saturday afternoon's vandalism spree. Herbie had a friend who had managed to come by and replace the studio's broken windows, but Stella knew the cost of the repair had set him back a bob or two, not to mention his losses from not being able to bill for the shoot.

Working with a tiny fine-tipped paintbrush, Stella tried to block out the image of all that shattered glass and instead carefully swept a pale blush of softest pink tint over the bride's cheeks. Her brow knotted in concentration as she gradually built up layers of fine colour using the brush and some blotting paper to control the intensity of the dye. With only one image to work with, she could not afford the slightest slip of the hand.

Stella had already successfully removed a few blemishes and an unsightly pimple from one of the bridesmaids, but when it came to the bride, she was so pretty, she felt as if she were only painting over her beauty. Still, as garish as it might appear to her, colour tinting was all the fashion and what the bride had requested. There was no imperfection that couldn't be remedied with Stella's careful hand. The groom's mum's double chin had been softened and Grandad's thinning hair shaded in. The shimmering silver of the sprayed lilies brought to life and the soft rose pink of the bridesmaids' tulips faithfully recreated. If only life were as easy to fix as a photograph.

By the time Stella had finished colouring in the exact same shade of the bridesmaids' lavender gowns, her temple was throbbing and she longed for a smoke. But the tiny office she worked from was right next to Herbie's darkroom and a naked flame near to all those chemicals would be nothing short of explosive.

Instead, she stretched her arms high above her head and, yawning, bent down and pulled her bag off the floor. She couldn't resist a little peek. Swaddled inside its leather case was her new camera, a Leica III. Stella felt the same jolt of joy she had experienced when she had first travelled with her mother up West and selected it from Wallace & Heaton on New Bond Street. A hand–held portable camera with celluloid film, a rangefinder and viewfinder! It was an object of total wonder to Stella.

Her father had died three years previously and Stella knew he had left her a sum of money. For months, she had been studiously saving what little she kept after her mother deducted her share of Stella's wage, but with her eighteenth birthday looming, her mother had taken pity and allowed her early access to the inheritance.

The camera had set her back the princely sum of

twenty-five pounds. It might have seemed like an audacious waste of money to some, but this camera was the future as far as Stella was concerned, and excitement thrummed in her belly. She took out a piece of lint-free cloth and carefully polished the lens as she pondered the possibilities.

It was 1936 and the world around her was changing dramatically, opening up through air and sea travel. Stella longed to be a part of it. Every Sabbath, when the rest of the East End worshipped then dined on the Sunday treat of cockles and winkles, Stella was to be found at Bethnal Green Museum, greedily absorbing every last detail of the wild and exotic stuffed birds in the Victorian dioramas and reading passages of books describing brave new worlds like Canada, America and Australia.

Stella closed her eyes and imagined what it must feel like to experience the dark underbelly of Berlin and the fleshpots of Paris . . . not just the timeslip streets of the East End. Life in all its edgy glory, that's what she yearned for. Not the static sentimentalism of portrait photography with its never-ending conveyor belt of beaming brides, sailors and seamstresses coming of age, stuffy town hall functions and church outings.

The sound of footsteps coming down the stairs forced her eyes open and Stella hastily slipped the camera into her bag.

'Got you a nice cup of tea, love – time to wet your whistle,' said Herbie, placing the cup and saucer carefully on the desk next to her. He leaned over her shoulder and regarded the freshly tinted bride.

'You've done a good job there, Stella love,' he said. 'You're better than I ever was.'

These days, Herbie left all the retouching and hand-colouring to Stella's dexterous fingers and fresh, young eyes.

'Nonsense,' she scoffed, gratefully sipping the hot, sweet tea. 'You taught me everything I know, boss.'

'That's what I love about portrait photography,' he said, picking up Beatrice's wedding picture and scrutinizing it. 'We captured that split second of time before the brick came crashing through and ruined everything.'

Herbie sighed. 'This, Stella . . . this is what makes my heart beat. I can freeze time with my wonderful machine.'

Stella smiled sadly. She had no wish to freeze time; she wanted to be out there experiencing it. Nor did she want to spend the rest of her days retouching and colouring wedding photos in this stuffy underground room.

'But I can't go on running this business forever,' he went on, putting the photo down and staring at her pointedly. 'Yesterday gave me quite a shock, I don't mind telling you.'

Herbie passed a hand over his mouth thoughtfully. 'It proved to me that I need to start thinking about the future of the business. The future is hand-held thirty-five milli-metre film cameras, not the old wooden-plate cameras I honed my craft on.'

'So . . . ?' Stella replied cautiously.

'I think *you* are that future, Stella Smee. You're my right-hand girl, so it makes sense to me at least that all this will be yours when I retire.' He hesitated. 'If you want it, that is?'

Stella was stunned. In the past, Herbie had only ever subtly hinted that she might one day be the person to take over, but now he had laid bare his vision of the future. The only problem being, it didn't chime with Stella's. But how could she tell him that? He had been so kind to her, teaching her all he knew and, in the absence of his beloved son, passing all his knowledge and wisdom down to her. To say nothing of his kindness! She had come to him, aged fourteen, a girl grieving for her father, and with his gentle paternalism, he had filled the aching void left behind. Stella had needed a father figure, as much as she sensed he needed a child to love.

To say no to his offer would be to throw all that back in his face. Instead, she mustered up her brightest smile.

'Thank you, Herbie. It means so much that you place your trust in me. I shan't let you down.'

'I know you won't, my dear,' he replied softly.

The four walls of the small underground office seemed to close in another inch, then Stella became aware of Winnie's voice calling down the stairs.

'Herbie, there's someone here to see you!'

Grateful for the interruption, Stella jumped to her feet. 'Shall we?'

Upstairs in the reception area stood a familiar, smartly dressed man, clothed in a pinstripe suit and a mustard-yellow tie, which did nothing for his sallow complexion. An oiled moustache twitched beneath the brim of his bowler hat.

'Mr MacNab,' Herbie said coldly. 'What can we do for you?'

'Mr Taylor, my dear man,' he said. 'I hear there was a spot of bother on Saturday, some of my chaps got a bit carried away. We certainly never meant to mix you up in all this. Please accept this peace offering, by way of an apology.'

He extended a decent bottle of Scotch whisky over the mahogany reception desk.

'I don't drink,' Herbie replied curtly.

'Better man than I,' Mr MacNab chuckled. 'In that case, I insist on paying for the damage.'

'It's already been repaired.'

'Well, in that case, how about we put some business your way in recompense? I need my official portrait done now that I'm a District Leader in the BUF.'

'We're busy,' Herbie snapped.

Mr MacNab shifted awkwardly and Stella saw his eyes harden under the brim of his bowler hat.

'Look here, Herbie—'

'Mr Taylor to you.'

A muscle in his cheek twitched and Stella could see Mr MacNab was working very hard to suppress his anger.

'Mr Taylor. My young men . . . how do I put this? They have fire in their bellies, spirit of youth and all that. They see this area being taken over by the Jews, encroaching on our territory, underpaying our women, overcharging our rents, and they are merely standing up for a cause they believe in.'

'Shall I tell you what I stand up for, Mr MacNab?' Herbie replied, coming out from behind the reception desk. 'I stand up for tolerance, peace and understanding. This area's been accepting immigrants since the dawn of time. Wherever a man lives and raises his family is his country, provided he works hard and contributes to the community.

'I'll tell you the real problem. Hitler and his dangerous anti-Semitic propaganda! Unlike Nazis, I don't decide people's worth on the basis of their race.'

'But what have the Jews ever done for you?' Mr MacNab snapped, exasperated. 'They don't belong here.'

'Goddamn it, man, how can you be so blinkered?' Herbie thumped his fist down on the counter, sending a pile of paperwork skidding over the parquet floor.

Stella and Winnie watched, flabbergasted. They had never seen their mild-mannered boss so riled.

'You're obviously not from around these parts,' he said. 'If you were, you'd have seen one thousand Jews standing in respectful silence at the death of our King last month. Or known about the Jews who took in the Irish dockers' children when they went on strike so that they didn't starve.'

Herbie threw open the door and swept his hand down the street.

'The Jewish traders who you terrorized on Saturday are my friends. We trade, laugh and graft side by side. They make me proud to be an East Ender. Whereas you . . .'

Herbie's voice trailed off, as he struggled to get his emotions back under control: '. . . your hatred is so far beyond my understanding, you may as well be on the moon. Now, if you'll excuse me, I've business to tend to.'

Mr MacNab walked stiffly to the door, but as he went to take his leave, Herbie blocked his way.

'One last thing. The streets may be narrow here in the East End, but I assure you, Mr MacNab, our minds are not.'

The bell over the door jangled as Herbie slammed it shut behind his unwanted visitor.

'Let's hope that's the last we see of him,' he said, bending to pick up the paperwork from the floor.

Stella was so stunned, she scarcely knew what to say. In three years of working with Herbie, she had not once seen him fly off the handle. Her boss was gently charismatic and dedicated to the church and community. He seldom put his views forward for fear of causing offence.

'Blimey, boss,' Winnie said admiringly, 'I didn't know you had it in you.'

A moment later, Gladys burst in, red-faced with excitement.

'Oh my days . . . please tell me that ain't who I think it was who just left here!' she puffed.

'Yes, but it's all dealt with.' Herbie groaned, rubbing his back and wincing as he straightened up.

'How very dare he?' Gladys thundered, ripping off her pinny. 'I'm going right round there now, give him a piece of my mind.'

'I can fight my own battles, Miss Tingle, thank you very much,' Herbie sighed, looking suddenly weary.

'He wants bringing down a peg or two, and I'm the woman to do it,' Gladys fumed, her pudgy fingers clenching into fists. 'I'm gonna ram that bowler hat right—'

Mercifully, Stella, Winnie and Herbie were saved from hearing precisely where when a woman who had crept into the studio unseen coughed behind Gladys.

'Sorry, sir, I can come back another time if you prefer?' she muttered.

'Not at all,' Herbie replied, hustling Gladys to the door. 'Miss Tingle was just leaving. Now, what can I do for you, madam?'

'I'm here about my daughter's wedding. I need a photographer.'

'Certainly, we can assist with that. When is the special occasion?'

'Five days from now,' she announced.

'Gracious,' Herbie spluttered. 'That is . . . well, short notice.'

The woman's face fell. 'Oh, I know, Mr Taylor, but you're our last hope. The photographer we had booked . . .' She shifted awkwardly and glanced about, her voice dropping to a whisper:

'He pulled out on account of finding out about my daughter's condition. She's, well . . . how can I put it, she's . . . yer know . . . carrying.'

The woman's fingers fluttered over her stomach and she nodded urgently again at Herbie. 'You get what I'm saying.'

'Aaah, I see,' Herbie replied, nodding thoughtfully as the penny dropped.

'The photographer says he wants nothing to do with it, but my daughter, well, she has to get married, it's urgent, and all we want is a memento of the day. Nothing fancy like, just a photo outside the church. I had hoped for so much more . . .'

She collapsed into floods of tears. Herbie shook out his pristine white handkerchief and passed it to her.

'Sweet tea with a drop of brandy for the lady, Winnie,' he ordered.

'My dear, of course I shall take her photo. Every bride deserves to be treated like a queen on her wedding day, regardless of her . . . condition,' he added delicately.

The woman looked up, eyes shining with gratitude, and trumpeted into the handkerchief.

'God bless you, Mr Taylor, sir, they're right about you. You're a true gentleman. The only problem is, I ain't exactly flush.'

'We have a wedding club to spread the cost,' Stella chipped in delicately. 'The three and six club'll get you mounted and framed enlargements and cartes-de-visite, or the shilling club offers a single parlour wedding portrait and six enamelled postcards.'

'Oh, miss,' she sighed, patting her apron pocket. 'I don't even have a brass farthing to spare at the moment.'

'Please don't trouble yourself about that just yet, madam,' Herbie soothed. 'I'm sure we can come to some arrangement. I always say, a little praise is of far more value.'

'Oh, but to do me such a kindness, sir,' she sobbed, a fresh deluge of tears flooding her face.

Winnie flicked Stella a look as she hurried to fetch the tea. Stella knew that this would end up being one of those jobs where the cost was spread so thinly it might as well be on the never-never, but she also knew her kindly boss would no more turn down this desperate lady's request than he would orbit the stratosphere.

*

Dinnertime. Over plates of steaming hot pie, mash and parsley liquor at Harry Charles' Pie and Mash shop on Green Street, the girls eagerly forked mouthfuls of food down and dissected the morning's events.

'A shotgun wedding, heh?' mused Winnie. 'We've never done one of them before.'

'That we know of,' Stella added, arching one eyebrow.

'Poor girl,' Kitty sympathized. 'At least he's agreed to marry her. Saves her shouldering the shame of a scandal alone.'

'Why should it be her shame to bear alone?' fumed Stella, flipping her pie over and stabbing her fork into the pastry base. 'Bleedin' men. He lands up cock o' the walk, meanwhile she's branded a fallen woman! Funny how there's no equivalent for "fallen man"? Proves it, though, don't it?'

'Proves what?' asked Winnie, looking up as she doused her pie in vinegar.

'Two minutes' fun, nine months' pain and a lifetime of shame.' Stella nodded knowingly as she shovelled a forkful of mash in.

'What did your Treacle have to ask you Saturday night that was so important?' Kitty asked, tactfully changing the subject. This talk was all a bit fast for a Monday dinnertime.

'He asked me to marry him,' Winnie sighed, putting down her fork and pushing her plate away.

'Oh, Win, I knew it!' Kitty gushed. 'What did you say?'

'No, of course,' she replied in a flat voice.

'Oh,' Kitty replied, feeling strangely crushed. 'How did he take it?'

'Says he shan't give up, but he's wasting his breath. Besides the fact that I can't leave Mum and the girls, I'm only seventeen.'

'Nearly eighteen,' added Stella. 'Old enough to know what you want out of life and work for it.'

'True, but how can I marry without my dad's permission? Even if Tommy were around, I can't see him agreeing to it, can you?'

'Funny how we're considered responsible enough to have worked from the age of fourteen, but not old enough to make our own choices over marriage 'til we turn twenty-one,' Stella remarked sourly, pushing her plate away and lighting up a cigarette.

'So what's going on with you, Kitty sweetheart?' asked Winnie breezily, keen to steer the subject away from marriage and her father.

'Actually, girls, I did want to show you something.'

Kitty pulled the letter she had found in the base of the sewing machine out and slid it across the marble-topped table.

'Blimey, what a thing to have found,' chuckled Winnie, her eyes gleaming, after she'd read it. 'This Harry sounds like a bit of a naughty so–and–so. Whatever did he do?'

'Perhaps he's a jewel thief?' quipped Stella.

'Give over, you daft sod,' giggled Winnie, pinching Stella's cigarette for a quick puff. 'But seriously, Kitty, you have to find him. That letter could make all the difference to him.'

'I know,' Kitty agreed. 'But how? His father left in such a hurry, with no forwarding address. All I know for certain is that his mother's called Agnes and Harry's in the Merchant Navy. Not a lot to go on, is it?'

Stella pinched back her fag, blew a long stream of blue smoke and, thinking hard, tapped the ash off her cigarette.

'Got it,' she said, so excitedly that Kitty jumped in her chair. 'We place an advert in the *East London Advertiser* personal column, called *Desperately Seeking Harry*.'

Winnie's mouth fell open and she started to laugh.

'You're wasted in the East End, Stella Smee!'

'Oh no . . .' Kitty quavered. 'I should never have the nerve.'

'Don't worry,' Stella grinned, as she took out a pencil

and started scribbling some words on the back of her fag packet. 'I'll do it for you.'

Her tongue poked out the side of her mouth in concentration as she wrote.

'How's this sound?'

Desperately Seeking Harry. Are you Merchant Navy sailor Harry . . . son of Agnes? If so, please get in touch with Kitty Moloney at Gladys Tingle's bridal gown workshop at 226 Green Street, Bethnal Green, and all will be revealed.

Stella lifted her eyebrows teasingly and their laughter rolled around the small dining room.

'Cross that last bit out,' Kitty giggled, blushing to the roots of her hair. Honestly, she didn't know where her friend got the nerve. 'He'll turn up thinking it's some sort of knocking shop.'

'Yeah, you know what sailors are like,' said Winnie, hooting with laughter. 'He'll turn up as randy as a rabbit in spring.'

'She's right,' added Stella, with a mischievous cackle. 'Most of 'em sail the seven seas, leaving a trail of broken hearts and broken hymens in their wake. Beer today, gone tomorrow – ain't that right, Win?'

'Stella!' Kitty admonished, taking a sip of her tea to calm herself.

'He better hope it's not Gladys who answers if he does show up,' Winnie shot back. 'She'll have him strung up by his dickie collar before you can say "Hello sailor"!'

Kitty couldn't help herself, and laughed so hard, she spat her coffee out.

'So go on then, Kitty, what do you say? Shall I put it in the paper?' Stella asked. 'I can nip down to the newspaper offices now and ask if they'll put it in the next edition. We've still got twenty minutes left of dinner break.'

Kitty had her doubts whether anything would come of Stella's madcap scheme, but in the company of two such vibrant, confident women, she suddenly felt as if anything were possible. Next to the burden of caring for her father, and a day spent entirely at his bedside yesterday, it felt good to laugh.

'Go on then,' she groaned. 'Gladys'll have forty fits if she finds out, but I suppose I have to try anything to get this letter to him.'

'You shan't regret it,' Stella said with a reckless grin as she jumped to her feet.

Impulsively, she reached over the tabletop, grabbed Kitty's head in both her hands and covered her in a shower of kisses. Kitty had to beat her off.

'Get away, you daft cow,' she giggled.

Stella scooped up her cigarettes and bag before strutting to the door, her blonde curls bobbing.

'Cover for me with Herbie if I'm held up, will ya, Win?' she called. At the last minute, she turned, whipped the small hand-held camera out of her bag and pointed it at the girls.

'Smile and say "Hello Harry",' she grinned, pressing the shutter release.

'Behave, you cheeky sod!' Winnie screeched, hurling a screwed-up napkin at Stella as she bolted out the door. 'I look a fright.

'That girl, honestly,' sighed Winnie, shaking her head. 'She's a case.'

They were still chuckling when the door burst back open. Both girls looked up as one, half-expecting it to be Stella, but the stricken face gazing down at them belonged to Mrs Flood's eldest son.

'Kitty, there you are, thank God,' he panted. 'You gotta come quick. It's yer dad. He's gone doolally!'

*

The rain was drumming on the cobbles outside Kitty's buildings as, breathlessly, she ran as fast as she dared along the slippery street. Panic slammed through her as she flew round the corner at high speed, holding onto a gas lamp to stop herself spinning out of control.

Please God, let Dad be all right.

But as she rounded the corner into the central courtyard of the tenement buildings, her heart lurched. What on earth?

Dressed only in a tatty white nightgown and urine-stained long johns, his white hair plastered to his head in the rain, her father twisted this way and that, cursing and lashing out at a group of five young lads.

'Ya little bleeders!' he screamed. 'Nicking my stock. I'll give you what for when I get my hands on yer . . .'

He reached out to cuff the nearest one, but quick as a flash, the boy ducked down out of reach, giggling, and Kitty's father slipped and crashed to his knees on the wet concrete floor. A thick slick of blood soaked his long johns, but he seemed oblivious.

'Look at my fruit,' he sobbed, bewildered, picking a stone

off the floor of the courtyard and holding it up with trembling fingers. 'It's all ruined. See, it's contaminated now. I'll never be able to sell that.' He started to cough, a deep and wrenching spasm, as he cradled the stone in his palm.

A terrible fear crawled the length of Kitty's spine. What was happening to her father's mind?

'Dad,' whispered Kitty, trying to keep the fear from her voice as she took off her coat and placed it round his shoulders. 'What you doing out here, you daft beggar? You'll catch your death.'

He stared back at her, unseeing, and Kitty saw her horrified face reflected in his pale, rheumy eyes.

'Kitty?' he rasped, confused. 'Is that you? Where's your mother? What's her game, eh? Leaving me to look after you and your sisters, when she knows I've got to be back at work. I've got to work twice as hard now they've put the rent up. Not that I've anything to sell,' he scowled, throwing the stone across the courtyard.

The boys fell about in howls of laughter. In the distance, a door slammed, and the tall, black upright figure of Auntie marched across the courtyard.

'You've had your sport, now go on, sling yer hook, or you'll get more than a fourpenny one!' she shrieked, cuffing the ringleader round the side of the head.

She and Kitty took an arm each and gently guided Mr Moloney back inside. As they walked, Kitty's eyes travelled up the building. On the outdoor balconies ringing the courtyard, she spotted a knot of women, sitting in a circle shelling peas into the laps of their coarse aprons, shaking their heads.

Auntie spotted them too. 'All right, you've had your

entertainment for the day, ladies,' she called up. 'There ain't gonna be an encore, so you may as well get back inside.'

*

An hour later, Kitty and Auntie, with Dr Garfinkle's help, had managed to bathe her father and dress the cuts on his knees. Now he was propped up by the fire in fresh clothing and wrapped in a warm blanket.

All traces of the wild and angry man of earlier had vanished, thanks to the barbiturate the doctor had administered. Now he sat smiling benignly as Auntie fed him sips of chicken broth, dabbing tenderly at his chin with a cloth.

'It's as I feared,' said the doctor quietly, leading Kitty to one side. 'Your father is greatly confused and his chest is worsening. I will keep a close eye on him, but should he deteriorate further it may be necessary to have him admitted to an infirmary.'

'But I promised Dad he'd stay here with me, in his own home,' Kitty protested, her eyes widening in panic. 'It's the recent illnesses he's had, messing with his mind, that's all. He'll recover his wits, I'm certain of it, Doctor.'

The doctor looked at her with compassion.

'My dear, your father needs unremitting arousing, an abundance of sleep, open-air exercise and nourishing food, to say nothing of supervision. You saw what happened. What if next time he wanders outside to the train line, or under a nearby tram?'

'With respect, Doctor, infirmaries are all well and good, but what about family love?' asked Auntie, who had been listening.

The doctor went to answer, but was interrupted by a sharp hammering at the front door.

Kitty's heart sank as she opened the door and found herself face to face with the mother of the boy her father had threatened in the courtyard earlier.

'Your dad's a bleedin' lunatic,' she ranted. 'He wants locking up in a loony bin. He's got no pride in himself, dirty old man. How dare he threaten my boy?'

'Don't you come round here shouting the odds,' interrupted Auntie. 'From what I saw, your boy was having a high old time, goading a sick man.'

'Rubbish, Auntie,' the woman blustered. 'I ought to get the law onto him. I will next time. Just you see if I don't.' She turned to the doctor, cheeks flaming with self-righteous indignation.

'You know me, Doctor, I say it as I see it. I call a spade a—'

'—a bleedin' shovel usually,' snorted Auntie.

''Ow dare you?' she screeched.

'Easily. Now, button it, unless you want a smack in the gob, ' Auntie snapped, slamming the door so hard in her face, the frame rattled.

'Cheek of her! Giving over like she cares about her boy,' she spat, the black feather on her hat quivering with rage. 'She only came over to stick her beak in. Honestly, that woman wants to know the ins and outs of a cat's arsehole . . . Apologies, Doctor.'

Dr Garfinkle shrugged. He had seen enough neighbourhood spats not to be shocked, just as he knew the two women would be friends again by morning; either that, or they would be going at it like cats in the courtyard.

'I shan't admit your father yet, Miss Moloney,' he said. 'But I'm afraid I will be powerless to intervene if she does get the constabulary involved and they deem your father a threat. Two doctors' signatures will be all that's required to admit him into a lunatic asylum.'

The doctor prescribed something to help Mr Moloney sleep, handed her a jar of calve's-foot jelly, the cost of which was borne from his own pocket, then took his leave, his dire predictions still ringing in Kitty's ears. Only once he had gone and her father was asleep did Auntie brew up a fresh pot and sit Kitty down gently by the fire.

'I have an inkling what sent your dad off like that,' she said, wearily pulling a crumpled letter from her pocket.

'What is it, Auntie?' Kitty sighed, feeling like she didn't have the breath in her body to cope with any more shocks.

'Your father probably opened this the same time as me and every other poor sod in the buildings, I shouldn't wonder.'

Kitty scanned the letter and felt despair tighten her throat. The tenant landlord of M. & P. Properties Limited was writing to inform them he had sold on the leasehold of the majority of the flats in the buildings to another landlord, who had promptly put their rent up to eleven shillings a week, an eye-watering sum to Kitty. No mention whatsoever had been made in the letter of tenants' repeated requests to repair the broken toilet door, the dilapidated rooftop washing facilities, broken handrails, or the crumbling steps, to say nothing of the damp, peeling walls.

'They can't do this,' Kitty choked.

'They're slum landlords, so crooked they can't lie straight

in bed,' Auntie muttered. 'They think they can do what they like.'

'But I can't move Dad,' Kitty cried. 'He's confused enough as it is, imagine if he had to move to new digs? I can't afford to stay here, but I can't move him either. Oh, what will become of us?'

At that moment, a steam train thundered past outside in a shower of smoke and smuts, its whistle blasting so loudly, Kitty's father twitched and stirred, even in his heavily sedated state.

The reverberations seemed to dislodge something deep inside, and Kitty broke down in Auntie's arms.

Auntie was a handsome, proud woman, not easily given to displays of sentiment; raising six sons had knocked that out of her. Easily in her late fifties, she still had jet-black hair, which she wore scraped back in a bun, an unlined face, bone-white teeth and hands as strong as a butcher's. She folded Kitty into her starched black skirts and rubbed her back firmly.

'Don'cha worry, girl,' she said. 'I'm gonna sort this. Ain't no one turning you and yer dad out of yer home, I promise. Not as long as my heart's still beating.'

Auntie's knuckles, as big as roots of ginger, twitched. 'We're gonna fight this!'

*

A mile and a half away, in Cable Street, another vow was being made.

'I must remember to take a jimmy riddle before I leave work,' Winnie vowed under her breath as she groped her way across the pitch-black yard, using the old lead piping that ran the length of the brick dividing wall to guide her.

Once in the freezing cold lavatory, she fumbled about for a square of newspaper. In the gloom, she felt for the note she had pinned there to cheer her mother up, but found it missing. Making a mental note to pin another one up for when her mother arrived home at the end of the week, Winnie yanked up her drawers and hurried across the yard, inside to the warmth of Treacle's arms.

No mention had been made of his proposal two nights earlier, with both of them content just to make the most of the precious few days of privacy that stretched ahead, until Jeannie and the girls returned to Cable Street. No mention, and yet there was a new thread of intimacy flowing between them. It had taken guts to lay his heart on the line like that, and even though she could never marry him, Winnie respected Treacle more than ever before.

'Look what I found on Sunday, buried beneath the mud at London Bridge,' Treacle said, glancing up as Winnie walked in.

'I think it's a Scandinavian axe,' he went on, excitedly. 'I showed it to a curator at Bethnal Green Museum and he reckons it could even date back to the late 900s and early 1000s. He was a smashing fella. Told me all about it, even lent me a book on it, so he did. Apparently, Scandinavian ruler Swein Forkbeard of Denmark tried to gain control of England. Swein's son Cnut eventually won the English throne.'

His eyes glistened, as animated as a child's, as he sat up in his chair. 'There were battles all along the Thames, Win, and around London Bridge – at one point, even the bridge was pulled down. These battleaxes and spears were found during building works at the north end of the bridge in the 1920s. They may've been lost in battle, or thrown into the river by the victors in celebration. The fella I spoke with reckoned this could even be one of 'em. Can you ever imagine, Win?'

'Don't forget to breathe, Treacle!' she laughed.

Winnie cocked her head, still smiling, as he cradled the ancient axe in his long, strong fingers. 'What is it about all this digging for stuff in the Thames that floats your boat?'

'It's pure magic, Win,' he breathed. 'When I'm alone at the water's edge, scouring the mud in a misty dawn, or at work, looking down at the swirling waters from the side of the docks, I just lose myself in the history of it. I love it, I do.' He shook his head in dismay.

'Old Father Thames is concealing hundreds, if not thousands of stories. So many generations of people have left their mark on the East End. Do you reckon in a hundred years' time, people will be talking about us and the way we lived?'

Winnie glanced around the poky room and wrinkled her nose.

'Yeah, they'll be saying, "How the hell did they survive in such a dump?"'

She grinned and carefully took the axe from Treacle's hands, before stowing it away on the top shelf, safely out of reach.

'Don't want my sisters thinking this is a toy when they get home,' she remarked.

'When is that anyhow?' he asked, pulling her down into his lap as she returned.

'Another four days – they're not back until Friday.'

'Smashing, so I've got you all to myself for a bit longer,' Treacle winked, a flash of mischief creasing over his face. Suddenly, he flipped her back onto the settee and covered her face with a shower of kisses.

'Stop mucking about, you daft sod!' she squealed, but Treacle was too strong and had her pinned fast with his broad chest.

'I ain't going to let you go until you give us a kiss.'

'Who do you think you are?' she laughed. 'King bleedin' Forkbeard.'

'Right here,' he said teasingly, tapping his mouth. 'Pretty please!'

'Very well,' she said, 'seeing as you asked nicely.'

Tilting her chin up, she brushed her lips against his.

Softly, Treacle kissed her back and within moments, Winnie forgot herself. All she was aware of was his warm mouth, tenderly kissing every inch of her face, exploring the curve of her neck, the lobes of her ears, her flushed cheeks, as he murmured her name over and over.

Threading his fingers through hers, his lips returned to her mouth, and teased it open. The physical sensations were overwhelming, the heat of his body, the sweet softness of his mouth exploring hers, her body succumbing to his. Something inside Winnie melted like warm honey and she no longer felt capable of concealing her love for this honest and decent man.

'I love you so much, Winnie Docker,' he whispered.

Looking back, Winnie wondered why she never heard the soft click of the front door. Maybe it was because she was unguarded, so caught up in the intimacy of that moment that she had taken leave of her senses? Or perhaps it was simply because, living cheek by jowl with their neighbours, she was used to the constant thud of footsteps and babble of Yiddish tongues.

Either way, she scarcely noticed her father until he was looming over her.

'I don't know who the hell you are, but you have five seconds to get your dirty paws off my daughter!' he thundered. 'Turn my back for a minute and you turn into some sort of whore hound.'

Tommy Docker spoke like a man who had just popped out for a packet of fags, not someone who had vanished without trace over a year ago.

Horrified, Winnie and Treacle scrabbled to their feet, smoothing down their clothes.

Silhouetted against the flames from the fireplace, her father's reddened face was more pinched, his eyes more sunken. He was also taller than Winnie remembered, and had grown a moustache since she'd last seen him: a small bristling red thing that clung to his top lip like a dead rodent. The same dark red hair though, slicked back over the crown of his head, and those curious circular bald patches either side of his temples, through which a vein throbbed alarmingly.

'Please, sir,' Treacle babbled. 'It weren't what it looked like. I promise I weren't taking liberties with your daughter. I'm in love with her and I want her for my wife. My name is Treacle—'

'I couldn't give a rat's arse who you are, sonny Jim,' Tommy interrupted coldly, without once taking his eyes off Winnie. 'Now piss off out of it.'

Treacle hovered next to Winnie, weighing up whether to front up to her father or do as ordered.

The tension was unbearable, as if the room might burst into flames at any moment, and Winnie burned with humiliation.

'I'll be fine, Treacle, honestly. I'll see you later,' Winnie said, as calmly as she could.

Without another word, Treacle left, but hesitated by the doorway.

'Please . . . just go,' she begged. Reluctantly, Treacle grabbed his coat and walked out.

Alone, Winnie faced her father, a groundswell of hatred and anger rising up inside her.

'How did you find us?' she whispered.

'I went back to our old buildings and you'd gone. So I went to a boarding house, next to the Salvation Army on Green Street, there a few days and that's where I spotted you, outside cleaning the windows, as luck would have it. Who's that fella you work for now? What is he? Bent, a faggot? Looks it.'

Tommy spoke fast, clearly agitated, as he fished about in his pocket, pulled out a Player's and lit it.

'You . . . you followed me home? You've been *watching* me?'

'Where's your mother?' he replied, ignoring her question as he started to pace the room, opening cupboard doors and flicking at the tatty drapes.

'She's on holiday,' Winnie replied.

Tommy stopped pacing and he stared at her unblinking, pale blue eyes gazing out through sandy, near invisible lashes.

'Holiday?' he rasped, as if he couldn't quite believe what

he had heard. 'So, I've been working away, slogging my guts out, and she's off having a nice *holiday*!'

'She deserves it, Dad,' Winnie protested hotly. 'She's done nothing but slave since you buggered off and left us high and dry.'

Winnie knew it was a mistake the minute the words were out of her mouth. Tommy drew back his fist and Winnie braced herself, but at the last minute, he drew back his hand and smiled instead, trailing one nicotine-stained finger down her cheek.

'Word from the wise,' he grinned, gripping her chin tightly between his fingers. 'I dunno who this Treacle fella is, but you need to keep yer hand on yer ha'penny, my girl.'

His ferrety features, pinched and red, loomed in front of hers.

'It's a woman's job to be pure when she marries. That ought to be the summit of all her ambition, her training . . . and that ring is her medal. But medals have to be earned, my girl.'

Winnie closed her eyes so she didn't have to see his mawkish expression, but still he kept on, his sour breath turning her insides.

'When your mother married me, half the girls down our turning were sick with envy. I was a catch, see, and your mother was over the moon to have claimed her prize.'

'Well, she don't love you now,' Winnie lied, jutting her chin out defiantly. Looking back, she didn't know where she summoned the bravery. 'I mean, look at'cha,' she went on. 'You ain't no catch now. If I were a fisherman, I'd throw you back.'

Her father laughed, a queer hollow splutter, like an automobile backfiring.

'And whose fault is that, heh?' Compulsively, he began to scrub at the strange bald patches either side of his head and Winnie watched in horrified fascination. 'She turned me into this,' he snorted. 'So no, you're right, it ain't love she feels. It's gratitude. Gratitude's what keeps her opening the door to me, with her face painted and her legs parted. Gratitude's what keeps a marriage going! 'Cause I'm her husband, and after all she put me through, she cleaves to my will, as it has always been. As it always will be.'

Winnie watched, transfixed, as her father pulled a crumpled note from his pocket. She recognized the handwriting instantly. It was hers, written to cheer her mother, keep her focused on the bright future Winnie had mapped out.

It's easy enough to be pleasant when life goes along with a song, but the man worthwhile is the man who can smile when everything goes wrong.

Tommy tore it to pieces and tossed it onto the fire. It was reduced to ashes in moments.

Five

Five days on, and the spectre of Winnie's father's sudden and sinister return still hung around her neck like a noose. The beat of her thoughts was like a ticking clock that would not be stilled, and as she, Herbie and Stella walked to the church for their next job, the same questions turned over and over in her mind. Why had Tommy returned out of the blue? What did he mean when he said it was all her mother's fault? And, more worryingly, how long did he plan on hanging around?

Her mother and the girls had returned home on the church charabanc from Suffolk the previous evening, and Winnie had never seen so many conflicting emotions crash over one woman's face: relief, fear, guilt, and the one which had felt like a knife in the guts to Winnie – joy!

How could her mother love such an utterly repellent man? Winnie had felt all her hard work of the previous year slip through her fingers like sand when Tommy had held out his arms and, without a word, Jeannie had walked into them. It wasn't that her mother wasn't a strong woman! God knows she had proved her mettle this past year by fighting so hard to keep the family together, it was simply that whatever hold her father had over her was far stronger.

Sensing her friend's silent distress, Stella slipped her arm through Winnie's and gave her a gentle squeeze.

'I know what you're thinking about, Win,' she said quietly. 'Has he, well . . . you know . . . laid a hand on you yet?' Stella and Kitty knew the painful details of her past, and they had been the first people she had turned to for comfort after her father's unwelcome return.

'No,' Winnie sighed, dodging a stream of kids charging up the sooty cobbles on their way to the twopenny rush at the bug 'ole. 'And that's the oddest thing, Stell. He's being as nice as pie, and Mum's acting like he's never been away.'

'And Treacle?' Stella ventured.

Winnie bit her bottom lip to stop the tears from coming, as they always did when she thought of the humiliating way her father had dismissed Treacle.

'I've told him to stay away for the time being. He seems to think he can win my dad round, but he don't know him like I do. He don't know what a sick man he is, how he—'

'Come on, girls, chop-chop,' called Herbie from ahead, as he swung open the gate to the churchyard. 'Let's not hang about like a bad smell on the landing. We have to be ready when the bride comes out.'

Stella placed a hand in the small of Winnie's back.

'Don't worry, sweetheart,' she whispered. 'We'll think of something. Come to ours after work for your tea if you want to stay away from home? Auntie's getting together all the tenants at hers for a meeting about what to do about these rent increases. Reckons she's got an idea on how we can give our greedy new landlord a kick up the bum.'

'Yeah, all right then,' agreed Winnie, silently wishing the reach of Auntie's boot could also extend to her father's backside. Someone needed to kick her rotten father clean out of the East End. For good.

*

The skies over St John's churchyard in Bethnal Green were dull, tarnished and threatening snow as the new Mr and Mrs Pickett emerged at the top of the church steps to cheers and applause. No one looked happier – *or more relieved* – than the bride's mother, Stella thought with a wry grin.

The groom was a spindly, bow-legged cabinet maker from Hackney, whose slight frame only served to make his new wife's burgeoning belly all the more prominent. As they reached the bottom step, she trod heavily on his toe and he hopped about in pain. Stella shook her head at the daft superstitions that East End weddings aroused. She could just picture the bride's mother, whispering knowingly in her ear on the way out of church: 'Tread on his foot on the way down the steps, love, and you'll always have the upper hand.' A harmless enough tradition, were it not for the fact that the bride was six months gone.

As Herbie rushed forward and began to arrange the wedding party in the grounds of the churchyard, a local newspaper reporter bustled around taking everyone's particulars. Stella could already picture the wording:

A most charming ceremony took place at St John on Bethnal Green on Saturday when the Reverend Stiles officiated at the delightful wedding of Mr Albert Pickett to Miss Maud Duggan. The bride presented an attractive picture in a becoming gown of white satin trimmed at the neck with silver lamé, a halo of orange blossom, a silk net veil and a five-yard train.

She was attended to by four bridesmaids; Misses Doris, Minnie, Connie and Violet, who all wore quaint little Quaker hats and carried posies of carnations. Master Charlie Wales drew many an admiring glance in his role of pageboy in a blue and white satin suit.

Nowhere in the gushing report would it say what the guests had so obviously guessed. As Stella helped Winnie and Herbie set up for the photos, she overheard a gaggle of brightly dressed female guests gathered round a tombstone, furiously smoking and gossiping. The noise of it all was enough to make the dearly departed turn in their urns.

She's knocked up or my name's not Edna . . . Look at them legs, he couldn't catch a pig in a passage . . . Look at that saucy piece from number 72 parading that young man about – trollop! . . . It was a gallstone, size of a boulder . . . Ten years younger'n what she is! I hope they've got trifle . . . Have you seen Pat's perm . . . ?

On and on they went, until Stella's head hummed with the noise of it all. Herbie's voice rose above the hubbub.

'Okey-doke, folks!' he bellowed. 'Come and gather round for the group photos. I know it's cold and you all want to get back inside.'

The congregation trudged reluctantly over and assembled around the newlyweds, the men scowling and stamping their feet to keep warm, the women jostling for key position as Herbie's finger hovered over the shutter release.

'I've just eaten a strong mint, so come and warm yer hands on my breath if you like,' he quipped and the crowd fell about. 'Lovely happy smiles, that's what I like to see,' he grinned, clicking away.

Stella smiled. Good old Herbie, he always knew how to get the best out of people. Just then, she spotted something unfortunate.

Discreetly moving forward, she nudged Herbie.

'Boss, let's shift the wedding party a few inches to the left, shall we?' she whispered, nodding at a nearby war memorial, a little to the right of the expectant bride.

In memory of the fallen, read the carved inscription.

'Oh crumbs, I didn't spot that! See, Stella, told you that you were my right-hand girl. You better not ever leave me.'

She smiled weakly, just as the clouds burst and snow fluttered from the dazzling white skies overhead, spiralling over the newlyweds like confetti. The bride and groom sealed the romantic picture with a lingering kiss and the crowd whistled and cheered their approval. Even the gravestone gossipers seemed to have changed their tune and were cooing over the pair.

'Good luck to them,' thought Stella, and she really meant it. Even Winnie managed a heartfelt smile.

War was brewing, violence was erupting on the streets, and down the docks, decent men were brawling over work; but for this young couple, kissing in the snow, their new lives were only just beginning. Who cared if they hadn't gone about things in the right order?

*

Later that same afternoon, Kitty was hard at work in the tiny workshop, machining lengths of white velvet for a wedding cape, her delicate fingers feeding the heavy material through her Singer. Velvet was a tricky material to work with and required every ounce of her concentration, but her mind was not on the job. Gladys had already torn a strip off her for not noticing that the lining of the cape had chewed up and had flung it back at her to redo.

The problem was, ever since Kitty had read the letter from her landlord informing them of the rent increase, she had been out of her mind with worry. She prayed Auntie had the solution. Between that and her father's loosening grip on reality, she was at her wit's end. His nocturnal wandering was getting worse, and he was growing increasingly paranoid, accusing Kitty of all sorts. Strangest of all though was how his memory had the ability to evoke recollections of long-past events with extraordinary detail, but his memory for recent names or faces was colourless.

The world he occupied now was shadowy and full of imaginary demons. She could deal with it, it was the others she worried about, and her mind cast back to her neighbour's veiled threats to call in the law.

'Are you listening to me, Kitty Moloney?'

Kitty looked up to find Gladys's round, red face staring back at her from her workstation near the door, one eye on the window, one on the veil she was embroidering. Kitty didn't know how she did it. Her pudgy fingers were as big as sausages, yet she was the most skilled seamstress in the East End, her hands so precise and unerringly nimble as she sewed. From her vantage point nearest the door, she also managed to keep half an eye on the comings and goings on Green Street and usually kept up a running commentary as she sewed.

'Sorry, Gladys, I was miles away,' Kitty admitted.

'I was saying how it's snowing again, and even that don't keep that lousy lot inside.'

She finished the seam she was sewing and snapped the thread off viciously between her teeth.

'Bloody blackshirts out on their weekly march again. I'll never forgive 'em for what they did last week. Poor Mr Taylor. All of us traders' reputations will suffer, you know.'

'They certainly don't give us much peace, do they?' Kitty agreed.

'Peace!' snorted Gladys, pushing back her stool and rubbing her back. 'Don't talk to me about peace. The only peace in Bethnal Green at the moment is the food. A little piece of this, a little piece of that. Still, least it's snowing and that will mean work clearing the streets for men and hopefully a decent feed for some nippers tonight.'

With that, she tied on her headscarf and grabbed her string bag from under her workstation.

'On the subject of which, I'm just nipping out, love, so can you hold the fort? I dropped that new Singer into Mr Moxhay's, so he could give it a once-over, and I want to see if it's ready.'

Kitty felt her stomach heave with guilt as she remembered the letter she had found in the base, which she still hadn't told Gladys about.

'Stay with me, girl,' Gladys tutted, snapping her fingers in front of Kitty's face, jerking her back to the moment.

'After that, I'm gonna pop to the butcher's. He promised he'd hold me back a nice bit of mutton, and Big Mickey's put aside some veg.'

Gladys smacked her lips together as she fastened the

buttons on her long black coat. 'I plan on doing up a big batch of pot roast, pad it out with some barley, taters and carrots, and then there'll be plenty to go round.'

She winked at Kitty. 'Some for your dad – nice bit of Gladys Tingle's gravy'll soon have him back on his feet – and some for Mr Taylor.'

At the mention of Herbie's name, the spinster's blue eyes lit up, twinkling out from the pudgy folds of her face. She crossed her arms and rested them on her gigantic corseted bosom, which jutted out of her sensible coat like a shelf. Quite suddenly, Kitty caught a glimpse of the young woman she must have been at twenty-one. The spinster still kept herself nice, with regular visits to the Italian hairdressers on Green Street, and she was never seen without a touch of rouge. Kitty suspected it was all for Herbie's benefit, though it was quite clearly wasted. Whatever had happened to his wife and son had left him numb to the attentions of middle-aged seamstresses.

Looking down, she felt like screaming when she saw the needle had chewed up the velvet again.

'Dearie me,' sighed Gladys. 'I don't know where your head is today, girl. Leave that and finish off the toile instead. Carry on in the mood you're in, and you'll have the needle through your thumb, I shouldn't wonder.'

Gladys disappeared out into the frosty hue and cry of the Saturday market. Sighing heavily, Kitty strung a tape measure round her neck and turned her attentions instead to the dressmaker's mannequin.

'You got any ideas how I get myself out of this mess?' she asked the dummy. 'No, thought not.'

Popping half a dozen pins in her mouth, she set about pinning lace to the collar.

So intent on not ruining another job was she, she didn't hear the stranger enter the workshop. Quite entranced, he stayed motionless by the doorway watching. The soft glow from the gas lamp lit up the downy hair on the back of her long, pale neck, her fine, slender fingers working with such deceptively casual ease, moving delicately across the folds of the material as she rhythmically pinned and tacked.

The stranger was so enchanted by the sight of this young woman, he didn't utter a word as he watched her in her endeavours. Her long hair, shiny as a polished conker, was scooped up on the top of her head in a bun, but fine tendrils had escaped and curled round her perfect cheekbones. He thought her quite the loveliest creature he had ever laid eyes on.

The cough startled Kitty and she jumped, whirling round to find herself face to face with a rakish young man in immaculate dark blue bell-bottomed trousers and a blue collar over a snowy-white vest. Two sea-green eyes shone mischievously from under a mop of blond hair and, in one hand, he clutched a natty blue-topped cap, and in the other, a copy of the *East London Advertiser*.

The penny dropped – and so did the pins from Kitty's mouth, scattering and pinging over the brown-paper flooring.

'Harry?' she murmured, feeling a deep flush prickle beneath her pinafore, as he knelt down to pick them up. His sun-kissed neck, which spoke of far-flung travel, and limber body didn't escape Kitty's attention. As he collected the pins, his uniform strained over a well-muscled back. Kitty held onto the mannequin to steady herself.

'At your service, miss,' he grinned, bouncing back up and placing the pins down on the cutting table. 'Apparently, you have been *desperately* seeking me out,' he said, raising one eyebrow, his grin spreading wide over his face like a Cheshire cat. Kitty thought back to the bold notice Stella had written out on her behalf, and inwardly cursed.

'Yes . . . Yes, that's right,' she replied, flustered. 'I got a letter of yours, by accident. I don't have it with me now. It's at home, under my pillow. For safekeeping.'

Kitty's flush deepened. Why had she said that?

'Well, now I'm intrigued,' he replied, edging a step closer to her, eyes sparkling. 'Miss . . . ?'

'Kitty. Kitty Moloney,' she gulped.

A strange physical sensation overcame Kitty. Her throat was dry and her pulse was racing unnaturally fast.

'Well, Kitty Moloney, there's a dance on next Saturday at York Hall Baths. Smashing band playing too, so why don't we meet there, say 7 p.m.? Then you can return my letter and do me the honour of being my date for the evening.'

'Oh, I don't know about that,' she mumbled, thinking of her father, to say nothing of Stella and Winnie's lurid descriptions of sailors.

'You do dance, I presume, Kitty?'

'Well, yes, but . . .'

'That's settled then,' he said, replacing his cap. 'You know, Kitty, I was watching you working before I introduced myself. You have quite a talent. Not sure about this wedding dress material though.'

'It's only a toile,' she giggled. 'We make it out of calico first to get the perfect fit.'

As they talked, a tiny spider crawled up the bodice.

'Not sure the bride'd be too happy with that,' he said, lifting the spider gently off the material.

'You'd be surprised,' she smiled, feeling herself relax a little. 'It's good luck to have a spider on your wedding dress.'

Harry took her hand in his and pressed it to his lips, his dancing green eyes never leaving hers.

'I think the good luck is all mine, Kitty. To have met you. Until next Saturday.'

A blast of cold air shot through the workshop as the door closed behind him, but Kitty still felt warm, the skin on her hand tingling where his lips had touched her skin. Sitting down on her stool, she fanned herself with a paper dress pattern, and with the other hand touched her throat. What had just happened to her? She was the same girl she had been five minutes ago, except everything *else* looked different. The familiar view outside the window was skewed, its colours more vivid; the orange glow of the market stall flares cloaking the snow-flecked gas lamps in a shimmering gold hue. Kitty's world shone a little brighter. Or so she fancied. Picking up the white velvet cape and smiling softly, she began to sew.

*

Later that afternoon, back in their buildings, Auntie stood astride an upturned orange crate slap bang in the middle of the courtyard, wearing her customary black floor-length, button-down dress and a militant expression. She cut a formidable figure, framed by the gloom of the soot-blackened tenements, and surrounded on all sides by her six protective sons.

The courtyard was filled with chattering residents, and

kids ran shrieking up and down the landings or sat dangling their feet and shelling peanuts over the balcony edges, while mothers with chapped hands and crossover aprons chattered and laughed.

Stella glanced at Kitty and Winnie, and grimaced. 'Don't know how Auntie's gonna make her voice heard over this din!'

From behind her back, Auntie pulled out a long wooden spoon and beat it loudly on the bottom of a saucepan until a hush fell over the courtyard. Only the sound of the broken toilet door banging in the wind cut through the silence.

'What is it that keeps the East End strong?' she hollered.

'A jug of Watney's and a port and lemon for the missus,' joked a wag.

'Solidarity, that's what,' Auntie boomed, ignoring him as she gazed around the crowd. 'The time has come to say, enough's enough! We can't carry on living like this.'

Heads nodded.

'Who here is sick of that bloody broken toilet door? Or the damp and the vermin? Or the peeling walls?'

More heads nodded and Stella felt a surge of impotence and anger bristle through the crowd. The kernel of an idea began to grow deep within; she did not yet know where it would lead, but acting on instinct, Stella took her camera out of her bag, raised it and silently began to take photos of Auntie on her soapbox. There was something so magnetic about the sight of her, she simply couldn't resist.

A wry smiled passed over her face as a sudden thought occurred to her. Over in the West End of London, society portrait photographer Dorothy Wilding's star was in the ascendant, as she became increasingly sought after by the Royal family. Over here in the less salubrious East End,

Stella Smee was also photographing royalty, of a sort – slum queens!

'Who wants wash facilities that don't keep breaking down?' Auntie bellowed, holding on to the feathered hat she wore like a crown to stop a gust of wind blowing it off.

'Me, Auntie,' piped up a woman. 'I've spent a bleedin' fortune dragging my laundry down to the washhouse every time they pack up.'

'And why should you have to?' Auntie railed, her eyes flashing indignantly. 'Who here thinks the open gas-jet flares that light the stairs and landings are dangerous?'

'They're an accident waiting to happen!' shrieked another woman. 'I caught some kids on each other's shoulders the other day, trying to light bits of paper off it. They could have been burned alive if I'd not stopped 'em!'

'So at a time when they ought to be coming round here and making repairs, upgrading us to electricity, what does our landlord do?' Auntie cried. 'Put our rents UP! That's how much him and his bloody kind care for our safety and comfort. What lessons are we teaching our kids, if we stand for this?'

She eyeballed the crowd. 'I raised my boys to have pride in themselves, pride in their district. How can we respect our homes and our neighbours if we don't respect ourselves?'

She slammed a bunched-up fist into her palm, before pumping it into the air.

'It's time to fight! Fight for our right to a decent standard of living!'

A great roar of approval ricocheted round the courtyard, and a flock of startled pigeons flapped off the broken rooftop washhouse, soaring into the zinc-coloured skies beyond.

'We may be working class, but we ain't the underdogs!'

Click. Stella caught the triumphant moment charismatic Auntie captured the hearts and minds of her neighbours. Up until now, she had been the community matriarch, turning her hand to everything from delivering babies to laying out their dead. Now, she was filling them with fight, an East End slum queen leading her troops to battle.

A lone male voice pealed out above the chorus of cheers.

'I hear you, Auntie, but what do we do about it? There's such a shortage of housing, they've got us by the short and curlies. We lose this place, there ain't nowhere else to go.'

'It's like what I first said,' she shot back, gesturing with flattened palms to quieten the excited crowd. 'We stick together. We only win when we stick together. Loyalty, comradeship, that's what will get us out of this mess.'

'But the landlord's got the law on his side,' called back the man. 'We're decontrolled tenants. We ain't got a leg to stand on.'

'But we have rights too,' she insisted. 'A right to live in decent housing, where the facilities we pay for actually work.'

Without a word, Stella slipped her precious camera back into its case, and together with Kitty and Winnie, watched with a deepening admiration as Auntie outlined her plans.

Turned out she had been busy. She had made contact with a friend who lived in Fieldgate Mansions in neighbouring Stepney, and discovered how they, with the help of the Communist Party, had fought and successfully forced their landlord to make repairs and bring in electricity.

'We band together and fight the slumlord like they did, and are continuing to do in Stepney!' she cried. 'We start by calling the sanitary inspector in and get him to send an Intimation Notice to the landlord . . .'

'That won't work,' heckled an older man. 'Sanitary inspector's bent as a nine-bob note, he's hand in glove with the landlord.'

'Then we bypass him and send a Statutory Notice direct to the landlord, instructing him to make repairs and demanding electric lighting. Another letter to the electric companies, calling for their help. Then we start to make a noise about the disgusting state of this place – we can all make noise, right?'

Another great wave of raucous laughter rang round the buildings.

'My missus has a voice that would stop Genghis Khan and the entire bleedin' Mongol empire in its tracks,' piped up a man at the back of the crowd.

'And we might need her too,' Auntie laughed. 'But, seriously, we organize ourselves properly like they're doing in Stepney,' she went on. 'We rally support – Dr Garfinkle has already pledged to help. We contact the local papers, the town hall; we make placards; we picket the landlord's office . . . but, above all, we don't stop making a noise until they come and make repairs.'

By the time the meeting disbanded and the buoyed-up tenants started drifting back to their flats, Stella felt a new wave of energy pulsing off the cobblestones. Auntie's speech had put fire and hope in their bellies.

Once they were finally alone in the darkening courtyard, Kitty turned to Stella and Winnie, her dewy skin glowing.

'I've got to get back inside to Dad, but before I go, I must tell you something,' she whispered.

Winnie glanced at Stella and winked.

'Judging by the look of her, I'd say it's something to do with our mysterious Harry.'

'How did you know?' she asked, gripping Winnie's arm. 'He saw Stella's . . . that is to say, my ad in the personal column and turned up at the workshop, earlier! He wants me to meet him at a dance next Saturday at York Hall. I've agreed to go, but please say you'll come with me. I shan't go without you two.'

'Course we will! We wouldn't let you trot off and meet a strange man without us having a chance to check him out. Us Wedding Girls gotta stick together, right, Stell?' Winnie remarked.

'What am I saying? I can't possibly go!' Kitty groaned. 'I can't leave Dad on his own when he's ill.'

'Then I'll sit with him,' Stella insisted. 'Treacle and Winnie can chaperone you and I'll look after your father. I'm a lousy dancer anyhow.'

'But I've not a thing to wear,' Kitty said despairingly. 'Every last penny's going on Dad's medicine and my rent. I've barely got enough to keep us in cabbage water.'

'I've got a little bit left over from Dad's inheritance. I'll buy you some material from Green Street and you can run yourself up a new dress,' Stella said.

Kitty opened her mouth to protest.

'No arguments,' Stella insisted, the timbre of her voice silencing Kitty.

'Good, that's settled then,' Winnie smiled. 'Cinderella here will go to the ball.'

From round the corner, the stout figure of Gladys hove into sight, huffing and clutching a pot in her hand.

'All right, girls, wot'cha all doing out here in the cold,

gassing? You'll catch your deaths. Now, Kitty, I've got your dad some stew, like I promised.'

'Take it right in, Gladys,' Kitty smiled gratefully. 'I told Dad you're popping round. I'll be in, in a bit.'

She turned back to the girls, blue eyes gleaming with excitement.

'Thank you,' she gushed. 'You're the best pals a girl could ever have.'

'And don'cha forget it,' Stella winked, pulling a cigarette out from underneath her cap and lighting it.

'He was ever so handsome,' Kitty said breathlessly. 'Oh, it's been an age since I've been dancing. I think I've forgotten how!' Her hand rested on her heart and she smiled dreamily. 'You ought to have seen his eyes, girls. The loveliest, deepest shade of green you've ever seen. Put me in mind of the ocean.'

Stella turned to Winnie and winked, before rubbing her knuckles playfully on the top of Kitty's head.

'Looks like someone's got it bad!'

But she was only teasing. She was thrilled to bits for their friend. Dear, sweet Kitty worked her fingers to the bone, and life had already given her so many problems to balance on her young shoulders. She deserved a new frock, and to dance her cares away with a handsome man.

A loud smash from inside Kitty's flat startled the trio.

'Dad!' screamed Kitty, her expression freezing.

In a flash, she was pelting towards the noise.

Stella mashed her cigarette out and she and Winnie followed.

It was not a pretty picture inside Kitty's shabby dwellings.

Stew was spattered over the walls and lino flooring, and an upended pot had skidded to a halt by the fire.

Gladys's face was blanched of colour and, trembling, she pointed over to where Kitty's father was sitting.

'I . . . I . . . I don't know what happened,' she stammered. 'I'm so sorry, Kitty, love, I was only trying to feed your dad a drop of stew.'

Stella watched in horrified silence as Kitty rushed to her father's side.

'Dad, whatever's wrong?' she said, putting her arms gently around his shoulders. 'It's Gladys . . . You know Gladys.'

His eyes, wild with fear, rolled around in his face as he jabbed a bony finger in Gladys's direction.

'She is one of them . . .'

'One of who, Dad?' Kitty cried, unable to keep the exasperation from her voice.

'The enemy! I am shadowed everywhere by my enemies . . . they have been charged with electrocuting me to death, or feeding me contaminated food.'

Stella watched in dismay as he went on with his bizarre rant, gripping his daughter's arm with trembling fingers.

'You must write a telegram to the King urgently, Kitty. He and I are in grave danger. The Kaiser is trying to poison us both. Please . . . Please, I beg of you, don't let them send me to the workhouse, Kitty. That's where they'll get me.'

Stella gulped fearfully. She had known Kitty's poor father was unwell, but this . . . ?

Winnie rushed for the doctor and together, Stella, Gladys and Kitty managed to pacify her father and clear up the mess.

After Dr Garfinkle arrived, Stella drew her exhausted friend outside to the courtyard.

'What on earth is going on, Kitty?'

Kitty hugged her arms around herself protectively, shadows from the gas lamp chasing over her pale face.

'He's got trouble with his chest, Stell. That's all. It's making his mind a bit, well, muddled.'

'I'd say it's more than a bit muddled, Kitty,' Stella replied.

'Oh please, Stella, not you as well,' Kitty sighed. 'He'll recover his wits. I just know he will.'

'And if he doesn't?'

Kitty stared out at the darkened courtyard, where only an hour earlier, Auntie had talked of the need for unity, to stand together in solidarity in the face of adversity. She turned back to Stella, but even in the shadows, Kitty couldn't hide the fear in her face.

'I . . . I can't send my father away, Stella. I promised him he would stay here with me. I'm all he's got. He's all I've got. We're family, and families stick together.'

*

'Isn't it lovely to have the whole family back together again?' Jeannie Docker trilled as she piled a mountain of mashed potato onto her husband's plate, before smothering it in onion gravy.

The slight quake in her mother's hand didn't go unnoticed by Winnie, nor did her smile, which looked like it had been nailed on.

She had got back from Kitty's and the tenants' meeting not half an hour ago and was amazed at the scene which greeted her. Her father, sitting in front of a roaring fire, polishing what looked to Winnie's eyes to be a pair of brand-new boots, her sisters sitting darning in silence, the smell of roasting pork scenting the air as Jeannie bustled about the tiny kitchen. To anyone else, it would have been the picture of domestic bliss. To Winnie, it spelt trouble.

'Where did we get the money for this?' Winnie asked, her eyes narrowing as Jeannie heaped her plate up with crisp, tawny sausages.

'Your father got a new job today,' Jeannie said with forced brightness, stepping back from the table and wiping her hands on her apron.

'You not eating, Mum?' piped up Sylvie, as she tore hungrily into hers.

'No, love, you go on, I had a kettle-bender earlier.'

Winnie lifted one eyebrow. A cup of crusts with some hot water, salt and a knob of marge might have been the only thing her mother had eaten all day, and that certainly wasn't going to keep body and soul together.

'Have mine, Mum,' Winnie said, glaring at her father as he shovelled the food in so fast, she was surprised he didn't choke on it.

'So what is this new job?' she asked.

'Security,' he mumbled through a mouthful of meat.

'Isn't it wonderful,' Jeannie gushed. 'Having his wage now will certainly help lighten the load, but your father's said I can carry on working too.'

'How generous of him,' Winnie said sarcastically. 'Did he also happen to mention where he's been this past year, or am I the only one allowed to point out the elephant in the room? Last we heard, Dad, you were going off to secure us one of them new nice new council houses in Dagenham – our chance to be respectable, you said. Oh, yeah, and not forgetting the shifts you'd picked up at May & Baker which would cover the down payment.'

She glared at him. 'Bloody long shift that!'

'Show some respect to your father,' Jeannie chastised. 'He's home now and that's all that matters. Home with his family, where he belongs, and with a new job too. We're all turning over a new leaf.'

'But, Mum, have you forgotten how hard we had to work this past year to keep the family together, all we went through?' Winnie cried.

'I said show some respect,' Jeannie warned.

'Listen to your mother,' Tommy grinned, picking up his plate and licking it clean, before setting it down in front of Jeannie to wash. 'I appreciate all you've done, Winnie, looking after your mother and sisters and all, while I was away, but I'm back now. Back in the bosom of my family.'

He smiled and winked at Winnie, a thick slick of gravy coating his bristly red moustache, and she felt her stomach heave.

'You've done a good job keeping things ticking over in my absence. Though you could have got a gaff up the Irish end of Cable Street, instead of the bleedin' Jewish end.'

He rose from the table, patted his belly and belched out the side of his mouth.

'After you with the trough, Dad,' Winnie said drily.

Quite suddenly, he began to cough, a terrible wrenching cough that drained the blood from his face. Shuddering slightly, he whipped a handkerchief from his pocket and clamped it over his mouth.

Winnie couldn't resist. 'See someone's forgotten to tell

your chest cough you've turned over a new leaf,' she quipped.

'It's nothing,' he mumbled, glaring at her from over the top of his hankie.

'Oh, I'm not so sure. You know what they say,' Winnie said breezily. 'It's not the cough that'll carry you off, it's the coffin they'll carry you off in.'

'Winifred!' Jeannie snapped, staring sharply at her eldest daughter.

Her father recovered his composure. 'Right, I'm off out now, off to sort a bit of business, but when I get back, see you've cleared your stuff from mine and your mother's room, Winnie. You can go back to sharing with your sisters again.'

Then he was gone and Winnie could do nothing but stare at her mother, frustration and anger fighting off her tears. Already, she could feel the bond they had forged this past year through overcoming adversity together melting away. They had not had one cross word in all the time her father had been away. Within five minutes of his return, a sheet of ice had gone up between them.

'See, love,' Jeannie muttered, unable to meet her daughter's gaze. 'I told you, he only needed some time away from the family, clear his head. He's come back a changed man.'

Winnie said nothing. She didn't buy it for a moment. Beneath the surface, demons were stirring, she was sure of it. Her father's dark, destructive moods could only be repressed for so long.

Six

Seven days later, a fierce, cold wind rushed through Green Street, rattling the shop awnings and sending the market traders' brown paper bags skittering and dancing up the cobbles. Perhaps it was the restless weather, or simply a need to be honest, but Kitty had finally confessed to Gladys about the secret letter she had found hidden in the base of the Singer sewing machine. The elderly seamstress had not been amused! Even less so when she had found out about the advert Kitty and the girls had placed in the local rag to track down the mysterious Harry, and had given her a right rucking. But Gladys was never one to hold a grudge, and now she was even quite curious about the prospect of Kitty's date that very evening.

'So, Dolly daydream, what you wearing then?' she demanded to know, looking up from the dress she was steaming.

Nervously, Kitty showed her the simple cotton dress she had run up.

Gladys took one look at it and her mouth puckered.

'Oh no! No, no, no . . . that'll never do. You want this chap to fall in love with you, you'll look a right plain Jane in that,' she remarked with her usual frankness. 'Besides, imagine if people see you, my apprentice, out in that frumpy frock. I'd never live it over!'

She bustled over to the heavy rack at the back of the room and pulled out a bolt of coral-coloured silk.

'Leave it to me, love,' she winked. 'I'll run you up a dress cut on the bias, show that Harry what a smashing figure you've got.'

She held the material up next to Kitty's face.

'You'll look an absolute peach.'

'But I've no money to pay you,' Kitty protested.

'Did I ask for any?' Gladys declared testily. 'Don't insult me. If I can't treat my hardest-working apprentice to a nice new dress for the dance, then what's the world coming to?'

Kitty couldn't help herself. Overcome with gratitude, she flung herself at her boss and knitted her slender arms around Gladys's neck.

'Give over, you daft ha'p'orth,' Gladys scolded. 'You nearly put me back out.'

'I'm sorry, Gladys,' Kitty wept, unable to stem the tears at her boss's show of kindness. What was making her so pink-eyed and lachrymose? Gladys drew back and took Kitty's hands in hers.

'And your dad? What news of him, love? I'm sorry if I upset him last week.'

'It's not you, Gladys, you've been nothing but kind,' Kitty replied. 'He's not himself at the moment, but he'll come right. He will! He has to, because, well, he's all I've got left now.'

Out of nowhere, she felt her face crumple in desolation, grief slicing through her.

'I can't lose another parent so soon,' she wept. 'I . . . I just wish my mum was here.'

'Oh love, God always takes the best first,' Gladys whispered, pulling out a handkerchief and dabbing away Kitty's tears. 'Your mum'd be so proud of how well you're caring for him, but hear this . . .' Her eyes shone fiercely. 'I made a promise to your mum that I would take good care of you after she'd gone. Both me and Auntie! We gave her our word, so you ain't on your own, see.'

Kitty digested her words over the soft pulse of the gaslight and drew comfort from them.

'Thank you, Gladys. That means so much. You're so kind, all of you.'

Kitty returned to her workstation and picked up the veil she had been embroidering with the bride and groom's initials. 'Stella's going to sit with my father tonight so I can go to the dance without worrying, and Winnie and Treacle are chaperoning me.'

'Aah, the Wedding Girls to the rescue,' grinned Gladys, picking up the dress and resuming her steaming. 'You're lucky to have those two in your life. I sometimes wonder whether friendship – not a husband – isn't the most precious thing in a woman's life,' she remarked knowingly through the clouds of steam.

Kitty knew she was being a bit bold, but her boss was obviously in an expansive mood.

'And what of you, Gladys? Is there not a special someone for you?' Her eyes strayed knowingly to the wall that separated the wedding dress workshop from Herbie's photographic studio. 'You're never too old for love, you know.'

Gladys gazed down at the soft folds of the gown and a flash of regret passed over her features as she let the material slip between her fingers.

'Love never came into my life, Kitty, as much as I'd have liked it to. The man I was courting went off to war and never returned, and after that . . . Well, you know the story. The Great War made spinsters of my generation. That's why I threw myself into this business and dedicated my life to building it up. Always the wedding seamstress, never the bride,' she joked weakly.

Kitty suddenly felt selfish for only considering her own troubles. 'But that ship hasn't sailed yet, Gladys – you're only fifty-five,' she protested.

Gladys shook herself, as if to cast off her sorrow, and quickly painted on her usual demeanour.

'Ships? Don't talk to me about ships, my girl,' she flashed back, holding an imaginary telescope to her eye. 'I don't see no ships, only hardships.'

And with that, Kitty knew she had shut the conversation down.

The pair were interrupted by the paperboy, sticking his head in and tossing a copy of the local paper onto the workbench.

'Read all about it, tenants in uproar.'

Gladys's cheeks flamed.

'How many times I gotta tell you, boy?' she shrieked, leaping to her feet. 'No newspapers in my workshop. I won't have it near the material.' She grabbed the paper, rolled it up and clouted him firmly round the head with it. 'How many times you seen a bride with the latest headlines printed on her behind?'

As the paperboy scurried off, rubbing his head, Gladys unrolled the paper and stepped out onto the kerb.

'Well I never,' she breathed, her outrage quickly forgotten. 'Good on Auntie. That takes guts.'

Kitty leapt to her feet and read over Gladys's shoulder.

There, on the front page, in unavoidable black and white was Auntie, arms folded, at the gates to their buildings. True to her word, she had gone to the papers and named and shamed their lousy landlord, as well as venting her spleen over the abysmal facilities: the rotting handrails, the broken toilet door, leaking drains, crumbling washhouse, and all the other things that made their daily existence a misery.

The paper had also quoted a reproachful Dr Garfinkle, who expressed his concerns over the residents' health and questioned why his letters to the landlord and sanitary inspector had thus far been ignored. It painted a damning picture.

Kitty quailed at the sight of it, and her father's frail face flashed through her mind. 'You don't think we'll get in trouble, do you? They might try and evict us!'

'Sometimes, Kitty, the only way to get anything in life is to fight for it,' Gladys remarked, looking across the bustling street at the sight of Miss Sugarman the milliner, who had repaired her vandalized shopfront and defiantly recreated her display with hats in a vivid rainbow of colours. Her headscarf ruffled in the wind as she vigorously polished her new glass window.

'Fight for it . . . And fight to protect it.'

*

By 7 p.m. that evening all thoughts of leaking drains and vermin were banished as Kitty sat in front of the vanity mirror in Herbie's studio dressing room. She squirmed in her seat as Winnie stood behind her, wielding a pin and an impish grin.

'I don't see why I can't look at my own reflection?' Kitty smiled quizzically, gesturing to the fabric Winnie had draped over the looking glass.

'Because, Kitty dear, I want you to appreciate the full benefit of your make-over. Trust me, you ain't going to recognize yourself.'

Kitty wasn't sure that was an entirely good thing, but she had agreed to put herself in Winnie's hands and for the last thirty minutes she had ministered to her like a fancy lady's maid. The dressing table was a clutter of jars, pots and potions, the contents of which had been smoothed and dusted over her face and décolletage.

'Hold still now,' Winnie warned, as she loomed closer and began to separate her castor-oiled glossed lashes with the pin. Standing back to examine her handiwork, a broad smile spread across Winnie's face.

'Perfect, lashes as long as a yard broom, now for the final touch,' she grinned, producing a lipstick of deepest carmine red.

'Isn't that a bit fast?' Kitty worried.

'Nah, all the actresses are wearing this colour,' Winnie insisted.

'Exactly!' she muttered.

When Winnie had finished painting on the vivid colour with a fine-tipped brush, she reached behind the changing room curtain and Kitty caught a flash of coral.

'Glad's done you proud. Come on then, get your pinny off.'

Self-consciously, Kitty tugged off her pinny and dress,

and stood naked and exposed, save for a pair of lisle stockings and her old cotton stays.

'And them too,' Winnie said smartly.

'W-what, my drawers an' all?' Kitty stammered, her rosepetal complexion flushing even under Winnie's liberal blotting of Papier Poudré.

'Gladys went to Ezther Groves at dinnertime – you know, the corsetière at number 40 – and bought you these. Said to say consider it a bonus for all your hard work.'

From behind the silky curtain, Winnie produced a white cardboard box, and untying the ribbon she lifted the lid with a coy smile. Nestled in the folds of soft tissue paper were a delicately embroidered pink slip and camiknickers, a garter and even a new pair of silk stockings.

'Oh, she never did?' Kitty gasped, and unable to help herself trailed her hands over the exquisite undergarments. She had never worn anything so fine in all her life, and as she eased the stockings up her pale thighs, she felt her flesh prickle with goosebumps at the touch of the silk.

The underwear was soon joined by the satin dress, which slithered over her taut torso like a second skin. True to her word, Gladys had run her up a divine creation. Goodness knows how, but in a matter of hours she had transformed a piece of fabric into a show-stopping gown, cutting the silk at an angle of forty-five degrees, so it draped her body in sinuous folds.

'I'm dressed but I still feel half-naked,' Kitty murmured, tugging nervously at her straps. The fluid fabric of her dress was precariously suspended from the thinnest of shoulder straps.

'You look sensational,' Winnie breathed, delicately

securing the straps to her undergarments by means of two tiny hidden poppers. She stood back to appraise her.

'It's missing something,' she mused.

'A white fox wrap and a diamond as big as an ostrich egg?' Kitty joked lamely.

'You don't need those things, you're beautiful enough as you are. This . . .' declared Winnie, taking a dainty sprig of lily of the valley from the bouquet on the dressing table and tucking it behind Kitty's ear, '. . . is the only jewellery you need.

'Now you're dressed,' she smiled, and with a flourish, tore the fabric from the mirror.

Kitty stared unblinking at her reflection. 'I-is that really me, Win?' she asked tremulously. Without her headscarf, and a mouthful of pins, she scarcely recognized herself.

'I-I look . . . I look . . .'

'Like Nancy Beaton, I know,' said Winnie admiringly.

From nowhere, Kitty felt her chin quiver and tears begin to seep from her eyes.

'Heh, what's all this about, you daft cow?' Winnie soothed. 'I thought you'd be thrilled. You're always going on about how beautiful Nancy is.'

'It's not that. I don't deserve this, any of it,' Kitty wept, thinking of her frail father, her responsibilities at home and to her neighbourhood.

Winnie's face clouded. 'Oh, but you do, and so much more besides, Kitty.

'Take a look at yourself,' she insisted, whirling her round until she came face-to-face once more with her own un-familiar made-up reflection. 'Really look at yourself . . .'

Hesitantly, Kitty reached out and wiped away the soft

dusting of powder that had settled on the looking glass. Winnie's eyes held hers, until her lashes fluttered and fell.

'You're not a fourteen-year-old girl no longer, Kitty,' Winnie whispered in her ear. 'You're a *woman* now and you deserve a life of your own choosing.'

Slowly, Kitty nodded and she lifted her gaze.

'Now come on, dry your eyes and paint on a smile,' Winnie said, tugging her handkerchief from the sleeve of her blouse. 'We don't wanna keep handsome Harry waiting.'

As Kitty reached for her purse she knew that it was *this* moment, and not leaving school at fourteen, which signalled the true start of her entry into adult life. She was transformed by the gown and as she and Winnie headed to the door, she realized she was even walking differently, her head higher, her spine straighter.

Outside on Green Street they linked arms and walked in silence, exchanging little grins at the admiring wolf whistles of the market traders, both secretly thrilled to be lifted out of the drabness of everyday life.

It was astonishing, Kitty thought, for suddenly she spotted glimpses of glamour where yesterday there were none to be seen. She saw it in the rose tucked jauntily under Miss Sugarman's headscarf, the gay red lips of the shop girls behind the counter at the haberdashery and the fluttering shawl of the watercress seller. As they neared the dance hall, there was even a queer kind of romance to be found in the very pavements on which they trod. Little Pearl Street, Fashion Street and Sceptre Street made Kitty feel like, this evening, the whole of the East End was putting on the glamour.

But by the time they reached York Hall and were joined

by Treacle, she felt her nerves creep up on her. Kitty fidgeted, tapping her heel on the sprung maple floor that covered the swimming pool.

'I don't think Harry's going to come, he's thrown me over,' she muttered, twiddling with a lock of fine brown hair as she scanned the sea of young people crowding the dance floor.

The band struck up a foxtrot and excited couples, done up to the nines, flocked to the floor in a cloud of eau de cologne, taffeta underslips rustling, chattering gaily. Kitty knew that, like her, every girl here worked in the rag trade, clocking up ten hours a day behind a sewing machine, and come Monday morning would be just another cog in the factory wheel, but tonight – Saturday night – they could be the East End's own Tallulah Bankheads. Tonight, the evening belonged to them.

Kitty suddenly felt out of place.

'I feel like a prize chump,' she said, chewing on her lip. 'Besides, I ought to go, Dad'll be fretting.'

'Don't talk daft,' Winnie scoffed. 'We ain't gone to all the trouble of dolling you up to have you go home again. You look smashing, Kitty.'

'Win's right,' remarked Treacle, who was looking pretty dapper himself, with his thick black hair slicked back and wearing an immaculately pressed suit, with just a quarter-inch of cuff on show.

'I didn't recognize you out of your pinny,' he grinned. 'You look the business – like a goddess, in fact – and if that Harry don't turn up, well, I have a feeling you shan't be short of dance partners tonight.'

'She certainly shan't,' piped up a man wearing a suit two

sizes too big and eyes that darted alarmingly in his head. 'The name's Christian. By name, not by nature,' he added with a lavish wink.

'Step aside, pal,' said a deep voice. Kitty whirled round and found herself gazing into a pair of sparkling green eyes.

'Harry,' she said nervously, as her shifty-eyed suitor slunk off with a scowl.

Harry pursed his lips in a silent whistle. 'I think I'm in love,' he declared, picking up her hand and kissing it. 'If you don't dance with me this moment, I shall die a thousand deaths.'

With that, the sailor swept her into his arms and straight onto the dance floor. Kitty barely managed a backwards glance at Winnie or Treacle, as the couples crowding the dance floor parted like the Red Sea at the sight of such a dashing young couple.

Harry was an energetic dance partner, his eyes scarcely leaving Kitty's as they waltzed, foxtrotted and quick-stepped with abandon through the next hour. The sailor led her firmly through a dizzying array of songs, until her legs felt weak and the dance floor was spinning.

Eventually, her heart pounding, Kitty held her hands up in surrender.

'Harry,' she laughed. 'Enough! I can't keep up. You might be Fred Astaire, but I'm no Ginger Rogers.'

She had come here to return his letter, and so far no mention of it had been made, and yet, she knew it was important.

'Please,' she whispered in his ear, 'can we sit this one out and talk?'

'Your wish is my command,' he replied, as he led her to the cluster of tables lining the dance floor.

'Please forgive me, Kitty,' he grinned, pulling out a chair for her, 'but when you spend so many months at sea in the company of nothing but men, to have a woman like you on my arm, well, I'm sorry, I got carried away. I'll fetch us some refreshments.'

Kitty sat fanning herself in the perfumed heat and waved to Treacle and Winnie as they waltzed past her, waiting patiently until Harry returned from the makeshift bar with a cool drink of sarsaparilla for them both.

'I must have had a brace of angels hanging off my bedpost the day I bought a copy of the paper and found your advert in it,' he said, staring at her intently. 'Do you believe in fate, Kitty? That there's one person out there for each of us?'

Kitty took a long sip of the icy cold drink to slake her thirst and pondered his question.

'I suppose so. Perhaps it is fate that led me to find your mother's letter and you to spot my advert?'

The colour leached from Harry's face.

'What do you know of my mother?'

'Oh, Harry . . . I'm . . . I'm sorry, I haven't yet had a chance to explain,' she stammered. 'The letter I found, it wasn't wrongly delivered, it was hidden in the base of a Singer sewing machine, which your father gave to Mrs Tingle. He obviously had no clue that the letter was in it. I feel so wretched for having read it, but I wasn't sure what it was.'

She leapt to her feet. 'It's in my bag. I'll run and fetch it from the cloakroom.'

Harry's hand shot out and gripped her wrist firmly.

'No,' he said sharply, then, sensing her alarm, his expression softened.

'Sorry, but no, Kitty. I have no wish to see anything my mother wrote. You can keep it.'

'But . . . But it's from your late mother,' she protested. 'She meant for you to read it. Surely you must respect her last wishes?'

Harry sighed and circled the rim of his glass. 'It's not that simple, Kitty.' There was sorrow and sourness in his voice. 'My mother and I were estranged when she passed.' His gaze slid down. 'I . . . I did something stupid and rash when I was younger – incredibly stupid, looking back – but my mother couldn't find it in her heart to understand my motives, or to forgive, and now it's too late.'

'But in her letter, she—'

'Please, Kitty,' Harry interrupted, his voice thick with emotion. 'I really don't want to waste any more of this magical evening talking about my mother. I want to dance with the most beautiful woman in the room.' Holding his hand out, he rose, and Kitty stood too. The air between them pulsed with uncertainty and unresolved anger. Kitty had no clue what secrets lay between Harry and his mother, but she had crossed an invisible boundary.

'I've so little time left of my shore leave,' Harry said, his charm recovered as he held out his arm to escort her back to the dance floor. 'And I don't want to waste a single moment. I want to hear everything there is to know about Kitty Moloney, and why such a talented seamstress isn't working in some grand store up West as a court dressmaker.'

He held her as if she were a duchess and they melted

into the sea of bare shoulders and carefree swaying bodies. In his arms, Kitty relaxed, and encouraged by Harry, she began to talk. He was as good at listening as he was dancing, and soon Kitty found herself telling him about her poor but happy childhood, life on Green Street and all about her good friends, the Wedding Girls. She even confided in him about her father's illness.

By the time Billie Holiday's 'A Fine Romance' floated over the dance floor, she allowed her head to rest on Harry's firm shoulder, exhausted but happy. She felt his breath, warm and tingling in her ear.

'I'm falling for you, Kitty Moloney.'

*

'There must be something in the air tonight,' Treacle grinned as he gazed down at Winnie. 'Look at Harry and Kitty, they can't keep their eyes off each other.'

Winnie *had* noticed. In fact, she had been at pains to keep a close eye on her good friend. Kitty might have grown up in one of the roughest buildings in Bethnal Green, but she lacked street smarts and, in many ways, was as green as they come. There was no doubt though, tonight, she looked so poised and beautiful in Harry's arms.

'But it's not Kitty I want to talk about,' he continued, and Winnie felt his strong body tense against hers.

'I've scarcely seen you since your dad came home, and it's killing me.'

'Oh, Treacle,' she sighed, feeling her throat constrict. 'It's . . .'

'I know, I know. Complicated, but it doesn't have to be, Win.'

Taking her hand, he pulled her through the throng of dancers to the door, sidestepping the stream of young couples who poured out into the night. Moonlight and mist bathed the cobbles a milky white and the fresh spring night air hit her cheeks.

'Let's just go,' he urged, his breath billowing like smoke as he gestured to the street.

'Go where?' she asked.

'Let's elope. Go to Gretna Green. We can hitch to the station now. This time tomorrow, we could be man and wife.'

'Are you knee-deep in the beers or what?' she laughed.

'No, I've never been more serious about anything in my whole life,' he said, gripping her face in his hands. 'I'm potty about you, Winnie Docker, in case you ain't guessed. I don't give a monkey's what your dad says – I ain't scared of him. All I want is *you*.'

Winnie's mind grappled with his words. His suggestion was ludicrous. Or was it? Since her father's return twelve days ago, a stifling tension had hung over the home, and her mother's simpering behaviour around him felt like such a betrayal after all they had been through. She had actually believed that, together, they had finally steered a path away from the twisted road of pain her father had dragged them along for so many years. More importantly, they had carved out a decent new life for her younger sisters. In accepting Tommy back into their safe house, Jeannie had shattered what hope they had for the future.

'Let's leave. Right now,' Treacle urged, sensing her hesitation. 'We don't need anything from home. I got enough money put by to see us right until I can get a new job. Just think, Win . . .

'We can start afresh. This place grows more dangerous by the day, what with them bloody fascists roaming the streets. There's trouble brewing, something bad's gonna happen. What happened the other day, outside the pub, that's only the beginning, Win. There's talk that another war is on the way.'

He was struggling to keep the emotion from his voice.

'I want to get out of it, I do, start a safe new life, away from the East End. Maybe in the countryside, the seaside . . . Who cares, Win, as long as I'm by *your* side. If war does break out, I'll be called up. We're living on borrowed time as it is.'

'Oh, Treacle,' she sighed, letting her forehead rest against his solid chest.

Every single word out of his mouth made perfect sense. Would it be so crazy to walk out into the moonlit night with a man she adored, and never come back? She could send tickets for her younger sisters to join them as soon as they were sorted. Maybe life really could be as simple as that.

A familiar voice cut through her tumbling thoughts and when she lifted her head from Treacle's chest, Stella was standing in front of her.

'Stell?' she exclaimed. 'What are you doing here? Who's looking after Kitty's dad?'

'Oh, Winnie,' she sobbed. 'Where's Kitty? It's too awful.'

*

By the time Kitty made it back to their buildings, she felt like her heart was going to explode out of her chest. She had registered nothing. Not the look of shock on Harry's face as she wrenched herself out of his arms and fled from the dance floor, or the voices of Treacle, Winnie and Stella, urging her to slow or else she would break her neck on the cobbles.

Nothing mattered, except getting home to her father. By the time she reached her front door the ambulance had already transported her father to hospital and Dr Garfinkle was waiting for her.

The blood in her veins turned to ice at the scene. A dark ribbon of blood ran the length of the greasy brick passageway and a cloying smell of gas lingered in the dark narrow space.

'What's happened?' she cried.

'Let's get in my car and I'll tell you on the way to the hospital,' said Dr Garfinkle. 'They're taking him to the London in Whitechapel.'

Stella's face, wrought with despair, hovered in the gloom.

'I'm so sorry, Kitty. I fell asleep. I didn't see him go. I'm so, so sorry.'

And then Treacle and Winnie were holding Stella back, folding the sobbing girl into their arms, as the doctor bundled Kitty into his car.

As they sped through the darkened streets, he explained everything. How Stella had drifted off to sleep and the neighbours had seen her father restlessly roaming the narrow passage and stairwell outside. How his tormented howls about the enemy hiding in the gas-jet flares, which lit the building's stairwell, woke the entire buildings. How Auntie had battled with him in vain as he attempted to extinguish them with his bare hands.

*

They found her father in a bed on a ward at the London Hospital, heavily sedated, both hands bandaged and suspended above the sheets in a cradle.

'You are Mr Moloney's physician?' questioned the duty doctor, standing by his bedside. 'His hands have sustained some very nasty burns and he appeared to be hallucinating on arrival.'

Dr Garfinkle drew the weary night doctor to one side and they conversed in hushed tones. While they talked, Kitty placed her hands gently on her father's ashen face and her tears dripped onto his starched sheets. The guilt was suffocating. How could she have been out dancing with a man, while her father roamed the building; scared, confused and alone? What kind of selfish daughter was she?

'I'm so sorry, Dad. I should never have left you. Please forgive me,' she sobbed.

Her words didn't penetrate the thick veil of medication. His face, alabaster white against the pillow, looked so old. So frail and paper thin, like he might blow away at any moment. Where was the buoyant giant of a man who used to throw her up on his shoulders as he worked his market stall and juggled fruit? The strong man who devoted every day of his life to being a good husband, father and provider. In her heart, Kitty knew that man was dead. The man lying here was a frail, bewildered old man, whose brain was slowly being leached away by something too terrible to contemplate.

She scarcely felt Dr Garfinkle's arms around her, leading her off the ward and into an office. Her legs seemed to move of their own accord as she took a seat opposite the duty doctor.

'Delusions and hallucinations such as the ones your father is experiencing are common with senile dementia,' he said. 'Dr Garfinkle tells me his decline has been rapid—'

'Senile dementia?' she gasped, snapping out of her torpor. 'That's what Dr Garfinkle thinks too. But he's only sixty, Doctor!'

'My dear,' said the duty doctor, regarding her with compassion. 'There are old men of sound mind who retain mental vigour until their last days, and then there are men who become physically old almost as soon as they reach maturity. I understand you lost your mother recently? This could have exacerbated his condition. In truth, though, the age of many is the age of their vessels, the degeneration of which for many is an index of senility.

'We shall keep him here under observation until his burns are healed, and then he will be transferred to an asylum dependent on his lucidity. At this stage, the best one can hope for is to keep him comfortable and safe.'

The sudden cognizance was breathtaking. He was right. Dr Garfinkle had been right all along. Her father *was* losing his mind. Life was slowly peeling away from him.

'What will happen to him?' she asked tremulously.

'He will become increasingly bedridden and practically unconscious. I'm afraid, Miss Moloney, that your father will never recover. As for how long he will survive, I'm afraid that is simply impossible to predict.'

Kitty looked down at her lap and started to shiver.

'You must be freezing, Kitty,' said Dr Garfinkle gently, removing his overcoat and placing it around her shoulders.

The sprig of lily of the valley which Winnie had tucked behind her ear only a few hours ago, though already it felt like a lifetime, slid from behind her ear and landed in her lap, limp and a little crushed.

It struck Kitty how absurdly out of place and vulgar she must have appeared, sitting in a hospital, in the flimsiest of silk evening gowns, a silly girl who had begun the evening reaching for the stars, and ended it with the cruellest of awakenings.

*

The next afternoon – a Sunday – Kitty, flanked by Stella and Winnie, began the walk down busy Commercial Road, in the direction of Poplar. They had already been to visit her father on the ward that morning, where, at Auntie's request, Stella had discreetly taken photographs of his burns.

'Auntie wants to use the photos as evidence of how dangerous the buildings are,' Kitty remarked over the hum of trams. 'The whole building's in uproar over it.'

She sighed and rubbed her stinging eyes. It had felt so strange, returning to her lodgings the previous night and sleeping there alone.

'That's the only good thing to come out of this whole terrible mess, I suppose. Hopefully, the landlord'll be forced to sit up and take notice now. It's a wonder Dad wasn't killed.'

Suddenly, Kitty and Winnie noticed Stella fumbling in her satchel for a cigarette, furiously blinking back tears as she sparked up.

'And if he had been killed, it would've been my fault,'

she wept, pulling an agitated hand through her unruly blonde curls. 'What sort of a friend am I?'

'Hey,' said Kitty, wrapping her arms around her. 'You're the very best friend I could ask for. None of this is your fault.'

'Kitty's right,' Winnie said soothingly. 'No one could've predicted what was going to happen.'

'If anyone's to blame, it's me,' groaned Kitty. 'I didn't want to believe Dad was that sick, so I buried my head in the sand, thought I was dealing with it, when in reality I was fooling myself. I know now that Dad ain't going to get any better.'

'So, what now, Kitty?' Winnie asked.

She shrugged. 'Who knows? I've written to my sisters to see if they can get leave from service, but I shan't hold my breath. I doubt on their wages they'll be able to afford the train fare up from Hampshire.'

'Well, you have us, and I promise we'll never let you down. We ain't going nowhere,' Winnie smiled, pushing down the nagging guilt she felt at how close she had come to running from the East End and all her problems the previous night.

'That's right,' grinned Stella. 'Us Wedding Girls gotta stick together. Best friends forever, right?'

'Right,' smiled Kitty, thankful for their support.

'So, where we heading then?' asked Winnie.

'To deliver this,' said Kitty, pulling a letter from her pocket. 'I never got the chance to give it to Harry last night after I had to run out on him. He seemed adamant he didn't want it, but I owe him this and an explanation for deserting him at the dance. He mentioned he was staying in a boarding house on Manchester Road, near the docks, while on shore leave.'

'You two certainly looked very cosy last night,' Winnie teased, nudging her playfully in the ribs as they resumed their journey.

'He was wonderful company, I'll admit,' Kitty blushed.

'And very easy on the eye too,' winked Winnie.

A twenty-minute foot-slog later, and the faint whiff of tar and salt told the girls they were nearly at their destination.

An immense sailing vessel was docked so close to the dry-dock wall, its bowsprit thrust out over the jumble of Victorian terraces on Manchester Road. A rigger balanced precariously on the bowsprit at least thirty feet above them whistled appreciatively at the sight of three such pretty girls. The sight of him and the gulls wheeling in and around his head made Kitty's own head spin as she knocked on the door of the boarding house.

A wiry woman in a wrap-over apron flung open the door, juggling a baby in one hand and a cigarette in the other.

'Excuse me, ma'am, I'm looking for Harry – he's in the Merchant Navy. I believe he's lodging with you?'

'Not any more, luvvie. You've missed him. His ship sailed this morning. I think they were bound for America.'

Seven

One week later, Sunday, 8 March, and Tommy Docker had his great big, brand-new boots slung up on the tabletop and was immersed in the paper. With her sisters in Sunday school and her mum doing the washing at the bottom of the yard, Winnie found herself in the uncomfortable position of being alone with her father.

Hurriedly finishing her breakfast of bread with a smear of marge and gulping down her tea, she pushed back from the table. Treacle would be waiting for her at the end of Cable Street. They were going to head over to Kitty and Stella's buildings to lend their support to a tenants' meeting, and she didn't want to be late. With any luck, she could escape without having to enter into conversation with her father.

Tommy lowered his paper, and his lips curled into a grin as he looked Winnie up and down. He had put on a good few pounds since his return to the East End, thanks to Jeannie's cooking. Ironic, given that half the East End were starving and Jeannie wasn't much further through than a coat hanger.

'Where you off to?' he growled, quick as a flash gripping

her wrist and pulling her back. 'You off to meet with that gutter rat Treacle?'

'What business is it of yours?' she snapped.

'Oh, but you are my business,' he said, slowly swinging his feet down from the tabletop. 'You're my daughter . . .' His eyes lingered on her. 'My possession, and I don't want no filthy man's hand going where it don't belong. I didn't like what I saw when I came home that day and caught you and Treacle at it.'

'We were hardly "at it",' she replied icily. 'We were only kissing – not that it's anything to do with you.'

'Now now,' Tommy interrupted with a mocking laugh. 'Don't go getting all excited.' Abruptly, his smile froze and the vein throbbed on the bald patch on the side of his head.

'This family belongs to me. *You* belong to me, and sooner or later, my girl, I'll be reclaiming what's rightfully mine.'

Winnie wanted to cry, to scream, to lash her fists against this repulsive excuse for a father. Instead, her feet remained rooted to the spot.

'Sometimes, force needs to be used to assert one's territory.' He gestured to the paper on the table. 'I've just been reading; did you know that Adolf Hitler marched his troops into the Rhineland yesterday?'

Winnie felt an uncomfortable prickle of fear.

'He's growing in power, claiming back what was so unfairly taken from him with the signing of the Treaty of Versailles. Thanks to him, the Germans are back in employment, their economy has never looked so good. The people have hope for the first time in a long time – which is more than can be said for us!'

Winnie's eyes widened. She had heard the news on the

wireless yesterday, and listened to Herbie and Stella discussing it in the studio. The name Hitler seemed to be bandied about a lot of late, always in conjunction with another word: war!

'Are you mad?' she gasped. 'He's a bloody German. How can you side with him?'

'Never felt more sane in my life!' he shot back. 'It's all becoming clear to me. The movement is stirring – social progress, my girl. Change is in the air.' He raised one eyebrow. 'Like Adolf Hitler, it's time to reclaim what's rightfully mine, outside and inside the home.'

With that, he swung his feet back on the tabletop with a thud and picked up the paper, just as Jeannie walked in the door, carrying a bundle of washing in her arms.

'Oh hello, love,' she said, licking her thumb and wiping a smudge from Winnie's cheek. 'You off out?'

Winnie stifled a sob, and pushed her mother's hand away.

Jeannie looked from Winnie to Tommy. 'What's wrong?' she asked warily.

'Stop fussing and go tend to your mangle, woman,' Tommie grunted, rustling the paper in irritation.

Winnie fled from the room. Outside, she drew in great lungfuls of air and tried hard to calm her wildly beating heart. Sunday morning and beyond the net curtains and aspidistras, front rooms remained cold and empty, for all life was outside. Cable Street was teeming with crowds of kids playing marbles in the gutter, hopscotch on the narrow pavement or running hoops up the long road. Dozens of dusty, scabbed knees pumped up the cobbles in pursuit of fun and excited shrieks bounced off the tenements. Winnie sighed. Had she ever enjoyed a freedom like the kids of

Cable Street? She cast her mind back to her own childhood. Funny, looking back, how little she remembered. There was one day, however, which stood out like candlelight in darkness.

They had been renting in Bow at the time, in one of the most notorious tenements, when word had got round that the Bundle Woman was setting up her arch at the Fern Street settlement.

Winnie felt a powerful wave of nostalgia wash over her as she cast her mind back to the little oak arch that straddled the cobbles of a shabby street in Bow. Now, what were the words inscribed on it? Like she could forget.

Enter Now Ye Children Small,
None Can Come Who Are Too Tall

Winnie chuckled out loud at the memory. She and every other snotty-nosed nipper in patched shoes and hand-me-downs had queued for hours, on tenterhooks to see if they could pass beneath that arch. Of course she had passed through, easily in fact, for she was nothing but a scrap back then.

In exchange for a sticky farthing she had been rewarded with a wrapped bundle containing a whistle, shells, beads, marbles, scraps of patchwork, cigarette cards and more. Odds and ends to a rich kid, but to Winnie, it had been treasure. Not only that, but a kindly lady had also ushered her into a warm kitchen, fed her porridge and honey, washed down with strong tea laced with condensed milk and sugar.

Looking back, she supposed it was charity, but it hadn't

felt like that to a six-year-old. It had just felt like kindness, pure and simple.

All these years on, Winnie could still hear her mother's voice, reedy and nervous in her ear, when she had shown her the Farthing Bundle.

'Don't let your father see that lot. He'll do for me if he knows you've been accepting charity.'

Winnie couldn't ever remember seeing her second-hand toys again after that. And right there and then on Cable Street, surrounded by hordes of playing children, she understood what she could *never* have grasped as a six-year-old. It was not pride that motivated her father, but jealousy. What kind of man could begrudge his six-year-old daughter a bag of broken beads and a hot breakfast? A fierce sadness scorched through her at the realization.

Her eyes settled on two young girls, sitting on a nearby doorstep. A little kindness had made such a difference to her at their age and, quite suddenly, she found herself walking towards them.

At the sound of her footsteps, one of the girls glanced up.

'Ha'penny for the grotto, miss?' she asked.

They had arranged an upturned orange box on the doorstep and covered it with a hotchpotch of items, from postcards to buttons, and even a bunch of weeds in a jam jar. Her pal protectively spread her arms wide in front of the grotto.

'Pay first, then you get a look, miss,' she said, wiping her runny nose with the sleeve of her cardigan and revealing the entire grotto.

'Very well,' Winnie replied solemnly, handing them both

a half a crown and the bag of toffees she had been saving to share with Treacle.

Winnie crouched down and as the girls proudly talked her through their display, she hoped this moment would lodge in their memories, the way the Farthing Bundle had hers. Childhood was so fleeting, so precious, and it must be protected from men like her father at all costs.

Once Winnie had finished chatting with the girls and reached the end of her long, shabby street, she spotted Treacle, joining in with a boys' game of street football, his lithe, athletic body zipping over the cobbles. Winnie leaned against a soot-stained brick wall, next to a couple of twittering sparrows pecking at a patch of dried horse dung, and watched his obvious enjoyment in the game. Nearby, a baby slept soundly in a perambulator parked outside on the street, a length of string tied to the pram's wheel and fastened to the door knocker of a house, to stop it blowing away in the breeze. Treacle would make a smashing father, she realized with a sharp pang. When he spotted Winnie, his entire face lit up and he jogged over to her, ignoring the chorus of wolf whistles from the young lads.

A group of giggling girls turning a skipping rope over the cobbles joined in:

'Rosy, apple, lemonade, tart,
Tell us the name of your sweetheart.'

'Don't mind 'em,' he grinned, taking off his cap and sweeping her into his arms. His kiss was warm and the feel of his embrace so comforting, but Winnie was unable to shake off her unease from her encounter with her father.

'What's wrong, my love?' he asked, his smiling brown eyes melting into concern. 'It's him, ain't it? What's he done now?' She felt his muscles tense. 'I'm going to go and see him, sort him out once and for all.'

'No, Treacle!' she cried in alarm. 'No, it's not him. I'm tired, that's all,' she lied. 'Now can we get going? I promised the girls we'd be there by ten.'

'All right,' he said. 'Perhaps this'll cheer you up.' He slipped a tiny medieval dice made from bone into her hand.

'Found it on the foreshore by Shadwell yesterday. Probably dropped from a sixteenth-century ship. Just think, someone could have made or lost a fortune on the roll of that dice.'

Winnie smiled weakly at the gift. Something told her she would need to throw more than a lucky six if she were to escape what lay ahead.

They set off, her hand warm in Treacle's as he protectively placed himself between her and the traffic. As they passed the boundary from Whitechapel into Bethnal Green, it occurred to Winnie that the mainly Jewish kids of Cable Street would never dare stray into these parts. It was so sad. Hatred was destroying their once-close neighbourhoods. Treacle was right. It felt like a state of civil war, with battle lines marked out, quarters to be kept to.

It wasn't long before they passed a group of blackshirts, setting up for a meeting on a street corner. Already a small crowd had gathered and the young men were thrusting pamphlets into hands and pasting posters to the wall. As they drew close, Treacle placed his arms protectively around her and hurried her past, but Winnie's eyes were snagged by a poster.

The British Union of Fascists.

The party of social progress.
Building a land fit for heroes.

She huddled in closer to Treacle.

'Still sure you don't want to leave the East End?' he muttered.

*

Stella spotted Treacle and Winnie, and waved them over to the patch of courtyard where she and Kitty were standing.

'Here you are,' she grinned, clutching her camera excitedly. 'Auntie's about to start.'

'Blimey,' breathed Winnie, looking about the place in amazement. 'There must be twice as many people here as the last meeting.'

Stella nodded. 'I've counted nearly a hundred and forty. That newspaper article, and all the interviews she and the doctor have done, haven't arf rallied support. There's a bloke from the town hall having a nose about, and I spotted some local councillors and a journalist from the *East London Advertiser*. Rumour has it, the Mayor of Bethnal Green might even put in an appearance! Smashing, ain't it?'

Auntie wasted no time. Helped by two of her devoted sons, she was hoisted high above the crowds onto a table, which had been carried into the centre of the courtyard. The chattering of the predominantly female crowd reached a fever pitch as she dusted down her skirts. Standing beside her like a centurion, Dr Garfinkle raised a hand and a hush fell over the crowd.

In Germany, the Führer may have been growing in power, and in parliament, debates might be raging over what to do about Britain's home-grown fascists, but here in the East End, a feisty matriarch was drawing her own battle lines!

'Yesterday, I went to see Mr Moloney in his hospital bed up the London,' she bellowed, whipping a copy of the local paper from her apron pocket and hoisting it up high for all to see. There was a photo of Kitty's father – the one Stella had managed to take in the hospital, his hands heavily bandaged, alongside a fresh article about their fight for repairs.

'I've warned our greedy slumlord, the town hall and the Inspector of Health, time and again, what would happen if those open gas-jet flares ain't replaced with electric bulbs. I told them they were an accident waiting to happen. In fact, I've shouted my mouth off to anyone who cared to listen.

'Now the worst has happened.'

Stella bowed her head, feeling the familiar tears of shame prick her eyelids. No matter how many times the girls told her it wasn't her fault, she felt the full burden of his accident. Kitty's fingers threaded through hers and Winnie reached over and squeezed her arm. United, the trio of friends listened in respectful silence to Auntie as she continued:

'Mr Moloney is a decent, law-abiding citizen who's spent his entire life working a market stall in all weathers to provide for his wife and three daughters. Never once has he been late with his rent or failed to pay his rates.

'Now he's frail, through no fault of his own. Because of slum living, he's frailer still, his hands burned, his lungs riddled with infection from the damp.'

Auntie eyeballed the crowd, her dark eyes flashing as she jabbed at the photo.

'We can't afford to ignore this. This could be any one of your nippers in that hospital bed!

'Our neighbours in Stepney ain't putting up with it no longer. They're going on rent strikes. They've had enough of being the underdog and – make no mistake, friends – that's all we are to them slumlords: dogs . . . lowlife . . . scum of the earth!'

Bodies pressed together in the courtyard stiffened at her unflinching words, frustration and anger coursing through them.

'But we know better, don't we? Us East Enders ain't scum of the earth, we're salt of the earth!'

Cheers and applause filled the courtyard, but Auntie wasn't done.

'I lay the blame for Mr Moloney's ill health and accident directly at the landlord's door. And if there are any further casualties, I shall hold him responsible. I say, enough! It's time for change. We need repairs and we need 'em now!'

A church bell chimed in the distance.

'Looks like He agrees with me an' all.'

'I hear you, Auntie, but look around ya, gal,' called a woman at the back of the crowd. Over the sea of outraged faces, Stella made out a local woman, Beattie, a mum of eleven. She knew Beattie and her entire family occupied two of the worst, foulest-smelling rooms in the tenement, eking out a pittance with the odd bit of homeworking. Everyone in the building rallied round Beattie, giving what food they could spare for her nippers, donating layettes and chipping in to help pay her doctor's bills, but the woman was only ever a heartbeat from destitution. Not that anyone pitied her: there was no shame in being poor, after all.

'Most of the people here are women and nippers,' she said despairingly. 'They ain't going to take no notice of us.'

'Then we force them to sit up and take notice, Beat,' Auntie shot back. 'It's us women who suffer, after all. We suffer in sweated labour in the factories, and we bear the brunt of the suffering in the home. But do we sit around grousing?'

'We ain't got time,' yelled back a voice.

'Exactly,' Auntie bellowed. 'It's *our* bartering skills at the market, *our* bargaining with the pawnshop assistant, *our* friendships with shop owners and the school board that keep all our heads above water!

'The slumlord don't give a monkey's about that! He don't care how hard it is for us to keep our children healthy and our homes sanitary, so long as he can extract his penny from our apron pockets with his grasping fingers.'

'You tell 'em, Auntie!' hollered a woman's voice from behind.

Stella whirled around to see Gladys and Herbie.

'What are you doing here?'

'I wouldn't miss this for the world,' Gladys replied, eyes gleaming.

'And I'm here to keep her out of trouble and support my girls,' smiled Herbie, the corners of his eyes creasing as he doffed his hat to Auntie.

'I'll need all your support,' she went on, nodding respectfully to Herbie. 'Because yesterday I received a telegram delivered straight from the offices of . . .' She broke off, and pulled the telegram from her apron pocket. 'Aah, yes,

Mr Richards, our new landlord, delivered straight from his offices in Highgate, North London. Apparently, I'm bringing his good name into disrepute and either I desist with this nuisance campaign and stop giving libellous interviews about the state of the building, and attracting unwelcome attention, or I'll face eviction next Wednesday.'

Stella felt her jaw slacken.

'Note the good doctor's not heard a whisper from him, only me, a working-class mother he thinks he can bully into submission.

'To him, I give this simple message . . .'

Auntie paused for dramatic effect, a malevolent smile touching the corners of her lips. Stella watched, rapt, as a local reporter waited, his pencil hovering over his notepad. The crowd waited. Even the birds perched on the wash-house roof seemed to have stilled.

'Shove your eviction up your backside, 'cause I ain't going nowhere!'

She tore up the eviction notice, threw it high into the air and watched it shower over the crowd like confetti.

Stella half wondered whether the thunderous roar of approval wouldn't be heard in Whitechapel.

'The bailiffs are coming next Wednesday at four p.m. I hope you'll stand with me in solidarity,' she called over the clamour.

Stella stared at the baying crowd of women and children, before turning to Kitty and Winnie in amazement.

'Like she even needs to ask!'

Stella gazed about the place and a warm glow of admiration filled her chest. Never had she felt more proud to be an East Ender. These indomitable mothers mightn't have a ha'penny to rub together, but there wasn't one amongst them who didn't wage an uphill battle trying to keep their homes clean and respectable, and their children turned out nice. They were born fighters. Auntie could count on their support.

*

The following Tuesday evening, the night before the eviction, Stella found herself out on the streets as dusk fell. She had always been a restless spirit, but lately a new urgency had taken hold of her and nightly she pounded the cobbles, photographing whatever caught her eye.

All their lives seemed to be on the threshold of something momentous. Daily, Stella photographed an ever-changing world and, with each image framed, saw a snapshot of a world gently melting away. Many of the young newlyweds whose images she retouched were starting their marriages with fresh lives mapped out in the burgeoning suburbs of Essex, in homes with neat gardens, indoor plumbing and high aspirations.

And yet . . . Was it too awful to admit that part of her so longed to break free that she secretly hoped for the winds of change a war could bring? Stella craved freedom, not the heavy burden of running a business. She was a woman now, skilled in her trade, but she felt as if she had experienced nothing of life.

A soft rain began to fall, transforming the dusty cobbles to a slick, shimmering landscape. Inside, beyond the Nottingham lace curtains, lamps were lit in cosy front rooms, families sat down for tea, music and laughter drifted out.

As she walked, Stella saw her shadow pass over the lace, dark and edgy.

At the end of the street leading to Victoria Park, a roast chestnut vendor poked his red-hot coals with a smouldering wooden stick. Caught up by the delicious aroma, Stella stopped and dug in the pocket of her fawn slacks.

'Penn'orth of chestnuts, please.'

The chestnut man heaped a generous portion into a rolled-up cone.

'Take my advice, miss, and turn back,' he mumbled as she paid him. 'There's going to be trouble in the park. Fascists got a big meeting, that ain't no place for a girl.'

Stella thanked him and carried on her way, the nuts burning into her palms, a curious excitement rising in her chest. She could no sooner turn back than fly to the moon. The vendor's worried voice called after her. 'On your head be it, love.'

Wolfing down her chestnuts, Stella checked her bag and patted the outline of her trusty Leica, the camera that had become like an extra limb to her. As she turned onto the main road that led into the park, she was stunned by the sheer size and seething mass of the crowds that moved along the road, sucking up all that strayed into its path.

On instinct, Stella tucked her blonde curls under her cap, pulled up the collar of her mackintosh and walked briskly. Somehow it felt safer to melt into the masses as an anonymous young man. Stella wasn't daft, she knew slacks on a girl were regarded by many men as an act of defiance, as risqué as red lips. Judging by the tension in the air, the last thing she wanted to do was draw attention to herself.

Flanking the crowds were blackshirts; it felt like hundreds

of them, moving in formation, jackboots thudding as one, eyes darting menacingly from under their peaked caps.

Once in the park, Stella ducked into the shadows of a bank of plane trees, pulled the collar of her coat up higher and watched from the safety of the leafy canopy.

Most of the blackshirts were nothing but young striplings, strutting about, filled with bombast and the self-importance a pseudo-uniform gave them. Her eyes zoned in on one: he scarcely looked old enough to shave, much less form an opinion. He and his pal were needling a couple of anti-fascist protestors, roughhousing them.

'Go home, Jew boy,' he growled, spitting squarely in the man's face.

'I am home,' replied the protestor bravely.

Stella turned away, unable to watch any longer. What sort of mind conjured up such hatred? Could this be the same boy who put a brick through Miss Sugarman's window?

The drumming and roar of the crowd intensified and, in the distance, over the sea of heads, Stella made out the figure of Oswald Mosley, climbing up the steps of a make-shift stage.

If you were watching from a distance, the whole scene could almost have appeared to be a carnival, with singing and drums beating, but on closer inspection it had a nasty, sour edge, like biting into an apple only to find it rotten.

Mosley began to speak, and protestors on the edges sang songs and heckled. Skirmishes between the blackshirts and anti-fascist protestors were breaking out all around her, police whistles piercing the gritty dusk.

Stella's head started to spin. She knew she ought to go,

but fear – and, if she was honest, excitement – was rooting her to the spot.

Mosley's magnified voice cut across the din.

'Fascism stands for free speech . . .'

'Does Hitler stand for free speech?' bellowed a voice to Stella's right.

In a heartbeat, the heckler was seized upon by a crowd of blackshirts, arms pinioned behind his back and marched behind the bank of trees, where he was beaten to the ground in a flurry of boots and knuckles.

Hidden from sight in the shadow of the trees, no one could see or hear his cries for mercy . . . No one except Stella. She heard the sharp crack of breaking bones as their heavy boots made contact with first his ribs, and then his back.

The beating went on and on, as they laid into him with fists, boots and coshes. Shuddering, Stella was filled with a poisonous anger.

The young man made a heroic effort to escape, scrambling through the blur of heavy black arms. For a moment it looked like he might get away, until the ringleader, his eyes obscured by the rim of his cap, grabbed him by his foot and hauled him back into the centre of the baying mob.

'Pin him down, lads,' he ordered, in a strangely familiar voice, as he pulled a knuckleduster from his jacket pocket.

Stella felt an unnatural calm descend upon her as she took her camera from her bag and began to take photos. The blood hissed in her ears as she clicked. She knew there was little she could do for the poor man, but somehow, she would get these disgusting images out. She wanted people to see the savagery she was witnessing, see what fascism really stood for.

The hand on her shoulder was accompanied by a throaty whisper.

'Hand the camera over, lad.'

Stella froze, felt the flesh on her back rise. Her indecision was momentary. A second later she was off, tearing across the dark damp earth of the park and leaping over tree roots, as she bundled her camera back inside her satchel. The shouts and hollers were close behind.

'Get him, he's been taking photographs, don't let him get away!'

Stella didn't know where she found the speed or strength; adrenaline shredded her lungs as she tore through the crowds, zipping this way and that in an attempt to outrun her pursuers.

Once out of the park gates, she realized her mistake. In the park, there were people and police who could have prevented a beating. Out here, the wet, grey streets were devoid of life.

She paused, clinging to a railing as she attempted to recover her ragged breath. Then, at the park gates, she saw them, five large blackshirted figures, and they saw her.

'There he is – get him!'

Terror propelled her forward again, down a smaller side road, plunging deeper into the maze of narrow streets and alleys.

Stella heard their angry cries growing closer as they pursued her through the darkness, hungry for revenge, their bloodlust up. Panic engulfed her: how much longer could she outrun them for?

With a last-ditch burst of speed she flew round a corner and that's when she spotted him. The chestnut man who had earlier warned her off going into the park! A desperate thought occurred to her. It was her only hope . . .

Reaching him, she skidded to a halt and sucked in as much oxygen as she could muster before tearing off her cap and shaking out her blonde curls. Next, she ripped off her mackintosh and thrust it and her cap under the chestnut seller's stand.

'Help me,' she hissed under her breath – and not a moment too soon, as a second later five blackshirts rounded the corner.

'You seen a young lad pass by?' one of them panted, his Adam's apple throbbing as he hastily stuffed something that looked suspiciously like a spindle from a bannister inside his jacket.

'Wearing a mackintosh and a cap, was he?' remarked the chestnut seller as he casually turned the coals under his grill tray.

'That's the one,' the blackshirt growled. 'Which way did he go?'

'Straight on up that way,' said the chestnut seller, pointing to the far end of the street.

'Thanks, pal,' the blackshirts muttered, and then they were off, jackboots thundering over the cobbles. Stella thought her legs might buckle in relief, but quite suddenly, one of them swung sharply back and stared at her closely.

'Hang about . . . It's you, ain't it?'

Stella could have wept and her legs began to shake violently.

His face drew closer out of the gloom, and a horrifying

bolt of recognition tore through her. She had thought the voice sounded familiar. It was the ringleader who had brandished the knuckleduster. It was also Winnie's father.

'Tommy,' she said weakly.

'Well, well, well, if it ain't little Stella Smee,' he grinned, removing his cap and pasting his sweat-stained red hair back.

'You go on, lads,' he shouted to the rest of the blackshirts. 'And make sure you catch up with and deliver the message to our young friend.'

Stella felt she had been rescued from the frying pan only to be tossed into the fire.

'I heard you were back,' she said coldly.

Tommy lit up a cigarette, the match crackling into flame, throwing up a flash of his new dark red moustache.

He looked her up and down with an amused expression.

'Slacks? What are you now, a suffragette?'

'I take that as a compliment,' she shot back.

'Take it any way you like. So, you missed me, gal?' he asked, offering her a cigarette.

She shook her head and jutted her chin out defiantly.

'Let's put it this way, Mr Docker, the world didn't stop turning.'

He laughed, a rasping splutter, which quickly dissolved into a phlegm-filled cough. Hoiking up, he spat hard onto the cobbles.

'You always had a smart mouth on you. Used to say to your dad, God rest his soul, that he ought to knock some respect into yer.'

'What, the same way you command *respect* from your family?' she flashed back. 'In my opinion, it was the best day of our Winnie's life when you did a moonlight flit out the East End.'

Tommy smiled, before viciously grinding his cigarette out beneath his jackboot.

'Is that so? Take my advice, sweetheart. Leave the opinions to the men, eh? Right, I've business to tend to. I'll be seeing you, Stella.'

Abruptly, he turned and walked away, leaving Stella and the chestnut seller to stare after him.

'I told you not to go in there,' he scolded, with a shake of his head. 'They're a bad lot.'

Stella thanked him, before putting her coat on and heading in the direction of home, her heart rate gradually returning to normal.

A gull wheeled overhead, its mournful cry providing an eerie backdrop to Stella's solitary footsteps. She walked fast and kept to the shadows, and as she walked her thoughts ran wildly. Tommy Docker. A blackshirt steward, a hired thug! How on earth would she break the news to Winnie?

*

The day of Auntie's eviction dawned and as Kitty had left for work that morning, excitement and tension were palpable in the occluded skies over the buildings. The whole place had been a hive of determined activity, with residents busy making placards in the courtyard and bracing themselves for the arrival of the bailiffs. Kitty had longed to stay and join in, but there was work to tend to, although Gladys had kindly said they could shut up early to lend their support to Auntie, provided the day's work was done.

Now, her boss had nipped out to the haberdashery, leaving Kitty in charge to finish off the final part of a wedding dress. Breaking with custom, the bride had actually come to the small workshop for the final fitting, despite Gladys and Kitty insisting they should come to her home and help dress her there.

As she waited for the bride to finish undressing, her thoughts turned to her father, who she had visited without fail every evening after work. Last night, the physician had suggested that, as her father had been in hospital now for ten days, the time had come to have him transferred to an asylum. His wounds were healing, but his mind was more fractured than ever, and when Kitty had visited him last night, he hadn't even recognized her. She knew the doctor was right, but in her heart, she felt she was failing her father.

A polite cough wrenched Kitty back to the present.

'Could you do the buttons up the back, please?' asked the bride-to-be, who had stepped from behind the changing-room curtain.

Kitty turned, and drew in a breath.

'Well, how do I look?' asked the young lady, self-consciously smoothing down her dress. By East End standards, the dress was understated. Her slim, graceful figure was draped in butter-coloured silk jersey, high-necked, with an elegant line of velvet-covered buttons that ran along the curve of her back. Nestled in soft folds of tissue paper in a box was a veil made of the most expensive Brussels lace Kitty had ever worked with.

'Oh, Miss Banks. You're a picture,' she breathed.

'Please, call me Celeste. I insist,' she smiled.

'Very well,' Kitty grinned back, as she began the fiddly task of doing up the tiny buttons.

Kitty found herself gazing, awestruck, at the beguiling sight of Celeste Banks reflected back at her from the looking glass opposite. Kitty was used to radiant young brides, of course she was. All the women who passed through these doors were beautiful, mainly because they were in love, but this lady was in a class of her own. Celeste had skin the colour of double cream, jet-black wavy hair that gleamed purple in places, and she held herself with an almost regal poise, her back so straight, Kitty could have laid a ruler flat against her spine.

When she had finished buttoning up the dress, Kitty got down onto her hands and knees to examine the hem of the gown. She noticed Gladys had left five inches unstitched. Tradition dictated that if the mother hadn't made the gown, then the last section of the hem should be hers to finish, as was her matriarchal right. East End mothers were held in high esteem and it was only fair they should leave their mark on the most important dress of their daughter's life. Although Kitty had observed more than one controlling mother who went beyond stitching hems!

Still, traditions were always observed in this corner of Bethnal Green. Leaving it this late, however, was un-orthodox. Kitty glanced at the clock. Ten o'clock. The bride was due to be married at one.

'Will your mother be here shortly, Celeste?' Kitty asked. 'Only I'm sure you're itching to get going and get your hair and make-up done.'

'I very much hope so,' Celeste whispered. 'I've sent word

to her.' Quite suddenly, her green eyes misted over and a solitary tear slid down her lovely cheek.

'Oh, miss,' Kitty gushed, leaping to her feet and pulling a clean handkerchief from her sleeve. 'It's perfectly normal to feel nervous. If I had a penny for every bride in here who cried.'

'It's not that, Kitty,' she said, twisting the handkerchief through her trembling fingers. 'Marrying Frankie is right. I'm not a bit nervous. In fact, I've never been more sure of anything in my life. The problem is . . . Well, my mother and I don't quite see eye to eye on it. She has threatened to boycott the wedding if it goes ahead. I sent her a telegram last night, pleading with her to see sense. I told her that I would be here this morning if she wanted to help stitch the hem. I thought the gesture might soften her resolve, and that seeing me in my wedding gown would help to change her mind, except . . .' Celeste faltered. 'It rather looks like I was wrong.'

Her beautiful face crumpled as she looked at the door. 'Once Mother's made up her mind on something, she'll rarely change it.'

'Pardon me for asking, miss – I mean, Celeste – but what does your mother have against the marriage?' Kitty asked.

'I suppose you could say I'm marrying out of my class.' Celeste's face flushed and her gaze slid to the floor. 'I'm the only daughter of Countess Bennito. My father is Lord Edward Forsyth-Banks. Our family seat is Berrington Manor in Sussex.'

'My days,' Kitty murmured, not knowing whether to cuddle her or curtsy.

'My fiancé is Frankie Butwell from Bow. Frankie's a

former welterweight boxing champion and the youngest boxing promoter on the British Boxing Board of Control. I think Mother had slightly higher aspirations for her only daughter than marriage to an East End boxer and a reception at the Merry Fiddler. I was educated in a convent in Bayswater, you see, then finishing school in Paris. I even came out in front of the King as a debutante.'

'How on earth did you two meet?' Kitty asked, intrigued.

Celeste's face softened at the memory. 'On a steamer coming over from the Continent last year. People talk of love at first sight, but in mine and Frankie's case, it was true. I've never met such a humble, honest man. He would do anything for me. I didn't even tell him who I was until we were engaged, for fear it might make a difference.'

'But surely, if you're happy, then your mother ought to be happy?' Kitty cried, secretly thinking it quite the most achingly romantic story she had ever heard.

'It doesn't work like that where I'm from, Kitty,' Celeste sighed. 'As far as Mother's concerned, Frankie was born on the wrong doorstep. It might have been better if he had been a butcher, say, instead of a boxer. It's his profession she really detests. She met him, just the once. It was excruciating. She kept staring at his hands. "Such rough, coarse hands, darling," she told me later.'

Celeste turned to look at Kitty, love and pride burning in her eyes.

'Those hands would hold up the sky for me.'

She shook herself a little and glanced at the clock.

'I'm afraid she's not coming. Would you be a dear, Kitty, and stitch up the hem and then help me out of my dress? I really must be on my way.'

Less than an hour later, Celeste was gone, one step closer to her new life, but Kitty would never forget the young woman's story. The old rhyme, *If you wed when March winds blow, joy and sorrow both you'll know*, certainly seemed to ring true in the case of Celeste Banks. But her obvious devotion to her fiancé, her determination to marry against the odds, were an inspiration.

Kitty's mind left behind the image of her ailing father, and instead travelled softly over the darkening oceans that lay between her and the mysterious Harry. She allowed herself the brief rush of pleasure from imagining herself in his arms once more, of having someone in her life to share her hopes and fears with. Someone who might, just might, love Kitty enough to hold up the sky for her.

That dinnertime, instead of popping to the dining room on Green Street with Winnie and Stella, Kitty caught a tram to the docks and delivered her letter to the Merchant Navy shipping offices, to be forwarded to Harry. Perhaps, like Frankie and Celeste, she should fight a little harder for her happy ending.

*

Three hours later, Winnie and Stella gazed with broad smiles at the fairy-tale wedding portrait sitting of the newlyweds, Celeste and Frankie Butwell of Bow. Herbie was, as always with such a large and colourful wedding party, not to mention the presence of such a beautiful bride, in his element, arranging numerous different groupings and bustling about the place full of bonhomie.

The bride's dress might have been understated, but the

five bridesmaids, all sisters of the groom, were doing a good job of making up for it. They had been paying into a wedding club for years, after all, and as such were determined to wring every last drop of glamour out of the momentous event. The studio was a sea of frothy organza, farthingaled frills and acres of tulle and swishing satin. And the flowers? Oh, but Winnie had never seen such displays; it was hard to tell the bride's bouquet from the bridesmaids'. Everywhere she turned, big luscious red roses trailing with silver ribbons and silver-sprayed carnations. The scent was making her quite heady, that and the hive of chattering Cockney voices.

Only the bride's family seemed curiously absent.

''Ere,' cried one of the bridesmaids. 'Anyone see old Mrs Brown outside the church?'

'Don'cha worry, Old Boots was there,' chuckled the groom's mother. 'No doubt she'll make an appearance at the reception too!'

'Thank Gawd for that,' said the groom, guffawing and breaking into a broad smile. 'It's bad luck if Old Boots ain't at yer wedding.'

'Not that we need luck,' he added, glancing at his new wife with a besotted smile.

Winnie laughed along too. Nanny Brown, or Old Boots, as she was affectionately known, was a large, jolly lady and a notorious flirt, who turned up without fail at every East End wedding or funeral, regardless of whether she was invited, or even knew the family. Mostly it was for a free feed, but she could always be relied on to hammer out a tune on the piano if required. Her presence was taken as de rigueur; almost, but not quite, as lucky as having a chimney sweep turn up at the church to shake the groom's hand and give the bride a kiss. Winnie still hadn't fathomed out how having a kiss off a sweep could bestow a bride with such good fortune, but no matter, married couples needed all the luck they could get as far as she was concerned.

By the time she had escorted the entire bridal party back out on to Green Street to a great cheer and a shower of rice confetti from the market traders, Herbie and Stella had already begun to pack up the studio.

'Anyone want a Rosie?' Herbie asked with a tired smile. 'I don't know about you, but I could do with a cuppa before we start processing.'

'That'd be handsome, boss,' Stella replied, wheeling the backdrop of a stately home in a mist-covered valley back into the props storeroom. 'I could do with wetting my whistle.'

'Lovely couple, weren't they?' Herbie remarked. 'I always knew young Frankie would marry well. I photographed him with his first trophy you know, aged sixteen. He might have a knockout punch, but he's got a heart of solid gold.'

'Rumour has it, she's the daughter of a lord and she's been disinherited,' said Stella knowingly.

'Thought she looked right at home against that backdrop,' Winnie chuckled.

'In this day and age, nothing'd surprise me,' Herbie replied sagely. 'Look at our new King, gallivanting about the place with an American. Folk don't seem to stick to their own these days.'

'Weren't you making tea, Herbie?' Stella winked.

'Hark at me, rattling on, so I was.'

When he left, Winnie turned to go back to reception, but Stella caught her by the arm.

'Win, there's something I need to tell you.'

'Can't it wait?' Winnie replied. 'I've got a stack of paper-work to sort.'

'Not really, Win, it's important. You see, last night—'

The door burst open, and Kitty and Gladys appeared.

'Girls, we've got to go,' Gladys puffed. 'It's the bailiffs – sneaky sods have come early. Auntie needs us.'

'What?' blurted Stella. 'But they're not due until later.'

'Well, they're on their way now,' Kitty replied breath-lessly. 'They were spotted walking up the end of Green Street in the direction of our buildings. Big Mickey tipped us off.'

'Then you must go, girls,' said Herbie who, overhearing the commotion, had rushed up from downstairs. 'Auntie will be relying on your support.'

'Sure you don't mind, Mr Taylor?' Gladys asked.

'What do you think?' he replied.

'Thanks, boss,' Stella grinned, planting a big kiss on his forehead and grabbing her bag. 'Come on, girls. Let's get on our toes, there's not a moment to lose.'

'I say, Miss Tingle . . . Gladys,' Herbie called after them. 'Look after them, won't you? They're all very precious.'

'With my life, Mr T . . . Herbie,' she replied, a soft flush colouring her plump cheeks. The two locked eyes, and Winnie noticed a look of unmistakable affection pass between the pair.

Eight

Less than ten minutes later, Winnie, Stella, Kitty and Gladys skidded to a halt outside their buildings. At least, it looked like their buildings, but the entrance was completely barricaded up behind old fruit crates and barrows. Beattie, and at least fifty other women, stood in front of it holding placards.

'Bleedin' hell, girls, it's like Fort Knox round here,' Gladys declared. 'Look at'cha. An army in aprons!'

'You betta believe it, gal! Now go round the back entrance,' Beattie said, eyes gleaming in anticipation. 'They'll let you in there. Auntie's waiting for you in her flat. Hurry up and shift your backsides, they'll be here soon.'

Winnie and the others hastened their way round to the narrow entrance at the back of the buildings, manned by yet more women and kids.

Once inside Auntie's flat, they found her cheerfully filling sacks with mouldy flour, while her sons emptied steaming hot potatoes into a bucket.

'Ain't no time to be making pie, Auntie,' quipped Gladys.

'Very funny, Glad,' she retorted. 'The only pie that lousy landlord's going to be eating is humble pie.'

'You're going to use weapons?' gasped Kitty.

'If I have to,' Auntie shrugged. 'Sometimes words alone don't butter no parsnips, know what I mean? I have to show that landlord I mean business.' Winnie couldn't hide her smile. Auntie was on fine form, her dander was up and she was ready for a fight.

Kitty gulped and, sensing her unease, Winnie drew her to one side.

'No one will mind if you want to wait in your flat,' she whispered.

'Win's right,' added Stella, as she took out her camera and polished the viewfinder. 'Besides, something tells me they'll have a job on their hands getting through the barricades.'

'No,' said Kitty firmly. 'Auntie's only in this predicament because she stood up for Dad. I'm staying put.'

'That's the spirit,' Stella smiled, tweaking her chin.

From outside, a woman's voice tore across the courtyard.

'They're two turnings away! Brace yourself, girls!'

'Just as well we've got our spies,' Gladys remarked.

Auntie rose to her feet, jammed on her hat and picked up a sack of flour.

'It's time. Come on, girls. Let's run 'em out the tenements!'

The girls followed Auntie and her sons out onto the narrow landing that overlooked the courtyard, and an unnerving silence fell over the buildings.

Then, an extraordinary thing happened. One by one, like dominoes, from the ground right up to the fifth floor, every single door onto the courtyard opened and, from each one, a woman emerged. More groups of women started to trickle down the stairwells and disgorge out into the courtyard. The trickle soon turned to a great, chattering tidal wave.

Soon, everywhere Winnie looked, there were women and kids, filling the courtyard, and completely lining the four sides of landings and stairwells that looked out over them. Young and old mingled together, a defiant human barricade. The whole place was alive with the noise of chatting, laughing, barking dogs and squabbling kids, and chiming over the noise of it all were the chants:

She will not, she will not be moved . . .

'Looks like they'll have a fight on their hands if they're going to kick you out, Auntie,' Stella breathed in astonishment.

Stunned, Winnie could only nod her head in agreement. The rapacious landlord and the dreaded bailiffs had no idea what was about to hit them. There was a tribe of angry women awaiting their arrival.

'I always said that power is in the group,' Auntie murmured, clearly moved by the show of support.

Just then, an almighty crash rang out from the entrance to the buildings, followed by shouts and bellows.

'It's the bailiffs!' yelled a woman near the entrance. 'They're here, and they're kicking in the barricade. They've brought blackshirts with 'em.'

'Blackshirts! Do you think we ought to call the police?' Kitty said nervously over the brouhaha.

'The police?' Gladys snorted. 'Don't make me laugh. This is frontline London, the only district they fear to come. Besides, even if they did turn out, they'd be on the bleedin' landlord's side.'

Within minutes, the scene had plunged into a state of

total pandemonium. Despite the best efforts of Beattie and her crew, pieces of splintered wood skidded across the courtyard as the barricade was forcibly kicked in. The landlord clearly had friends in low places, as a minute later, the bailiffs, two big swaggering toughs, forced their way into the courtyard, accompanied by three blackshirts.

The noise was deafening. Howls of outrage filled the air as they were set upon by hordes of angry women, leaping on their backs and whacking them with their placards. The women on the balconies above went wild, sending down a hail of missiles and showering the eviction posse in mouldy flour.

Startled at first to meet such resistance, the blackshirts and the bailiffs quickly regained their composure and showed no mercy, shoving any woman who got in their way to the floor, as they furiously attempted to hew a path through the angry mob.

Standing beside Winnie, Stella caught the lot on her camera. A blackshirt hurling a woman to the floor. *Click!* The bailiff's mouth twisted into a determined grimace as he repeatedly booted the door to the stairwell. *Click!* The twisted jumble of bodies, fighting and writhing as great clouds of flour drifted down over them. *Click!*

It was astonishing and, for a moment, Winnie felt paralysed by the scene. Then came the noise. Great thunderous roars and caterwauling screams which snapped her out of her stupor. Bending down, Winnie picked up a potato from the bucket and, with all her might, flung it over the side of the balcony. It landed with a resounding thud against the side of a bailiff's head and, for a second, he staggered back.

'That's the spirit, gal!' bellowed Auntie. Reaching into

her pinny, she pulled out another spud and hurled it full force at the nearest blackshirt's head. It smashed everywhere, showering the bailiffs with hot potato.

'You want that mashed or boiled?' she screeched. 'Take that, you rotten swines! Now go on, clear off, get outta my buildings.' She lobbed another potato over the balcony like a grenade, smacking him straight between the legs. Groaning, the blackshirt crashed to his knees, coated in flour, onto the concrete floor.

'Bullseye, Auntie!' Winnie hollered. The crowd of kids went wild, leaping around the mob with delight.

Gladys swiftly followed that up with a well-aimed hot potato straight to the other blackshirt's ear, which sent him staggering sideways.

'Life in the old gal yet,' she cackled with glee. 'The years are melting away.'

'Cor, not much, Glad,' Auntie muttered, as she stepped forward and gripped the edge of the balcony.

'Perhaps you'll think twice next time you come round here, intimidating innocent women and children. Now you'll remember me every time you take a leak, you dirty little bugger. I ain't going nowhere, you hear me? Nowhere!

'You tell that rotten, rent-racketeering landlord to come and fix this building up and make it a decent and safe place to live. And while you're at it, tell him this . . . He knows the cost of everything, but the value of nothing!'

Sensing that breaking through the mass of women around the stairwell door to Auntie's flat would be impossible without extreme force, to say nothing of further injury to themselves, the lead bailiff gestured to the rest of his crew.

'This shan't be the last you hear, Mrs Flood, of that you can be certain!' he called up to her.

'I don't doubt it, love,' she laughed, giving them a two-fingered salute as they left, pursued by a crowd of booing, hissing women.

Winnie watched them beat a hasty retreat, the blackshirt at the back limping slightly. The battle might not have been won yet, but something told her they could claim today as a small victory. Another thought struck her. Somewhere along the way, the fight for better housing had become entwined with the fight against fascism. If folk could live in safe and peaceful communities, tolerant and respectful towards their neighbours, then something good would have been forged from the dark crucible of pain that held them all in its grip. Was it Winnie's imagination, or were heads held a little higher as the women drifted back indoors?

When the eviction posse reached the gates, they paused, turned and looked back up to where Winnie, Stella and Kitty were still standing on the landing. One of the blackshirts was gesturing furiously back to the courtyard, in a heated debate with the lead bailiff. Spitting on the floor, he removed a handkerchief from his jacket pocket and angrily wiped away the thick coating of mashed potato and flour that covered him. In the flour-filled frenzy, she hadn't got a proper look at his face, but suddenly Winnie found she could see – really see – clearly for the first time. Her lungs emptied and she gripped onto the edge of the landing wall for support. Beneath the grime was her father, Tommy. He was a blackshirt! So this was why he had returned to the East End. This was what he meant when he said his new job was in 'protection'!

Winnie felt Stella tap her on the shoulder. Her sympathetic face swam into view.

'That's what I was trying to tell you earlier, Win. Your dad: he's one of them.'

*

Thirty minutes later, still buoyed up from the eviction battle, Kitty, Winnie and Stella scurried up the corridor at the London Hospital as fast as their legs could carry them, oblivious to the trail of flour they left in their wake. Kitty knew that today was the day the hospital authorities were planning to transport her father to the asylum, and she prayed she was in time to go with him in the ambulance. Winnie and Stella had insisted on coming with her for moral support, though Kitty had a sneaking suspicion Winnie was trying to avoid going home to her father.

But it was her own father Kitty was preoccupied with. There was so much she wanted to tell him, so many words still unspoken. She couldn't wait to tell him about how they had successfully beaten back the bailiffs and defended Auntie, and about the disinherited bride she had helped to dress earlier. Maybe she would even confide in him her decision to pursue her dreams of love.

Goodness only knew if he would hear, or for that matter understand any of it, but Kitty knew she had to try. When it came to her father, she would never stop trying.

As she walked briskly onto the ward, the girls close behind, it occurred to her with a fierce pang how very much she loved her gentle father. They had always had a special bond that transcended the one he had with her elder sisters.

When she was little, he had been the one to sneak her arrowroot biscuits when he thought Mother wasn't looking, and she in turn had spent hours at his market stall, patiently watching as he showed her how to stack oranges into mountains and lay out glistening piles of dates. It wasn't only his family he doted on. George Moloney adored his beloved community and understood the need for tolerance, turning a blind eye to the kids that pilfered fruit from his stall, and holding back the slightly bruised vegetables to give to the hard-up women in the building. Now it was his turn to be looked after in his dotage.

Kitty saw the outline of his body in the hospital bed as she drew closer and felt a burst of relief. They hadn't left! Her steps hastened up the ward.

'Dad . . . Dad!' she cried excitedly, as she neared his bedside. 'Oh, Dad, you ought to have seen it today. Auntie was like some sort of mighty warrior queen – marvellous, she was. We beat them back. We won, we . . .'

Kitty's steps faltered as she reached him and her voice trailed off. As dusk seeped through the high hospital windows she took in the familiar sight of her father in his bed. Familiar, yet something had irrevocably altered. The sunken eyes, the distended limbs, the perfect stillness, which told Kitty that what was laid out before her was nothing but mere remains.

'I'm so terribly sorry, Miss Moloney. Your father passed away a few minutes ago.' For the first time, Kitty became aware of a nurse standing on the other side of his bed. She felt herself slip into a chasm of deep shock and was aware of nothing; not the arms of her friends holding her as her legs crumpled beneath her, nor the nurse drawing the curtain around his bed, before silently pulling the sheet over his face.

'No . . . No, wait!' Kitty choked, recovering her senses. 'Please . . . Please, mayn't I have some time with him?'

'Of course,' said the nurse gently, before guiding Winnie and Stella away.

Alone with her father, Kitty laid down beside him. In her heart she knew he was gone, but somehow, if she kept talking she thought she might rouse him. She told him everything about the day, leaving out no detail. Tears slid down her cheeks as she recounted their triumph. The old George would have revelled in the minutiae.

It could have been a minute or an hour. Time lost all meaning as Kitty lay next to his body, rubbing his cold cheek, trying to warm him up, breathe new life into him, but deep down, she knew. It was too late. He was gone.

That's where they found her . . . the nurse, Stella and Winnie. Tenderly, they transported her home, where Auntie, Gladys, Treacle and Herbie were waiting with a cup of tea, stiff with sugar and laced with brandy.

Comforting arms were placed around her, the hot cup pressed into her hands. 'For the shock,' said a distant voice.

It was only then, as she sipped the scalding liquid, that a thought occurred to her.

'Dad always said he'd sooner die than enter an institution,' she whispered. 'At least he managed to avoid the very thing he dreaded.'

'Perhaps there is some dignity in dying after all, Kitty love,' said Herbie tenderly.

*

By the time Winnie and Treacle stumbled in exhaustion from Kitty's flat, where they left her still being looked after by Auntie, a thick cloak of velvety darkness had descended over Bethnal Green. After the ear-splitting din earlier in the day, Winnie found the silence in the darkened courtyard eerie; the only noise was the sound of their muffled footsteps echoing off the flour-dusted cobbles.

Treacle insisted on walking Winnie all the way back to Cable Street. A greasy yellow fog clung to the gas lamps as they set out hand in hand through the deserted streets in the direction of Stepney.

It was quiet, so quiet that, for a moment, Winnie felt that she and Treacle might be the only two souls alive in an East End of grime and grief. In the perfect silence she could sense Treacle had a question on his lips.

'Stella told me about your father being at the eviction, that he's—'

'One of them?' Winnie shot back into the darkness. 'Please, Treacle, I don't want to talk about it. I'm ashamed and . . .' Her voice trailed off.

'Scared?'

Winnie didn't get the chance to answer. Out of the fog they heard the clattering of horses' hooves and the dark silhouette of a horse and cart drew up alongside them.

'Bit late for you two to be out, ain't it?' Big Mickey's voice rang out. 'Come on, hop on the back. I'm just off to Spitalfields to get the best pickings. I'll drop you off on the way through. The streets ain't safe.'

Gratefully, Winnie allowed Treacle to help her clamber onto the back, and with a bone-grinding jolt they set off, sparks shooting out from the cobblestones as they clashed with the metal rim of the cart wheels.

'Look at that,' Treacle said, nudging her as he gestured up.

A patch of fog had cleared and a brilliant moon had washed the night sky silver. Hundreds of stars danced and shimmered as they clattered through the dark streets.

'Just think, Win, if we lived in the countryside, we could look up at skies like that every night.'

She turned and stared at his face in the gleam of starlight, so handsome and full of hope that it made her heart swell. It was pointless resisting it any longer and the realization made her shake. She was brimful of love.

By the time they reached her front door and bade farewell to Mickey, Winnie was dead on her feet. The fog had caused her hair to plaster itself to her face and she could feel the freezing tendrils snaking down her neck. Treacle pulled her shivering body into his arms, draping his warm coat over her shoulders and smoothing back the wet hair from her cheeks.

'Please, Winnie,' he whispered, his breath warm in her ear, 'let me come in and speak to your dad. I'm worried about you going in by yourself.'

'No, Treacle,' she said, pulling back sharply. 'He'd fly off the handle if you came in.' She glanced up at the window above the rag shop sign and sighed. 'Besides, it's late. They'll be asleep by now, I shouldn't wonder.'

'Very well,' he said reluctantly. 'But I'm going to wait right here, until you can give me a sign that everything's all right. I shan't sleep until I know you're safe in your bed.'

Winnie looked up at her stargazing sweetheart. He was so handsome, it made her dizzy sometimes. Those dark eyes,

his loose-limbed walk, the easy smile he had for everyone
. . . It was an intoxicating package.

Reaching up onto her tiptoes, she kissed Treacle's freezing
cheek, causing a soft flush to bloom across his face.

'Oh, how I love you, Michael Brody. How I love you!'

Treacle pulled back, his face crinkling into a delighted
but puzzled smile.

'Is it queer to hear me use your real name?'

'No, no, it's not that,' he laughed. 'You've never actually
told me you loved me before. I must have told you – a
million times over. But you've never said it to me. Until
now.'

'Well, I do, Treacle,' Winnie said solemnly. 'I love you
dearly.'

Before she could say another word, Treacle gathered her
into his arms and swept her high up into the air, giving her
a kiss so passionate, it crushed the breath from her body.

'You don't know how long I've waited to hear you say
that,' he murmured as his mouth left hers. Gently he placed
her back on the cobbles and slid his hands through her wet
hair, tilting her face so that her gaze met his in the moonlight.

'I'll never give up on you now, Winnie. You hear me? I'm
going to find a way to a better future for us both.'

Bending down, he kissed every inch of her face; her
cheeks, her eyelids, the sweep of her brow, until Winnie felt
light-headed with exhilaration and the stars above their
heads began to spin.

She pulled back, laughing.

'You're potty you are.'

'Potty about you.'

With a wrench she pulled herself free from his arms, kissed her finger and pressed it against his lips.

'Night-night, Treacle.'

'I'll not leave this spot until I know you're safe,' he said, settling himself down on the freezing step and pulling his overcoat around himself for warmth. 'After all, gotta look after my girl.'

Winnie drew the front door closed with a soft click and ascended the dark staircase to their rooms with a smile playing on her lips. She heard the cry of a baby call out from the floor above, shortly followed by the tread of its mother's feet and a soft Yiddish lullaby.

Winnie paused at the door and her hand went to the small bone dice that Treacle had given her three days before, still nestled in her coat pocket. She had been right to finally reveal her true feelings for him. Treacle was as safe a bet as any man and as soon as she had spoken with her mother – let her know *exactly* what sort of new job Tommy had – she intended to leave and accept Treacle's offer of marriage. Who cared if they had to wait, or even elope? She adored her mother, but taking her father back the way she had felt like a betrayal.

As soon as she had enough money, Winnie would send for her sisters and build a secure home for them. The events of that strange day had made her realize . . . If you wanted anything in life, you had to fight tooth and nail for it! She could not allow the past to dictate her future a moment longer.

Winnie turned the handle and stepped indoors into the smoky darkness.

'Look what the cat dragged in,' rang out a hollow voice. 'Been out with that gutter rat Treacle, have ya?'

Her father was sitting in the easy chair by the dying embers of the fire, playing with a half-empty twist of snuff in the palm of his hand. Her mother was sitting opposite him, her face pinched and white with fright. Jeannie shot her a look Winnie recognized all too well, then turned back to staring at the floor. Scattered around their feet were all the gifts Treacle had unearthed from the Thames.

Winnie instinctively froze, her mind grappling with what to do or say, but her father was on his feet in a flash, dragging Jeannie up with him by the collar of her dress.

'I saw you there today at the eviction, alongside that law-breaking old crone,' he seethed, one hand clamped round Jeannie's neck, the other pointing a finger in her direction. 'I don't even know what to say, Winifred. You're a bloody disgrace . . . carrying on in such a ridiculous fashion! You've brought shame on the family name.'

If it hadn't been so utterly absurd, Winnie would have laughed.

'Me, carrying on in a ridiculous fashion?' she spluttered. 'You're the one goes out dressed head to toe in black, saluting some strange fella who wants to march us straight into another war.'

She turned to her mother, fury rising in her chest.

'Did you know that, Mum? Dad's wonderful new job is as a blackshirt steward? That's why he's really come back to the East End. Not 'cause he gives two hoots for his family, but 'cause he gets his kicks terrorizing innocent men, women and children. Mind you, don't know why that should come as a surprise, he's spent his whole life terrorizing us!'

Tommy took a step closer, his moustache twitching in anger.

'How dare you talk about the leader like that! If it weren't for Mosley, I'd be with all the other down-and-outs in Itchy Park or queuing on the stones for work,' he shouted, flecks of sour spittle peppering Winnie's cheek. 'That man is our saviour. The British Union of Fascists and National Socialists is this country's only hope now – and, by God, I'm proud to serve them.'

'But what have they ever done for you?' Winnie cried.

'I'll tell you what! I've got hope for the first time in years. When I came home from the war, it was to the promise of a land fit for heroes.' Her father laughed scornfully and immediately began to cough; great rasping, juddering spasms that rocked his body. Winnie and Jeannie watched in silent horror as he clung to the mantelpiece, gasping for breath.

'Land fit for heroes – that bloody well never materialized, did it?' he wheezed, once he had recovered himself. 'Bleedin' dirty Jews – they've taken our jobs and our homes. What's left for me, except shovelling shit and snow or hanging round the bomping box? Me and hundreds of other poor chumps hoping to clock on down the docks for a days' work.

'Mosley's given me a uniform to feel proud of, a shirt on my back, new boots on my feet and I've got my dignity back. One and three-quarter million unemployed, and I ain't one of them. I'm strong again. Powerful.'

Winnie didn't see strength or power in his eyes, only the glint of madness.

'You're a bloody fool!' she yelled, convulsing with despair. 'That hope is as fake as your uniform. He's playing on people's fears, serving the Jews up as a scapegoat, stirring up bad blood, and you're just his puppet. Don't you get it, Dad?'

His fist caught her mother off guard and Jeannie spun

round three hundred and sixty degrees, before landing in a heap on the hearthrug. Instinctively, Jeannie curled into a ball and started to whimper as Tommy laid into her.

Winnie's hands were trembling as she plucked back the collar on her blouse as if it were strangling her and watched, mute with horror. With every blow he rained down on her mother, more childhood memories came hurtling back, but these ones were far darker, more wretched than confiscated marbles.

Aged six, hiding under the kitchen table . . . Trying to hit her father with a shoe to stop him punching her mother . . . Aged eight, watching him swing her expectant mother about the room by her hair, Jeannie desperately trying to shield her swollen tummy . . .

The awful, brutal details of her childhood ran through her brain like a never-ending newsreel, until finally, something inside her snapped.

'Stop, stop, STOP!' she bellowed, jumping on his back and pummelling him with her fists. 'Please God, think of the girls.'

Tommy staggered back, giving her mother the chance to scrabble out of reach of his boot.

'God?' he laughed manically. 'God! He was blown out of my head years ago.'

Slowly, he passed the back of his hand across his mouth, straightened his tie and smoothed back his hair.

'Now you listen here. I'm the man of this house and my word is law. I'll see to it, Winnie, that if you or your mother ever leave, it'll be Treacle they'll be dragging out the Thames next, not these poxy things.'

A cruel smile split his face in two as he ground the heel

of his boot down on all of Treacle's treasures. Precious pieces of Bellarmine jug, clay pipes and rare pieces of Tudor pottery were all reduced to dust.

'End it with that gutter rat, or I'll end him.'

And then he was gone, tearing off his shirt and retreating into the bedroom.

Once the bedroom door was closed, Winnie began to follow the practised routines she knew all too well from childhood. Preparing the poultice to tend to her mother's wounds, fixing her hot, sweet tea, clearing up the damage and holding Jeannie until the shaking had subsided. But this time felt different. This time they had known a life away from her father's violence. For one precious year they had tasted freedom.

Waiting until she heard her father's snores, she led her mother to the chair by the fire and covered her with a rug. Next she stirred sal volatile into a glass of water and held it gently to her mother's bruised lips.

'We don't have to put up with this any longer,' she whispered as her mother took a shaky sip from the tumbler. 'We've managed without him once before, and we can do it again. I'll talk to Treacle, warn him to stay away until we've escaped.'

'You don't understand, love,' her mother replied. The drink revived her somewhat, but her eyes remained bleak and defeated in the firelight. 'I can't ever leave, it's . . . It's my fault he's like this.'

Winnie felt herself tense in frustration.

'*He* is the only person responsible for his actions!'

'No! No, it's not true, it was the war, it changed him. He came home with a head full of mud and smoke.'

'I know you're prepared to take the blame for a lot of things, Mum, but even you can't shoulder the blame for the war,' Winnie insisted, 'or Dad's part in it.'

'But it's my fault he went,' she sobbed. 'I've never told you this before. When I met your father, he was a clever young man, nineteen years old – the same age as your Treacle. Handsome and clever like him, too. He'd got the scholarship to go to a grammar, but there was no money for books. Despite that, he had managed to get a good job, training to be a pharmacist. He was doing ever so well too, I was so proud of him.'

'So what happened?' Winnie asked, struggling to reconcile the image of her father to that of a respectable young pharmacist in a white coat.

Jeannie's careworn face fell, her livid pink hands searching out the hem of her apron and twisting it compulsively between her fingers.

'By 1916, we'd been married two years, your father was twenty-one and had avoided conscription, on account of being slightly short-sighted. One dinnertime – I remember it like it was yesterday – I'd popped in to drop his sandwiches off, when a woman came into the pharmacy. She didn't say a word, just looked at your father and placed a white feather onto the counter.'

'An emblem of cowardice,' Winnie breathed.

Jeannie nodded and closed her eyes.

'So help me God for saying this, but back then, I was young and self-righteous. I was embarrassed, couldn't stand to think of the neighbours calling my Tommy a coward behind my back. He was the only man under thirty left on our street, see. I told him that, unless he joined up, he'd be less of a man in my eyes.

'I knew he wanted to stay and continue his apprenticeship, but 'cause of me, he left his job that very afternoon, went straight to the nearest recruiting office and enlisted there and then. By that stage, they cared nothing for his short sight. They just needed bodies.'

'And?' Winnie whispered into the darkness.

'Your father was on the front a week later, straight into the Battle of the Somme as a stretcher-bearer.

'I . . . I sent him to his death, Winnie, and not a day goes by when I don't hate myself for it.' Tears slid down Jeannie's cheeks, but she made no effort to brush them away.

'But he didn't die, Mum,' Winnie replied. 'Surely, he was one of the lucky ones? He came home!'

'The man who came home wasn't your father. The real Tommy *did* die. God alone knows what he saw, but he left his sanity at the bottom of a trench in France.'

'So what happened next?' Winnie asked, already fearing the answer.

'I didn't recognize him. His war didn't stop when the guns stopped firing. Hysterical madness, the doctors called it; the papers called it something else – shell shock, I think. Either way, he was in a dreadful state. He hid under the bed for a week, rigid as a statue. The doctors came and he was packed off to The Maudsley in Camberwell, a hospital for soldiers returning from the front. I wasn't allowed to visit him, they told me he was in solitary confinement as part of his treatment. When that didn't work, they gave him torpillage.

'Electric-shock therapy,' Jeannie added, when she saw the look of confusion on Winnie's face. 'It was supposed to shock him out of his state. Goodness knows what it did, but the hair never grew back on either side of his head, where it was shaved to place the electrodes. After seven months, Tommy came home, supposedly "cured", but he weren't, not really. Not deep down where it counted.'

'Oh, Mum,' Winnie stammered. 'Wha-what did you do?'

'What could anyone do, but get on with it?' she sighed. 'He couldn't return to his old job at the chemist, his hands shook too much, so he had to take whatever manual work came his way – we needed the money, especially when I found I was expecting you. You were ten when the Depression set in, but his depression had set in long before that. The war destroyed him, and I have to hold myself accountable for my part in making him go. It was me who sent him to the front.'

'Mum, that . . . that is a terrible story,' Winnie said haltingly. 'I don't even know what to say, it's shocking and sad, and wrong, but—'

'But what?' Jeannie snapped.

'Sooner or later, he would've been conscripted. So it had *nothing* to do with you. You can't take the blame for the madness inside him, Mum. Plenty of men who fought came home and dealt with their demons instead of taking it out on their wives!' Winnie realized she was actually shaking with emotion, but by God she meant every word. 'You don't deserve to be his punchbag,' she insisted.

'Really?' Jeannie replied with a brittle laugh. 'Well, climb inside my skin, love, tell me how it looks when you've seen it from my angle. If I hadn't forced him to go to war, none of this would've happened. He may have left me, but I can't leave him. Ever.'

Winnie shook her head as the terrible realization dawned

on her that nothing she could ever say or do would dislodge the burden of guilt from her mother's mind. Jeannie Docker's remorse was a disease, and after suffering with it for twenty years, she was riddled with it. Another thought struck her: it surely suited a controlling man like her father to have a wife who truly believed she deserved no better than the violence he served up to her.

'Why've you decided to tell me this now, Mum?' Winnie asked.

''Cause I'm scared of what'll happen if you leave us,' she shrugged. 'And the irony is, we're heading for another war, just as the legacy from the first one looks like it's finally catching up with your father.'

Winnie felt confused and so very tired.

'What do you mean?' she whispered, wiping her eyes with the heels of her hands.

'Gas. Your father inhaled gas in the trenches. His lungs'll never be the same.

'The older he gets, the worse it becomes. I'm so worried for him . . .' Jeannie choked back a sob. 'I don't know how long he's got left.'

Winnie folded her heartbroken mother into her arms, as her own heart splintered into thousands of pieces. The destiny she had dreamed of mastering not one hour before, on the doorstep with Treacle, had vanished.

Jeannie drew back and stared at her eldest daughter, her eyes pale and haunted.

'You shan't ever leave us, will you, Win? I couldn't stand it if you left.'

'No, Mum.'

Wearily, Winnie clambered to her feet and walked to the

door, the remnants of Treacle's tokens of love crunching under her feet.

'Where are you going, love?' blurted Jeannie, alarmed.

'To call it off with Treacle, Mum. He's still waiting outside.'

'Good girl,' said Jeannie shakily. 'I think it's for the best, don't you? Your father's taken against him.'

Winnie picked her way down the stairs and out into the damp, coal-scented night, where Treacle was still patiently waiting on the step. She couldn't stand to see the look on his face as she spoke, so the words tumbled out as she stared hard at the glistening cobbles.

Ten minutes later, the terrible deed was done. Treacle was as destroyed as she had known he would be, but throwing him over was the sacrifice she had to make for her mother's safety.

*

Stella had imagined herself the only person awake at this hour, so she'd been surprised to see Treacle emerge out of the mantle of mist that cloaked Green Street, his hands thrust deep into his coat pockets, his face a mask of misery.

The moonlight etched dark shadows on his face. He looked like a man who barely had the strength to pick his feet up off the floor, but when he drew closer to Stella, he kicked angrily at a stray stone. It ricocheted off a rubbish bin with a clatter, sending a stray cat who had been picking at old fish bones darting up the street.

Stella ducked back into the doorway of the portrait studio, and Treacle walked past without spotting her. Goodness only knew what he was doing, pacing the streets at this unholy hour. Not that Stella had much time to contemplate it. It had taken her a long time to process all the photographs she had taken from the eviction battle earlier that afternoon, and she wanted to deliver them safely.

Just to make sure, she patted the inside of her coat. The brown paper envelope was safely stowed away, ready to deliver to the offices of the *East London Advertiser.*

How Stella wished she could be there to see the editor's face when he opened the package to find a ready-made front-page exclusive. The evidence against their landlord was damning. In crisp, pin-sharp detail, the violence of the bullyboy bailiffs and blackshirts he had employed to forcibly evict Auntie was laid bare.

Stella's quick eye and steady hand had grasped every favourable opportunity. Her personal favourite had been the one of Tommy Docker's boot smashing through the barricade, scattering women and children to the cobbles. In case there was any doubt what else his thugs were capable of, Stella had also included the photos she had taken at the Victoria Park rally the previous night, showing Tommy and the other blackshirts laying into a defenceless man. Just twenty-eight hours ago, but so much had happened since, it already felt like a lifetime. She felt a frisson of excitement pulsing inside as she pulled up the collar of her coat and set off into the night. Now this was the kind of photography that set her blood racing.

*

Six days later, Kitty buried her father under a dazzling March sky. An insurance policy George Moloney had insisted on paying into before illness stole his mind, ensured he was at least given a decent send-off.

Kitty had felt genuine pride and a lump in her throat when two beautiful gleaming black horses, harnessed in black leather and silver livery, pulled a black carriage containing his coffin right into the centre of the tenement courtyard.

It was quite the sight. The carriage was polished to such a high shine, the spring sun dazzled off the surface. The purple-feathered plumes on the horses' heads ruffled slightly in the morning breeze. Every resident of the tenement block came out onto the landings that lined the courtyard and bowed their heads as a mark of respect. Stella and Winnie, who had scarcely left Kitty's side all morning, stuck to her like glue. She was so grateful to them for their support, as she was to Auntie. It was she who had insisted on sprinkling sawdust on the cobbles to muffle the horse's hooves as the cortege moved off, and it was Auntie's they returned to afterwards to a tremendous spread of sandwiches, tea and cake.

It was there, after the speeches and songs had died down, that they received the news they had all been waiting for.

'Auntie!' Stella called, weaving her way through the throng. 'A telegram's just arrived for you.'

Ears pricked up and conversations trailed off as Auntie read the message. Placing the telegram down on the table, she made her way to Kitty's side.

'I have some good news, but is it all right to announce it at your father's wake?' she whispered in her ear.

'I think Dad would probably like that, don't you?' Kitty replied with a tremulous smile.

'In that case . . .' said Auntie, tapping a spoon against

the side of her glass of ale. 'It gives me great pleasure to announce that, from tomorrow, there'll be plenty of workmen around these parts, replacing the gas lighting with electric ones, repairing broken doors and handrails, tackling the vermin – and the wash facilities will be fully operational from next week . . .'

A stunned silence fell over the wake.

'After careful consideration, our landlord has withdrawn my eviction notice. Anyone with any further grievances is invited to meet with him in his offices, and there will be a full rent review to follow.'

'Wouldn't be anything to do with this, would it?' crowed Beattie, holding up yesterday's copy of the *East London Advertiser*.

Stella's photographs were emblazoned over the front page under the headline *Slumlord Scandal . . . lousy landlords in bed with fascists*.

'I mean to say, it don't make him look too good now, does it? One in the eye to them bleedin' blackshirts 'an all!'

A chorus of laughter and cheers rang round the room as, one by one, the residents got to their feet and embraced. Kitty sat and watched in silent wonder, even casting a wink Stella and Winnie's way as they watched Herbie and Gladys give each other an awkward hug. Only Treacle didn't join in, standing with his back to the wall, barely able to muster a weak smile.

'I say we go on a rent strike next, like they're doing over in Stepney!' cried Beattie.

'One step at a time, Beat,' laughed Auntie. 'I think we should remember this victory's a hollow one. It's come too late for Kitty's father.'

Kitty coughed nervously and rose to her feet.

'I'd like to say thank you, to you all, for your support. I can't ever bring Dad back, but to know I'm surrounded by such a close community, who'll fight for one another when the chips are down . . . Well, that means the world.

'Before he took ill, Dad knew the value of standing together, and I reckon he'd be ever so proud. We may be poor, but we're rich in so many ways.'

'Hear hear!' cried Gladys. 'Well said, my girl.'

The residents of Kitty's buildings may have grieved together, but they also rejoiced together, and the celebrations went on well into the night. Laughter and victory songs drifted over the tenements.

Long past midnight, Kitty, Stella and Winnie said their goodbyes and made their way back along the landing to Kitty's flat. Once there, Stella insisted they stay the night and made up beds on the floor next to Kitty, while Winnie fixed them all cocoa. Kitty's sisters had made it to the funeral, but time off in service was rare and so they'd had to race off to catch last trains.

'No-one should be alone after they've buried their father,' Stella said, as they snuggled down for the night under their coverlets, cradling milky drinks.

Kitty felt her eyelids grow heavy, but there was a question she had to ask.

'Winnie, what's going on with you and Treacle? He had a face like a man who'd won the Football Pools and lost the coupon.'

'Yeah, what's going on, Win?' Stella asked. 'You've been out of sorts all week.'

Kitty couldn't read her friend's expression in the dark ened room, but her voice was loaded with pain.

'We've gone our separate ways. He was getting too serious. Marriage equals—'

'Yeah, yeah, we know, drudgery – and I'm with you on that,' Stella interrupted, 'but Treacle's different. It's obvious you're in love with him, Win, and he's potty about you.'

'He's a good man,' Kitty insisted.

'Well, like I say, it's over,' Winnie said crisply, blowing the steam off her mug. 'Besides, there's more to life than courting.'

'Nothing to do with your dad then?' Stella asked. 'We ain't daft. You can't pull the wool over our eyes, Winnie Docker, we've known you too long, remember? He comes back and you two split up? It don't add up . . .'

Winnie said nothing, just kept on staring at the skin that had formed on her cocoa.

'Perhaps it's time to leave home, Win?' Stella said. 'You can come and stay with me.'

'And there's always a place for you here too, Win,' Kitty added.

'I said leave it, will you? You don't know what you're talking about!' Winnie snapped, setting her cup down abruptly and drawing the covers around herself defensively.

Stella shot Kitty an alarmed look.

'Let's get some shut-eye, shall we?' Kitty suggested tactfully. 'We're all tired.'

Outside, the gas lamps hissed and flickered for the last time and, as Kitty finally surrendered to sleep, she wondered what all their tomorrows held.

Nine

August arrived and the mercury on the thermometer climbed, enfolding the East End in an oppressive blanket of heat. A summer so tinder-dry and tense, it felt like all it would take was a single spark and the whole district would go up in flames.

Winnie was still pretending that it had been her decision to cool things off with Treacle. He, in turn, was a broken man. Stella was edgy and restless. Herbie's nerves were shattered from witnessing the constant vandalism along his beloved Green Street. Kitty was emerging from a thick cocoon of grief and felt like she could think clearly for the first time since her father's death. The seamstress could see now that the East End was living on a knife-edge. Despite this, they had never been so tearing busy. Wedding season was in full flow, and it was almost as if the more volatile and dangerous the streets became, the more couples passed through their doors, desperate for marriage and security.

Since Auntie's triumphant campaign, to everyone's amazement, Kitty's landlord had made good on his promise and ordered the repairs to their buildings, but on hot summer days like this, bedbugs were rife and people stayed outside for as long as possible. Tonight, after work, Kitty longed to escape to the shade of a tree in Victoria Park with a book and blanket to sleep out under the stars, but she knew the girls and Gladys would never allow it. It simply wasn't safe to be out alone after dark any more, and besides, Stella had told her she had plans for them all.

'So, where you off to tonight, ducks?' mumbled Gladys, through a mouthful of pins.

'Not sure, Gladys,' Kitty replied. 'Stella says she's got something planned.'

'Well, why don't you knock off as soon as the girls have finished their last portrait sitting? It's like a bleedin' furnace in here,' Gladys grumbled. The elderly seamstress made a comical sight. Both her feet were plunged into a bucket of cold water under her workstation and she had attached old rags to the wheel of her sewing machine, which gave off a limp breeze as it spun round.

'Don't be out too late though – remember we said we'd help Herbie and the girls out tomorrow. His church has organized a summer fete for the kiddies at the children's home in Shoreditch. They're taking photos and we're serving refreshments.'

'Oh crumbs, I forgot about that,' Kitty replied.

Gladys removed the last pin from her mouth and pinned it to a length of red felt material.

'I'm running them all up a glove puppet each. Poor little mites ain't got much. Do you think they'll like 'em?' she asked, holding up a cheerful red puppet with buttons for eyes. 'Herbie asked if I'd do 'em.'

Kitty smiled at Gladys fondly from over the top of the

gown she was working on. Silk jersey with sleeves tapered to below the wrist and tiny mother-of-pearl buttons. Lamé was out – or so the bride-to-be had confidently announced as she'd produced a copy of the *Daily Mirror*, showing some society sort in a Victor Stiebel gown for Kitty to copy.

'I think the sooner Herbie Taylor comes to his senses and realizes what a catch you are, the better,' Kitty added.

'Ooh, don't talk daft, you saucy little madam,' Gladys tutted. She paused, there was a moment's hesitation and Kitty saw a brief flash of vulnerability. 'H-has he ever said anything to Winnie and Stella in that direction?' she asked hopefully.

Kitty wished she had never brought the subject up. 'No, sorry,' she said. 'He never discusses his personal life with them.'

Gladys's face fell.

'No . . . No, course not, love, and even if he were to take a wife again, what on earth would he want with an old woman like me?

'Oh, I nearly forgot, love, a letter arrived for you today.'

Gladys fished an envelope from her pinafore and handed it to Kitty.

'Well,' she grinned expectantly. 'Ain't you going to open it? It could be from that sailor chap of yours. Remember, I still need to find out who his father is, thank him for his generous gift.'

'Later,' Kitty mumbled, popping the letter in her handbag. If it was from Harry, she certainly didn't want an audience whilst reading it. But as Kitty returned to the gown, a shiver of excitement ran through her and she began to sew like she had never sewed before, imbuing each tiny, delicate stitch with that most tender of emotions: hope.

*

Next door at the reception desk, Winnie braced herself for their fifth and fortunately final wedding of the day. It was wedding season so of course the pace had picked up, but Winnie felt she had no sooner finished sweeping up the confetti from the cobbles outside than the next bridal party was descending.

Herbie had photographed more weddings in a day, but for some reason, Winnie felt exhausted to her bones. The fierce heat meant a sticky ring of sweat had formed around her stocking tops and her cheeks ached from the effort of smiling; the happy, carefree mood of the day felt deeply at odds with the darkness in her heart.

The only good side effect of wedding season, she supposed, was that it left her little time to dwell on Treacle. The pain of letting him go was exquisite. She had seen him often since that awful night, walking past the studio on his way home from the docks, and each time her body ached to go to him. The effect of seeing his tall figure loping down Green Street was mesmeric; like a needle to a magnet she fought the urge to weave through the market stalls and throw herself into the safety of his arms. The only thing stopping her was her promise to her mother. Only a week ago she had looked up from arranging the wedding portrait displays in the window to see him chatting with Mickey on the other side of the street. For the briefest of moments their eyes had collided. Winnie had attempted a smile, half-raised her hand in greeting, but his gaze quickly slid downward and he had turned his back on her. How could she blame him? She had broken his heart on the doorstep with absolutely no explanation.

Five months on from that night and still her loneliness was unabating, memories running through her mind on a loop. The evening when he had proposed to her from the window ledge, the heart-stopping softness of his kisses, his strong hands cupping her waist at the dance, and the most bittersweet of all: their last night together, clattering through the deserted streets on the back of a cart gazing up at the stars. For the briefest of time, she'd had hope. Treacle had cherished her so much that she had believed anything was possible, even escape from her father. Now there was no relief from the nightmare. Her love was gone and she had to stand here at reception, smiling at happy newlyweds day in, day out. 'Yes, your daughter does look radiant . . . no, I can't remember the last time I saw such a happy couple . . .' She uttered the words expected of a receptionist at a wedding portrait studio, but inside she was silently weeping, grieving for the love she had lost and the wedding day that would never be hers.

'All right, folks, to your stations please – last wedding of the day just pulled up outside,' Herbie announced, breezing into reception, smelling of mint and cologne, all sharp creases and crispness, despite the wilting heat.

'Are you well, sweetheart?' he asked, touching her forehead. 'You look peaky.'

'I'm fine, boss,' she said, painting on that all-too-familiar fixed smile and standing up ready to greet the newlyweds. And then, she wasn't . . .

The door opened to a great cheer and the infectious energy that always accompanied a big wedding. First came the bride, a coalman's daughter from Shoreditch, looking charming in a cloud of tulle, a gown Winnie knew Kitty had copied from one Carole Lombard had worn in *The Gay Bride*; then came the matron of honour, who Winnie recognized as the bride's older sister, Queenie. Winnie groaned inwardly. Queenie certainly lived up to her name and fancied herself as the East End's answer to royalty.

Queenie was swathed in so much satin and tulle there was little difference between her and the bride, and she was holding on to the best man as if it were she who had just got spliced and not her younger sister.

'Treacle,' Stella said, greeting him warmly. 'You didn't tell me you were the best man.'

He answered Stella, but it was Winnie he couldn't tear his gaze from.

'Sorry, Stell,' he replied awkwardly, plucking at his collar as if he were trying to escape his suit. 'I meant to come in, only I've been feeling out of sorts lately.'

Winnie felt a hot flush scorch her cheeks and with a heroic effort stretched her plastic smile until she felt her face might crack.

'Hello, Treacle . . . you look smart.'

'Doesn't he scrub up well for a stevedore?' Queenie cooed, tightening her grip on his dinner jacket.

The wedding party proceeded upstairs and Stella flicked Winnie a look as they followed.

'Blimey, Queen's got her talons in,' she muttered under her breath.

Upstairs, the torment continued.

'Well now, doesn't everyone look handsome,' Herbie declared, as he arranged the bridal party in front of the camera.

'I'm the happiest chap in the world and I don't mind admitting it, Mr Taylor,' the groom chuckled. 'I've got my beautiful new wife, Pamela, tomorrow we're off on honeymoon to Bournemouth, and when we get back I've landed a new job at a brewery.'

'Well, it don't get much better than that,' Herbie agreed, slapping him on the back. '"Whoever wed in August be, many a change is sure to see," or so they say.'

'Change is as good as a rest – ain't that right, Treacle?' Queenie chirped, casting him a cheeky wink from over the top of her bouquet of red carnations. 'I hear you're single again.'

Winnie felt Stella's hand softly on her back as she fought the urge to ram Queenie's carnations where the sun don't shine.

After the group photos, Herbie began the individual and the smaller groupings.

'Maid of honour and best man next, if you please.'

Queenie bustled Treacle into the spotlight and snuggled in close, sucking in her diaphragm and thrusting out her best assets. Winnie had to concede, with Treacle's jet-black hair and Queenie's platinum finger waves, they made a striking couple.

'Oh yes,' said the bride's mother approvingly. 'Yes, yes, yes. Don'cha make a lovely couple! If only my husband, God rest his soul, were here to see this.'

'Legend says single women will dream of their future husbands if they sleep with a slice of wedding cake under their pillow,' Queenie whispered into Treacle's ear, but loud enough for the whole studio to hear. 'I know who I'll be dreaming of tonight.'

It was too much. Winnie fled from the studio and clattered down the stairs into the dressing room one floor down. She just about managed to shut the door before a great sob escaped her lips.

'Whatever's wrong?' came a voice.

Winnie looked up in surprise. The bride was sitting at the dressing-table mirror, blotting her cheeks. By the looks of her red-rimmed eyes, she too had been having an unbridled meltdown.

'Pamela,' Winnie ventured. 'Never mind me, are you all right?'

'Never better,' she said, a fresh deluge of tears dampening her lovely cheeks.

'Sorry,' she sniffed. 'I *am* happy, truly I am, but I miss my dad and, well, I can't let Mum see me like this. It'll only upset her.'

'Oh, Pamela,' Winnie said, pushing aside her own heartache. 'Weddings are emotional. You're allowed to cry at your own.'

'Really?' the bride replied, absent-mindedly fingering the creamy flesh around her pearl earring. 'Perhaps I shouldn't have worn these. Queenie did warn me against it. "Pearls for tears, Pamela," she told me. "You might as well wear a black veil and have done."'

Pamela mimicked her older sister's pert voice so perfectly, Winnie couldn't help but snort with laughter.

'That's nothing but a daft wedding superstition,' Winnie scoffed, handing Pamela a clean handkerchief to mop up her tears. 'Right up there with rain on your wedding day being good luck. Trust me, I've heard 'em all.'

Pamela managed a weak smile and dabbed at her eyes.

'But surely we only cling to the old ways 'cause nothing in life is certain?' she said softly. 'Look at my dad. I used to think he was the strongest man in the East End. He could carry a two hundredweight sack of coal on his back up the stairs of our buildings like it was nothing. Picture of health, he was. Six months ago, he went to sleep and never woke up. His heart, the doctor reckoned.'

Pamela shook her head as if she still couldn't quite believe it.

'It ain't fair, Winnie. It ain't bloody fair. It should've been him walking me down the aisle. He'd be up there now, cracking bad jokes and getting nervous about his speech.'

She looked up, bewilderment etched in her hazel eyes.

'All my life I've dreamed of my wedding day, Winnie, and so did Dad. As soon as I was born he and Mum took out an insurance policy, which they cashed in a year ago to pay for the wedding. So you see, even when I was a little girl he longed for this day.' She faltered. 'I . . . I never imagined for a moment that he wouldn't be a part of it.

'Although maybe he is, in a small way,' she smiled sadly, picking up the hem of her gown. 'Here's me with the superstition again, but when Kitty made my dress, I asked her to sew five inches of the hem with hair from Rosie.'

'Who's Rosie?' Winnie asked.

'Oh, sorry,' Pamela grinned. 'Rosie's Dad's old horse. He loved that nag so much he used to bring her home for dinner. Used to drive my poor mum mad.'

Winnie chuckled. 'I can imagine, but why the horsehair? Believe it or not, I ain't never heard that one.'

'Horse's hair – you know, to give your marriage strength. But mainly 'cause I know Dad would've loved it. He'd have loved it all, in fact.'

Sighing, she let the hem of her dress float to the floor. Taking a fortifying breath, she pushed back from the dressing table.

'I better go. Queenie'll have eaten poor Treacle alive by now – but thanks for listening, Winnie.' Pamela hesitated at the door, her silhouette framed by the soft folds of her veil.

'True love is so precious, don't you think? It's obvious he loves you very much. Don't squander it, sweetheart.'

*

Outside, despite the lengthening shadows drawing up Green Street, the heat bounced off the confetti-covered kerb and the acrid smell of melting pitch drifted up to meet Kitty. Finally, the day's work was done and for a few brief hours, freedom was hers.

Stella and Winnie were already waiting outside the studio, clutching lemon ices in paper cones. Winnie thrust one at her and Kitty gratefully took it.

'Blimey, I'm boiling,' she sighed, licking the ice and fanning herself with her hand. 'How did the last wedding go?'

'Oh, don't ask,' Winnie sighed.

'Emotional,' Stella admitted. 'Bride looked a picture

though. Talking of which, do you know, Kitty, you look ever so pretty of late yourself. You're sort of glowing.'

'Don't know about that,' Kitty scoffed. 'I'm so hot, I look a fright.'

A workman repairing the tramway nearby unscrewed a turncock in the road and passed her a tin of cool water, with a mock bow.

'I'd marry you on the spot if you'd have me, sweetheart,' he winked.

Winnie and Stella hooted as Kitty blushed to the roots of her hair.

'Come on, let's get going,' she blustered.

'So, you gonna tell us where we're going, Stell?' Winnie demanded as they weaved their way up the busy street.

'Abbott Road,' Stella replied. 'Poplar Municipal Alliance Club.'

'Dancing?' Kitty asked hopefully.

'No. It's a debate. "Should Women Stop at Home?"' Stella replied.

'Sounds a bit jam and Jerusalem, if you ask me,' Winnie replied with a roll of her eyes. 'After the day we've just had, I was hoping to let my hair down.'

'Oh, please say you'll come,' Stella pleaded. 'I need some moral support, only, well, the editor of the *East London Advertiser* got in touch – he wants me to cover it for the newspaper and take photos . . .' She hesitated and for the first time ever, Kitty detected a hint of nerves in her plucky friend.

'Please don't tell Herbie, but the editor says he was impressed with my photos of the eviction and the rally, even seems to think I might have what it takes to be a news photographer and journalist. Says if this goes well, there might be a job for me at the end of it.'

'You're going to leave Herbie?' Winnie gasped.

'No . . . Well, maybe,' Stella blurted. 'Oh please don't be cross. It'd be a dream come true for me. Who knows?' she breathed. '*East London Advertiser* today, tomorrow the *Daily Sketch* . . .'

'And the *New York Times* right around the corner,' Kitty insisted. 'Fancy! Well, we're thrilled for you, ain't we, Win?'

'Yeah, course,' Winnie smiled. 'I just couldn't stand to think of you ever leaving the East End.'

'Thanks, girls, your support means the world to me,' Stella replied. 'On the subject of leaving . . .' She hesitated. 'Winnie, did you know Treacle's going?'

Winnie started to choke on her lemon ice.

'Going?' she spluttered. 'Where? When?'

'Start of October,' Stella replied. 'His uncle's opened up a motor-car business in Hampshire that's doing well, wants Treacle to come and work for him. He's got a smallholding too – few cows and sheep, that kind of thing. He told me earlier in the studio.'

'Sounds idyllic,' Winnie snapped, furiously wiping down her skirt, which was covered in dribbles from her melting ice. 'I'm happy for him. He always did want to get out of the East End. Perhaps he could take that blousy Queenie with him 'n' all.'

'Are you really? Happy for him, that is?' Stella probed.

'Why wouldn't I be?' Winnie said briskly. 'Now come on, let's get going.'

By the time they reached the Municipal Alliance Club,

it was heaving, full of agitated ladies in floral dresses and hats, fanning themselves in the heavy blanket of heat.

'The paper's reserved us places,' said Stella, motioning them to three empty wooden chairs. 'But I've got to stay up the front to get a good view for photos.'

Kitty and Winnie took their places and looked around.

'Half the women of Poplar are here; it would be a brave man to come up against these lot,' Winnie grimaced.

A suited man seated at a trestle table at the front rose to his feet, and Stella began snapping away.

'Good evening,' he said with a nervous cough. 'My name is Mr Arkwright. I propose a motion that the entry of women into business affairs is detrimental to the family life of the nation. Woman was created from the fifth rib of Adam and she has been a pain in the ribs of man ever since.'

A great groan rang around the hall, but the man gamely soldiered on.

'Humour aside, I'm all for women educating themselves, but one should always remember that the hand that rocks the cradle, rules the world.'

'Not in my bloody house,' Winnie said under her breath.

'Today we are facing a serious crisis, and women have been instrumental in creating that crisis. It would never have come about if women had stayed at home. Why, only last week, a woman member of the House of Commons was concentrating so much that she drove her car past a set of red traffic lights.'

'Shame you weren't crossing at the time, mister,' hollered a voice from somewhere at the back, and the stuffy room filled with cheers.

'Carry on like this and he's gonna get lynched,' Winnie commented as Mr Arkwright fingered his speech nervously.

'I deny no woman the right of the vote, but I do deny women the right to neglect their homes . . .'

His voice was drowned out by a chorus of boos.

'They wouldn't leave the home if men weren't so bloody useless!' called a woman over the hubbub. The temperature seemed to soar another few degrees. When Kitty fished in her handbag for her handkerchief, she felt the letter. She knew she oughtn't to be thinking of romance at a time like this, but she couldn't resist. Surreptitiously, she slit the envelope open and began to read. Her heart thumped. It *was* from her Harry.

Dearest Kitty,

I can't tell you how happy I was to read your letter, which finally reached me onboard. I had it in mind you'd run out on me because I had bored you rigid. That night lives on in my memory as one of the best of my life. I hope that doesn't sound too soppy, but I can't shake the image of you in my arms. I could've danced all night with you, and the next, but it was not to be and I understand why you left in such a hurry. I hope your father's recovering well.

Kitty bit her lip and blinked back a tear.

You're lucky to be so close to him. Treasure him, you don't realize how special parents are until they are gone. And that, Kitty, is how I feel about you. I know

*it sounds like madness, only having met you the once,
but I must see you again. I'll tell you what happened
between me and my mum, to force our estrangement, I
must be honest with you, especially if we are to have
any future, for that is my dearest wish, Kitty.*

*My boat is due to dock in the East End on the morning
of Sunday, 4 October. I plan to take a look at the new
kit bags and uniforms in the windows at Gardiner's
Department store, Gardiner's Corner. Say you'll be
there to meet me outside the entrance at 2 p.m.? I'll be
waiting, Kitty.*

*Who knows where my ship will be by the time you read
this, but wherever I am in the world, I'll be sailing
back to you.*

In anticipation,

Harry

Kitty smiled as she folded the letter neatly and slipped it
back into her handbag. Nothing would keep her from being
there and hearing what Harry had to say. *This* was her chance
at happiness, and this time she would not be running.

Kitty glanced to her left, eager to share her news with
Winnie, when she noticed the stricken look on her friend's
face.

'I don't believe it,' Winnie muttered. 'Did you plan this?'

A moment later, Treacle edged his way along the line of
seats, apologizing to everyone he passed, before removing

his tie and sliding in the spare seat on the other side of Winnie.

'What you doing here?' she said sourly. 'I thought you'd be doing the two-step with that pushy piece.'

'Oh, don't be a goose, Win. I ain't interested in Queenie. You know you're the only girl I love,' he pleaded, his voice thickening. 'It's you. Only you for me.'

'Go back to your wedding, Treacle,' she replied dully.

'Please, Win, I've left me best pal's wedding to come and see you, so at least hear me out, and don't be mad with Stella. She thought this was a safe place for us to meet.'

Winnie said nothing, just stared hard at her hands, her face rigid and unreadable.

'I'm leavin',' he whispered. 'The first Sunday in October, the fourth, at midday, to join my uncle in Horndean. I've borrowed a motor car from him. There's room enough for you, your mum and your sisters.' He shifted nervously in his seat. 'It's the perfect opportunity to start afresh, Win, away from here, for *all* of us.'

'You oughtn't have come here. It's over!' Winnie blurted.

'Keep it down, will ya?' scolded a woman behind. 'Some of us are trying to listen.'

'Sorry, miss, it's my fault,' Treacle said, before turning back to Winnie and lowering his voice.

'Don't, Win. Don't say another word. Just promise me you'll think about it. I'll *never* stop loving you.'

Picking up his tie, he smiled weakly at Kitty. She had never seen such heartbreak etched on a man's face. 'Sorry to have interrupted your evening, Kitty.' And then he was gone.

'Please don't say a word, Kitty, or I'll cry,' Winnie pleaded under her breath. In silence, Kitty took Winnie's hand in hers and squeezed it tight.

Mr Arkwright had concluded his argument and now Mrs Bouttell, Chairman of the Ladies Committee of the Alliance, was putting forward her case.

'During the last war, everything that was good in women was brought out and everyone who could do a man's job did it. Now women whose husbands were maimed in the war ought to do anything they can to get a few more shillings for the children. But ultimately, ladies, it comes down to this: a woman's place in the world is wherever her heart is.'

'A fine sentiment . . .' Winnie whispered, blinking back angry tears, '. . . if we weren't born into a man's world.'

Ten

The next morning, Stella was bubbling over with excitement and nerves. The job at the *East London Advertiser* was hers if she wanted it – at least, that's what the editor had said when she had dropped her report and photographs of the previous evening's debate into his offices on the way to work that morning. She replayed the conversation over in her mind again. What was it he had said? 'You are a bright young talent, Stella Smee. Fearless, with a superb eye for a story. Exactly what I look for in my reporters and photographers.'

He had laughed out loud when he came to the photograph of a beleaguered Mr Arkwright scurrying out the back door of the Municipal Alliance Club, hotly pursued by a dozen angry matrons.

The debate had not gone Mr Arkwright's way and, sensing he would be looking for a quick escape route, Stella has positioned herself by the exit at the back, capturing the precise moment the Deputy Chairwoman had brought her parasol crashing down on his head.

'Marvellous stuff,' the editor had declared. 'I need fresh young blood like you on my team, you're wasted in that photographic studio.'

This was the opportunity Stella had been searching for.

Her excitement burst the moment she pushed open the door to the studio and spotted Winnie's downcast face behind the reception desk. She glanced up when Stella walked in and then went back to her copy of the *Eastern Post and City Chronicle.*

'Oh, Win, sweetheart, have you got the dead needle with me for inviting Treacle last night?' Stella asked.

'Says here in the "Grains of Knowledge" section,' said Winnie, without looking up, 'that there is a machine now in use which can wrap toffees at a rate of five hundred a minute. Fancy that.'

Stella walked round behind the desk and seized the paper out of Winnie's hands.

'Oi! I was reading that,' Winnie protested.

'And I don't want to talk about toffees,' Stella replied. 'What's biting you?'

'You went behind my back, Stell,' Winnie said quietly, refusing to meet her friend's gaze. 'I told you not to get involved.'

Perching on the side of the desk, Stella tilted Winnie's chin up so that their eyes met.

'Please don't be browned off, Win. I only did it 'cause I think the world of you both and 'cause you're both miserable without each other. I had hoped hearing Treacle's news might bring you to your senses.'

'To my senses?' Winnie echoed.

'Yes! I've known you since we was nippers and I know when something is wrong. But even if I hadn't, it don't take no detective to work out you're miserable. I've heard you,

Win! Crying down in the darkroom, when you think no one's about.'

Tears instantly sprang into Winnie's eyes.

'I don't know why you're putting up with your father, but I do know that he's a dangerous man. And you . . .' Stella shook her head, suddenly overwhelmed at the strength of her affection for Winnie, 'you . . . you're kind, funny, sweet and loyal. Maybe *too* loyal.'

'Mum'll never leave him and I can't leave her or the girls. It's that simple,' Winnie shrugged. 'I've no choice but to put up and shut up.'

No more words were said, but Stella had the nastiest of sensations that her friend was hiding a secret from her.

The bell over the door tinkled and in strode Herbie, still wearing a dark suit, tie and hat, despite the fierce glare of the late August heat. He took off his hat and fanned down his face.

'It's cracking the cobbles out there. I've just bought some sweets for the kiddies at the children's home.' He dumped bag after bag of tiger-nuts, sherbet-dabs, gobstoppers and liquorices over the desktop with a satisfied smile.

'Blimey, boss,' Winnie grinned. 'Was there anything left in the shop?'

'I confess, I got a bit carried away,' Herbie chuckled. 'I even got some for your sisters,' he added, slipping a brown paper bag into Winnie's handbag. 'I can't help it. I just love the summer fete at the orphanage. You'd have to have the hardest heart not to feel moved when you see how much it means to those that have so little.'

'Before we leave, might I have a quick word, Herbie?' Stella ventured, feeling her heart quicken.

'Can it wait until we get back, my dear?' Herbie replied, as he headed down to the steps that led to the darkroom. 'You won't believe it, but that bride we photographed yesterday, Pamela, she only came in this morning with a photo of her late father Joe – says she can't bear that he missed the day, so she's asked me to superimpose him onto the back of the wedding photo.'

He shook his head in dismay. 'Don'cha just love our job? No two days are ever the same, are they?'

'How you gonna do that then, boss?' asked Winnie.

'Combination printing, or else I'll cut, paste and re-photograph.'

'Sounds fiddly,' she replied. 'Shall I bill for the extra work?'

'No, I don't think so,' Herbie replied, stroking the end of his moustache thoughtfully, 'it's not the sort of job you can put a price on, is it? Now then, Stella, are you quite sure it can keep, love? Only I want to get going on Pamela's photos. She's a smashing girl and I said I'd try my best for her.'

'Quite sure, boss,' Stella replied with a weak smile. 'If anyone can bring a man back from the dead, it's you.'

*

Next door, Kitty hummed a Billie Holiday tune, a whisper of a smile playing on her pretty face as she gently treadled her machine. She couldn't quite tug her mind free from the music, or Harry's letter. What was it he had said?

Wherever I am in the world, I'll be sailing back to you.

Up until now, Kitty had lived her romantic notions

vicariously, pouring all her tender unused love into every stitch. But finally it felt like life was offering her an opportunity.

Harry had been so handsome, so smart. She had no idea what he and his mother had fallen out over, but how bad could it possibly be? Tucked in her pocket was her response to his letter, assuring him that she would most certainly be there on the fourth of October to greet him.

'Someone's in a bank holiday mood! Good to see you with a smile on your face again, love,' Gladys remarked. 'Now come on, let's hop to it. Herbie and the girls'll be waiting. I've invited Auntie too. I think she's at a bit of a loose end since she won the eviction battle.'

The Wedding Girls, accompanied by Herbie, Gladys and Auntie, wove their way through the crowded street in the sunshine. By the time they reached their tram stop by the Salmon and Ball, their arms were groaning with yet more gifts; everything from apples and oranges to ribbons and marbles. Word had spread that they were going to the home for Waifs and Strays in Shoreditch, and the traders and shop owners of Green Street had proven yet again what big hearts East Enders had.

It was a joyous occasion and Kitty loved every minute of the afternoon, dishing out jelly, ice cream and currant buns.

When the photographs were done and the children had said their goodbyes, Kitty, Auntie and Gladys wandered over to where Herbie, Winnie and Stella were packing up.

'You all right, Mr Taylor?' Kitty enquired. 'Working with children is exhausting, isn't it? My ears are ringing.'

'Herbie, your hand!' Gladys shrieked.

His right hand was red raw and the skin had bubbled off.

'Please, Gladys, don't make a fuss,' he replied in a shaky voice, but it was too late and soon all the girls had gathered round.

'Herbie, have you burned yourself?' Stella asked.

'It's nothing, just a little slip,' he said, squeezing his eyes tightly shut in pain. 'I used flash powder and I'm afraid I misjudged it and some ran down my hand.'

'Why ever didn't you say?' Winnie asked, shocked.

'I didn't like to, in case I alarmed the children,' he admitted.

'So you carried on taking photos, even though your hand was burning?' Auntie exclaimed in astonishment.

'It wouldn't have been fair, it would only have panicked them. Really, ladies, I'm quite all right. I need to run it under cold water, that's all.'

'Nonsense, you're coming with me,' bossed Gladys, fetching his jacket. 'I'm taking you straight to Dr Garfinkle – and no arguments.'

*

'What a day,' Winnie sighed, feeling utterly exhausted as she trudged up the steps to their rooms.

'Mum!' she called out.

'You'll never guess what happened to poor old Mr Taylor,' she babbled, before remembering her mother was doing a shift at a local cafe.

'Girls! Anyone about? I've got some sweets for you!'

The flat was deadly silent. She supposed the girls must

be playing out on such a warm summer's evening. Ripping off her headscarf, Winnie heard a faint rustling coming from the cupboard under the stairs.

The noise, muffled to begin with, grew louder and only as she drew nearer did she realize to her horror that it was the sound of sobbing.

Wrenching open the cupboard, Winnie gasped in shock. For there was her sister, Bertha, squashed into the darkness, tears streaming down her face. Bertha took one look at her and flung herself into Winnie's arms.

'Dad was cross, 'cause I was playing with Mari over the road,' she managed, between sobs. 'He told me never to play with dirty Yid kids and he chucked me in the cupboard.'

'How long have you been in there?' Winnie asked, taking in her little sister's tear-stained cheeks and swollen eyelids.

''Bout an hour. Oh, Win. I'm sorry, I didn't mean to upset him. What if he comes home and finds I've come out?'

'Ssh, you're safe now,' Winnie soothed. 'Don't you worry about Dad. I'll deal with him.'

'So ought I to stop playing with Mari?' Bertha asked, gazing up at her in confusion. 'Only, she's my best friend.'

'Absolutely not,' Winnie replied, unable to hide the quake from her voice. 'You mustn't listen to Dad. Not ever.'

Later that night, under the veil of darkness, as she lay in bed listening to the soft breathing of her three sleeping sisters, a violent hatred clawed Winnie's chest. This could not be allowed to go on. At no cost could history be allowed to repeat itself. She did a mental count in her head . . . Just over one month. Five weeks until Treacle left Bethnal Green. Forever. What would it take to get her mother to join him?

The whole situation was an impossibly dark and tangled mess. The only thing that stood out with any clarity, like a single golden thread, was her love for Treacle.

*

The next day in the studio, Stella came in early, hoping to catch Herbie alone. The photographer was hard at work already, setting up for the day ahead, his right hand swaddled in a bandage.

'What a clot I am!' he remarked, holding up his hand and gesturing to the velvet chairs he had set up in front of a painted backdrop of a mist-covered valley.

'Come and sit with me, Stella. I need to talk to you, love.'

'Good, 'cause there's something I want to talk to you about actually, Herbie,' Stella said softly, pulling her chair a little closer to Herbie's.

'I've been thinking . . .' they both said at exactly the same time.

'You first,' Stella smiled.

'Very well,' Herbie said, in a way that sent a ripple of dread spiralling through her. 'We talked in the spring, didn't we, about me retiring?'

He held up his hand and grinned ruefully. 'I think the time's come, don't you?'

'What?' Stella spluttered. 'It's only a little injury. You ain't ready for the scrapheap just yet!'

Herbie chuckled and clasped his hands together in prayer. 'From your lips to God's ear, eh, love! Seriously, though, I've made up my mind, Stella, and I shan't change it.'

He hesitated, fixing his brown eyes on hers to check he had her full focus.

'I want *you* to take over and run this place as you see fit. I'll set it up so I can help to manage things in the background, but the day-to-day running of it will be down to you. And after I die, well, it all goes to you.'

'Herbie!' she gasped. 'I . . . I don't know what to say.'

'Just say yes,' he smiled, smoothing back a stray blonde curl that had fallen over her eye. 'I've never really said this before, but since your father passed, I've felt very protective over you. You have such a talent at your fingertips, but more than that, you feel like a daughter to me.'

Stella couldn't help her burning curiosity and the words slipped out before she could stop them.

'What happened to your wife?'

Herbie's face paled and he reached down to pick up a glass of water from the floor, but his bandaged hand fumbled and failed to grasp it.

'Forgive me, I've no right,' said Stella, handing him the glass, from which he took a long shaky sip.

'No . . .' he whispered. 'You have a perfect right to ask. She . . . She died in childbirth. We thought they had managed to save our son, but it was not to be. He breathed for twelve minutes before dying in my arms.'

Herbie's voice broke on the words and tears flooded his cheeks.

Stella watched, horrified and deeply ashamed of herself for dredging up the past.

'You think,' he wept, 'that your brain will eventually find a way to come to terms with it, erase the memories, but after all this time, I can picture my baby's face more clearly than ever. He was born with his eyes open, the clearest blue eyes, and then they closed to the world forever. I remember every single last detail: his perfect skin, those tiny scrunched-up fingers . . . the softness of his head. My brain replays over and over, every single second I held him in my arms.

'Oh, Stella,' he moaned, shuddering and squeezing his own eyes shut. 'My boy . . . My beautiful, beautiful boy. Yesterday was the anniversary of their death. Thirty-five years, and yet he still visits me in my dreams.'

'Oh, Herbie, I'm so sorry,' Stella wept, feeling her heart contract.

'People told me I ought to move on, take a new wife, but I never could – silly, stubborn old fool that I am.' He smiled weakly and trumpeted into a handkerchief. 'Instead, I threw myself into this place. And through my work, I found comfort.' He cast a hand around the studio. 'Photography is my way of freezing time. Unlike us mere mortals, an image can live forever, can't it?'

Stella nodded sadly, suddenly understanding. Understanding with perfect clarity his passion for documenting life in the community; the way he had not rested until Pamela's father, Joe, was cut and pasted into the wedding, which death had stolen his chance of attending. Life was random and, at times, spectacularly cruel. Portraiture was Herbie's way of redressing the balance, enshrining memories under glass so that they might live forever.

'But the world around me is changing at such a pace,' Herbie went on. 'Do you know, I read the other day in my *National Encyclopedia of Photography* that two and a half million people in this country drive a motor vehicle and double that amount now use a camera, would you believe! I can't keep up, Stella!'

Herbie patted the lace antimacassars that covered the arms of his velvet chair and sighed.

'I like to cling to the old ways, as you know, but what this business needs is someone like you at the helm. Someone with vision and guts, to embrace all those changes.'

'But surely there must be a man to inherit?' Stella murmured.

'Well, I've a nephew who works in the print, but he's got no interest in photography. Besides, Stella, this is *your* place. It's only right I bequeath it to you, my right-hand girl.'

A soft smile lit up his weary face. 'I've been thinking: why don't we change the name of the business?'

He held up his bandaged hand, as if framing an imaginary sign. 'Herbie Taylor & Daughter? Got a ring to it, ain't it?' he smiled.

The smile faded. 'It's time for me to let go of the past.'

After all she had heard, Stella knew there was no way on earth she could leave. As she nodded her agreement, it felt like the ground beneath her feet was crumbling away.

'So what was it you wanted to speak to me about, love?' he asked.

'Oh, nothing,' she mumbled. 'Nothing important.'

Eleven

Four weeks later, the paperwork had been filed and management of Herbie Taylor & Sons had passed to eighteen-year-old Stella Smee. Her future was now a fait accompli.

With one crass question, Stella had ripped open all Herbie's old wounds, and in return he had bestowed upon her his greatest treasure – his business. She felt deeply humbled and selfish, but above all, determined to make the very best of it and pull herself up by the boot straps. In this day and age, she was lucky to have a job, never mind a business! So why had it felt so gut-wrenching when she had called on the *East London Advertiser* to inform them she would not be taking up the position as junior news photographer after all?

It was a Thursday afternoon and in a break between bridal and baby portraits, she and Winnie had popped next door to Gladys's workshop for a quick cuppa with the girls.

'We ought to celebrate, love,' said Gladys. 'I want all the Wedding Girls at mine for your tea tonight. I'm doing liver and bacon followed by apple fritters, and I've invited Auntie and Herbie. That man don't eat, he's wasting away!'

'Smashing, I'll be there,' smiled Kitty. 'I must admit, without Dad, I do get a bit lonely in the evenings.'

'Count me in too,' said Winnie. 'Dad's about tonight so I'd like to make myself scarce.'

Once again, Stella felt humbled. What was a lost opportunity when she compared her problems to the grief and heartache that her two best friends were going through?

'And your young beau, Treacle?' Gladys asked Winnie as she reached for her pinking shears. 'Kitty mentioned you ain't stepping out no longer. Please tell me that ain't true, love.'

Winnie's face fell. 'I'm afraid it is true, Gladys. It's over.'

'But why?' Gladys shrieked, dropping her pinking shears on the cutting table with a thud.

'It's complicated,' Winnie muttered defensively.

'I don't know . . .' Gladys tutted. 'You girls. Don't know how lucky you are to have all these nice young chaps about the place. You wanna be careful you don't all end up old maids like me.'

Kitty paled. 'That's what I worry about.'

'Behave, Kitty,' Stella chuckled. 'You've only just turned eighteen, you're hardly on the shelf. Besides, you're meeting that sailor chap Harry on Sunday, ain't you?'

'On the subject of which,' Gladys interjected. 'I'm going to insist that one of you girls chaperone her. After all, we don't know the first thing about this Harry.'

'That's right,' Stella said, casting a wink at the girls. 'He could be any old Tom, Dick or . . .'

'Harry!' Kitty and Winnie hooted.

'You may mock,' Gladys said, pointing her shears at them knowingly. 'But he could be a right villain for all we know. Besides, you know what sailors are like. Also, the streets just ain't safe at the moment. Did you hear about that massive fight in Shadwell between the fascists and the anti-fascists? Some of them Jew baiters were carrying bars of iron wrapped in paper, and razors blades hidden in potatoes!'

'Don't worry, I'll go with Kitty on Sunday,' Stella said, placing a soothing hand on Gladys's arm. 'I'll make sure she's not sold into the slave trade or caught up in any riots.'

'Good, that's settled then,' remarked Gladys. 'Now, chop-chop, back to business, everyone – let's sort the workers from the shirkers.'

As they made their way back to the studio, Stella caught Winnie by the arm.

'You sure about you and Treacle? He's leaving this Sunday. Forever.'

'You sure about this job, Stell?' Winnie shot back. 'Seems like we're both turning our backs on a lot.'

Sensing they had reached a stalemate, the girls headed into the portrait studio.

*

Kitty drained her cup and returned to the bridesmaid's dress she was putting the finishing touches to.

'I must admit, I don't completely approve of you meeting this Harry fella on Sunday, but I do feel comforted to know Stella will be going with you,' Gladys remarked as she took their cups to the small scullery out back to rinse out.

'Honestly, Gladys, I'll be fine,' Kitty replied as she deftly threaded her needle. 'We're meeting in broad daylight and outside the busiest department store in the East End. What could possibly go wrong?'

Gladys bustled back in and picked up her string shopping bag.

'Don't start me off, love,' she replied, with a heavy sigh. 'I can feel one of my heads coming on! I'm gonna nip out for some shopping and get a bit of fresh air before it takes hold.'

Kitty nodded and returned to her sewing.

Gladys hovered on the doorstep, for the first time ever looking at a loss as to what to say.

'I . . . I know I come over like some fussy old aunt,' she said, 'and you're probably thinking, "What can a spinster like Gladys know of what it feels like to be young?" But, trust me, Kitty, I . . . I know what it feels like to be lonely. I'm surrounded by young women enjoying the biggest love affairs of their lives, and not a day goes by when I don't wonder what that feels like.'

'You don't—'

'Please, love, let me finish,' Gladys whispered. 'I ain't daft. I know it's too late for me. I got varicose veins on my legs and the conductor don't call me "Miss" no more, but . . .'

She hesitated and her eyes filled with tears. 'Romance doesn't just belong to the young.'

Choking back a sob, Gladys disappeared out into the busy street.

Kitty stared after her, open-mouthed. A moment later the door swung back open and a pretty young lady paused expectantly on the threshold.

'Cooey! Shall I call back later?'

Kitty wrenched her mind from Gladys's halting confession and back to the present.

'I'm ever so sorry, miss, I don't know what's wrong with me today,' she blustered.

'You and half the East End,' the woman laughed, tugging off her gloves. 'There must be madness in the air today. Looks like there's going to be murders on Sunday, judging from the talk on the market.'

Kitty smiled and nodded, even though she had not the faintest notion what the woman was talking about.

'What can I do for you, miss?' she smiled. 'It's Joyce, Joyce Spicer, isn't it?'

'That's right,' Joyce smiled, unpinning her hat next and placing a large dress box down on the cutting table.

'I'm getting married on Saturday and you've made me the most heavenly dress.'

'I remember it well,' Kitty gushed. 'White satin, sweetheart neckline, inlet of lace, cathedral sleeves with a loop for the finger and twenty-two satin buttons on the back.'

'Hark at your memory,' Joyce grinned.

'Oh, I never forget a gown,' Kitty replied, 'especially not one as dreamy as that. I can't wait to see you in it . . .' Kitty's voice trailed off in alarm. 'Is everything all right, with the dress I mean, only . . .'

'Ooh, rather,' Joyce soothed. 'I couldn't be happier, only I was just wondering if you could make a small alteration.'

Kitty gazed at her tiny frame, wondering if she needed it taking in. She was such a slip of a thing. All tumbling blonde curls and dewy skin, so petite she looked as if she could fit in Gladys's coat pocket!

'I wondered if you could sew this ring into the lining?' she asked huskily.

Joyce fished in her pocket and pulled out a tiny ring with

a fake blue gemstone stuck on it and handed it to Kitty. It was no bigger than a child's ring.

'It's worth nothing, at least not in financial terms,' Joyce said apologetically, 'but it's priceless. To me, at any rate.'

Kitty gazed at it, intrigued.

'Course I can, Joyce,' she replied. 'You wouldn't believe what we get asked to sew into dresses. Only the other day, a bride had me sewing a tiny leather doll that belonged to her nan into the hem.'

'Fancy that! Ain't that sweet?' Joyce replied brightly, and then burst into tears.

'Oh, Joyce,' Kitty exclaimed, jumping to her feet and rushing to her side. 'I didn't mean to upset you.'

'Ignore me,' she wept, waving her hand and trying to dab at her eyes. 'I'm such a twerp. I've just done me lashes an' all.'

'Joyce,' said Kitty. 'Tell me to mind my own business, but who did the ring belong to?'

Joyce hesitated. 'It . . . it belonged to my fiancé's twin brother, Billy.'

'Go on,' said Kitty gently. Through more tears, the whole story came tumbling out.

'Me and Billy was neighbours and childhood sweethearts,' Joyce said, her face lighting up. 'We used to play in the alleyway that ran between our houses. Ooh, he weren't half a soppy sod, even as a kid. The first time he proposed he must have been all of eight years old. Went down Woolworths and bought the ring himself, he did, got down on one knee on the roof of the washhouse in the yard.'

Joyce smiled.

'I thought he was the most handsome boy on the street,

so I said yes, of course. Only fly in the ointment was his twin brother, Alan.' Joyce grimaced. 'Ooh, I hated Alan. Stuck up, he was, always had his nose in a book, aloof, know what I mean? He and Billy were that different, I couldn't for the life of me fathom out how they were related, never mind twins.'

Kitty shook her head, confused. 'But, Alan . . . Isn't he your intended?'

'That's right,' Joyce nodded. 'So time goes on, and me and Billy started work, both of us got a job down at Tate & Lyle so we could be near each other. He'd meet me every morning and evening after work, so he could carry my bag back. Soon as we turned eighteen, we were to marry. Billy had it all planned out, see. Alan had left home by this time. All those hours with his head in a book had paid off and he'd got a scholarship for some fancy school.

'Billy and me opened up a wedding club, started paying in regular like, so we could afford something decent; the wedding was booked, Alan was to come home and act as best man, and then . . .'

'What happened, Joyce?' Kitty asked.

'Billy was killed, a month before we were due to get married. Stepped out in front of a tram on the Commercial Road. Killed on impact. Daft sod. He always did have his head in the clouds, probably dreaming about our wedding.'

Kitty's hand flew to her mouth to prevent her cry of shock.

'Oh, Joyce . . . What did you do?'

A tear slid down Joyce's cheek and angrily she brushed it away.

'I . . . I thought I was drowning. No one tells you how

close grief feels to tear, Kitty. I was so scared after Billy died, scared of living . . .'

Joyce looked up and the guilt in her eyes took Kitty's breath away.

'I couldn't leave the house, couldn't even wash meself. I was like a child again.'

'So how did you carry on?'

'In a word: Alan. He turned up out the blue and he never left my side. Sounds strange, but he was the only person in the world who really understood what I was going through. He'd loved Billy just as much as I had, see. We found solace and understanding, and gradually, I began to realize that Alan wasn't snooty or rude. He was shy and gentle and kind and . . .'

A smile played on Joyce's lips.

'. . . and over time, understanding blossomed to . . .'

'Love,' Kitty murmured.

'That's right, Kitty,' Joyce smiled tremulously, turning to face her. 'You don't think me awful for marrying him? Our families understand, but many down the street and in the factory think it's wrong to be marrying my fiancé's twin. I've heard the whispers. "Ignore 'em," Mum says, but I can't. I have this horrible nagging guilt that Billy'll be watching and he'll hate me . . .' Tears splashed down Joyce's face and suddenly Kitty found she too was blinded by tears.

'How could he possibly hate you, Joyce? He obviously worshipped the ground you walked on. I think that you and Alan have both suffered an awful, crushing loss and you've found comfort in one another. Where's the sense in you both going to your graves miserable and lonely? Your Billy would never want that, surely?'

Joyce sniffed and blew into her handkerchief.

'I think you're right, Kitty,' she said shakily. 'Thank you. I never really saw it that way before.'

Kitty held up Billy's ring.

'I think this ring ought to play a part in your day. I'll sew it into the lining, right next to your heart.'

'So you think I'm doing the right thing, marrying Alan?' Joyce asked, hesitantly. 'The wedding should go ahead?'

A pair of pinking shears dropped from the shelf above their heads and landed with such a clatter on the workbench next to them, dislodging a small box of sequins that showered over the floor around their feet like confetti. For a second, both girls sat in stunned silence, before bursting into a hail of nervous laughter.

'Dodgy shelf?' Joyce grimaced.

'Perhaps . . . Or maybe that's Billy's way of saying he approves?' Kitty smiled.

Half an hour later, Joyce was on her way, with a lightness to her step she had not felt in a long while, and Kitty set to work sewing the tiny ring into the lining.

Over the years, Kitty had often found herself acting as unofficial agony aunt to the droves of young girls who passed through the workshop. Something about her presence and light touch as she measured and pinned seemed to invite trust and confidence. But of all the stories she had heard, nothing spoke to her heart like that of Joyce and Alan.

As Kitty delicately plied her needle she wondered whether it was possible to transfer emotion through her fingertips, into the very fabric of the dress. Superstitious Gladys believed that all negative emotions, from anger through to jealousy, could be sewn into a gown, like poison seeping into an apple, and as such insisted that neither of them sat down to a day's work unless it was with a good heart.

If that were true, would Joyce feel the love – and if she were honest – longing, she had stitched into the soft folds of satin? Kitty was suddenly gripped with a strong ache of desire. When . . . *When* would it be her turn to experience a passionate, sweeping love like that of Celeste and Frankie, Joyce and Billy, and, even though it seemed doomed, Winnie and Treacle?

Sighing gently, she finished unpicking the lining and carefully slipped the ring under the sweetheart neckline. Kitty ran her hand over the satin bodice and shivered. Maybe her destiny was to follow in Gladys's unfulfilled footsteps.

*

Later that evening, Winnie arrived home from work and, shrugging off her coat, called out to her mum from the gloom of the passage.

'Don't worry about any tea for me, Mum. I'm not stopping, I'm only here for a quick wash. Gladys Tingle's invited me over to hers . . .'

Winnie's voice trailed off as she stepped into the kitchen to find her mother being quizzed by a man from the Relief Office.

'What's he doing here?' Winnie asked warily.

'Winifred, where's your manners?' Jeannie scolded.

'Sorry . . . But, well, it's a shock. We haven't claimed

relief in over a year now. We're all in employment and we're up to date with the rent . . .'

Jeannie's head dropped.

'Aren't we?' Winnie asked, feeling a deep dread crawl up her spine.

'Mum?'

Jeannie said nothing, just kept on staring bleakly out of the window.

'Please say you've been paying the rent, Mum?'

'Well, since your father's been back, naturally I've let him take over the finances again and I think he may've missed a couple of payments and we're a bit short, so I've had to get a few things on tick and . . . It's mounting up a bit.'

Winnie felt her legs weaken as she slumped into a chair. 'Oh, Mum . . .' she breathed. 'Mum, after everything we've been through to get ourselves respectable again, you let that man take control of the purse strings?'

Suddenly, she was on her feet, anger fizzing.

'Growing up, what were the four things you always drummed into me?' Winnie demanded. Not that she needed Jeannie to answer her, she could remember them by rote. *Work hard. Speak the truth. Never borrow money or be late with the rent. And if you get lost, don't ask a policeman or a priest, ask a tramp to show you home, then give him money for a cuppa.*

Who was leaching away her values? The door thudded open and her father appeared.

Kicking off his boots, he sat down heavily without bothering to close the door behind him. 'Put the wood in the hole, Jeannie,' he ordered gruffly, before turning to the Relief Officer with an icy expression.

'And who might you be?' he asked coldly.

'Aah, Mr Docker, I presume. My name is Mr Lacey and I'm from London County Council. I am responsible for the Means Test—'

'I know who you are. Now go on, get out of it! We don't need no charity,' Tommy scowled.

'You are an impecunious family, are you not?' the Relief Officer asked, shifting uncomfortably.

'I don't like that word.'

'Needy then . . .'

'Nor that.'

'Insolvent then . . . Look here, Mr Docker. Your wife tells me you are behind on the rent and you have mouths to feed. There are a number of items that will need to be sold in order to claim relief and—'

'We don't need your bloody charity!' Tommy thundered. 'Get out!'

Mr Lacey sighed and rose to his feet, but not before he had scribbled an address on a piece of paper and handed it to Jeannie.

'This is your nearest soup kitchen. You'll be able to feed your children there.'

'She don't need to go to no bloody soup kitchen,' Tommy ranted. 'They're all run by the bleedin' Jews anyhow.'

As the door slammed behind Mr Lacey, Winnie turned on her father, shaking with rage. How was this ignorant man her flesh?

'Mum works all the hours, holding down three jobs, and I work, so where's all our money going? How could you let us fall behind on the rent? How?'

'Show me some respect,' Tommy growled.

'When you've earned it, I will,' Winnie replied, thrusting her chin out.

A smile crept over his face.

'You'll have to show me respect soon, my girl. Judgement day is coming and then we'll be out of this dump.' His voice dropped an octave and he started to sing, his voice gravelly and tuneless as he rocked back on the balls of his feet.

'When once Olympia is past,
then, boys, the spring clean comes at last,
then we'll have one more glorious go.
And set about the Jewish foe.'

'You've finally lost your marbles,' Winnie snorted.

'Have I?' he grinned. 'You wait and see on Sunday, my girl. It's all happening on Sunday.'

He paced the airless room above the rag shop, the gloaming light casting his face into shadow. 'We shall rise victorious and legends shall be born!'

Winnie turned and, with her father's taunts still ringing in her ears, she fled. Outside on Cable Street, the road was humming with a strange activity, a feeling of defiance and anger pulsing off the cobbles. Winnie leapt out the way as a motor car cruised past, a boy clinging to the running board, scattering handbills like confetti.

A loudspeaker was fixed to the top of the car, its message crackling ominously up the long narrow street.

All out against the blackshirts! They shall not pass!

A handbill fluttered through the air, landing at Winnie's feet. Intrigued, she picked it up.

All rally to Gardiner's Corner – 2 o'clock, Sunday 4th

Winnie felt her head start to spin. Sunday again! What on earth was happening on Sunday?

As she walked back in the direction of Bethnal Green, nearly every wall and kerbstone in Whitechapel was painted with slogans. *No pasarán! . . . They Shall Not Pass . . . Bar the Road to Fascism.*

Walls coated with centuries of industrial grime and coal dust had been whitewashed out of recognition. There must have been a hundredweight of chalk and gallons of white-wash used to transform East London. The very air she breathed was electrified. Winnie didn't know what was about to go down, but something momentous was brewing.

*

In Gladys's flat above the wedding workshop, the girls gathered. The tidy parlour room gleamed like a new pin and warm, spicy cooking smells drifted in from the kitchen, but it did little to disguise the tension cloaking the room.

Herbie sat at the small table, a copy of the *Daily Herald* spread out before him. Auntie sat beside him, bolt upright, wearing her customary black and a deep frown.

Kitty didn't really understand what was going on, politics meant little to her, but she was bright enough to know that something serious was about to erupt in the East End. A sense of foreboding had hung over her buildings as she, Stella and Auntie had left earlier, the air thick with whispers. What was it Joyce Spicer had said?

There's going to be murders on Sunday.

'I'd like to take this,' Auntie scowled, as she extracted the steel pin from her black hat, 'and teach that Mosley a lesson in manners.'

At that moment the door opened and Winnie burst in.

'Have you seen this?' she exclaimed, clutching a handbill.

'That we have,' remarked Gladys, bustling into the room, holding a steaming pot in her podgy fingers. 'As if the streets ain't dangerous enough as it is.'

'What does it all mean?' Kitty ventured.

'This Sunday, Oswald Mosley is planning a huge march through the streets of the East End, and has invited every blackshirt and fascist in the country to celebrate the fourth birthday of the movement,' Herbie remarked, looking up from the paper. 'Says here, the fascists will assemble at Royal Mint Street near the Tower of London, then there'll be four marching columns, which will end in four massive rallies, each of which Mosley will speak at.'

'Bloodshed is where it will all end,' Gladys remarked, as she set her pot down on the table and wafted away the steam. 'Why can't he just stay indoors and blow out the candles on a bleedin' cake, like everyone else does on a birthday?'

'That's right, Glad,' Auntie nodded. 'Instead, he wants to terrorize East London into submission.'

'Well, he's got a fight on his hands,' Stella remarked. ''Cause from what I've seen on the streets, folk ain't prepared to sit back and let him march. Apparently, the Jewish People's Council took a petition with nearly one hundred thousand signatures to the Home Office, calling on them to ban the march, but they've refused. They're even giving Mosley a mounted police escort.'

'Why?' gasped Winnie.

'Some rot about how they ought to be allowed to exercise

their right to free speech,' Stella snorted in disgust. 'Excuse my French, but that's a bloody abuse of words. It's not free speech that mob want, but free punch-ups. Remember what happened at Olympia two years ago?'

'Erm, I don't,' Kitty admitted.

'Mosley held a big meeting and every time he was interrupted by a heckler, his Biff Boy blackshirts smacked the living daylights out of them!' Stella railed. 'Anyway, word on the streets is that there's to be a counter-rally at Gardiner's Corner to prevent the fascists getting through. Everyone who is against fascism is being encouraged to get out and defend their streets.'

She said it again, slower this time, looking pointedly at the girls. 'Everyone . . . That's men *and* women!'

Her eyes sparkled with excitement, and Kitty was in no doubt where Stella Smee saw herself going after church on Sunday!

'So what should we do?' Kitty quavered.

Herbie gently tapped his purple-stained fingers together several times as he thought it over.

'We stay in and lock our doors,' he said eventually.

'What?' Stella shrieked, leaping to her feet. 'And give them free passage through the East End? That's . . . that's just plain wrong!' she spluttered.

'And two wrongs don't make a right,' Herbie said wearily, pointing at the newspaper. 'Says right here, a deputation of the five East London mayors are appealing for calm, they want people to keep away on Sunday.'

He eyeballed each of the girls in turn.

'Stay away and stay safe . . .'

'Is that an order?' Stella demanded. 'We're supposed to

back down and follow the Germans into slavery? What was the war about then?'

'Calm down, madam, and don't go working yourself into a lather,' Gladys tutted. Stella sat back down and folded her arms testily.

'Herbie cares about all of you,' Gladys said, laying a hand on his shoulder. 'He's not trying to lord it over you, he's simply showing concern for your safety, that's all. Come Sunday morning, there'll be coachloads of fascists descending on the East End from every corner of Britain, and you can bet they ain't come in peace.'

'Gladys is right,' Herbie added, smiling gratefully and patting her hand. 'In all your cases, I like to think I'm the closest thing you've got to a father, and I should never forgive myself if any harm were to come to you.'

Herbie glanced over to Winnie. 'I know you already have a father, Winnie, so I hope you don't take offence.'

'None taken, I can assure you, Herbie,' she replied. 'You've shown me more love and guidance over the past year than that man's shown me in a lifetime.'

'Well, I, for one, happen to think Stella's right,' Auntie piped up. 'We faced down them greedy landlords and stood together to fight injustice. We have to take a stand, otherwise we'll have another Hitler on our hands. I'll be out on Sunday, defending our streets.'

'I respect that, Auntie, but I'm afraid neither my knees, nor my nerves, are up to watching thousands of wannabe Nazis marching on a day of rest,' said Gladys.

'Nor me,' muttered Winnie. 'I don't want to run the risk of bumping into my father.'

'And you, Kitty? What'll you do?' Stella asked. 'It's the

same time and place you're supposed to be meeting Harry, in case you'd forgotten?'

'I haven't decided,' she replied honestly. 'If I don't go, Harry will think I've run away – again – and how can I possibly get word to him before then? His ship doesn't dock until that morning. But . . . I've been trying to think about what my father would have done. I think . . . I think he would've made a stand, like Auntie. He loved his East End and would have done anything to protect it.'

'Kitty, love,' Gladys cried. 'Your father worshipped you and would never want to see you in harm's way, and nor do I. Please, don't go, love. You'll meet another chap. I beg of you, don't go.'

Gladys looked utterly stricken and, in that moment, Kitty knew how strong the depth of her feelings must run. Her and Herbie were like substitute parents to all of them, and to go on Sunday would be to cast aside their feelings.

'Very well, I shan't go,' she smiled.

'Good,' Gladys replied shakily. 'Now, shall we eat?'

As she served up tea, a heavy silence descended on the room, each of them lost in their own thoughts.

*

By Saturday morning, the tension in the streets had reached a fever pitch. The whole of the East End was in a ferment and Kitty realized you would have to be either deaf or blind not to be aware of the march, for it was being discussed in every street, tram, bus and cafe.

Loudspeaker vans toured the districts, and the streets

had been whitewashed with that much paint it looked as if Christmas had come early.

As Kitty walked to work with Stella, her friend tried to pin her down.

'So what are you going to do, Kitty? Are we going to meet Harry tomorrow and get involved in the march, or what?'

Stella ran a hand through her bouncy blonde curls and fixed Kitty with one of her inscrutable looks.

'See what it says?' Stella persisted, tearing down a hand-bill that had been pasted to a gas lamp outside the studio. *All Out!* All, Kitty. That includes you and me.'

Kitty scuffed her shoe against the kerbstone.

'I don't know, Stella,' she mumbled, wishing she shared her friend's bravura outlook on life. 'You heard what Gladys and Herbie said. The authorities are warning people to stay away.'

'Don't mean they're right,' Stella replied, jutting her chin out.

Kitty hesitated. 'I really do want to meet Harry and, besides, I don't agree with the march and I know Dad wouldn't.'

'So let's go,' Stella urged, unable to keep the note of excitement from creeping into her voice.

'But I told Gladys I wouldn't,' Kitty quavered. 'I really ought to ask permission.'

'Better to ask forgiveness than to seek permission,' Stella shot back with a capricious smirk.

Kitty opened her mouth, but found there was nothing she could say in the face of Stella's irrefutable logic.

'Come on,' Stella said, ruffling Kitty's hair and swinging

open the door to the workshop for her. 'You best get to work. At least think about it, though.'

Kitty did think about it. She thought of little else and, by the time the newly married Joyce and Alan pulled up in Green Street for their official wedding photographs, she would have missed it altogether, had it not been for Gladys and her beady eye.

If there was one thing Gladys couldn't bear missing, it was the sight of one of their creations on a bride.

'They're here!' she screeched, so loud that Kitty nearly ran the sewing machine needle through her thumb.

'Come on, ducks, shake a leg!' Gladys was already piling out of the workshop door with a bag of confetti to join the market traders and shop owners who were clustered round the ecstatic couple. Kitty picked up the present she had made for them and timidly followed Gladys through the crowds.

A lump lodged in her throat when she spotted Joyce in a swirling cloud of confetti. Tears blurred her eyes as she watched the radiant bride, so petite and happy, nestled into the crook of her new husband's arm. Joyce was showing off her ring to the small crowd of cooing shop owners as a shy, bespectacled Alan had his back slapped by the enthusiastic traders.

Three young bridesmaids ran rings around the couple, giggling and tying lace-covered horseshoes to the bride's bouquet.

Everyone loved a wedding in the East End, and no one could resist the sight of a newlywed couple. There was something infectious about their happiness. Kitty's turmoil over whether to turn out on the march tomorrow melted at the sight of Joyce's happiness.

Kitty hung back and watched. Joyce had actually done it. She had married the man who had saved her from her grief and, judging by the way he was gazing at her adoringly, he clearly worshipped her as much as his twin brother had. She couldn't hear what Joyce was saying over the hubbub, but one gesture needed no words. Slowly Joyce raised her hand and placed it over her heart, trailing her fingers over the ring that only she, Alan and Kitty knew was hidden under the lining.

Joyce looked up and spotted her through the crowd.

'Kitty!' she cried, beckoning her over.

Kitty made her way to the bride's side and instinctively they moved into each other's embrace. Kitty found herself wrapped in clouds of chiffon and violet water.

'I don't know how to thank you,' Joyce murmured in her ear.

'Whatever for?' Kitty replied.

'For the other day – being so kind and not judging me,' Joyce whispered, pulling back and placing her hand over her breast. 'A part of my heart will always belong to Billy, but my future is with Alan. I know that now.'

'I'm so thrilled for you, Joyce,' Kitty replied. 'You deserve your happiness. Here, this is for you.'

Kitty placed a small, hand-stitched bundle into Joyce's hands.

'There's salt, so you may always have food. A piece of coal, so you will always be warm, and a bar of soap, so you can always be clean.'

She hesitated, smiling shyly. 'Something tells me you'll never be short of love.'

'You're an angel on earth, I swear it, Kitty,' Joyce beamed.

Suddenly, they both became aware of Winnie and Stella standing beside them.

'Congratulations, Joyce. The studio's ready, would you like to come and have your photographs now?' Winnie smiled, gesturing to the door.

Joyce and Alan made their way through the crowd to the studio entrance, but at the last moment, Joyce paused and turned back, her brown eyes glowing with love.

'I know you're not supposed to do this until later, but hang it all . . .'

Stretching her arms out wide, Joyce tossed her bouquet of dusky pink tea roses high up over Green Street. Every shop girl in the vicinity craned her neck as the flowers soared through the air, jostling for position. But it was straight into Kitty's hands they sailed.

Joyce winked as she disappeared into the studio.

'You're next.'

Kitty and Gladys returned to their workshop, back to their needle and thread and their unfulfilled dreams and, in that moment, Kitty knew. Like Joyce, it was time to take a risk on love.

*

As darkness fell over the East End that night, Winnie lay awake in the bed she shared with Sylvie. Bertha and Betty were tucked up in their bed on the other side of the tiny bedroom. All three of them were sound asleep.

Winnie wished sleep would come as easily to her, but her thoughts were like a ticking clock, all counting down to the moment when a new day dawned and Treacle would leave the East End. Winnie felt her chest heave. The pain of his departure was tormenting. Treacle was her man, her gentle, strong, decent man. No one even came close.

Next door, through the paper-thin wall, she heard the creak of bedsprings as her father grunted and rolled over and, just like that, Treacle's face vanished.

The crack at the window startled her.

Winnie stumbled from her bed and wiped a trail through the condensation on the window. In the backyard, she made out the outline of a man and her heart lurched.

'Winnie!' hissed a voice. 'Winnie, wake up.'

Treacle!

Winnie pulled up the sash and leaned out, the cold night air sucking the breath from her body.

'What you playing at?'

Treacle stamped his feet and rubbed his biceps to keep out the cold. At his feet lay a duffel bag.

'I've come to say goodbye. I'm leaving.'

'But I thought you weren't going until tomorrow?'

'I weren't, but what with the trouble expected at this march an' all, I don't want to risk waiting, so I'm going now. I've got the motor parked out front.'

He paused and gazed up at her, his face illuminated by a bright sickle moon hanging in the inky sky.

'Come with me. I'm lost without you, Winnie.'

'Why have you come here?' she cried. 'You know I can't.'

'You can,' he implored, his fists bunching in frustration. 'You can. It's as easy as walking out the door.'

Winnie's mind felt slow and muddy as she turned over his proposition, but before she had a chance to speak, she felt a presence behind her.

A heavy hand shot out. Winnie just about made out Treacle's dismayed face, before her father wrenched the curtain across the window.

'Get back to sleep,' he ordered. 'I'll deal with you in the morning.'

Climbing back into bed, Winnie's limbs felt as heavy as lead. A minute later, a car engine fired up and she was helpless to stop the deluge of tears.

All night Winnie lay awake, feeling like she was hanging on the edge of a great precipice. After Treacle's car had gone, the sounds of the night tortured her. The distant crackle of fascist amplifiers, the shattering of breaking glass, woken babies crying in the rooms above and, somewhere in the distance, the low wail of a ship's foghorn as it sailed into the docks. All along the narrow, smoky street, the inhabitants of Cable Street lay breathless in their beds, waiting for the break of dawn, but for Winnie, nothing mattered any more. Treacle had gone and a part of her would be broken forever.

Twelve

Sunday the fourth of October dawned bright and clear, with not a wisp of cloud in the sky. Kitty got back from church, changed out of her Sunday best and fixed herself a cup of strong, sweet tea and a thickly sliced piece of bread scraped with marge. When she had finished eating, she brushed down the crumbs from her fawn cotton dress, went to the outside tap and filled a pail, before steeping her hands into the icy-cold water and splashing her face.

Already, the tenement courtyard was filled with the scent of boiling cabbage, but dinner was the last thing on Kitty's mind as she strode purposefully up the flight of steps and landing that connected Stella's lodgings to hers.

'Kitty!' Stella exclaimed as she pulled open the door. 'What you doing here? I'm just on my way to the march.'

'I'm coming with you. To Gardiner's Corner . . . if that's all right?'

Stella's mischievous lips curled at the edges. 'Do they have ponies down a pit?'

Stella grabbed her cap and her camera, then linked her arm firmly through Kitty's in case she changed her mind.

'Let's go!'

Both girls found their hearts were in their mouths as they tripped down the tenement steps.

'What changed your mind?' Stella asked, blinking as they emerged from the gloom of the stairwell and out on to the dazzling street.

'Let's just say, I had a sign from above,' Kitty replied, casting her mind back to the previous day when Joyce's bouquet had sailed straight into her hands. 'Also, my dad. Before his mind went, he was a freethinking man, who believed in tolerance. He stood up for others as a matter of principle and belief.'

'I think you're doing your dad proud,' Stella replied softly.

After that, neither said a word as they bounded up the Bethnal Green Road, anticipation burning in their chests, arms linked tightly. Nothing but blue skies stretched out over the market stalls. It was turning out to be a fine, bright autumn morning, but for once, the weather didn't seem to be the right topic of discussion.

'Gardiner's Corner' were the only two words on people's lips, and as the girls turned left down Brick Lane, the crowds were already growing.

To Kitty, it felt like the East End was emptying itself and her blue eyes stretched wide with dismay. Folk spilled from narrow courts and side alleys, or streamed past on bicycles, calling to friends, holding flags and banners aloft. Nervous, excited chatter bounced off the high walls of the factories and shops.

Kitty gripped Stella's arm a little tighter as the fast-moving crowd of people jostled against her.

'Blimey, I never expected it to be so busy,' she murmured.

'You wait until we get to Gardiner's Corner,' Stella panted, as she walked briskly along to keep pace with the flow of human traffic streaming down Brick Lane in the direction of Aldgate.

'How will I spot Harry in this crowd?' Kitty panicked.

'Don't worry, we'll find lover boy,' Stella grinned, taking out a cigarette and lighting it with trembling fingers that belied her breezy manner. 'But whatever you do, Kitty, don't leave my side.'

'I should never dare,' Kitty gulped, holding onto Stella's arm like it was a life buoy.

When they reached the intersection with Whitechapel Road, Kitty felt the breath stop in her lungs and the cigarette dangling from Stella's lips dropped onto the kerbside.

'My days!' Kitty gasped. 'I've never seen so many people.'

There must have been thousands, if not tens of thousands of people jammed along the Whitechapel Road; in fact, Kitty could barely see to the end of the broad street.

'Come on, this way,' panted Stella, mashing out her cigarette, before grabbing Kitty's hand and pulling her through the thickening crowds in the direction of Petticoat Lane.

Faces blurred as they weaved their way through the seething mass of men and women. It all started to feel like a dream to Kitty as she took in the sea of flags and banners, the terrific roar of the crowd.

They Shall Not Pass was the slogan of choice and the crowd chanted it as one, their voices euphoric at the tremendous turnout.

Finally, when they reached Gardiner's Corner, where Commercial Street, Leman Street and Commercial Road joined Whitechapel High Street, the crowds were simply too thick to pass and they were wedged in solid.

'Stella, I can hardly breathe,' Kitty rasped, feeling a prickle of panic.

Stella's head darted this way and that as she sized up the situation.

'Here, mister, give us a hand getting up there, would you?' she asked a man, pointing to a broad awning that ran over a shopfront.

'Course, darlin',' he grinned, rolling up his sleeves. 'Bloody marvellous, ain't it? Like being at Wembley on Cup Final day. Come on then, I'll give you a bunk-up.'

'Oh no . . .' Kitty trembled, trying to back away, but escape was impossible and, a moment later, Stella and the man had wrestled a leg each and she found herself hoisted high up onto the thick metal ledge of the shop awning. A minute more, and the man and his mate had helped jump Stella up.

With their feet dangling over the edge, Kitty's head spun as she gripped the sides for dear life and took in the astonishing sight.

'Oh just look at it, will you, Kitty?' Stella exclaimed, pulling out her camera. 'So many people! We've got a bird's-eye view up here!'

In all her days, Kitty had never seen the like, and doubted she ever would again. A curious excitement took hold of her. The intersection was crammed solid as far as she could see in all directions. Men, women and even children stood defiantly, backs ramrod straight. Kids clung to the top of lampposts and others, like them, had scrambled onto shop awnings. There were faces glued to every window, looking out on to the streets in dismay.

Kitty's eyes roamed over the sea of heads and gradually began to focus on the faces in the crowd.

Tough dockers brushed shoulders with Orthodox Jews wearing long silk coats and soft black hats. Grandfathers who remembered the Boer War stood side by side with housewives from Bow and Bethnal Green. There were Irish voices, communist flags, trade unionists, old girls in cross-over aprons with grim glory etched on their faces, merchant seamen, giggling factory girls, shop owners, tailors, council workers, railway men, foremen, navvies and more.

Never had Kitty seen so many people from all walks of life. Men and women, young and old, were united in a human barricade and a lump formed in her throat. What her dear old dad wouldn't have given to see this!

Her eyes rested on two familiar faces in the crowd. It was Celeste and Frankie Butwell, the debutante and the boxer who had overcome such odds to marry seven months ago. Frankie had his arm protectively slung around his new wife's shoulder, and the pair looked so happy, their eyes lit up as they joined in the singing in the crowd.

'Celeste!' Kitty yelled, waving her hand in the air, but her cries were snatched by the breeze and went unheard. No matter, it was good to see them both there, clearly as besotted with each other as they were the day they married. And suddenly it struck her: Celeste and Frankie were born on different sides of the divide, but they had found common ground in love and their beliefs.

And so it was happening here today, except on a far larger scale. The realization sent a delicious warmth rippling through Kitty's tummy. Decent folk, regardless of their background, creed, colour or belief, were sick to the back teeth of the fascist bullies flooding their streets with violence and hatred. Kitty sensed that this moment had been months in the making. She felt her father's spirit and, for one glorious moment, she had never felt so dizzyingly alive. The noise, the colours, the sheer energy and spirit of the crowd coalesced into one huge, happy mass of humanity.

'Look at that,' Stella blurted, breaking off from her photos for a moment to point out a tram that had been parked smack-bang in the middle of the intersection. It looked as if the driver had just stopped and walked off. More trams were doing the same.

'Mosley'll have a job on his hands, getting his mob through here all right,' she laughed, her quick eyes gleaming in the pale autumn sunshine.

But her hollering was drowned out by a sudden clattering and a dark shadow flashed over their heads.

Both girls craned their heads skywards. Cutting through the roar of the crowds was a police autogyro, circling overhead.

'Heavens above, what's that?' panicked Kitty, grabbing Stella's arm. 'Are they going to shoot us?'

'Don't worry, it's only a police observation plane,' Stella laughed, raising her camera up to snap a picture. 'Yeah, that's right!' Stella bellowed into the air. 'We're watching you 'n' all!

'And look – talk about well prepared, they've even got a first-aid station over there,' Stella gushed, pointing to a shop doorway and raising her camera again.

Kitty's eyes travelled to the doorway near Gardiner's department store and that's when she spotted him. Fresh off the boat in his merchant navy uniform, a kit bag slung over one shoulder and a look of total bewilderment etched on his face.

'Harry! Harry, up here!'

Kitty saw his face whip round. 'Look up!' she yelled.

Harry spotted her, and a bemused smile creased his face.

'You came!' he hollered back, removing his cap and holding it over his heart. 'Picked a right day for it, didn't I?'

'Wait there,' she said breathlessly. 'I'm coming down.'

Stella's voice, thick with alarm, cut through her thoughts.

'Don't be daft, Kitty,' she urged. 'Wait here until the crowds die down.'

'I must go to him,' Kitty insisted, easing herself along the awning and preparing to drop herself down.

'No, Kitty!' Stella screamed. 'Wait!'

Suddenly, the crowd surged forward, the ground seemed to tremble underfoot . . . and that was when they heard it: the sound of horses' hooves. A thick blue line of mounted police was advancing on the crowded intersection from two directions and the atmosphere changed in the blink of an eye.

A scream caught in Kitty's throat as she watched a police constable swing his long, leather-bound truncheon high up over his head, before bringing it down with a sickening crunch onto the skull of a man at the front of the crowd. He dropped like a sack of potatoes.

A woman's howl of pain filled the air, followed by the smashing of glass. Kitty and Stella watched in horror as a young woman and her friend were charged through the plate-glass window of Gardiner's by another mounted policeman. Men fought with policemen, punches were thrown, caps were dislodged and the air was filled with the sound of breaking bones as police on horseback tried to hew a way through the impenetrable crowd.

'Why are they doing this?' Stella cried, bewildered, as

she photographed the blood-spattered shop window. 'It's obvious they shan't get through.'

Kitty didn't know. She only knew she had to get to Harry. Taking a deep breath, she released her grip and slipped down off the awning into the seething crowd below.

*

Half a mile away, in Cable Street, it sounded like all hell was about to break loose. Tentatively, Winnie opened the window and leaned out. Already the barricade outside the builders' yard at the top end of the street had grown since she last looked.

All morning, Winnie, Jeannie and the girls had watched in disbelief as men and women had swarmed below, hauling anything they could find to shore up the barricade that blocked the narrow street. Bricks, ladders, old broken furniture and mattresses had been stacked in a heap and covered in planks of wood and corrugated iron. Now, there was even an over-turned flatbed truck in front of it, and a second and third barricade of corrugated iron had been built a hundred yards back. *Remember Olympia. They Shall Not Pass* was chalked over one.

The girls were full of excitement – all except Bertha, who was sitting silently away from the window. Sylvie had kept up a running commentary all morning of the events unfolding outside.

'How many times have I got to tell you? Come away from the window, Sylvie,' Jeannie ordered, looking up from her darning.

'I don't believe it!' Sylvie shrieked, completely ignoring

her mother. 'The Irish are coming. All the dockers are coming up from their end of the street, and look, they've got pickaxes . . . They're tearing up the cobblestones to put on the barricades.'

Winnie jumped at her sister's shrill voice. The sleepless night had sharpened her senses. Every cry, every thud and crack from outside was magnified tenfold in her mind.

Ever since her father had left at the crack of dawn, much to her relief, she could see something momentous was brewing. If her rotten father and the rest of his blackshirts tried to march down Cable Street, they would certainly have a fight on their hands.

'Look, there's Kathleen and Alice from three doors up, they're helping to build the barricades,' Sylvie went on, leaping from foot to foot in her excitement. 'And look, Bertha, there's your Mari's mum, she's out too!'

Bertha said nothing, just stared glumly at the floor.

'Bertha, sweetheart, what's wrong? You've barely said two words all morning,' Winnie said, crouching down by her little sister's side. Bertha bit hard on her lip and refused to meet Winnie's eye. An uneasy feeling twisted inside her, and she was aware Jeannie had put down her darning and was looking over at them.

A tense silence filled the room, the only sounds the crack, crack, crack of the dockers' pickaxes reverberating up the street.

'Bertha, it's me, your big sister,' Winnie coaxed. 'You can tell me anything.'

Tears filled her sister's eyes and her face crumpled.

'Oh, please don't be cross, but Dad caught me playing with my mate Mari again and he was mad. He belted me one. Told me not to play with Yid kids, else I'd cop it.' She dissolved into floods of tears and Winnie wrapped her in her arms.

'There, there, no one is cross with you,' she soothed, staring pointedly at her mother. 'You've done exactly the right thing, telling us what Dad did.'

Tears pricked Winnie's eyes as she tried to hold back the tide of anger. Something stirred inside Winnie: an instinct to protect her sisters so primal it took her breath away. All their lives depended on her finding her backbone.

'Girls, go and wait in your bedroom,' Winnie ordered. 'I need to talk to Mum. Alone.'

Sylvie could tell she meant business by the timbre of her voice and, without complaint, she shut the window and silently led her two younger sisters into their bedroom.

Winnie turned on her mother. Maybe it was the tension from the streets spilling over into the tiny airless room, or perhaps it was her heartache at being forced apart from Treacle, but months of grief and bitterness crystallized together into a bolt of pure emotion. Winnie had reached her tipping point.

'I'm sorry, Mum. I know you love Dad, but your guilt is playing with your mind. I'm going, and what's more, I'm taking the girls. You can come, you can stay, I no longer care.'

With a shaking finger, Winnie closed her eyes and pointed to the bedroom door.

'My *only* concerns rest with those three girls. That man has destroyed your life and he ruined my childhood. I'm not sitting by while he wrecks their lives as well. I'm sorry for what he went through in the war, Mum, truly I am, but it's not our fault – or yours, for that matter.'

Jeannie rose unsteadily to her feet.

'Very well . . . I . . . I'll come.'

Winnie's eyes snapped open.

'You mean that?'

Jeannie nodded slowly, her baggy eyes teeming with fear.

'Yes . . . Yes,' she wept. 'What can I say, love? I'm so sorry. I ought to have listened to you, but I'm not as strong as you. I just kept hoping your father would change . . .'

Winnie's heart started to thud in her chest like a jack-hammer.

'All right, Mum, don't worry about all that now. The main thing is, we have to stay calm and we have to leave. Right now.'

Jeannie started to shake violently and Winnie realized what an enormous task she had ahead of her.

'Oughtn't we to wait?' Jeannie trembled, jerking her head at the window. 'At least until the streets have cleared a bit.'

'No,' Winnie said firmly. 'In fact, this is the perfect time – there's so much confusion, no one will see us leave. And Dad'll be away all day on his hateful march. I've got enough put by to book us one night in a boarding house near the station, then at first light we'll get a train out to Horndean.'

'And then what?' whimpered Jeannie.

'Then we go about finding Treacle. Now come on, there's not a moment to lose. We have to go.'

Something pierced the fog in Winnie's brain and she felt as if her blood were on fire as she wrenched the bedroom door open. It was happening, it was finally happening. They were leaving.

'All right, girls, pack one small bag each. I'll explain later, but we're going to the countryside. There's no time to waste.'

*

When Kitty landed from the awning onto the pavement beneath, she felt as if she was being sucked down a giant plughole. Her dress skirts billowed out as she fell and within moments the crowd had consumed her. The sheer weight of so many jostling bodies pressed together was over-whelming. Panic flared. She had no sense of her bearings. Elbows, cloth caps and Brylcreemed hair flashed before her, and she couldn't think for the clatter of the autogyro circling relentlessly overhead. A young man clinging from the top of a lamppost called out to the crowd. 'Come on, don't let them push yer back, come forward.'

It was an unholy din. Shouts and jeers rent the air, mingling with the clanging of ambulance bells and shrilling of police whistles.

'Harry!' Kitty screamed, frantically twisting this way and that in an effort to free her body from the crush. 'Harry, where are you?'

'Kitty!' called a voice over the roar. 'Over here.'

Suddenly, the crowd parted and Kitty saw a gap open up on the street in front of her.

'Thank God,' she gasped, clutching her chest as she felt the oxygen flood back into her lungs. Her relief was short-lived. In dismay, she realized why the crowds had scattered. Her pupils dilated as she saw the steaming flanks of an enormous grey dappled police horse bearing down on her, its hooves drumming over the cobbles. The world seemed to go into slow motion and, to her horror, she found she was rooted to the spot.

Kitty couldn't make out the police constable's eyes under the rim of his helmet, but his mouth was fixed in a grim slit of determination as he raised his truncheon aloft.

'Move! GET OUT THE WAY!' screamed a voice.

Poor beast, Kitty thought, absurdly, as the shadow of the powerful horse swallowed her. *He probably don't like this any more than I do.*

Suddenly, Kitty felt a strong hand wrench her back and she fell with a thud onto the cobbles as the horse flashed past with inches to spare. The breath was crushed from her body and she was so winded that all she could do was close her eyes, but when she opened them, she found she was folded in a man's arms. A pair of concerned green eyes hovered over her.

'Harry?' she whispered. 'Harry, is that really you?' For a moment, she wondered if she hadn't died, so unreal did the moment feel.

But if this was Harry, then his ghost had a very grimy face and a bleeding knee.

'Hello, Kitty,' he grinned, pushing back his mop of blond hair. 'This weren't quite the reunion I'd imagined. I spotted you as soon as you came down off that awning. I had a right game getting through the crowd to reach you, mind.'

'Thank goodness you did,' she said, suddenly feeling like a perfect fool. Why hadn't she just stepped out of the way?

'Don't worry. It's the shock. I'd have been the same,' Harry said kindly. 'Hark at the state of us.'

He nodded down and Kitty suddenly realized that she too had nasty gashes on both her knees.

'Come on,' he smiled, gently helping her up to her feet. 'I heard someone say there's a first-aid post in Curly's Cafe, down Brick Lane. I want to get you away from here and somewhere a bit safer.'

Carefully, he draped his sailor's overcoat around her shoulders, before looping his arm around her waist and guiding her away from the chaos.

'And once we've got ourselves patched up and a cup of tea, I want to tell you everything about why my mum washed her hands of me, and then . . . Well, then you can make up your own mind about me.'

*

Stella waited until she saw Kitty limping off, supported by Harry, before jamming her cap over her head and heading in the other direction. She had fought like fury to reach Kitty's side, but Harry had beaten her to it, and now that she could see Kitty was safe in his arms . . . well, three was a crowd. Besides which, this crowd was on the move and she wanted to be a part of it.

She had watched, horrified, as time and again the mounted police had tried to force a path through the immense crowd using baton and lathe charges, but the sheer weight of people and the parked trams meant there was no way they were getting through.

The irony was, Stella had scarcely seen a single fascist or black uniform; they were all still stuck down on Royal Mint Street, waiting for the police to clear a path for them to march.

Her heart had hardened at the scenes; police lashing out

indiscriminately at anyone, women going down under the horses' hooves, terrified children's faces gazing down at the bloodshed from a Sunday afternoon dance class at the top of Gardiner's department store.

Stella had no idea how long they had been out on the streets. It felt like mere minutes, but the clock in a shop window told her it was longer. Eventually, she could see the thick blue line of police thinning out.

Boos turned to cheers and a great wave of jubilation rushed through the crowd. 'They're turning back!' yelled the man clinging to the top of the lamppost.

The chanting grew stronger.

They did not pass!

Then another voice, louder still, reached Stella: 'They're heading to Cable Street, they're going to try and get through there!'

Stella had no idea why the police were heading there, but that was where Winnie lived. She had to get down there. Fast. Her heart picked up speed as she started to run, along with streams of others.

As she rounded the corner into Cable Street, she skidded on an upturned cobblestone and crashed to the ground, quickly rolling into a doorway before she was trampled underfoot. From her vantage point, it looked like the scene of an almighty fight, even more incredible than the sights she had already witnessed, and she wound her camera on with trembling hands, before edging as close to the barricades as she dared.

In the narrow street, the noise was even more deafening than at Gardiner's Corner, the men and women manning the home-made barricades gripped with a fever of passion and excitement.

One, two, three, four, five, we want Mosley dead or alive!

Herbie's words of caution drifted into Stella's mind – *Stay away and stay safe* – and straight out again. Stella's tenacious spirit kicked in and Herbie's voice vanished as she raised her camera. Her Leica was perfect for this, with its wide-aperture lens and high-speed shutter, suitable for capturing every electrifying moment of the battle.

With each frame she shot, Stella's astonishment grew. Ducking a hail of flying debris, she inched closer to the action.

More police on horseback repeatedly charging the barricades . . . Missiles flying through the air . . . Kids hurling marbles under the horses' hooves . . . And the sight she found most amazing of all: women from the tenements above the shops emptying the contents of their chamber pots out of the windows over the heads of the police beneath. One old girl she recognized from visiting Winnie yanked open her window and dumped a bucket of rotten vegetable peelings and fat right over a copper's helmet.

'Go on, clear off!' she scowled, hugging her shawl about her. 'What you helping that lousy lot for? We don't want 'em down our street. I've got a paralysed son-in-law and six grandkids in here what need protecting.'

The window slammed, and a few seconds later opened again.

'Have that 'n' all,' she cackled, emptying the slops from her teapot over his head for good measure.

Stella heard the crunching of glass behind her.

'Mind how you go, love, I got wounded coming through.'

She hopped out of the way just in time, and was stunned

to see Ted, a well-known winkle seller, ferrying casualties up the road in his cart. He winked at her as he passed, his cartwheels slipping on the briny cobbles.

'Beats a day at the seaside, don't it, love?'

Ducking into a shop doorway, Stella paused to take a breath and tuck her blonde curls back up under her cap. A familiar figure skirted the pavement on the other side of the street, hunched over with his cap pulled down low over his face. Where did she recognize that walk? It came to her. It was Tommy, Winnie's father. What on earth was he doing back in Cable Street so soon? She had supposed he would be up near Tower Hill with the rest of his blackshirts. He had at least had the good sense to remove his uniform.

*

Less than two hundred yards away, Winnie's sense of urgency was mounting.

'Mum, please, will you hurry up?' she begged. 'We have to be on our way.'

'I . . . I'm sorry, love. I'm not as fast as you, my nerves are shot,' Jeannie mumbled, trying to pack her needle and thread into a sewing bag. Her hands were shaking so much, she couldn't do the zip up.

'Here, let me do the packing, Mum,' Winnie said. 'You go and make us a flask of tea for the journey.'

Like a child, Jeannie nodded . . . And promptly walked into the girls' bedroom. Winnie sighed and tried to control her panic. Her mother was so terrified, she didn't know whether she was on her heels or her head. Between her and the girls, who were flapping about over their packing, this was taking far too long. They ought to be long gone by now. The terrific roars and crashes from outside weren't doing anything to help matters and Winnie's nerves were at breaking point.

Five minutes later, she had their meagre possessions packed and was waiting by the door, tying her hair back in a headscarf, when the girls came out.

'All right,' said Winnie, blowing out a long, slow breath to calm her pounding heart. 'Everybody ready?'

'I haven't done the flask,' Jeannie shrieked.

'Mum, don't worry about the bloody tea,' Winnie snapped. 'We'll grab a cup when we get to the station.'

'It's all right, love,' Jeannie stumbled, her eyes filling with tears. 'When your father left this morning he told me not to expect him until late and . . .'

Bang!

The front door downstairs thudded. Jeannie gripped the wall, her face as white as bone.

Silence . . .

Winnie waited a beat. 'It's all right, it's all right, it's only the noise from the barricades. Let's go.'

She reached down to pick up her bag, but as she turned round and yanked open the door, a figure slid out of the shadows.

'Go where?' asked her father, his voice dripping poison.

Winnie stood stock-still and took in the stricken faces of her mother and sisters.

'Sh . . . shopping,' she stuttered eventually.

'Oh yeah?' he sneered. 'What for, pigeons' milk and rubber mallets? I weren't born yesterday, Winnie.'

Winnie cursed herself. They had been tumbled. Lying

was pointless. They were each clutching their worldly possessions, for heaven's sake.

Instead, she sucked up what little bravery she felt and gripped her bag for support.

'Move out the way please, we're leaving.'

A smile curled over her father's face and he started to laugh: a cold, mechanical noise that turned her insides.

'And where might you be off to, Winifred? Off on yer holidays, are ya?' Abruptly his laughter trailed off and he poked her hard in the chest, pushing her backwards into the room.

'Get. Back. Inside. NOW!' he bellowed, smacking his palm hard against the wall behind Winnie's head.

At that moment, Winnie's last shred of bravery left her; panic, dark and electric, prickled and the room seemed to shrink. Her father was angrier than she had ever seen him. He clamped his mouth shut in a tight line, blew noisily out of both nostrils. Whatever had happened outside on the streets had stoked his temper, and now this . . .

The blood-curdling thought occurred to her that there was little point in screaming for help, for who would hear them over the noise from the battle outside?

His hand shot out and clutched her mother's throat so tightly, the skin around his fingers faded an unnatural white.

'Dad . . . Dad please,' Winnie pleaded, her heart smashing against her ribs. 'Not in front of the girls.'

'Go to your room,' he ordered.

Sylvie, Bertha and Betty didn't need to be told twice, and scuttled off to their bedroom.

Tommy's eyes moved from Winnie to Jeannie, and in that moment, he looked demented, his eyes glazed over with fury, his cheeks blazing. Outside, a cobblestone cracked against the wall. The sound acted as a disturbing mnemonic.

'Get down!' Tommy roared, clamping his hands tighter round Jeannie's neck. A sudden shudder rushed through Winnie's body as the dreadful realization dawned on her that her father was no longer in Stepney, but back on the Somme. The tremendous noise of the riots outside was triggering a flashback to the battlefield. In his mind, the cracks and thuds of torn-up cobblestones were exploding shells. He was once against in the grip of madness. All his intelligence, his personality, the attributes her mother had fallen for, had been stripped away by his experience. Like a train that had lost its driver, he was hurtling through life, out of control.

Her mother's face was draining of its last remaining bit of colour, her legs twitching, her eyes turning milky and clouded, as his fingers squeezed tighter.

'Get off her!' Winnie yelled, jumping on his back and pummelling him with her fists. Her bodyweight caused him to stagger and lurch sideways, dislodging her mother's bag from the table. Her sewing kit crashed to the floor, and burst open, showering the floorboards with hundreds of buttons and pins. Gasping for breath, Jeannie slid down the wall, clawing at her throat, and collapsed in a heap amongst the pins. It was too grotesque for words.

Like a dreadful scene from a Western bar brawl, they crashed around, bumping into furniture as Tommy wrestled to get Winnie off his back. The room filled with thuds, grunts and the sharp cracking of pins underfoot. At last, with a ghastly howl, Tommy wrenched Winnie off and threw her against the wall. Her back hit the skirting board with a crack, the pain forcing the breath from her body. For a moment, she lay winded and unable to move a muscle.

Tommy smirked, fished a cigarette out of his pocket and lit up. Inhaling deeply, he blew out a long stream of blue smoke through his nostrils and looked down at Winnie through the haze.

'You wanna fight like a man? Well, you better be prepared to hurt like one.'

'No, Dad,' she whimpered, as he hauled her to her feet by her collar and backed her up against the wall. Bolts of pain sliced through her head as he placed his hands around her neck, the tip of his cigarette burning just inches from her eye.

Winnie heard her mother's pleading screams give way to sobs, then the noise seemed to tune out, like someone turning down the volume on a wireless. A strange thud, wet and liquid-sounding, reached her ears. The walls rushed in. Blackness engulfed her.

*

Winnie came to on the floor by the door. Rubbing her neck, she struggled to sit up.

At first, as her vision swam back into focus, she didn't see her mother. Then she spotted her, sitting at the kitchen table, groaning quietly and rocking back and forth. Laid out before her was an axe. The same axe Treacle had fished out from the Thames and Winnie had stowed away up high on a shelf. Winnie felt like she had stumbled on an unfinished scene from a play. The blood-curdling fear that filled the room had dissipated, in its place confusion and disbelief.

'Mum . . . Mum?' she rasped, staggering to the kitchen table, still clutching her tender throat. 'Where . . . Where's Dad?'

Her mother said nothing, just kept staring down at the axe as if she couldn't work out how it had got there, and suddenly it dawned on Winnie, the tip of it was slippery and red. Her heart stumbled and then began to race.

'What happened?' she whispered. In mounting disbelief, Winnie's eyes scanned the room and then she saw it – a trail of dark-red blood streaking the linoleum floor, from the kitchen to the open doorway.

The bedroom door opened a crack and Sylvie peeked out.

'Has Dad left, can we come out now?'

'No!' Winnie gabbled in panic. 'Get back in your room.'

The door banged shut and Winnie turned to her mother, a feeling of hysteria crawling up her spine.

'M-mum, what happened?'

Finally, Jeanie looked up from the axe and stared at her daughter, her eyes haunted.

'I . . . I think I might have killed him.'

Winnie slumped into her seat and started to shake.

'He . . . He was going to kill you, Win,' she wept. 'He wouldn't stop. I . . . I had to make him stop, love.'

'What did you do?' she whimpered.

'I can't remember. I . . . I spotted the axe, next thing I know it's in my hands. I warned him, said to let you go or I'd hit him. He was wild, I don't even know if he heard me, it was like I weren't even in the room.'

Jeannie was babbling now, hysteria overcoming her.

'He just kept squeezing your throat . . . So I hit him

from behind and he went staggering out the room. I heard him, Win. Falling down the stairs. What if I've killed him?'

A look of sheer terror crashed over her mother's face.

'I'll hang for it . . .'

'Oh God,' Winnie moaned, letting her head slump into her hands. 'Oh God, no.'

In despair, she began to cry, great heaving sobs. What if her father was lying dead outside on the doorstep, what if she really had killed him?

Just then, she heard the door bang open, heard her mother's gasp of shock. Winnie didn't know what she feared the most, the police or her father's return.

'Dad,' she gulped, whipping round.

But it wasn't her father's face she was gazing upon, it was Treacle's.

In that moment, it was hard to say who looked more shocked. Winnie didn't know what he was doing there, or why, but never in all her life had she been so pleased to see anyone.

'I couldn't go, Winnie, not without you,' he cried. 'And when I heard about the fighting going on down Cable Street, I had to come back. One last time, just to make sure you're all right . . .'

His gaze rested on the bloodstained axe sitting on the table between Winnie and her mother, and his voice trailed off in dismay.

'But you're not, are you? What the hell's been going on?'

By the time Winnie had wept her way through the whole story, or what she knew of it, Treacle had regained his composure.

'First things first,' he said decisively. 'You're going to get your mum a drop of brandy. I'm going to take this,' he said, removing the axe from the table and shoving it into his bag, 'and bury it right back where I found it.

'When I've finished there, I'll go and try to find your father and see what's happened. In the meantime, you get the girls their tea and you try and act normal.'

Normal! Winnie wanted to laugh. What the hell was normal?

Instead she blurted: 'But you will come back, won't you, Treacle?'

Treacle gripped her face in his hands.

'Yes. And you have my word that I will never leave you again. You hear me?'

Winnie closed her eyes and nodded. The future had never looked so terrifying or confused, but thank God she had Treacle by her side to face it.

*

Back in Curly's Cafe, with their wounds bandaged, Kitty and Harry sat facing one another across a Formica-topped table, steam from their cups of Bovril curling between them. They had sat at the quietest table they could find in the corner, but the cafe was packed with injured protestors, trading tales and comparing battle wounds, while the singing from the streets grew steadily louder. Fear had given way to unprecedented scenes of jubilation. Hats flew in the air and throngs of people streamed up the narrow street, faces etched with glory.

'It looks like a carnival out there,' Kitty said, smiling shyly at Harry through the steam.

Harry's head dipped as he stirred his drink, unable to return her smile.

'You're the sweetest girl I've ever met,' he mumbled. 'You deserve better than me.'

'You don't have to do this now,' Kitty said. 'We've just met, and besides, it's hardly the right time.'

'On the contrary, Kitty,' Harry blurted, looking up sharply. 'It's quite appropriate, as you'll find out in a minute.'

'Very well,' Kitty replied, shifting uneasily in her chair. 'Go on.'

Harry's voice lowered. 'Three years ago, I was one of them,' he whispered.

'One of who?' Kitty replied, confused.

'I was a blackshirt . . .'

'A blackshirt!' Kitty blurted, choking on her Bovril. People on the neighbouring table looked over curiously.

'Keep your voice down,' he urged, 'or we'll get lynched.'

'Sorry . . . But . . . But I don't understand,' Kitty stuttered.

'Look, I'm not proud of it,' he muttered. 'It was over two years ago, I was a skinny seventeen-year-old who thought he knew it all. I couldn't find work at the time, so I was larking about in the park with my mates. Some fella came over, asked us whether we would like to join the party of the future. Told us such tales of how they were creating wealth and jobs for the youth. How did we fancy a half a crown, and the glory of building a land fit for heroes?'

'So what happened?' Kitty asked.

'Well, a few days after that I came home like the conquering hero in my new black uniform – brimming over with pride, I was. Mum took one look at me and did her nut.

'I was always getting into scrapes when I was younger, but I had never seen her as angry as that moment. She went berserk, Kitty – ripped the shirt clean off my back.'

Harry's face clouded and he took a shaky sip of his drink.

'We had a right row over it. My poor dad, he was stuck in the middle. We both said things we didn't mean, and then she threw me out on the street. Told me that she was ashamed of me, and that if I didn't leave the blackshirts there and then, I was no son of hers.'

'Oh, Harry,' murmured Kitty. 'What did you do?'

'I was a silly, stubborn sod. Told her she was no mother of mine.'

A silence fell between them and Harry sighed, wiping his blond hair back from his face.

'Soon after that, Mosley spoke at Olympia. It was a bloody shambles. When I saw what went on – the violence, women getting beaten up for daring to speak, men thrown down stairs . . .'

He shuddered. 'I can't even describe the sights I witnessed, Kitty. It was a bloodbath.'

'My friend Stella was telling me about it only the other day,' Kitty replied.

'Yeah, well, suddenly I didn't feel like such a big tough man. Mum had been right all along.'

He gave a brittle laugh. 'She'd been right about a lot of things, in fact, but in my infinite bloody wisdom, I thought I knew better.

'I left the blackshirts, of course, but it was too late for Mum and me. Shortly after, I heard through Dad that she had cancer. I blamed myself.'

'But why?' Kitty asked.

''Cause if I'd been a better son, not put her through so much, she wouldn't have got ill.'

'You can't surely believe that?'

'Can't I?' he said sharply, his green eyes clouding over. 'In the finish, I joined the Merchant Navy. A uniform to truly be proud of,' he said, lightly touching his breast pocket.

'When I came back from a trip to the Far East, I went to make my peace with Mum, but it was too late . . .' Harry's voice broke off, choked with emotion. 'She had passed. To this day, I blame myself for her death. It was shame what killed her. If I had been a better son, she'd still be here, Kitty. I've been a selfish fool and I don't blame her for feeling ashamed of me. *I'm* ashamed of me!'

With that, Harry started to cry, fat tears coursing down his cheeks and, embarrassed, he dashed them away with his sleeve.

'I . . . I just miss my mum,' he confessed.

The charming, confident man Kitty had met at the dance all those months ago was scarcely recognizable in the defeated, broken wretch sitting in front of her now, and something about his plight resonated deep within her. Kitty felt the sharpness of his grief, but suddenly she realized that she had it within her power to help.

'But don't you get it?' she gasped, grabbing her coat from the back of her chair with fumbling fingers. 'She felt the same – she felt exactly the same way you did.'

'That's sweet of you to say, Kitty,' he said, smiling through his tears. 'But you can't possibly know that.'

Without a word, Kitty removed his mother's letter from her pocket and slid it over the countertop.

'It's from your mum. I found it in the base of the sewing

machine your father donated to Mrs Tingle, remember? I
tried to give it to you when we met at the dance. Won't you
read it? Please?' she implored.

Gulping deep in his throat, Harry took the letter out and
started to read. Kitty watched in fascinated silence, too
scared to interrupt, but she could almost hear his mother's
words in her head, she had read it that many times.

*I am deeply ashamed that I have allowed matters to come
to this.*

And the part that filled her with the most bittersweet
emotion . . .

*This is a queer letter to write, because I know that if you
are reading it, I will be dead, but know this, Harry:
wherever you are, whoever you have become, I love you.
I have never stopped loving you, son.*

When he had finished reading, Harry folded the letter and
replaced it carefully in the envelope, before tucking it in his
jacket pocket. 'So you see, Harry,' Kitty whispered, brushing
a tear from his cheek with her thumb before tilting his chin
up so that their eyes might meet. 'She *did* love you, so very
much. It's time to stop blaming yourself.'

Harry nodded, his eyes glistening with more tears and
the pair moved instinctively towards each other, their fore-
heads gently meeting over the tabletop, their hands tightly
clasped.

'Thank you,' he whispered into the space between them.

All around the East End, the celebrations and fighting continued, but in one quiet corner of Brick Lane, Kitty and Harry remained locked in a world of their own, two children who simply missed their parents.

*

Stella could scarcely wipe the exuberant grin from her face. The joy of the crowds was infectious.

'We only bleedin' well did it! We stopped 'em marching!' gibbered a young lad, grabbing Stella and planting an impulsive kiss on her lips, before lifting her clean up off the cobbles.

'Oi, mind yourself,' she giggled as her cap flew off.

The street spun out of focus as he whirled her round and round before plonking her back down and running off up the street to join his pals.

Stella stared open-mouthed after him and started to laugh as all around her perfect strangers rejoiced and embraced.

It was now 5 p.m. The fierce fighting had gone on down Cable Street for hours before word had finally reached the barricades that the Commissioner of Police had ordered Mosley to turn back and march the other way, through the deserted streets of the Embankment. The roads into the heart of the East End were now barred to him and Stella knew the defeat would be a bitter and humiliating one. She half-wondered if Mosley and that horrible scar-faced crony of his couldn't hear the triumphant roar from the other side of London!

'Now he's got his marching orders!' shouted a wag.

'Yeah, all dressed up and no place to go!' shouted another.

In a stroke, the tension lifted. A fear-haunted East End

had beaten the bullies. The usually peaceable citizens had reclaimed their beloved streets from the fascists and, as the crowds dispersed, was it her imagination or were chests puffed out and heads held higher? Stella knew it hadn't been a case of politics at work that day but working-class solidarity, the people coming together to right a wrong. Mosley had set out to breed hatred, only to find himself defeated by ordinary folk coming together as one: men *and* women who believed in tolerance, respect and peace.

Shaking her head at the extraordinary turn of events, Stella reached down to pick her cap up. When she stood back up she caught a glimpse of herself in the window of a pawnshop, lit up by a column of gauzy sunshine. She looked a fright! Her blouse was sticky with perspiration and her hair a dusty, dishevelled mess, but despite this, or perhaps because of it, Stella had never looked, or felt, so alive.

As the sun set over Cable Street, drenching the barricades in a fiery glow, the East End basked in its finest hour. She breathed in the jubilation that seemed to bounce off the cobbles, aware that she could never go back to the narrow life now.

Stella longed to join the masses who were streaming to Victoria Park Square for a victory celebration that would doubtless go on long into the night, but she knew finding her friends was more important. She didn't have to wait long. It seemed Kitty had had the same idea!

Stella squinted her eyes against the setting sun and spotted her oldest friend limping up the road, both her knees swaddled in bandages, supported by Harry. Judging by the way the handsome young sailor was gazing at her, the pair's unusual second date had clearly gone well.

'I shan't ask!' Stella called to the pair. 'Let's just get inside and check on Winnie, shall we?'

'Stella, this is my Harry,' Kitty smiled bashfully, her pretty face flushing.

'Your Harry, eh?' Stella winked, ruffling Kitty's hair and extending her hand to the beaming sailor.

'Good to finally meet you,' she grinned. 'You better take care of this one, she's very special to us.'

'On my honour,' he replied, glancing down at Kitty with a tender smile. 'She's quite special to me, too.'

'Oh, hush now, you two,' Kitty scolded, but she couldn't wipe the daft grin from her face as she pushed open the door to the side of the rag shop. A minute later, Stella, Kitty and Harry's smiles froze on their faces as they walked into Winnie's kitchen and took in the bloodstained lino, the scattered pins and upended furniture.

*

By the time they had learnt the whole story, Stella felt her fingers curl in helpless anger round the mug of tea Kitty placed in front of her.

'This is all my bloody fault,' she trembled. 'I saw him, I saw him walking up the street and I ought to have run and warned you. All the while I was out there taking pictures when you . . . You were in here . . .' Her voice splintered.

'Please, Stell, there's no point blaming yourself,' Winnie replied, exhausted. 'How were any of us to know what would happen? My father's a maniac, and if it weren't for Mum, I might well be dead by now.'

A dreadful silence descended on the room as Winnie

touched her neck. A deep purple bruise was already blooming across the pale skin of her throat.

'I'm going to the police,' said Jeannie suddenly, scraping back her chair. 'I'm gonna tell 'em what I've done. I could never live with myself if I've killed him.'

Just then the door swung open and Treacle returned. All heads in the room swivelled and waited expectantly. Poor Jeannie looked like she might faint on the spot.

'Well?'

'He's alive . . .'

'Oh thank God!' Jeannie and Winnie gasped as one.

'I asked a mate of mine who's a porter up the London Hospital, and he says your dad's been admitted with a head injury – along with dozens of others from Gardiner's Corner and Cable Street. He was found unconscious on the doorstep and scooped up by a St John Ambulance man.'

'But how do they know who he is?' Stella asked.

'They found his blackshirt membership papers in his pocket. The medics are assuming he's a victim of a cosh over the head with a police truncheon, another victim of the fray. It's chaos up there, apparently, and the ward's full to bursting.'

'So what now?' asked Kitty.

'I say we consult Herbie and unless he says otherwise, we say nothing,' Stella interjected. 'There's no sense telling the police, especially if your dad doesn't remember anything.'

'I . . . I don't know,' Jeannie wavered. 'I hit him over the head with an axe, for goodness' sake. How's it going to look if I don't tell the police?'

'Mum, you had no choice. He would have killed us! You saw the state of him, it was like a switch had flicked inside his head,' Winnie protested. 'Besides, you know fine well how the law will regard what you've done. Do you think they'll care, or take into account the fact that he's knocked *you* black and blue for the last eighteen years? No. They'll only judge you by your actions, not his! The law don't give two hoots for men who get handy with their wives, but a wife who fights back . . .'

Treacle nodded gravely. 'She's right, Mrs Docker. Winnie and the girls need their mother here, not locked up behind bars.'

Jeannie scrubbed at her face wearily. 'Very well. I'll say nothing. For now . . .'

Thirteen

It was mid-morning on Monday as Stella set up the studio for a wedding that afternoon. As the winds battered at the windowpanes, she pondered the strange week that had passed since that momentous Sunday.

The ramifications of the battle that had taken place at Cable Street were far-reaching. Eighty-four arrests, of which thirteen were women – or so Stella had read in the papers – were going through the local courts. Eighty people had been given medical aid at police stations, and many more treated at the London Hospital, including one Tommy Docker. Word had reached them via Treacle's pal that Tommy had regained consciousness, but was groggy and could remember nothing of the events leading up to the attack. How Stella prayed for Winnie and Jeannie's sake that it remained that way.

Treacle had paid their rent arrears and moved in with Winnie, Jeannie and the girls, sleeping on the parlour floor and refusing to leave Winnie's side, except to go to work. Winnie was fragile, and Stella doubted she would have survived any of it were it not for his close care.

As for Kitty . . . Stella smiled to herself as she arranged sweeping white velvet drapes in the pale autumn sunshine that filtered through the large studio windows. The girl was absolutely smitten with her Harry. Stella didn't know what had happened to bond the pair so fast, but she was thrilled for her dear friend. After the agony of caring for her father, Kitty deserved a happy, settled future.

Her smile gave way to a heavy sigh as she stared out of the window, down at the bustling street below. What of *her* future? It was she, Stella Smee, whose life could perhaps be most profoundly affected by what had come to pass.

Soon after the battle, Scotland Yard had released a statement. Stella could still remember it word for word. *Owing to one of the finest days of the year, many people were attracted to the counter-rally, including a large number of women and children.* They had made it sound like a day out at a pleasure beach, not a day of struggle and swinging truncheons! In a fit of pique, Stella had caught a bus in the direction of the Strand and delivered all her photographs from Gardiner's Corner and Cable Street to the offices of the Fleet Street Bureau News and Photographic Agency, with instructions to distribute. To her amazement, some of her photos had actually been printed in the national press. To her even greater shock, forty-eight hours later, the editor of the agency had sent her a telegram offering her a job as a press photographer!

The proposition had knocked her for six, but she had recovered herself by the time she visited his offices to thank him and tell him she had commitments in Bethnal Green, but would seriously consider his offer.

'Don't take too long,' he had warned her. 'I'm taking a risk on employing a girl, but I'm doing it because I see you have talent.'

Three days on and she had thought of little else. The Agency was a reputable one, with offices in Paris and New

York. This could be her chance, her big opportunity to make it, to maybe even see something of the world and prove what she was capable of.

Stella rested her forehead against the cool window and images of clashing hooves and flashing truncheons spun through her mind. It felt like she was waging her own battle, with loyalty to her friends on one side, versus an exciting, bright future of opportunity on the other. Was that why she hadn't told anyone of the job offer?

Despairingly, she threw open the window and looked to the gusty blue skies for a sign, anything that would give her some clue as to the right path to take.

Nothing . . . Except the rich and meaty scent of cooking wafting from Gladys's kitchen window and the lively cries of the market traders lacing the air.

'Tomorrow,' she vowed, closing the window, and racing down the stairs. Tomorrow, she would decide where her future lay.

Stella took the stairs two at a time, bounding into reception just as Gladys pushed open the door with a tinkle of the bell.

'Do the workers fancy a spot of dinner?' she smiled, wiping her hands on her apron. 'Beef pie made with dripping and lard, followed by spotted dick with plenty of currents, exactly the way you like it, Mr T.'

'Sounds delicious, Mrs T! Lead on,' twinkled Herbie, putting on his hat and opening the door for Gladys.

Stella handed Winnie her coat and winked.

'What is it they say? "The way to a man's heart is through his stomach." Is it my imagination, or do you think Gladys is winning Herbie over, one puddin' at a time?'

Winnie smiled weakly and instinctively her hand moved to her neck. Her bruises were fading from livid purple to green, but she still insisted on covering them with make-up, not that it did much to conceal the savagery of the attack.

'Oh, Win,' Stella gulped, throwing her arms around her friend. The way Winnie and her mother had suffered at that man's hands left her breathless. To Stella's mind, it always came down to the same thing: it was women who paid the price for men's mistakes. But she suppressed her feelings; anger would not serve her friend in her time of need.

'You keeping your end up?' she asked instead.

'It's been tough,' Winnie admitted. 'It's been eight days now and every day I wonder, will today be the day the police come?'

'The longer you hear nothing, the better, surely?' Stella replied. 'Besides, it's unlikely he'll remember anything. He sounded like he weren't in his right mind. If he knows what's good for him, he'll steer clear.'

Winnie's face darkened. 'You don't know the man like I do,' she whispered, playing with a small crucifix necklace around her neck. 'We're his possessions and he won't let us go without a fight. Treacle's insisting that if we leave the East End, it will just look worse and that we should stand our ground, you know, like folk did at Cable Street and Gardiner's Corner, but . . .' Her voice faltered. 'I've a nasty feeling about it, Stell. It's not the last we've heard of him. I'm scared.'

'I know you are, Win, but we're all here for you,' Stella replied quietly. 'We love you dearly.'

'Thanks,' Winnie replied gratefully. 'You really are a pal, I honestly don't know what I'd do without you and Kitty.'

'What are friends for?' Stella smiled, feeling her insides knot. 'Now come on, let's go and eat.'

They stepped outside onto Green Street and walked the few yards next door to Gladys's. Two young men stood huddled on the kerbside, heads knotted together. As Stella walked past, she caught a snippet of their conversation.

'I don't suppose we shall get a chance tonight,' one muttered under his breath.

'Did you hear that?' Stella hissed as she and Winnie pushed open the side door to Gladys's workshop.

'No,' Winnie said, shaking her head. 'What'd he say?'

'Not a great deal,' Stella murmured. 'He sounded like he was up to no good, though.'

'I think we're all so jumpy right now that evil lurks in every shadow,' Winnie replied.

'Yeah, perhaps you're right,' Stella agreed. So much had happened lately, she was imagining the worst in every conversation.

*

After Gladys's succulent pie and stodgy pudding, what Kitty had really longed for was a lie-down, but there was a wedding to tend to, and what a wedding it was!

The bride and her entourage of bridesmaids' were such a striking sight, they had literally stopped the traffic as a line of automobiles, delivery boys on bikes and costermongers pushing carts had ground to a halt to observe the spectacle.

Kitty could scarcely believe her eyes as Evelyn March stepped from the wedding automobile onto the kerb. Evelyn might only have been a shop girl on Petticoat Lane, but she had looks to rival Carole Lombard or Dorothy Lamour. She positively oozed glamour. Lustrous dark, wavy hair gleamed in the soft autumnal light and her luscious lips were painted a rich berry red. If silver lamé really was out, someone had forgotten to tell the bride, not that Kitty suspected she would have much cared.

Evelyn's slinky gown was as delicate as tissue paper and clung to her curves like warm toffee on an apple. A head-dress with matching silver leaves and an enormous sheaf of silver-sprayed arum lilies completed the look.

It was as if a Hollywood picture had burst into life right here on Green Street. Evelyn might spend Monday to Friday serving pastries and confectionery in her father's Petticoat Lane business, but today she was the sweetest star of her own matinee film.

Bright blue belladonna eyes sparkled under expertly plucked eyebrows as Evelyn gripped her proud bridegroom's arm and waited for her two pageboys in adorable blue-and-white satin sailor suits and the never-ending procession of bridesmaids to disgorge from the car.

There were six of them, and Kitty knew this because she had painstakingly hand-stitched each of their lilac silk dresses, matching picture hats and floral fans trimmed with silver-sprayed ostrich feathers. As they clustered round the bride, babbling away like a flock of brightly coloured birds, the barbs of their feathered fans quivering in the pale sunshine, Kitty couldn't hide her delight. She sighed deeply.

'Oh hark at this one, she's gonna keel over,' teased Stella, pretending to fan her down. 'Your time'll come, Cinderella.'

'I can't help myself, it's just so dreamy,' Kitty gushed,

clutching her chest. 'Look how happy she is. They're so in love.'

Evelyn's husband, Albert, a clerk at Bethnal Green Town Hall, immaculate in evening dress, gazed down with a tender, proprietorial smile and cupped his hand round his new wife's tiny waist.

'Do you know, her father's been saving for this wedding since she was a little girl,' Kitty went on. 'They're having a reception up at the Embassy Rooms in Bow, seven days in Canvey Island, and as soon as they're back, they're moving out to a new-build in Dagenham.'

'Charmin', I'm sure,' muttered Gladys under her breath, 'and so we lose another East Ender to Corned Beef City.' Gladys had never hidden her disapproval of anyone who left. Her roots were deeply embedded in East End soil.

'I went to Dagenham once,' she sniffed, 'brought me out in hives.'

'But surely you can't begrudge anyone a fresh start, Gladys?' Kitty protested. 'It's been like a civil war round here lately. People are still afraid to leave their homes. Did you hear about the vandalism spree down the Mile End Road last night?'

'No,' Stella frowned.

'Fifty shops smashed up, hardly an inch of glass left, and a man and child thrown through a shop window! Retribution for Cable Street, so they're saying.'

Kitty trailed off and, in silence, she, Gladys and the rest of the girls looked at the thick steel grilles that had popped up over the windows of D. Gotlieb's the tailors, Fisher's the perfumers and Miss Sugarman's milliners. It was quite a contrast to Evelyn's dazzling looks and carefree happiness.

'I don't blame Evelyn for wanting to escape,' Winnie murmured, fiddling with the top button of her blouse.

'I don't know what the world's coming to, really I don't,' Gladys tutted, before lowering her voice. 'I do think she wants to try eating more of her dad's buns, mind you. I've seen more meat on a butcher's apron.'

A paperboy was weaving his way through the wedding throng. 'Read all about it!' he hollered. 'King's moll set to divorce.'

A scowl flashed over Gladys's face and, seizing the rolled-up paper from his hands, she clouted him hard round the side of the head with it.

'Wot'cha do that for?' he protested. 'I ain't left the paper in your workshop.'

'Show some respect,' she ordered. 'We're in the middle of a wedding 'ere. Go on, hop it!'

Rubbing his head, the paperboy scuttled off, and Gladys dusted her hands down.

'Hell'll freeze over before I accept that hard-faced hussy as our queen,' she snapped. 'Slutty eyes 'n' all!

'Right, enough of this verbal, let's get back to work.'

Gladys disappeared back inside her workshop. Kitty was about to follow her, but someone called her name from the street and she turned round. At first, she didn't spot him, but as the crowds dispersed, her eyes met his across the street.

'Harry!' she exclaimed. 'I thought we weren't meeting until tonight?'

Harry was clutching a wind-up gramophone and wearing a hopeful grin.

'We weren't, but I can't wait that long.'

'W-whatever are you up to, you daft beggar?' she stuttered.

'You'll see,' he said mysteriously.

Harry placed the gramophone down on Big Mickey's fruit stall and slipped him a coin. Mickey slapped him on the back and winked at Kitty.

Harry had his back to her, fumbling with a gramophone record, but as he turned back round, the crackly strains of 'Pennies from Heaven' by Bing Crosby floated out over the market stalls.

'May I have the pleasure of the last dance, Kitty?' Harry asked, holding out his hand to her.

'Have you lost your marbles?' Kitty laughed, placing her hands on her slender hips.

'Nope. Never been more sane in all my life,' he replied, striding towards her. 'Seven months ago, I met a girl and lost my heart. She left me standing on a dance floor.'

Suddenly he was towering over her, all shiny blond hair and glinting green eyes. Kitty felt as if she were in a dream as his hand snaked round her waist and pulled her firmly into his arms.

'That girl was you, Kitty Moloney,' he breathed, 'and now I should like to have that last dance. May I?'

Speechless, Kitty allowed herself to be led over the cobbles, her heart thudding against her ribs, the hem of her pale yellow cotton dress flipping in the breeze. They began to move, their steps as light as air, swaying in gentle rhythm. Kitty was in such a whirl, she didn't see Gladys or Herbie watching from the doorway with sentimental smiles, or the eager faces of the wedding party, clustered round the studio window two floors up, or Big Mickey pretending he had something in his eye. Kitty was aware of nothing but the feel of Harry's firm arms tightly wrapped around her, the heat of his chest under his shirt, the exquisite tingling of her skin as he pressed his lips to her ear.

'The world lost all its purpose after Mum died, but you've brought me back to life, Kitty. I know it sounds barmy, but I think I knew we were meant to be together the minute I set eyes on you. These last eight days being with you have been among the happiest days I've ever known.'

He paused, his eyes boring into hers.

'I have to set sail again soon, but please say I'll go with the knowledge that you're my girl, 'cause I'm yours, Kitty!'

Kitty's skin bloomed like a ripe peach and a soft smile spread across her face. She nodded, a girl in the full flower of her beauty.

'I'm your girl, Harry,' she vowed.

And then he kissed her and under a hazy Indian summer sky, Kitty lost her heart for good.

*

Stella was so cold, she had lost all feeling in her fingers, and the rank smell of chemicals was making her head swim. She glanced at the clock. Ten past two in the morning. The realization that she had been down here, in this unheated underground darkroom, for over six hours now was a startling one.

After the wedding party had departed, she had watched wistfully as Kitty and Harry had left hand in hand for their evening at the pictures, Treacle had collected Winnie to escort her home, and Gladys and Herbie had gone back to hers for tea. Not that she should grumble. She was a business proprietress now. Someone had to develop the glass-plate negatives from Evelyn's wedding and a portrait of the Mayor of Bethnal Green she had taken that morning up at the Town Hall.

It had taken an age to do all the developing, and there was still the retouching and colouring to do. Stella decided that could wait until morning.

Turning off the red safelight, she switched on the overhead bulb and blinked like a mole coming to the surface, as a flickering light illuminated the darkroom.

Up on the drying line, Evelyn the silver goddess gazed down at her, in front of a cream archway with a wispy, white cloud backdrop. Behind the dreamy soft-focus expression, a steely inner core glinted. Evelyn was a girl who knew exactly what she wanted out of life and how to get it; more than could be said for Stella. Eight days ago, she had been so sure and now . . .

Reaching into her bag, she pulled out her photos of the Battle of Cable Street as she had heard someone refer to it earlier, and pegged one of the photos next to Evelyn. A police horse, all steaming flanks and flaring nostrils, was bearing down on a scattering crowd, the officer's truncheon a dark, solid flash in the corner of the photograph.

In truth, Stella had slipped on the cobbles and the camera shutter had accidentally gone off, capturing the dramatic scene, but the slip had turned into the most dynamic and revealing picture she had ever taken. An accident, but then, didn't the world turn on such small chances? Stella was a hundred times prouder of that image than the sugary, staged photo she had taken of the Mayor in his ceremonial robes. So what now?

Stella was growing in confidence and skill, changing . . . Into what, she did not yet know, but she liked the woman she was becoming. A slice of history had played itself out against the setting of her life, and she knew the ripples would change her destiny forever. That day, at the barricades, she had felt so alive, as if a fire were burning beneath her skin. How could she just forget it, go back to the girl she once was?

With a jolt, Stella realized they had passed into a new day and she still hadn't made a decision over the job offer. Taking this opportunity would mean turning her back on the Wedding Girls, on Herbie . . . on the East End. It was an impossible choice.

Rubbing her stinging eyes, she flicked off the light and wearily climbed back up the stairs to the darkened reception.

Stella had been so immersed in her work, she hadn't heard Herbie arrive home from Gladys's, but as his hat was on the coat stand by the door, she guessed he must have gone straight upstairs to his attic bedroom above the studio.

Shrugging on her coat, Stella locked up and stepped out into the crisp night air. She loved seeing the busy market street by night, so still and serene, blanketed in moonlight, but tonight she felt the frisson of something else. Stella couldn't put her finger on it, but something felt wrong. Her sense of disquiet grew as she stared at the steel grille over Miss Sugarman's window.

A whisper of wind ruffled the shop awnings, but other than that, there wasn't a sound. Suddenly, a blanket of cloud passed over the pale moon, and the street darkened. Stella shivered. She had the strangest sensation she wasn't alone. Winnie's words from earlier came back to haunt her: *We're all so jumpy right now that evil lurks in every shadow.*

Stella turned and, with her heels clicking on the cobbles, hurried for home.

Once in the safety of her kitchen, she threw some coal on the dying embers of the fire and fixed herself a cup of Ovaltine.

The milky drink had no effect. Half an hour ago in the darkroom she had been virtually asleep on her feet, now she felt wide-awake and queasy with anxiety.

Stella drummed her fingers against her mug and, just like that, it snapped into her mind.

I don't suppose we shall get a chance tonight.

Yes! That was what she had overheard the young man saying to his pal on the street outside earlier. A sudden dread enveloped her. Stella shot to her feet, sending her drink skidding across the table, but there was no time to mop it up, she had to get back to Green Street. Something dreadful was about to happen. She felt it in her bones.

With her breath ragged in her lungs, she tore down the stone tenement steps and pounded down the deserted streets.

Rounding the corner of Bonner Street into Green Street, she smelt something sharp and acrid in her nostrils. Petrol!

Panic flared in her chest and Stella picked up speed. In the gloom ahead, she spotted two figures hunched in front of the doorway to the offices of the BUF, thick scarves obscuring their faces. One was splashing liquid from a can over the doorway. A match crackled into a flame.

'Hell's teeth!' Stella cried, hurling herself into a doorway. A second later, a solid sheet of bright white flame leapt up from the pavement. The fire took hold instantly, devouring the front door of number 222a, the Bethnal Green offices of the BUF, and catching the awning of her photographic studio next door.

Stella watched as if in a trance as the flames licked greedily across the canvas awning, reducing it to flying molten ash. A dense black smoke billowed out in whorls and tangles, sparks flying up into the night sky.

The sound of breaking glass snapped her from her reverie as the studio's glass windows blew out. Through the shower of glass she saw a dark flash of movement, heard the revving of a car engine.

Anger mobilized her and Stella stepped out into the street, holding both her hands aloft. Someone had just set fire to her studio!

'Stop!' she yelled.

But the unlit dark saloon car didn't slow. It gunned towards her, a dark figure clinging to the running board, picking up speed.

Stella tried to make out the number plate, but it was too dark, the car moving too fast; all she could see were the arsonists' eyes, burning over the tops of their scarves.

'STOP!' she screamed, as the dark car swallowed the ground between them.

A shrill whistle pierced the air, the screech of brakes, a flash of orange flame as Stella flung herself to the ground. The car clipped her leg as it sped past and a shooting pain sliced through her hip. For a moment, she lay motionless in the gutter, winded and confused. Then the stench of petrol brought her to her senses.

'Herbie!' she croaked, ignoring the immense stabbing pain as she hauled herself to her feet. 'I'm coming.'

She staggered up the street and by the time she reached the studio, men and women, clutching children in blankets, were flocking onto the street, bewildered faces reflected in the glare of the fire. Men raced to fetch buckets of water and a human chain was quickly assembled to pass it along.

Miss Sugarman, dressed only in a nightgown and metal curlers, was blowing hard on a whistle. When she spotted Stella, wild-eyed and dazed, heading for the studio door, she reached for her, tried to hold her back.

'What you playing at, Stella?'

'It's Herbie,' she panted. 'He's inside.'

'For pity's sake, love, wait for the fire brigade,' she protested, plucking at Stella's blouse.

Stella shrugged her off.

'There's no time,' she cried, before plunging into the smoky building.

The reception was filled with smoke and, in the window display, flames leapt and danced as the fire took hold. The sight was extraordinary and Stella watched, stunned, as one by one flames devoured the display photographs.

First Celeste, then Beatrice, Pamela, Joyce and Doris shrivelled and curled as the flames greedily licked at their faces. Their images melted to ash on the green baize cabinet floor.

It was a disturbing, macabre sight, but Stella's concern lay with the flesh and blood, not in salvaging photographs.

'Herbie!' she yelled, whipping out a handkerchief from her sleeve and clamping it over her mouth. 'I'm coming.'

As she ascended the staircase to his living quarters, a dense layer of smoke swirled and crept up the stairwell behind her, and she knew her time was limited. Any hesitation would cost them their lives and instinctively she kept low, moving stealthily up the staircase.

A sudden thought occurred to her and a scream caught

in her throat. If the fire reached the basement darkroom it would be nothing short of lethal. All those highly flammable chemicals sitting stoppered in glass bottles . . . All were potential bombs waiting to blast them sky-high.

Picking up the pace, she wrenched open the door to Herbie's bedroom and shut it quickly behind her. Fortunately, the smoke hadn't permeated the room yet, but it wouldn't be long. Already, wisps were creeping in under the door frame, and rising up the walls like a curtain.

Stella's eyes adjusted to the gloom of his bedroom. Herbie was motionless in his bed, asleep – or had the deadly smoke fumes already reached him?

'Herbie, wake up!' she screamed, shaking him vigorously. 'Wake up!'

His eyes flickered open, startled.

'Stella? What are you doing here?'

'There's a fire,' she panted. 'We've got to get out.'

Confusion, then panic crashed over his face.

'W-what?' He rose to his feet unsteadily and reached for his dressing gown. 'We must get to the studio, rescue the cameras, the . . .'

'No,' Stella shot back in alarm. 'No. Herbie, there's no time. It's already taken hold.'

She gripped him by the shoulders. 'We have to leave. Now.'

Ignoring the throbbing in her hip, she gripped Herbie's hand and led him to the door.

With her hand poised over the handle, she hastily grabbed a handkerchief off his dresser and handed it to him.

'Now listen. I'm going to open the door, but it's really important you stay calm and keep this over your mouth. There's already a lot of smoke. Understood?'

He nodded.

'Good. Now take a deep breath, and let's go.'

She flung open the door and together they picked their way down the stairwell. Stella could feel the poisonous smoke, gritty in her nostrils, seeping into her skin, and her thoughts grew muddy, confused, like she was sinking to the bottom of a dark ocean.

As they descended, the blanket of black smoke grew thicker still and for a terrifying moment she lost her bearings.

What floor were they on? Panic slammed through her. She couldn't tell up from down. She was smothered, the smoke suffocating her, blocking out all her senses. She felt Herbie's hand grow clammy in hers.

The old building seemed to swell and groan around her, creaking in its ancient joists and joins, like a ship about to go under.

From above, she heard the shrill tinkling of glass and a sudden roar, and in relief she realized it could have only been the vast studio windows on the second floor. They were on the first floor.

'Nearly there,' she croaked through the darkness to Herbie. 'Keep going.'

'Don't leave me, Stella,' he rasped, his hand trembling in hers.

'I ain't going anywhere, boss.'

Suddenly a face appeared out of the smoke, then arms, and a fireman was leading her to safety. Stella tried to talk, but out on the street as the air flooded into her lungs, the pavement rushed up. Darkness swamped her.

Stella came round and found herself horizontal, suspended in mid-air.

'H–Herbie?' she gasped in fright, gripping the metal poles that were supporting her as she grappled to sit up.

'The gentleman you were with is on his way to hospital,' came back a voice. 'Which is where we're taking you now, miss. Now lie back on the stretcher and try not to panic. We'll have you there in a jiffy.'

Just before she was loaded into the ambulance, Stella strained her neck and caught a last glimpse of the studio – her studio. The fire had claimed its prize. Firemen had their hoses trained on the building, but blood-red flames roared and bellowed from every window. The noise from the pumps was deafening and the whole street was lit with a ghastly, garish light as if morning had come early. All was heat and chaos.

A voice pealed above the noise. 'Stand back! Get well back. The roof's about to give way!'

An immense and aching sense of loss swamped Stella as she collapsed onto the stretcher. Tears washed crooked white runnels down her soot-stained cheeks as the ambulance doors slammed shut on the whole sickening scene. She wept like a child all the way to the London Hospital.

Fourteen

Four days later, Stella's tears had dried up. In fact, her eyes had never felt so dry, almost as if her face had been baked by the heat of the fire. Stella's entire body felt tender and stiff, especially her left hip, her hair was singed and she couldn't move without collapsing into a convulsive coughing fit. Yet despite all this, the hospital staff assured her she was lucky to have survived with only smoke inhalation. X-rays showed her hip wasn't broken, just badly bruised.

The hero of the hour! That's what Kitty, Winnie and Treacle had called her on their daily visits. Apparently, the whole of Bethnal Green was talking about how she had rescued Herbie from the fire. Even the doctors and nurses seemed to be in agreement.

'You're made of tough stuff, young lady,' the doctor had assured her, when he informed her she would be kept in for seven days' observation and bed rest. Stella didn't feel very tough and she certainly didn't feel like a heroine. In fact, lying in this hospital bed, she felt weak and emotional. It had given her time to think, however, and now she was desperate to see Herbie. She waited until the nurse came on her morning rounds.

'Please, Nurse,' she begged. 'I really need to see my

friend. Herbie . . . I mean Herbert Taylor. I believe he's on the next ward?'

'You can't possibly leave your bed, Matron would string me up,' the nurse admonished, taking out her thermometer and shaking it vigorously.

'Not even for five minutes? He's a dear friend . . .' Stella pleaded. 'I feel fine, honestly. In fact, I feel like a perfect fraud, taking up this hospital bed.'

The nurse regarded her curiously.

'Aren't you that young lady everyone's talking about, the one who rescued that chap from a fire down Green Street?'

Stella nodded.

'Go on then,' the nurse smiled. 'But five minutes, no longer, and I insist on helping you down there.'

Stella's legs felt like cotton wool as she allowed the nurse to lead her to Herbie's bedside, and she sank gratefully into the chair next to his bed.

'Oh my dear,' Herbie whispered, his brown eyes brimming over as he clamped his hands over hers. 'I . . . I really don't know how I'll ever thank you.'

Stella tried to hide her shock at the sight of him in his hospital-issue pyjamas. Without his dapper suit, he looked old and vulnerable.

'You don't need to, Herbie. I just thank God that you're all right. I shudder to think what would have happened if I'd been a minute or two later. How are you feeling?'

'I've felt better,' he admitted, rubbing his chest. 'I dare say I look a fright.'

'Nonsense, you're as debonair as ever,' she smiled, gently smoothing back his hair.

'Gladys is in here every available opportunity with food

parcels,' Herbie went on. 'She even had a stand-off with Matron yesterday, told her she doesn't trust the hospital to feed me properly.' He grinned ruefully. 'I don't know who came off worse!'

Stella chuckled and then began to cough.

'I can imagine,' she wheezed, reaching for the jug of water by his bedside and pouring herself a glass. 'Don't be too hard on her, Herbie. She'd take the moon out of the sky for you if you asked.'

'I know that,' he replied softly. 'And I'm quite sure I don't deserve a woman like her. But listen, it's not Gladys I want to talk to you about. I'm glad you've been allowed down here, love, there's something I've been meaning to discuss with you. I know you were at Cable Street.'

Stella nearly choked on her water.

'You do?'

'Yeah. After you left the studio, the night of the fire, I heard you leave and I went down to the darkroom.'

'Checking up on my work?' she asked, raising one eyebrow.

'Maybe,' he admitted. 'Old habits die hard, Stella. I've worked in that studio every day for the last forty-six years, don't forget.'

He raised his hands, his fingertips still stained from the silver nitrate chemicals he had worked with day in, day out. 'It will always be a part of me.'

Stella didn't know what she found sadder, the fact that no end of scrubbing would ever remove those stains, or the slight quake in his fingertips.

'Anyway,' he went on, 'while I was there I came upon

a photo taken from the disturbances at Cable Street, a mounted policeman. I take it you took that?'

Shakily, Stella put down her glass and nodded.

'It's good. I taught you well.'

'Y-you're not cross?' she stammered.

'I'm disappointed that you felt the need to hide your involvement from me, but I'm not angry. In truth, I think I've known all along your heart wasn't in the studio. But I wanted so desperately to hand the business over to someone who felt like family that I allowed that to blind me to my instincts.'

He stared searchingly at her.

'If I was acting like a true father, instead of forcing you to follow in my footsteps, I should have allowed you to follow your heart. It was selfish of me, and I'm sorry, Stella.'

Stella shook her head, stunned.

'No . . . No, Herbie, don't you see?' she cried. 'I've had a lot of time in here to think, too. Watching the studio go up in flames made me realize how it's a part of me. Green Street, Bethnal Green – why, the whole East End . . .' Her hand flew to her chest. 'It's in here. My heart and soul belong here, to this community, to you, Gladys, Auntie and the girls . . . My people!'

Her throat felt raw and her eyes stung with unshed tears, but the words were tumbling out of her and the decision, now she had voiced it, was the right one.

'It all makes sense to me now. Going to Gardiner's Corner on the day of the demonstration . . . It was about wanting to defend my streets. I'm proud of what I saw that day, proud to call myself an East Ender. I see that now and, well, it's really quite simple. I can't leave. I want to carry on

Herbie Taylor & Daughter. Continue your family name. If . . . If you'll allow me, that is?'

Once Stella had finished her stumbling speech, she gazed up at Herbie, hope and fear burning in her eyes.

'Very well,' he said, reaching his hand out over the starched sheet, and lacing his fingers through hers. 'When the insurance money comes through, it's yours to set up a new studio with. Just promise me one thing . . .'

'Don't tell me,' Stella replied, thinking of Herbie's favourite saying. 'To always remember, that a little praise is of far more value?'

He shook his head.

'To use tact, diplomacy and a soft-focus lens?'

'Those things are important,' he chuckled, 'but no . . . not that. Just promise me, love, that you'll do it your way.'

Stella's gaze softened and she nodded her head.

The emotion of the moment had taken it out of her and without another word she laid her head on his chest.

*

Winnie paused at the end of the bed, flanked by Treacle and her mother, and observed the touching scene. Stella curled up in Herbie's arms, the pair of them looking for all the world like a father and daughter.

'Cooey,' she called. 'Feel up to some visitors?'

The bedside lit up with smiles and kisses as everyone embraced.

'Good to see you both looking like you're on the mend,' Treacle said. 'You gave us quite a scare.'

'Well, it takes more than a fire to see us off, don't it, Stella?' Herbie winked, wincing as he struggled to sit up.

'Any word yet on the bastards that did it?' Stella asked.

''Fraid not, Stell,' Winnie replied. 'I was over at Gladys's yesterday with Kitty. Fortunately, the firemen tackled the worst of it before it spread to hers. Anyway, the police turned up, asking all sorts of questions. Had we seen or heard anything suspicious in the days before, that kind of thing.'

Stella nodded. 'They've already been up to see me in my hospital bed, asking the same thing. I told her about those two men I overheard on the morning of the fire.'

'They've been to see me too,' Herbie admitted. 'Told me they rushed carloads of police to the street, and a wide net was spread around the area to trace the saloon car, but nothing's turned up so far.'

'It's such a shame I couldn't make out the number plate, but it was too dark and the car was moving too fast,' Stella said.

'Don't blame yourself, love,' Herbie soothed. 'You did more than enough that night.'

'That's right,' Treacle agreed. 'Besides, the law seem to think it was intended to burn down the BUF offices next door, and the studio was just an accident. They reckon it was a revenge attack for Cable Street. All the anti-fascist groups have denied it point-blank. To be honest, I wouldn't put it past the blackshirts to have started it themselves in order to blame others. You know, like Hitler did at the Reichstag.'

'What do you mean, Treacle?' Winnie asked.

'Three years ago, the Reichstag, the building where the German parliament sat, burned down. Hitler used it as an excuse to round up all his political opponents, have them arrested and seize power for the Nazis.'

'Who knows?' Herbie frowned. 'But it's all very queer.' He lowered his voice. 'Any news on Tommy?'

Winnie paled. She felt Treacle's hand reach for hers and their fingers slid together.

'My pal seems to think he's on the mend. His head wound's healing, though he don't remember a thing about what happened,' Treacle interjected. 'Who knows, may even have knocked some sense into him and he'll stay away. Let's hope we've heard the last of him.'

Jeannie stared bleakly out of the window at the bustling Whitechapel thoroughfare below, seeing nothing but the depths of her own misery.

Just then, there was a cough from the end of the bed. Everyone looked up to see the ward sister, accompanied by two men.

'These gentlemen would like to speak with you,' she said, pulling the curtain around the bed, before discreetly leaving.

'Good afternoon,' said the older man. 'My name is Detective Inspector Hughes of Leman Street Police Station and this is my colleague, Sergeant Williams.'

'Good afternoon, Detective,' Herbie smiled politely. 'How may we help you? We've already told your colleagues over at Bethnal Green everything we know about the arson attack. Although my young friend Treacle here has a most interesting theory you may wish to explore.'

'Actually, Mr Taylor, we're not here about the arson.'

The Inspector turned to Jeannie and a bottomless pit opened up in Winnie's stomach.

'Mrs Jeanette Docker?'

Jeannie nodded, her eyelid twitching.

'Could you please step this way? There's an office off the ward at our disposal.'

'It's all right,' she trembled, 'you can talk to me here.'

'So be it. Mrs Docker, we would like to question you at the station in connection with a serious assault on your husband. Would you come with us?'

She nodded like a woman resigned to her fate.

'Let me fetch my coat. Winnie, would you see to my washing and make sure the girls get tea?' Her voice cracked and tears spilled from her red-rimmed eyes.

'Let me come too,' Winnie begged.

'Wait!' Treacle blurted. 'Everyone, please . . . please, just wait.'

Everyone froze and looked, startled, at Treacle.

'It's me you need to speak with, Inspector, not Mrs Docker. You see . . . it was me who hit him. There's a very good reason, but I can't deny it, it was me, Jeannie weren't even there, I swear.'

Blindly, Winnie reached for the bedside table to steady herself as the air around her seemed to thin.

'Treacle,' she managed. 'W-what are you playing at?'

'I ain't playing, I'm confessing to what I did,' he replied in a low voice, staring hard at Winnie, before turning back to the Inspector.

'I hit him with an axe. I can even show you where I hid it, if you like. It'll probably still have my fingerprints on it 'n' all.'

'You do realize the severity of the crime to which you are confessing?' asked the Inspector. 'A charge of grievous bodily harm with intent carries with it a maximum sentence of life imprisonment?'

'I do, Inspector,' Treacle replied gravely. 'But, like I say, I had good cause. Do you want to lead the way?'

And then they were gone, leaving Winnie and the others staring after them in stunned disbelief.

*

Three days later, Stella and Herbie were discharged from the London Hospital and took a tram back to Bethnal Green. It felt odd, emerging back into the real world. Just one week since the fire, but it felt like a lifetime to Stella. The trams, billowing smoke and cries on the street, felt bewildering after the crisp, clean and ordered serenity of the hospital wards.

The clippie on the tram recognized Stella and refused to take her money for a ticket. 'Good to see you out, gal. We need more of your kind.'

'Don't talk daft,' Stella blustered. 'I only did what anyone would've done.'

'She's right, Stella,' Herbie agreed, clutching her arm as the tram rumbled through the busy Whitechapel streets towards Bethnal Green.

'You ought to go and see your mum, she'll be desperate to have you home,' Herbie said wearily, as they gingerly alighted at the end of Green Street. 'And get some rest.'

'I will, Herbie, but I must see the studio first,' she replied.

He knew better than to argue with his headstrong young protégée. As they walked, they noticed the street was curiously quiet for a Tuesday dinnertime. 'Where is every-body?' Herbie frowned.

'Gawd only knows, perhaps . . .' But her words trailed off as they paused in front of the remains of the studio.

Herbie Taylor & Sons Photographic Portraiture, a family business, proudly trading since 1860, was no longer. All that remained was a pile of charred wood and shattered masonry scaled off behind a *Keep Clear* sign.

The stench of burnt timber hung in the air, and here and there lay a curled and water-sodden photograph. It turned Stella's heart over to see the anatomy of the studio laid bare, to look upon so many precious memories, now shrivelled and ruined.

How ironic, she thought to herself, silently reaching down and picking up a warped picture frame, the faces within blackened beyond recognition. *I only realize what it truly means to me once it's gone.*

In silence, Stella tossed the frame back onto the debris and reached out and took Herbie's hand. She felt his frail body lean in towards her. Something inside the elderly gentleman seemed to recoil, and Stella felt every ounce of his pain. So much of Herbie was bound up in the fabric of the building. His lifeblood had pulsed through every joist and join. Stella didn't know if a building could take on the features of its owner, or vice versa, but the two had seemed intertwined somehow and the awful thought dawned on her: Herbie hadn't just lost his possessions, he had lost his heritage.

They stood in silence for a long time, absorbed in their own memories of the studio, before a sudden thought occurred to her.

'You do think the insurance'll pay out, don't you?' she blurted.

Herbie drew in a deep breath.

'They bloody well ought to,' he replied. 'They increased the price of the policy right after Cable Street.'

They lapsed back into silence, before Herbie shook himself.

'This is a bitter pill to swallow, and I'll admit, I never thought for a moment this would be the future of the studio, but we must be thankful for what we have. No one died and, 'cause of you, the studio has a chance to be reborn.'

Stella nodded, understanding.

'The business has a future,' he went on. 'Unlike . . .'

His words trailed off.

'Treacle, you mean?' Stella replied sharply, turning to look at him.

Herbie frowned and looked about before lowering his voice.

'Whatever is the lad playing at?' he muttered. 'I know he loves Winnie dearly, but taking the blame for a crime he didn't commit? Isn't that beyond the pale?'

Stella shrugged. She too was still attempting to fathom the shocking turn of events. Winnie had been in to see her in hospital since the arrest, still clearly in a state of disbelief. She'd been shaking as she told Stella that Treacle had formally been charged with Grievous Bodily Harm after he led the police to where he had buried the axe, and they were able to identify his fingerprints on it.

'She thinks she'll get him to change his mind, but he's as stubborn as the day is long. Besides, it's too late, surely?' Stella remarked.

Herbie nodded. 'I hate to say it, and admittedly I don't know much about the law, but now he's confessed and the police think they have their man, then probably, yes.'

'Added to which,' Stella went on, keeping her voice low, 'apparently, Tommy can't remember anything about the attack, only that he was struck from behind, so Jeannie's alibi will be that she wasn't even there.'

'So what now?' Herbie asked.

'He's due to appear at Bow Street Magistrates soon for the committal hearing and then we'll see,' Stella replied. 'Winnie reckons he'll claim he was defending her against her father. Treacle knew every last detail of how Tommy strangled Winnie, after all – she told it all to him. Poor Jeannie's in bits about it, apparently. Says she'll never forgive herself if Treacle gets jailed on her behalf.'

'Let's hope he tells a convincing story,' Herbie said, his frown creasing into a deep groove across his forehead. 'Otherwise . . .'

'Oh don't, Herbie,' Stella groaned. The thought of such a loyal man behind bars on Tommy Docker's account was too much to bear.

'Well, we shall all just have to rally round Winnie and Jeannie as best as we can to prop them up in their hour of need,' Herbie replied, putting his arm around Stella. 'You Wedding Girls have never let each other down yet, have you? Friendship is what will get her through this.'

'Indeed it will, Mr T,' sang out a familiar voice. 'Good to have you back.'

Stella and Herbie turned to find Gladys, Kitty and Auntie standing on the pavement behind them.

Kitty flung herself at Stella, nearly knocking her over.

'Oh, I'm so pleased you're home,' she gushed, hugging her so tightly, Stella winced.

'Thanks, Kitty,' she grinned. 'It feels good to be back.'

'Now then, Herbie, I've run you up a couple of suits and shirts to see you through until the insurance pays out, and I can easily make you up a spare bed in the parlour,' Gladys said.

'That's kind of you, Gladys,' he replied. 'But I don't want to set tongues wagging. I'll be perfectly comfortable in a lodgings house, but I'll certainly avail myself of your excellent cooking.'

Gladys blushed. 'You can count on that.' The two locked eyes and the look that passed between them didn't go unnoticed by the girls.

'Come on now, there's a few people who want to welcome you home,' Auntie said mysteriously. 'Follow me.'

Intrigued, Stella and Herbie followed them up the still strangely silent street to the Rising Sun pub. Once the door was thrown open, a great cheer went up from the crowded room. Stunned, Stella looked round and felt a lump lodge in her throat. The saloon bar was packed and it was standing room only. No wonder the street was so quiet, half the market traders and shop owners of Green Street were crammed into the smoky pub!

Stella spotted Big Mickey from the fruit stall, Miss Sugarman from over the way, and Tubby the tobacconist. As well as the local traders, it felt like every bride they had ever photographed was assembled under the same roof. There was Doris, clearly with child, beautiful Beatrice and, oh look! There was Maud – proudly rocking a baby over her shoulder – Celeste, Pamela, Joyce and even their newest newlywed Evelyn, fresh from a week's honeymoon on Canvey Island.

'It's a bridal reunion,' she laughed out loud.

Customers old and new were gazing fondly at them, arms laden with gifts of food and clothing for Herbie and Stella.

'Word got round about the fire,' Auntie winked. 'And people wanted to show you their support, in the way you've supported this community over the years.'

'That's right,' Gladys grinned, handing him an envelope. 'We've started a club, and everyone's paid in, so there's enough to see you right, until you're back on your feet.'

'I . . . I don't know what to say,' Herbie stuttered, his kindly brown eyes moist with tears. 'You're all so . . . so kind. I don't know how I'll ever repay you.'

'Nonsense,' Gladys scoffed. 'The East End lives collect-ively, *not* individually. You've always been the first person to step in and help someone. If we can't help *you* out for a change and show you what you mean to us all, well, it's a bad show, Mr T! Besides, what is it you've always said?'

'A little praise is of far more value,' Stella cut in, happily finishing the sentence off for Gladys.

'Everyone just wants to see the studio up and running again, and preferably not too far from these parts,' Auntie said. 'After all, what's Bethnal Green without a portraiture studio? You ain't got no shortage of brides and babies!'

'That's right, my little Albie needs christening, and I need you to take the photos, Mr Taylor,' piped up Maud.

'And my youngest sister's getting hitched soon 'n' all,' Joyce chipped in.

'That's up to Stella and her assistant Winnie now,' Herbie

grinned, 'but rest assured, everyone, you're in safe hands. Stella's a far better photographer than I ever was.'

Herbie was quickly sucked up by the eager throng, but Stella was happy to stand back and observe from the doorway.

Women of all generations had gathered together, many had even brought in their wedding photos and were eagerly leafing through the albums, comparing dresses in an impromptu reminiscing session. Stella smiled as she spotted Kitty in the thick of them, eagerly pointing out the gowns she had helped to create.

Excited voices pealed over the clamour.

Took my sister a whole hour to button me into that dress, couldn't do it now, mind you . . . Oh, Mum, don't you look beautiful . . . Will you look at the embroidery on that veil? . . . Ooh, I'd forgotten your father scrubbed up so well . . . I felt like a princess for the day . . .

The gates to Memory Lane had been thrown wide open, thanks to Herbie's lovingly taken photos.

It was such a joy to watch women trade stories of the most important day of their lives. A day she was proud to have had a hand in. And it struck Stella – Herbie was right! He had always been right. As portrait photographers, they could freeze time and capture fleeting memories forever, so that they might be cherished for generations to come. How had she ever imagined that to be dull?

Suddenly a voice piped up over the comforting swell of background chatter.

'This party looks like a hoot!'

'Winnie!' Stella exclaimed, grabbing her by the hand excitedly. 'I was wondering where you were.'

'I've been up visiting Treacle. He's being held on remand at Pentonville. It's taken me an age to get back on the trams.'

'Oh, Win,' Stella cried as she took in the dark shadows under her friend's eyes. 'What can I do to help?'

'Nothing, Stell. There's nothing anyone can do now but pray. I wish to God he hadn't taken it upon himself to take the blame, but he has, the daft sod, and now I just have to hope that . . .'

Her voice cracked as tears seeped from her eyes.

Stella folded her into a hug and her mind scrabbled with what she could do or say to ease her friend's misery.

'Can anyone join in?' Kitty asked.

'Course,' laughed Winnie, dabbing at her eyes as she pulled Kitty in.

'You'll get through this, and me and Kitty will be right there with you every step of the way,' Stella vowed.

'That's right,' Kitty nodded solemnly. 'This year has already thrown so much at us, but it takes more than that to finish the Wedding Girls off, don't it?'

'Dear sweet Kitty,' Winnie smiled sadly. 'You're such a treasure, you both are. I honestly don't know what I'd do without you both.'

From somewhere in the corner of the room, a spoon tapped against a glass.

'Can we get a little order here please?' Herbie boomed.

A hush fell over the room.

'I just want to say thank you to you all,' he said haltingly. 'Green Street has seen many changes over the years, and God knows we've had more than our share of trouble this year, but seeing you all here, drawing together in times of need, makes me realize we'll be all right, come what may.

Whatever dark clouds might be brewing, we'll weather the storms. 'Cause we're a proper community.'

'Hear hear!' echoed the room.

'I know most of you grew up with cardboard-patched shoes and hand-me-downs, yet there's not one among you who didn't look and carry yourself like a king or queen on their wedding day, and that's because you dare to dream.'

He raised his glass. 'To dreams!'

'To dreams!' came back a solid chorus of voices.

Herbie's face was flushed as he took a shaky gulp.

'While I'm at it, I want to thank four special ladies in my life.'

He turned to the girls.

'My Wedding Girls: Stella, Winnie and Kitty, turning out beautiful brides time and again . . . And . . .'

Herbie paused and scanned the room until his eyes searched out Gladys.

'To Gladys Tingle! Sometimes, you're so busy you don't realize you have a diamond shining right under your nose.'

Gladys flamed and her mouth opened, and then closed.

'Cat got your tongue for once, Glad?' Auntie quipped, and the whole room fell about.

'Ooh, you wicked rascal,' she scolded, wagging a finger at Herbie, but it was as plain as day she was thrilled to bits.

Once glasses had been refilled, Gladys and Herbie joined the girls.

'Nice speech, boss,' Stella said.

'I think it's time you stopped calling me boss,' Herbie replied, loosening his tie. 'You're going to be proprietress of your own new business premises soon enough. Talking of which, have you any thoughts on that? Or perhaps it's too soon?'

'Not at all, I was going to head down Bethnal Green Road tomorrow actually,' Stella replied. 'There's a lease come up on a building that might be suitable.'

'Oh please don't go too far,' Kitty groaned. 'It'll feel so strange not having you right next door.'

'Something tells me you're going to have plenty else on your mind to keep you occupied,' Gladys said mysteriously. 'Do you miss your Harry?'

'Something dreadful,' Kitty admitted. 'His boat set sail six days ago and I've already written to him three times.'

'Perhaps you might wanna take a look at this then, ducks,' Gladys said, smiling knowingly at Kitty as she handed her a copy of the *East London Advertiser*. 'And turn to page thirty-four. The personal column.'

Bemused, Kitty turned the pages and then read.

A moment later, her cornflower blue eyes widened.

'I . . . Oh . . . I don't believe it . . .'

'Whatever's wrong, Kitty?' Winnie asked in alarm, gently prising the paper from her fingers and reading out loud.

'Desperately Seeking Kitty, the most beautiful girl in the world' – Winnie's voice rose – *'to be my wife. Marry me? Yours in anticipation, Harry.'*

Winnie's scream of excitement was so loud, Stella was surprised it didn't blow the roof off.

'Well?' Gladys asked. 'Will you, girl? Marry him, that is.'

'Yes,' Kitty replied, looking around the group tremulously. 'Yes, I will marry him.'

In the absence of an actual fiancé to hug, Kitty stifled a

sob and threw her arms around the next best thing, her Wedding Girls.

'I don't believe it,' Gladys sobbed, pulling out her lace hankie and dissolving into a soggy mess in Herbie's arms. 'Our Kitty's getting spliced!'

While the smoky pub erupted into rapturous cheers, and a wag whistled the tune of 'I'm Just Wild About Harry', the Wedding Girls remained locked in the tight embrace of friendship, and Stella realized there was nowhere else on earth she would rather be.

Fifteen

Winnie looked bleakly up at the high prison walls to the leaden November skies beyond and drew in a deep juddering breath as she made her way to the visitors' entrance. Guilt crawled down her spine as she looked at the lines of tiny windows, staring down like so many mean, dark eyes, and she found herself wondering, which one was Treacle's cell?

It had been a little under one month since her mother had inflicted a grievous wound on her father, and four days since Treacle had officially confessed to it at Bow Street Magistrates.

The committal hearing on a dreary Wednesday morning should have made little impact, but the lurid headline in the local paper announcing the arraignment of *The Cable Street Axe Attacker* had ensured the stalls in the public gallery were full of eager onlookers to the spectacle.

As Winnie took her place in the queue of crying babies, bored-looking children and harassed mothers, all waiting to pass through the heavily guarded gate into the prison, she shuddered at the memory of it.

Treacle had openly confessed to the crime, but the basis

of his defence was that the blow had been dealt to prevent Winnie from being throttled by her father. But with no witnesses beyond Winnie, who couldn't remember anything after she blacked out, Treacle's future looked anything but secure. Winnie had wanted to scream out loud when the prosecution had painted her father as a frail war veteran, set upon by some marauding young brute, hell-bent on luring his daughter into eloping. The entire proceedings had felt like a charade.

The magistrates, having found there was sufficient evidence against Treacle, committed the case for a full trial at the Old Bailey for 7 December, five weeks from now, and denied Treacle bail, for fear that he might pose a threat to Tommy Docker. Treacle, a threat? What a joke. As she had watched her father playing the wounded war hero, helped from the court with his head wrapped in bandages, she had never felt so much disgust for a human being. The last time she had seen that face was when it was hovering over hers, his eyes bulging with fury as he tried to squeeze the life out of her. Tommy had brutalized her and her mother for years, nearly killing them both in the process, and now it looked as if his wish to have Treacle off the scene permanently was about to come true.

Winnie found Treacle sitting at a chipped varnished table at the furthest end of the visitor's room, but despite this the noise was tremendous. The sound of babies crying and nervous chatter echoed off the tiled walls, and try as she might, Winnie couldn't think straight. The astringent smell of carbolic, with a sour undertone of unwashed armpits, was making her feel queer.

'You came,' Treacle said softly.

'Of course,' she gushed over-brightly, folding her coat to disguise her trembling hands.

'Fill me in on what's been going on down Green Street. They caught anyone yet for the arson?'

Winnie made to reply but was drowned out by the shrieks of the woman on the next table:

'And if you think I'm going to sit around while your lousy tart runs me down all over town!'

'Sorry,' Treacle said, his face creasing into a smile. 'I think her poor husband only committed forgery so he could get some peace. Actually, he's not such a bad fella, once you get to know him.'

'Oh, Treacle,' Winnie cried, feeling her chirpy demeanour abandon her. 'I can't stand to think of you in here with villains and thieves.'

'Hey. Come on now, it shan't be for much longer, Win,' he soothed, his deep voice reassuringly solid. Winnie found herself drinking in every detail of him, from the dark hairs on his strong forearms, to his firm jaw.

'I'm sorry, Treacle, I'm trying to be strong, it's just . . .' Winnie's head slumped into her hands.

'Dear God,' she mumbled, 'if you're found guilty, you could go to prison for life for this, so they're saying . . . *For life!*'

'So don't listen to them. Listen to me instead, Win,' he said gently, tilting her chin up to meet his steady gaze. 'It ain't gonna happen. You hear me? My uncle visited. Says he's holding the job open for when I'm out. That's what you should be thinking about: a new start in the countryside and all the fresh air we can breathe.' He stroked her cheek, made a heroic effort to smile. 'Come on, gal. Chin up. This'll all feel like a bad dream soon enough. You'll see.'

'No touching,' barked a passing guard, and Treacle reluctantly pulled his hand back.

'Tell me one thing, Treacle. Why did you do it?' she whispered. 'What made you confess like that?'

'Simple,' he replied. 'I couldn't let your mum go through it. She'd never have survived prison. Your sisters would've been taken off you and you'd all have been split up. I love you too much to allow that to happen.'

He shrugged. 'Besides, where's the sense in ruining four lives, instead of one? You have to convince your mum that she *must* stick to the story that she wasn't even there. They have to believe it was me if we're to have any chance of getting her off the hook.'

She nodded, in a state of utter disbelief. Treacle's love for her was so pure, and now, so self-sacrificing. He was willing to forgo his liberty so that her family might stay together.

Winnie didn't know where the words came from.

'Marry me?' she blurted. 'It's a leap year, ain't it? So I can propose to you. I only wish I'd done it months ago, or eloped when you first suggested it, and then maybe . . .'

A wan smile chased over his face.

'Oh, Win. A year ago, I'd have jumped at that chance, but now . . .' He straightened up, gave her a look of mock disapproval. 'Now you look here, I'll be the one to do the proposing, all right? Give a fella that much to look forward to, at least.'

Winnie nodded. At that moment the guard checked his watch and pulled out a handbell.

'Time's up!'

The ringing bell chimed loudly and, instantly, the room was filled with the scraping of chair legs, and the noise level went up another notch.

Winnie leapt to her feet and touched her hand to his.

'Very well, and this time I'll say yes. I swear it.'

She turned and walked quickly from the room without once glancing back. Winnie could feel his eyes following her all the way to the door, but she couldn't look round, couldn't let him see the tears already spilling down her cheeks.

*

Kitty was all of a tizz. She had only popped round to Gladys to drop off a veil, before going on to meet Stella and Winnie for a bit of dinner before they headed to the Sunday afternoon matinee. Somehow though, she had let Gladys talk her into a couple of custard creams and an impromptu dress-fitting. A BBC light entertainment show was playing softly on the wireless in the corner, but Gladys meant business, and was circling her with a tape measure and a beady eye.

'First things first, we'll need to start a wedding club and book the church – you'll do St John, of course – and the dress . . .'

Gladys puffed out her cheeks.

'Now, I know you youngsters like this fashion for silver lamé, but honestly, with your colouring, Kitty, you might as well go in the altogether.' She paused only to wrap the tape measure round Kitty's waist.

'Hmm, twenty-three inches. Don't worry, we'll get you down to twenty-two with a decent girdle. The most important thing, my girl, is the dress. It has to be a showstopper, otherwise people will only talk. I don't want no one saying you ought to have gone to Hetty Dipple. I'd never live it over.'

Kitty opened her mouth to reply, but Gladys was in a garrulous mood.

'My personal favourite was Joan Crawford's wedding dress in *Letty Lynton*. Organza, ruffles, mutton sleeves, ooh-ee, now *that* was a dress. I went to Miss Sugarman's niece's nuptials last week at La Boheme and, honestly, talk about posh, you ought to have seen it, Kitty . . .'

Gladys shook her head at the memory. 'The bride was a picture in lace. Four-foot train and a rock as big as your eye! We had a sit-down meal, would you believe – must have cost 'em a pound a head. Sandwiches – all the fillings you like – lobster patties, fruit jellies, meringues . . .' Kitty zoned out, only coming to when Herbie strode in from the kitchen carrying a tray of tea.

'I think Kitty is perfectly able to decide what's right for *her* wedding, don't you, Gladys? You sound like one of them overbearing mother-of-the-brides you're always complaining about. Besides . . .' he paused and winked at Kitty. 'Kitty might not even like lobster.'

Gladys's face fell.

'Do I? Oh, love, I'm sorry,' she blustered. 'I only want what's best for you.'

'Don't worry, Gladys,' Kitty smiled, as she began to pour tea into three rose-patterned cups. 'I'm grateful for your help, but it's all a bit previous. I doubt Harry will have even received my letter of acceptance yet.'

'But I will be involved, won't I, love?' Gladys asked worriedly.

Kitty laughed. 'Do East End women drink tea?'

Gladys relaxed, and sank back onto the chaise with her cup and saucer.

'Herbie!' she screeched, looking down into her cup. 'Whatever do you call this? I can pee stronger!'

Heaving herself to her feet, she whisked the pot back to the kitchen.

Herbie smiled wryly once she was out of earshot.

'Seems I've got a lot to learn.'

'Are you ready?' Kitty chuckled.

'Her bark's worse than her bite,' he smiled back, stroking the tips of his moustache, a habit Kitty knew was a prelude to a question.

'The question is, are you ready, Kitty?' he asked. 'You haven't known Harry long.'

Kitty smiled and laced her fingers around her teacup.

'Quite sure, Herbie. From the moment Harry saved me from going under that police horse, I've felt so safe with him. He made a mistake in his past, but he's been brave enough to admit to it. Now *I* need to be brave and trust that I'm doing the right thing.' She faltered. 'Besides, I think Dad would've liked him, don't you?'

Herbie nodded. 'I'm sure he would, love. I dare say he'll be looking down when you pledge your troth, as proud as any father can be.'

Kitty smiled quizzically.

'Where does the word "troth" come from?' Sounds daft, but I've never really thought about it until now.'

'Why, it's the old English word for truth,' Herbie replied.

Kitty thought for a while, cast her mind back to Harry's heartfelt letter. *I must be honest with you, especially if we are to have any future.*

'Then I really do know it's right, Herbie,' she exclaimed. 'Harry's honesty is what I admire most about him.'

'Then just promise me, you'll keep being honest with one another throughout your marriage, love. If you do, you can't go far wrong,' Herbie smiled, patting her knee.

Kitty smiled back at Herbie and felt a sudden rush of gratitude and love. You could hang your hat off Herbie Taylor. The Wedding Girls would be nothing without him and Gladys to look out for them. Most girls their age had bosses who looked on them as no more than cheap labour, but to Herbie and Gladys they were so much more than piecework hands. They were brains and mouths, with opinions worth listening to.

'Herbie, would you give me away?' Kitty asked suddenly.

Herbie slapped his knees and his face crinkled into a broad smile. 'Why, Kitty, I'd be honoured, my dear.'

Kitty smiled contentedly and let her gaze rest on Gladys's pride and joy, three china ducks on the wall. For the first time in her life, she felt herself in upward flight too.

'No prizes for guessing who the bridesmaids'll be.'

'Well, of course, it has to be Winnie and Stella, but how can I possibly ask them with Treacle's trial hanging over us all? In fact, how can I be sitting here making plans and discussing my future, when theirs is so uncertain?'

'In times of uncertainty, nothing is more important than

friendship and the joy and comfort it brings,' Herbie stated. 'They'll be thrilled for you, love.'

'You're right,' she said, rising to her feet and placing a gentle kiss on the older man's cheek, which sent a soft flush creeping over his skin.

Gladys walked in with the refreshed tea tray, just as Kitty was pinning her hat on.

'And where might you be off to, madam? I wanted to talk to you about the wedding breakfast.'

'Sorry, Gladys,' she grinned, pinching a biscuit off the tray. 'I've got something important to tend to.'

*

Stella and Winnie looked up from their tea as the dining room doors swung open and Kitty hurried through the steamy room.

'Hello, sweetheart,' grinned Stella, glancing up from her Leica, which she had been polishing on the tabletop.

'All set for the pictures? I thought we could go and see *The Charge of the Light Brigade*, it's got that dishy fella in it: Errol Flynn.'

'Will you be my bridesmaids?' Kitty blurted before she had even taken her coat off. 'I promise not to bore you rigid about it and I shan't mention the "W" word again, but I just have to know that you two'll be there by my side.'

'Breathe, Kitty,' Stella cut in.

'Oh you daft nitwit, of course we will, we thought you'd never ask,' Winnie laughed. 'In fact, I dare you to try and get married without us.'

'Oh, that is a relief,' Kitty gushed. 'I felt so rotten,

bringing it up, now of all times, but I had to know. Now please, Winnie, tell me: how's Treacle?'

Winnie's mouth tightened.

'He's being typical Treacle,' she replied. 'Refusing to be downhearted about it, convinced that the jury will see through my father, but . . .' Her shoulders slumped, and Stella realized that, in Winnie's mind, Treacle was already a condemned man. 'Mum and me were interviewed by Treacle's defence lawyer last week. Nice enough chap, but he's quite junior, took the brief on a nominal fee. Whereas, God knows how, Dad's got some top KC – a King's Counsel – as a prosecutor, a "most experienced advocate", apparently.'

'Money talks, bullshit walks,' Stella snorted angrily, shaking a cigarette loose from her packet and sparking up. 'He sounds like a right flashy bugger.'

'Exactly,' Winnie said miserably. 'He's going to make out like Treacle was trying all year to lure me into eloping with him. Reckons they've got a witness who says he saw Treacle scaling the side of the house and climbing through the window. And, as if that weren't enough, this witness also heard Treacle begging me to run away with him, the night before the battle down Cable Street.'

She paled further. 'They're going to claim that Treacle burst in and attacked Dad in some sort of fit of revenge.'

'But that's poppycock!' Kitty protested. 'It's your father that's the violent one, not Treacle. Treacle was trying to get you to run away to safety.'

'We know that, Kitty,' Winnie sighed. 'Just as we know it was Mum who actually hit him. But Treacle's confessed to it and, on paper, Dad's the respectable one, the former chemist, served his King and country and all that. No one, apart from Mum or me, can testify that he's dangerous.'

'I can,' piped up Kitty.

'Bless you, Kitty, but you ain't never actually seen him get handy with his fists. We need . . . what was it that lawyer said? . . . a "similar fact" witness.'

'Someone must have. A temper like his can't be concealed,' Stella mused, thinking back to the grotesque evening in Victoria Park when she had seen Tommy lay about an inno-cent man, his wiry fists encased in a steel knuckleduster. The blood-curdling image of that savage attack still flashed through Stella's mind as fresh as if it happened yesterday, not eight months ago.

'If only I'd managed to get a decent picture of his face that night at the park,' she groaned. 'But his cap was pulled too low and the photo's too dark and grainy to be able to tell it's him.'

Stella shuddered angrily. 'If the jury could only get a chance to see what I saw, we'd have him bang to rights.'

'What about friends of his?' Kitty asked, placing a soothing hand over Stella's.

'Dad never had any, unless you count his lousy blackshirt mob, and I don't fancy our chances there,' Winnie said, shaking her head. 'No, I've gotta face facts. Apart from that year he went AWOL, on the face of it, he's led a blameless life.'

'That's it!' Stella blurted, feeling her mind start to race.

'What's it?' Winnie asked blankly.

'That year he vanished, where did he go? Up the line, weren't it?'

'That's right,' Winnie replied. 'Said he'd read in the local rag about some new scheme London County Council were building out near Dagenham. Homes for Heroes . . . now what was it called?'

'Becontree Estate,' Stella interrupted. 'I read about that too. They finished building it last year, thousands of new-build homes.'

'That's where half our brides have been disappearing off to after their weddings,' Kitty exclaimed. 'The houses are supposed to be ever so smart. Indoor lav, sparkly kitchens, even a bath . . . If you've the money for a down payment, that is.'

Winnie nodded.

'That's what Dad said. Reckoned there was some new pharmaceuticals factory opening up near there and, with his background, he might be in with a shout. Said he'd try for a job, then apply for one of the new-builds, and as soon as he got it all sorted, he'd send word for us. A "pathfinder" he called himself.'

Her lip curled in contempt. 'Except, of course, he never found the path back to the East End. We didn't see hide nor hair of him until he turned up that evening out the blue.'

'It makes no sense,' Stella puzzled, squashing the tip of her cigarette into a small tin ashtray. 'Why leave somewhere that sounds like Arcadia to come back to a family you'd run out on and these narrow streets?'

'And he never said anything about his time away, Win?' Kitty asked.

'Mum never dared to bring it up in case she got a hiding, and I could hardly stand to look at him, much less talk to him,' Winnie replied. 'Whatever happened that year in the suburbs is a mystery.'

Stella straightened up in her seat and eyeballed the girls. 'Well, it's time for the suburbs to give up their secrets!' Kitty and Winnie stared at her blankly.

'We're going to go there ourselves, girls, and ask about, see if we can't find anyone who knows Tommy.'

'It'll be like searching for a needle in a haystack,' Winnie protested. 'There's thousands of homes there – all identical, from what I've heard. Besides, chances are, he got a job, then got bored and missed his punchbag and decided to come back to Bethnal Green. That's if he even went there at all.'

'Call it a hunch,' Stella replied breathlessly. 'That editor said I had a nose for a story and my instincts are telling me we need to head to the suburbs and find out what your dad really got up to. How about it, girls?'

'I'm not sure that it'll do any good,' Winnie protested. 'Besides, I can scarcely afford to put food on the table, much less fares. I've got factory work to tide me over until you get the studio back up and running, Stella, but it would be reckless to spend that on a wild goose chase.'

'I happen to think Stella's right, Winnie,' Kitty said. 'Have you got a better idea to help Treacle?'

*

The following Sunday, Stella sat between Winnie and Kitty on the train as it screeched its way out of East London. All three were quiet, lost in their own thoughts, and Stella gazed out of the rain-spattered window at the grimy rooftops as they flashed past.

London was an unforgiving place; a seething metropolis

where the narrow streets lay hugger-mugger with factories. Row upon row of smoking slums pressed up against great blocks of Victorian charity and tenements. Flannels and sheets flapped in thousands of identical backyards. It might have been a dark, dirty sprawl, but it was Stella's city, the place she loved the best. She watched in fascination as the city peeled back and the dark mean streets gave way to red Edwardian villas and gradually to fields.

The rain dried up and a pale November sun struggled through the clouds. She glanced at Kitty, who was absorbed in her copy of *Peg's Paper*, and Winnie, who had her eyes closed, her face doughy with exhaustion under the brim of her cloche hat.

Was she being reckless to bring the girls here on their day of rest? Was this all a 'wild goose chase' as Winnie had so glumly predicted? Possibly, but as the train clattered down the tracks into open countryside, she had this feeling she couldn't explain, that somewhere out here in London's overflow lay the answer. Did the clue to Treacle's freedom lie here, at the end of the line?

The train rattled around a corner and suddenly, in the distance, Stella could see the outer smudges of the council estate, a great tide of identical housing ringed by green fields. So neat, so orderly, so perfect . . . Too perfect. A curious feeling stirred in Stella's chest. She was willing to bet that the suburbs had their secrets, perhaps even more so than Stepney.

As they neared their stop, her eyes chanced upon a huge hoarding by the station. *Own Your Own House. Price £449. Deposit £20. Repayments, rates, taxes, 18s weekly*. She sighed as the train slowed to a halt. Could you really buy the dream for 18 shillings a week?

'We're here – look lively, girls,' Stella announced.

By the time the girls had disembarked, they felt crumpled and in need of a cup of tea. A walk into the centre of the estate quickly disabused them of that notion.

'Where are the cafes and shops?' Winnie asked, looking about.

'And the pubs!' Stella gasped. She'd never seen anything like it.

There were no cobbles, or markets, no kids out playing in the streets or washing flapping on lines. Where were the barrows piled high with meat, fish and clothing, the cries of the costermongers, the quarrels and laughter, the every-day hustle and bustle that spoke of a thriving community? There was nothing but long, broad concrete streets, flanked with identical pebbledash houses, huddled behind perfectly manicured privet bushes. And the silence! Save for the birdsong, it was deafeningly quiet.

'I'd go off my head living round here,' Stella laughed, glancing at a small municipal park at the entrance to the street with its officious sign – *No Cycling. No Ball Games.* 'It don't exactly look much of a hoot, does it?'

'I'd never find my house,' Winnie whispered. 'They all look exactly the same.'

'Why are you whispering, Win?' Stella asked.

'I don't know!' she whispered back, and they immediately broke out into nervous giggles.

'Well, I think it's smashing,' Kitty announced, her blue eyes shining as she gazed up and down the street. 'It's like . . . Like, oh I don't know . . . paradise with the gates off!'

'Pull the other one, Kitty,' Stella scoffed, but one look at Kitty's enchanted face told her she wasn't joking.

'What I wouldn't give to live here, the chance to better myself,' she breathed.

'Wouldn't you miss your people?' Stella asked. 'Being around the folk you were born and bred amongst?'

'Of course, but just imagine, Stell. No damp or bugs, or sharing a lav. No more walls so thin you can hear next door stirring their tea! Instead, warm rooms, cupboards, a little patch of lawn to call your own . . . Heaven!'

'I don't know,' Stella sniffed, eyeballing a semi nearby optimistically called 'Grey Gables'. 'It's all a bit "kippers and curtains", if you ask me.'

'May I help you?' rang out a shrill voice. The voice belonged to a woman clipping her privet bush, looking at them from over the top of her shears as if they had just crawled out from the drains.

'I hope so, ma'am,' Stella replied politely. 'Don't suppose you've ever heard of a man named Tommy Docker?'

'Where does he live?' she said crisply.

'Becontree Estate,' Stella replied. 'Or rather, he did. Moved out last February. I'm afraid I don't know the street name.'

'Do you know how many houses there are on this estate?' she asked, curling her slightly feathery lip.

'No, madam, but I feel sure you're about to enlighten me,' Stella said with a fixed grin.

'One hundred and ten thousand, I believe. Good day to you,' she retorted, snapping her shears shut and hurrying inside.

'Good day to you too,' Stella sang back, and then under

her breath, 'Grumpy old bat. Honestly, you'd think she was living in Buckingham Palace, not reclaimed marshland.'

'Friendly sort, ain't she,' Winnie laughed. 'The airs and graces on her.'

'Come on,' Stella said, looping her arm through the girls'. 'We got doors to knock.'

*

Five hours later, the balls of Stella's feet were throbbing and she was beginning to see the foolishness of her quest – not that she could admit as much to the girls. They were flagging just as much as she was. They had already finished off their hard-boiled eggs, apples and slices of seed cake but she knew both, like her, were gasping for a cup of tea in the warmth.

After splitting up, they had combed through the estate, taking a street each, but after knocking on what felt like thousands of doors, they were still no nearer to finding out where Tommy Docker had lived. With the factory where he had allegedly found work shut, and so few pubs or shops to ask in, it was proving to be far harder than she had imagined. Besides which, folk out this way weren't quite as friendly as East Enders and at most doors they knocked on, they were treated with suspicion at best.

'Look here, Stell,' Winnie said, stifling a yawn. 'I appreciate you trying, but I don't really think we're getting anywhere here. It's going to get dark soon. Every time I shut my eyes, all I can see is pebbledash.'

'I'm sorry, girls,' Stella sighed, shaking her head. 'I feel wretched, dragging you all the way out here for nothing.'

'Don't be daft,' Kitty soothed. 'You could never have known the estate was so big. Can we go home, though? I don't think I've got any feeling left in my feet.'

Stella stared up at the sky as the last of the daylight faded behind the rows of neat saplings, and shivered.

'Come on. Let's get back to the East End. I reckon even the mice are friendlier there.'

They had reached the outskirts of the estate when Stella decided to have a last cigarette before the train journey home.

'Bugger,' she declared loudly. 'I'm out of matches and I'm busting for a smoke.'

'Sssh,' laughed Winnie. 'If they can fine you for not keeping your hedge at regulation height, I'll bet you swearing's not allowed!'

'No, it bloody well ain't,' a voice rang out from behind them and all the girls whipped round.

'A rent collector with a sense of humour,' Stella grinned. 'There's a first.'

'Can I help you, girls?' the man smiled back, shifting his money satchel from one arm to the other. 'You look like you're a bit lost.'

'Don't worry, sir,' Stella replied. 'We're on our way to the station to get a train back to London. Don't suppose I could trouble you for a light, though, could I?'

'Go on then,' he grinned, pulling some matches from the pocket of his gabardine trench coat.

As the match crackled into flame, Stella drew heavily on the cigarette.

'What brings you girls all the way out here?' he asked.

'Don't ask,' Stella grimaced, blowing out a long stream of blue smoke. 'We're chasing a ghost.'

'This ghost have a name?' he replied, amused.

'Tommy Docker. Thanks for the light. Ta-ta.'

Stella and the girls turned, and began to trudge up the street.

'Wait! This Tommy fella have red hair and a moustache? Come from Bethnal Green?'

Stella whirled round.

'Yes . . . And yes,' she gibbered in astonishment. 'Please, sir, do you know him?'

The rent collector shook his head.

'I did have the misfortune. You want number 11 Walnut Tree Avenue, two streets up. But don't tell 'em I told you.'

'Quick, girls,' Stella said excitedly. 'We ain't got long, the last train's going soon.'

She stamped out her cigarette and the girls began to run through the twilight, feet drumming on the deserted concrete street.

The house was as innocuous as all the rest. Same privet hedge and creosoted gate.

'I can't knock,' Winnie exclaimed, her face pale with fright. 'I should never dare.'

Kitty cowered behind her and Stella realized she would have to find the nerve. She cleared her throat, before rapping twice on the knocker.

The door opened and a pleasant-looking woman in her forties smiled back at them. She was wearing a maroon blouse with a pretty green jade pendant at the neck and was clutching a pair of oven gloves.

'Hello. May I help you, girls?' she asked. The scent of

something roasting drifted out from a plush carpeted passage and, along the hall, Stella spied a glass-fronted cabinet filled with china figurines and a silver horseshoe.

'I hope so, ma'am,' Stella replied. 'I understand you know a Mr Docker. Tommy Docker?'

It was like a switch had been flicked. The woman's face drained of colour. Her oven gloves landed on the doormat with a soft thud.

'No . . . No, never heard of him,' she muttered tightly, wincing slightly as she retrieved the glove.

Stella recognized fear when she saw it, and this woman was plainly terrified.

'Are you quite sure, miss?' asked Kitty, stepping out of the shadows. 'Only, we've come a long way . . .'

'Look here! You think I don't know me own mind?' she shot back, her fingers leaping defensively to the pendant at her neck. 'Now if you'll excuse me . . . '

She began closing the door and a sudden burst of despair flooded through Stella. This couldn't be it. They had come such a long way. Quick as a flash, she lodged her foot in the door.

'Please, miss,' she cried. 'We mean you no harm. We only want to talk. It's important!'

The woman's fingers curled tightly round the door frame, a tiny vein in her neck jumping in agitation, but Stella sensed a moment's indecision.

'I beg of you. Please, give us fifteen minutes.'

The woman's eyes, dark and uncertain, flickered up and down the deserted street.

'What's your business with Tommy?' she whispered.

'I'm his daughter,' Winnie said tremulously, breaking her silence. 'I . . . I have questions about my father.'

The woman's eyes widened in disbelief. 'His daughter!?' she exclaimed, unable to keep the quake out of her voice. 'You better come in. Quick, before the neighbours see.'

Sixteen

MONDAY, 7 DECEMBER 1936

Rex v Brody

Day One

The air hung like lead as Winnie and her mother made their way up the steps of the Old Bailey, flanked protectively on all sides by Stella, Kitty, Herbie and Gladys. They cut a sombre group, their black clothing stark against the Portland stone facade of the ancient courthouse.

The memory of their trip to Dagenham; that dreadful, gut-churning confession they had heard in the front room of a suburban semi in Essex, just four weeks ago but a whole world away, still burned fiercely in Winnie's mind. She would never forget what that woman had divulged to them, but would it be enough to secure Treacle's freedom?

God only knew. Casting her eyes up to the towering dome of the courthouse, her gaze rested on the statue of Lady Justice, holding a sword in one hand and the scales of justice in the other. She stared down grimly at Winnie, her gold crown silhouetted against the gritty December skies and the full enormity of what was about to occur hit her.

'Defend the children of the poor and punish the wrong-doer,' Herbie said, reading out loud the inscription over the main entrance.

Stella gave them a shaky smile as she pushed open the heavy door.

'Ready?'

As they passed through the entrance and into the grand baroque marble foyer, with its high vaulted ceiling, ornate mosaic arches and imposing air of grandeur, all six of them stared up, stunned into silence.

'Blow me,' breathed Gladys at last. 'This is a different gravy, ain't it?'

Everyone laughed nervously, grateful for something to break the tension, everyone except Jeannie. Winnie glanced over at her mother. Her lips were bitten white against the pale of her face as she mumbled the Lord's Prayer, and in that moment Winnie knew: Treacle was right! Her mother would never have survived being a defendant, much less a prisoner.

'You sure I look smart enough, love?' she fretted, breaking off from her fevered recitation to nervously pluck at the sleeves of a borrowed black blouse. It was far too big for her and swamped her skinny frame.

'Yes, Mum,' Winnie soothed, wanting to scoop her mother into her arms and protect her from all this. 'Ever so smart.'

As they made their way to the public gallery of courtroom number 2, Jeannie was shaking so much, she tripped up a step, cutting a nasty gash in her shin. Sticky beads of blood seeped through her stockings, and Gladys hastily fished a handkerchief out from her sleeve and began dabbing at the cut.

'Don'cha worry, love,' she soothed, 'it's not that bad, it's just the blood that makes it look worse.'

But Jeannie wasn't listening, she was staring up at Winnie, her eyes bleak holes in her head.

'It's an omen,' she cried, her tremulous voice growing louder in the hushed corridor. 'It'll all be my fault if Treacle goes down. May the Lord have mercy on my soul.'

Two passing court clerks looked at her with bemusement.

'Mum!' Winnie hissed. 'Keep your voice down.'

'Court is about to commence!' boomed the voice of a clerk down the oak-panelled corridor. 'The Crown versus Brody.'

*

Stella watched from the public gallery as the prosecution outlined the case to the jury, with an increasing sense of unreality.

'The facts are these,' declared a barrister wearing black robes and a silky smile.

'Never trust a man in a wig,' Gladys muttered under her breath as she unwrapped a toffee.

'On the afternoon of Sunday the fourth of October, the defendant, Mr Michael James Brody, a stevedore by trade who resides at 14 Globe Road in Bethnal Green, did gain unlawful access into the home of Mr Thomas Docker. Armed with a stone axe, his sole intent was to lure Mr Docker's eldest daughter into elopement, and no one was to stand in his way.

'In the eight months leading up to the attack, Mr Brody waged a concerted campaign to entice Miss Winifred Jeanette Docker away from her respectable family home and into a dubious marriage. Despite Mr Docker expressing concerns over the suitability of such a match, the defendant would stop at nothing to achieve his aim.'

Stella glanced at Treacle, sitting in the wooden dock, his head bowed, his eyes squeezed tightly shut as if somehow it would block out the prosecutor's voice. She wanted to scream at him, 'Hold your head up high!'

The prosecutor was clearly enjoying himself as he began to pace the courtroom like an actor treading the boards, rubbing his chin thoughtfully.

'You will hear from a witness today who will testify to seeing Mr Brody making a nocturnal visit to the home of Miss Docker on the night before the attack and begging her to flee her family and run into the night with him. On a separate occasion, some eight months earlier, he was even spotted scaling the side of the house in the manner of a common cat burglar, in order to procure her hand in marriage.'

The barrister stopped pacing and paused by a female member of the jury, his tone sincere yet grave, as he looked her square in the eye.

'Please allow me to disabuse of you of any notions of romantic grandeur over such gestures. The man in the dock is not some latter-day East End Romeo, and the tawdry tale you will hear today has its roots in neither love nor fidelity.'

The barrister's voice rose suddenly as he swept one black-robed arm dramatically in the direction of the dock.

'The man you see before you now is spontaneous,

impulsive and, if thwarted, a highly dangerous, violent and calculating individual. He is a scourge of young women and protective fathers.'

'What bloody rot!' Stella hissed under her breath as she saw the female jurors' eyes narrow.

'Buoyed up by a violent demonstration on Cable Street and unable to control his blood lust, Mr Brody broke into the home of Mr Docker with one sole aim. Vengeance! This was ruthlessly executed with the use of a blunt stone axe to the back of Mr Docker's head.

'It is nothing short of divine providence that he wasn't killed and we are not gathered here today for a murder trial instead.'

'My lord, I object to this,' said Treacle's barrister, leaping from his seat. 'This is highly speculative and not relevant to the issue at hand.'

'Anybody who dares interrupt leading counsel during an opening speech to the jury in my courtroom better have a good reason,' snapped the Judge, glaring down at him through a pair of half-moon spectacles, 'and you, Mr Worthers, have come up short. Mr Harrington-Smythe, please continue.'

Stella's stomach twisted unpleasantly.

'Thank you, my lord,' said the prosecutor, shooting a triumphant look at Treacle's barrister before continuing. 'By some miracle, or perhaps the bravery born of his time in the trenches, Mr Docker valiantly staggered from his home onto the street outside, whereupon he collapsed and was conveyed to the London Hospital with a fractured skull and excessive blood loss.

'It was believed by hospital physicians and the

constabulary that Mr Docker was merely another victim of the Cable Street fray when he was found unconscious and bleeding in the gutter. Which is, of course, exactly what Michael Brody would have had everyone believe.'

The barrister paused to inject maximum drama into his oratory, his sharp eyes gleaming.

'Imagine Mr Brody's delight at the fortuitous turn of events. To put it in common parlance: he thought he'd got away with it! Except . . . Mr Docker regained consciousness . . .'

He turned back to the jurors, his chest swelling.

'Ladies and gentlemen of the jury. During the course of this trial, the defence will seek to point the finger of blame at Mr Docker, in an effort to persuade you that the blow was dealt in order to somehow protect Miss Docker from her father. The truth, as is so often the case, is far simpler than that.

'Mr Docker is a respectable man, a war veteran, a man who has served his country and struggled to find employment during the Depression. A man who has cleared snow from the streets in order to put food on the table for his wife and four daughters. A father who simply wanted to safeguard his daughter's innocence.'

The barrister paused and said gently, regretfully, 'A man who thought his fighting days were over.'

He paused and bowed his head obsequiously to the Judge.

'My lord, may I be permitted to call my first witness?'

'You may,' replied the Judge.

'The crown calls Detective Inspector Hughes of Leman Street Police Station.'

As the Inspector to whom Treacle blurted his false confession stood and the court clerk made his way to the stand with a Bible, Stella became aware of a commotion to her left.

'I-I can't stand to watch this no longer . . .' Jeannie choked, jumping to her feet in the public gallery. The acoustics of the room carried her cries around the court and all eyes turned in their direction. Even the courtroom stenographer looked up from her typing.

'Sit down, Jeannie,' Gladys begged, her cheeks burning as she frantically tugged on Jeannie's hand. But it was no good. Jeannie fled from the hushed courtroom, tears coursing down her cheeks, with Gladys in hot pursuit. Journalists looked up from the press bench and eagerly began scribbling in their notepads, their instincts for a juicy story aroused. One even left the courtroom after them. Stella felt a dreadful prickle of foreboding up her spine. What a wretched start!

FRIDAY, 11 DECEMBER 1936

Rex v Brody

Day Five

By Friday evening, Winnie didn't know how much more any of them could endure: five bruising days the prosecution's side had been going on for now. No one had dared voice it, but after hearing of Tommy's testimony, as well as that of the physicians at both the London and the Chest Hospital, and the witness who had seen Treacle crawling through the window, his predicament was looking dire. The prosecution had painted a truly dreadful picture of Treacle, while, so far, her father had emerged as clean as a choirboy. Not being permitted to sit in on the trial until she herself gave evidence meant that, so far, Winnie had been shielded from the worst of it. She had relied on the girls for daily updates, but Winnie knew this was a comfort blanket she would not be able to wear for much longer. Her time to give evidence was looming, as was Treacle's, and the thought made her feel helpless with anxiety.

The problem was, Treacle had not been able to give the police a clear answer as to why he had not simply restrained Tommy to prevent him strangling Winnie. Why instead, he had struck him with the axe, or why he had buried the axe in the foreshore at Shadwell . . .

The truth, of course, was that he had not been there at the dreadful moment Tommy had staggered bleeding into Cable Street.

It was her mother's hand that had brought the axe crashing down on Tommy's skull. Not Treacle's . . .

The witness to his unsavoury-looking nocturnal visit, the fact that the axe had originally been pulled from the Thames by Treacle . . . these were nothing but terrible coincidences, which when pieced together presented a damning picture of guilt.

Winnie let out a long slow breath as she opened the door to her mother's bedroom and saw the real perpetrator curled up fast asleep on the bed. Thank goodness for Dr Garfinkle, who had kindly called on them and prescribed a sleeping draught for Jeannie. He had offered one to Winnie too, but she wanted nothing to dull the edges of this ex-perience. She deserved to feel every raw and ragged moment.

If the truth came out, she would lose the mother she loved. If the lie persisted, she would lose the man she loved. It was a bleak, hopeless situation. The rest of the trial stretched ahead like a dark, exhausting vacuum.

Smothering a yawn with the back of her hand, she walked to the copper and filled up a bowl with hot water. Winnie closed her eyes and drew a warm flannel over her face, relishing the feel of nothing but warmth and darkness, comforted by the smell of spicy chicken broth wafting up through the cracks in the floorboards and distant laughter.

The soft crackling of the wireless cut through the noise.

'At 10 p.m. on Friday the eleventh of December we bring you this special broadcast from Windsor Castle. His Royal Highness Prince Edward will now address the nation.'

Winnie wrung the flannel out and listened, rapt. Even her neighbour's laughter trailed off.

A few hours ago I discharged my last duty as King and Emperor, and now that I have been succeeded by my brother, the Duke of York, my first words must be to declare my allegiance to him. This I do with all my heart.

You all know the reasons which have impelled me to renounce the throne. But I want you to understand that in making up my mind, I did not forget the country or the empire, which, as Prince of Wales and lately as King, I have for twenty-five years tried to serve.

But you must believe me when I tell you that I have found it impossible to carry the heavy burden of responsibility and to discharge my duties as King as I would wish to do without the help and support of the woman I love . . .

Winnie felt tears, hot and fierce, splash down her face

and she pressed a knuckle into her mouth to prevent a loud sob escaping.

Her tears weren't for their former King, but for the sacrifices some men were prepared to make for love. Except in hers and Treacle's case, there would be no reward at the end of it. No shared future to map out. No comfort or privilege to soften the blow of his sacrifice. Treacle was about to spend the rest of his life behind bars, while her father would walk free.

MONDAY, 14 DECEMBER 1936

Rex v Brody

Day Six

By the second week of the trial, it was the defence's turn to question their witnesses, which meant of course one thing. It was Treacle's turn to give evidence. As Kitty took her place in the public gallery alongside Stella and Gladys, she felt as nervous as if it were *she* about to be questioned.

'This better start to go Treacle's way,' Gladys muttered grimly. ''Cause if I was sitting where the jury's sitting, I'd believe he was some sort of sex-crazed brute.'

'Gladys!' Kitty gasped.

'She has a point, Kitty,' Stella sighed, gesturing to where Tommy was sitting meekly, his head still wrapped in bandages and his eyes downcast, the very picture of frailty.

'He comes out like the victim in all this,' she said, angrily drumming her fingers on the wooden pew in front. 'This is all . . . all like some sort of, I don't know, fairy tale! And that flashy prosecution fella's running rings round Treacle's barrister.'

Her mouth tightened. 'Don't forget, I've seen the *real* Tommy Docker,' she hissed. 'I saw the bruises he left on Winnie's neck, and what a mess he made of that poor fella's face in the park with his knuckleduster, and . . . '

'Calm yourself, Stell,' Kitty whispered, laying a hand over Stella's jittery fingers. 'I'm sure now that Treacle is going to have his say, things will all start to look a lot brighter. It's important we stay positive, for Winnie and Jeannie's sake.'

She said the words, even though she didn't really believe it herself. Stella was right. The prosecution chap was good, very good. He had such a theatrical way with words and seemed to know instinctively how to put things to paint Treacle in the worst possible light.

'Just as well Winnie can't watch until she's given her evidence,' Kitty said, changing the subject.

'Which is when?' Gladys asked.

'Tomorrow, I believe.'

Stella nodded. 'It would've been too difficult for her to see Treacle on the stand anyway, and after Jeannie's outburst I know she's worried about what . . .' She glanced nervously, '. . . what her mum might blurt out . . .' Her words trailed off as the private door to the Judge's chambers opened and the atmosphere stiffened.

'All rise for His Honour, Judge Askew,' ordered the court clerk. Kitty stood, and fought the urge to run from the chilly, imposing room as the scarlet-robed judge took his place under the Sword of State.

*

Two hours later and all Kitty's innate positivity had deserted her.

Treacle was coming apart at the seams under cross-examination.

'You were courting the plaintiff's daughter in the months leading up to the attack, were you not?' asked the prosecution barrister, Mr Harrington-Smythe.

'We was – rather, we are stepping out, and I made an offer of marriage to Win – I mean, Winifred,' Treacle said, stumbling over his words.

'And to procure Miss Docker's hand in marriage, you climbed the side of her buildings and clung to the window frame on the evening of Saturday the fifteenth of February, correct?'

'Erm, yeah, yeah, I did . . .'

'How terribly flamboyant of you, Mr Brody,' the barrister remarked acerbically, one hand nonchalantly clasping the lapel of his gown. 'Do you have an aversion to stairs?'

A ripple of laughter rang around the court. Kitty and Stella exchanged a nervous look.

'And what exactly did Miss Docker say to your offer of marriage?'

'Erm . . . Well, she knocked me back,' Treacle mumbled, running an agitated hand through his hair.

'For the benefit of the jury, the defendant says his proposal was declined,' the barrister said crisply, turning on Treacle.

'What did you say to Miss Docker when she turned you down?'

'That I weren't going to take no for an answer,' Treacle replied.

The barrister raised one eyebrow. 'I see.'

'Not 'cause I can't take a knockback,' Treacle blurted angrily, 'but 'cause I knew she felt the same as me.'

'Stay calm, Treacle,' Kitty urged under her breath.

'Two days later, on the evening of Monday the seventeenth of February – presumably, this time by means of the stairs – you were back. Only on this occasion your intentions were less honourable.'

'I-I don't understand,' Treacle stuttered.

'What I mean, Mr Brody,' the barrister replied forcefully, 'is that even though your offer of marriage had been declined, you were found in a compromising position with the plaintiff's daughter.'

'What?'

The barrister pinched his nose between his fingers, a pained expression on his face.

'I had hoped to avoid this delicate subject with ladies present and in the jury, but you were caught in a state of sexual arousal on top of Miss Docker.'

'What? No! No! Not at all. We was only kissing!' Treacle cried, knuckles turning white as he gripped the edge of the stand.

'I put it to you that, even though this young lady had turned down your advances, you were unable to accept this and you turned up once more, frustrated and determined to get what you had come for . . . By any means possible!'

Treacle looked flabbergasted as the barrister circled the dock, his expression as hard as a hatchet.

'If Mr Docker had not returned home and interrupted

you, one shudders to think where it would have ended. At the very least, Miss Docker's reputation would have been left in tatters and her honour smirched.'

'NO!' Treacle yelled, thumping the stand angrily. 'It weren't like that. I told you once, we was only kissing.'

'Let's talk about this temper of yours, Mr Brody,' the barrister said coolly. 'Does it often get you into trouble?'

'W-what?'

'You box, do you?'

'Yeah, at the Repton, but so do half the men in Bethnal Green.'

'You like to fight?'

'In the ring only. I ain't no cobblestone brawler, if that's what you're driving at.'

'How tall are you?

'Um, six foot one,' Treacle replied, bewildered at the sudden change in questioning.

'Age?'

'Nineteen.'

'And you weigh?'

'About eleven, maybe eleven and a half stone . . . Look here—'

'Pack a punch, can you?'

'When I need to, yeah.'

'Fighting fit, one might say?'

Treacle shrugged, baffled, but Kitty felt a deep fear grip her. She knew exactly where the barrister's questions were leading.

'Please help me out here with something I am struggling to understand, Mr Brody,' snapped the barrister. 'In contrast to your robust strength, Mr Docker is forty-one years of age, five foot six and weighs nine stone.

'We have already heard evidence from a physician at the London Chest Hospital, describing Mr Docker's condition. The gas he inhaled as a stretcher-bearer has left him a frail and sickly man.

'Who would be the victor in the boxing ring, Mr Brody? You, or Mr Docker?'

'I would,' Treacle mumbled.

'Say it louder, please, for the benefit of the court.'

'I would!' Treacle replied, oozing angry resentment.

'So, with this knowledge, why, if Mr Docker was throttling his daughter, as you have claimed, did you not simply overpower him and restrain him until the constabulary arrived? It would have been easy enough for a man of your stature, surely? After all, as you yourself have admitted, he posed no physical threat to you.'

Treacle's mouth opened and closed as he scrambled to think of a reason.

'I . . . I don't know,' he said eventually.

'You. Don't. Know?' the barrister exclaimed scornfully. 'Well, I do, Mr Brody. Admit it, there was no attack on Miss Docker that day, or any other, was there?'

'There was!' Treacle yelled, starting to shake.

'No, there wasn't, Mr Brody,' he replied calmly. 'It's nothing but a poorly conceived and feeble excuse, conjured up as mitigation for your actions when, overcome with a vengeful rage, you crept up behind Mr Docker and delivered a violent blow to the back of his head.'

He turned to the jury with a sorrowful shake of his head.

'Ladies and gentlemen, this is no crime of passion. As

you have heard for yourselves, this is a man who simply cannot take no for an answer. A man who will use extreme and premeditated force to get what he wants.'

He turned and bowed slightly to the Judge.

'My lord. I have no further questions.'

As Treacle sank trembling to his chair, dragging a hand-kerchief across his brow, Kitty turned to Stella and Gladys.

'I hate to say this,' Gladys muttered, with a shake of her head, 'but he's going down.'

Seventeen

WEDNESDAY, 16 DECEMBER 1936

Rex v Brody

Day Eight

The day they had all been waiting for had finally arrived. Stella found she was quite possibly as jittery as Winnie, who, having given her evidence, was sitting between her and Kitty in the public gallery for the first time, feverishly turning a small bone dice between her fingers.

'Will this work, Stell?' Winnie murmured, without once taking her eyes off the empty witness box.

'Of course, Win. She's good for her word,' Stella replied, crossing her fingers under the wooden bench.

'All rise for His Honour, Judge Askew,' the court clerk announced, and the room filled with the sounds of creaking, rustling and throat-clearing.

Once seated, the Judge began his preamble to the day's proceedings and Stella closed her eyes, casting her mind back to the moment Ada had opened the door to number 11 Walnut Tree Avenue. As soon as she had spotted the green jade pendant – believed to ward off bad luck – nestled at Ada's neck, she had known that the woman from the suburbs had a reason to feel afraid. Ada's faltering story, when at last it had come, had confirmed Stella's suspicions.

Stella had never gone in for superstitious mumbo jumbo, she had always left the horoscopes and tea leaves to Gladys and Kitty, but right now she wished she had some sort of talisman to grip on to, if only to stop her hands from shaking. She opened her eyes. Treacle's defence counsel was rising to his feet, fanning out his black robes as he approached the bench.

'My lord. With your permission, I have a late witness I should like to call.'

'Objection! Inadmissible,' spluttered Mr Harrington-Smythe, leaping to his feet. 'This is far too late. We haven't been served with any witness statement.'

'Counsel for the defence and prosecution, approach the bench,' the Judge demanded. Both sides rushed forward and huddled round him.

'What's going on?' Winnie hissed.

'I'm guessing they're trying to get rid of our witness,' Stella replied, her heart beating a tattoo against her chest.

'But they can't do that!' Kitty exclaimed.

Five muttered minutes later, Treacle's counsel returned to his seat with a look of quiet triumph.

'My lord, I should like to call Ada Elms to the witness box.'

An expectant hush fell over the courtroom. Journalists in the press bench leaned forward eagerly. The clock ticked loudly. Kitty coughed nervously.

'Counsel, where is this witness of yours?' asked the Judge

irritably, peering down from behind his high vantage point on the dais. 'She may rule herself inadmissible by virtue of not actually appearing.'

'Where is she?' Kitty panicked under her breath.

Without saying a word, Stella rose to her feet and quietly edged along the row of seats in the public gallery, muttering apologies.

She found Ada sitting on a padded bench outside court-room number 2, nervously folding a handkerchief into pleats.

Stella paused, and then placed a gentle hand on her shoulder.

'Ada, they're waiting.'

She jumped, recoiling at Stella's touch.

'I know, I've been told. But I'm sorry, Stella . . . I-I just can't do it! I can't see that man again. Ever . . .'

Her voice cracked on the words as she made a grab for her handbag.

'I don't even know why I'm here . . .'

'Please don't leave, Ada,' Stella pleaded. 'I understand how you must be feeling.'

'No you don't,' Ada said sharply, whirling round. 'Unless you've been through it, you can't ever know.'

Her hand clutched at the neck of her blouse, the delicate skin at the base of her throat scorching pink beneath the pearl button fastenings.

'Th-the fear . . .' she stammered, 'it knocks the stuffing out of you. That man took everything from me, Stella. Everything!'

The flush deepened to an angry red rash, spreading up her neck, encircling her delicate flesh like fingers.

'I . . . I can't believe he's the other side of that door,' she gasped, as if choking. 'If I see him again, Stella, I-I shan't be able to force out a word.'

Stella moved towards her, took both her hands in hers, looked her squarely in the eye. They stood facing, a yard apart, the tension of the moment suspended in the air.

Stella's mind spun. Ada's fingers were as cold and rigid as steel, her pupils constricted to pin-pricks. What, if anything, could she say to breathe life back into this vulnerable, broken woman?

'I-I know you have no reason to trust me, Ada,' she said haltingly. 'You only just met me, but please believe me when I say you're not alone. Tommy took something so precious from you. Something you can never get back.'

At that, a tear broke and slid down Ada's cheek, her anguish so raw it seemed to come off her in waves.

Stella paused, placed the cool flat of her palm against Ada's flaming cheek, and stopped the tear in its tracks. 'In your mind, you're defeated. In your heart, you're sick.' She gestured to the door.

'Yes, the man that made you that way is in there, but so too are two women who know *exactly* how you have suffered. Together, you can make him pay, I swear it. If you don't . . . well, the brutality, it will all continue. Nothing'll change. Nothing.'

'But it's hopeless, don't you see?' Ada wept despairingly. 'They'll always take a man's word over a woman's. Even if it were one man versus an entire bloody army of women, it don't make no difference in the finish. Men always come out on top. Always have and always will. It's a man's world, Stella.'

'No!' Stella blurted, her mind scrabbling. This woman

was Treacle's only hope! She could see the court clerk approaching up the corridor out the corner of her eye.

'That's not true.' She cast her mind back to Auntie's eviction fight, the Battle of Cable Street, Green Street's reaction to the fire . . . 'Power comes when women stand shoulder to shoulder. Solidarity will win out.

'If you leave now, you'll never be free of that man. But if you can find the courage to speak out against what you know to be wrong, why . . .' her voice trailed off as she searched for the right words. 'You could know peace again.'

Stella paused, gently placing her hand on the space over Ada's heart.

'We stand beside you.'

In that moment, there was a tangible shift in the space between her and Ada, a quickening, a connection, call it what you will, Stella felt it in the slowing of Ada's heart rate, saw it in the dilation of her pupils.

'Mrs Elms, are you ready to give evidence?' The clerk's voice hung in the air.

Ada tilted her chin forward and her hand searched out Stella's.

'Yes.'

*

Winnie wasn't watching as the slight form of Ada Elms shakily took the stand. She couldn't wrench her gaze from her father's extraordinary reaction. She'd heard that, throughout the entire proceedings, he had remained a model of composure. But now, as Ada's tiny voice tremulously echoed throughout the courtroom, his face snapped up in shock.

'I swear by Almighty God that the evidence I shall give shall be the truth, the whole truth and nothing but the truth,' Ada vowed.

With every syllable she uttered, his face drained of colour, and by the time Ada had finished swearing on the Bible, he was as pale as ivory. And then Winnie saw it . . . That vein in her father's temple pulsing. She could read his face like a map. Years of looking out for his moods meant she knew every nuance of his expression.

Tutting heavily, Tommy passed his hand over his mouth and accidentally dislodged a sheaf of papers from the desk in front of him. As they glided over the parquet flooring, his counsel laid a cautionary hand on his arm.

'Looks like someone's rattled,' Stella whispered, as she slipped back into her place beside Winnie.

'Where've you been?' Winnie whispered, clutching her arm. 'It's about to start.'

'Never mind that now. Let's listen.'

'Could you please tell the court your maiden name and where you live?' asked Treacle's barrister.

Ada cleared her throat nervously, her small frame almost lost in the grandeur of the courtroom.

'My name is Ada Elms and I live at number 11 Walnut Tree Avenue, Becontree,' she replied, almost inaudibly.

'Who do you live there with?'

'With my mother, Renee, father, Albert, and until ten months ago, my husband.'

'And who is your husband?'

'Have a look for yourself,' she said. 'He's sitting right over there.' With that, she pointed to Tommy Docker.

A commotion immediately swept over the courtroom. The stew of noisy chatter rose up to the ornate ceiling.

'He's already got a wife!' screeched Gladys, unable to contain herself as she leapt to her feet in a shower of sweet papers.

'Silence in my court!' ordered the Judge.

Winnie reached out and threaded her fingers through her mother's. She could not bear to look at her face. After her initial outburst, they had successfully managed to keep Jeannie away from the court, but today she had insisted on attending. God alone knew what heartbreak her mother must be feeling at the announcement. She had stayed with Tommy through thick and thin, but still she wasn't enough.

'Just to be absolutely certain,' the barrister asked, once order had been resumed. 'You are married to Mr Thomas Docker?'

'Yes . . . Yes, sir. I am.'

'May I ask where and when you married?'

'Objection,' the prosecution cut in quickly. 'My lord, I hesitate to interrupt my learned friend, but this line of questioning is completely irrelevant. On what possible basis can a wedding date have any connection to the brutal assault on Mr Docker?'

'My lord, this goes to both the chronology and the credibility of the prosecution witness,' Treacle's barrister insisted. 'The jury need to hear the background to this witness.'

Winnie's heart was pounding like a piston as she, along with the rest of the courtroom, waited for the Judge's answer.

'You may continue, Counsel,' said the Judge.

'Thank you, my lord. I shall repeat my question. Where and when were you married?'

'We got married on the fourteenth of May 1935. A civil ceremony in Romford. It was supposed to be in Dagenham, only there was some problem with the papers.'

'I see,' the barrister mused, before adding delicately. 'You do realize, Mrs Docker—'

'Elms,' she interrupted sharply. 'I go by the name of Elms now.'

'Of course. You do realize, Mrs Elms, that there may be some question mark over the legitimacy of your marriage?'

'I do, sir. I understand . . . Rather, I was told just over six weeks ago by his daughter and her pals when they visited me at my home.'

'I have to ask this, Mrs Elms, but were you aware of the existence of another Mrs Docker, or that she had four daughters with the plaintiff?'

'Course I weren't! Do you think I'd have married him if I'd known he already had a wife?' she shrieked, affronted.

'I'm sorry. I had to ask. Their visit must have come as a considerable shock to you.'

'It did,' Ada admitted, swallowing hard. 'But, to be perfectly honest with you, when it comes to that man, nothing'd surprise me.'

Winnie could see Ada was starting to relax, opening up.

'You see, he ain't right in the head,' she went on. 'Marry in the month of May and you shall surely rue the day. Ain't that the truth!'

'She's a bleedin' liar!' Tommy screamed, leaping to his feet.

'Counsel for the prosecution, can you please tell Mr Docker to control himself?' the Judge ordered.

Tommy glared at Ada as his barrister pulled him back down and muttered furiously in his ear. The vein in his temple was throbbing.

'That's it, you bastard,' Winnie murmured under her breath. 'Show 'em your true colours.'

'Can you please tell me how you met?' Treacle's barrister went on.

Ada nodded and glanced nervously around the courtroom. 'I work at May & Baker, doing the wages. Tommy joined the firm in the February and he caught my eye when he came up to the offices. He said he'd not long moved to the area, he was ever so polite . . .' her voice trailed off. 'To begin with.'

'And what happened next?'

'There was a factory social one evening, and we got to talking and, well, I liked him. He paid me a lot of interest. I was flattered.'

'It was a fast courtship?'

'Very. Set my head spinning, but Tommy, well, he seemed in a hurry. We'd only been courting six weeks when he proposed.'

'Did this not strike you as somewhat hasty? You scarcely knew him.'

'Look, love,' she sighed, exasperated, forgetting for a moment where she was. 'I'm thirty-five, a surplus woman. Do you know how many women there are like me out there? Trust me, opportunity don't knock that often at my age!'

Her cheeks coloured. 'Besides. My dad – he works over at Ford's in Dagenham – and my mum, they was all in favour of it. Said we could live with them after we married, until we'd saved up enough for a place of our own. The daft thing is, I weren't even really hoping for marriage, not at my age, just companionship, but Tommy was insistent.'

'And you had high hopes for your marriage?'

'I did,' she said softly. 'All I wanted was to keep a nice home, be a good wife. Tommy didn't like to talk about his past much; I knew he'd been in the trenches and I didn't like to pry. I just hoped being with me in Walnut Tree Avenue would be enough.'

'And was it? Enough, that is?'

She shook her head, and Winnie watched as a flush of colour spread up her neck. For the briefest moment, her gaze slid over to Tommy and her hands began to tremble. She paused, took a shaky sip of water and replaced the glass with a chink.

'It quickly became obvious that he had a chip on his shoulder. Jealousy, it's a disease, you know . . .' Her voice trailed off.

'Can you elaborate?'

'Tommy felt, living with my parents, that he lacked status. He grumbled when the neighbours got a bigger lawnmower, when Mrs Brown up the road had a new hat. And when a work colleague purchased a motor car . . . Well, you ought to have heard him. He was boiling. He was never happy with his lot. He also had a problem with . . .' her voice trailed off nervously. 'Can I say this here?'

'You are free to say whatever you like in this courtroom, Mrs Elms.'

'He had a problem with the Jews. Forever ranting on about how they were taking over. Held them responsible for all life's ills.' She chewed her lip. 'It caused no end of problems between him and my dad.'

'When did you begin to realize you might have made a mistake in marrying Mr Docker?'

'Almost immediately,' she admitted. 'But you know what they say: marry in haste, repent at leisure. I'd made my marital bed and I had to lie in it.'

'How would you describe your relationship with Mr Docker?'

'Well, sir . . . it was what you might describe as, erm . . .' Ada's voice quavered, lowering to a whisper. 'Physical.'

'Physical?'

'Yeah, you know, violent.'

'I see. In what way?'

'In the way that really bleedin' hurts. Usually with his fists.'

'Do you remember the first time he struck you?'

Ada visibly winced.

'I-I do, sir,' she gulped. 'It was over such a trifling little thing. Mum and Dad had taken a trip out to the seaside one Sunday, I took the opportunity of having the house to ourselves to cook a nice roast, filled the house with sweet peas from the garden. I wanted to remind him of the simple pleasures in life.'

The detail plucked at Winnie's heart and she listened, spellbound, to the woman as she poured out her pain. The account she gave was all too familiar to Winnie.

'I accidentally mixed up the carrots and peas. Tommy don't like peas. He threw the bowl against the wall . . . It smashed everywhere. I just remember watching all these peas bouncing off the wall . . . Broken bits of china . . .'

she shook her head. 'All I could think was how cross Mum would be. It was her best china, see.' She closed her eyes so tightly, her forehead puckered, and a tear slid down her cheek.

'Then . . . then he grabbed me by my hair, swung me round the room. He must have punched me, I–I don't know, it felt more like an explosion. Next thing I know, I'm lying on the carpet, blood pouring out my nose.'

Ada shook her head, eyes still clamped shut, unable to look at the crowded courtroom.

'I sat there for what felt like hours, surrounded by them bloody peas. I . . . I felt so wretched, kept thinking what a terrible mess I'd made of things. I suppose . . . I felt, well, shame. Yes . . . I felt ashamed that I'd driven him to it and, deep down, I know this is going to sound daft, but I loved him.'

Winnie gulped hard in her throat at the familiarity of Ada's confession and tightened her grip on her mother's hand.

'She's right,' Jeannie whispered, without once taking her gaze from Tommy. 'How can you love a man and hate him, all at the same time?'

'And when you had gathered your wits?' the barrister continued gently.

'I cleaned myself up, scrubbed the blood off the carpet. Tommy came home the same time as Mum and Dad later that day and no more was said. I told Mum I'd accidentally tripped, dropped the bowl and banged my nose on the table as I went down. She and Tommy even laughed at what a butterfingers I was.'

'You did not think to confide in your parents?'

'Are you bloody mad!' she cried. 'S-sorry, your honour . . .'

'No, no chance, I couldn't of. Besides, I blamed myself. Told myself I wasn't a good enough wife. Many women have put up with far more.'

'But not many women would put up with what happened next, surely?' he probed softly.

Ada shook her head. 'You'd be surprised what some wives put up with behind closed d—'

'Objection,' protested Mr Harrington-Smythe, leaping to his feet before she'd even had a chance to finish her sentence. 'That was a leading question. If Mr Worthers wants to give evidence himself, then maybe he should take the oath!'

'Mr Worthers,' said the Judge wearily. 'This is a criminal trial, not a coffee morning.'

'My lord, I apologize. I shall rephrase my question. Mrs Elms, can you please describe to the court, in your own words, what happened on the morning of February the fourteenth, 1936?'

She drew in a deep breath, gripped the stand for strength.

'My monthlies were late. The doctor had confirmed it. I always thought I was too old to have a baby. Once I'd got over the shock, I was so happy . . . It was smashing to know there was a little life growing inside me.' Ada's face lit up briefly and Winnie got a glimpse of what a pretty woman she must have been, before she met Tommy.

'I thought a baby would be just the thing to get my marriage back on track. I-I, well, I had the notion Tommy would be made up to be a father.'

'When did you tell him?'

'I waited until I felt the quickening . . .' her hand fluttered to her belly. 'You know, when I was sure it had caught, taken like. I waited until Valentine's Day morning to break the news, I kept thinking to myself what a lovely present it would be, better than a card at any rate. I fetched him up a cup of tea in bed and then I broke the news . . .' Ada's voice trailed off and, for a long time, she stood in silence.

'Mrs Elms, was he angry?'

'No . . . No, he weren't angry. He was absolutely livid.'

A sudden shudder ran the length of her body and Winnie longed to go to her, to comfort her.

'Told me I had no right. I'd tricked him, he didn't want no baby. He had me up against the wall and he started strangling me . . . Oh God, no . . .'

A wail of anguish erupted from her lips. For one dreadful moment, Winnie thought she might be about to crumple to the floor, but somehow she kept going, her words tripping over themselves to escape. 'He was strangling me . . . H-he was crazy. It was like he wasn't there . . . He was there in body, in his hands, in his grip, but his head was gone . . .'

She gasped for breath, clawed at the neck of her blouse.

'He'd have killed me, I know he would, if Dad hadn't come in and pulled him off.'

The barrister waited a while. Allowed a court clerk to fetch her more water, and then . . .

'Are you able to continue?'

'Yes . . . sorry . . .'

'Can you tell us what happened next?'

'I-it's a blur, to be honest. My dad threw him out the house, told him to sling his hook and never come back.' Her voice flattened.

'And the next day, I started to bleed. My doctor said he couldn't be sure if it was down to the attack, or my age . . . You know, nature's way.' She gave a brittle laugh. 'But I know, all right. I lost my baby because he couldn't control his temper.'

'Mrs Elms, did you ever see your husband again after the attack?'

'No, not until now. We heard a rumour he'd returned to the East End and I was glad of it. I-I thought I knew fear, until I met Tommy Docker.'

Her words had a finality to them. The grief etched on her face spoke volumes.

'I have no further questions, my lord,' the barrister said. As he returned to his place at the counsels' bench, Winnie felt Stella's arms around her shoulders, holding her gently.

'Was it like that for you too, Win?' she whispered, tears filling her eyes.

Winnie simply nodded, exhausted, her spirit too broken to reply, and allowed herself to be folded into Stella's safe embrace. She had known all along what her father had been capable of, how many lives he had destroyed with his violent temper, and now, thanks to Ada's heart-wrenching testimony, the jury had had a glimpse of it too. The similarities between her and Ada's story were many. The question was, would it be enough to secure Treacle's freedom?

Rex v Brody

Day Ten

The Verdict

Two days later, in the wedding dress workshop, Kitty ever so carefully lifted the catch on the sewing machine's hidden compartment. As the old brass catch eased back and the drawer sprang open, Kitty's heart lifted. The old Singer gave her a physical connection to the woman who would have been her mother-in-law, but more than that, it spoke to her soul.

To use Harry's mother's machine, to place her feet where Agnes had gently treadled, was to journey back in time. Through the simple act of sewing, she could connect to a woman she had never met. At times, in quieter moments, Kitty fancied she could feel Agnes's presence at her shoulder, her immortal spirit making itself known in the tiny workshop. She was a strong believer in fate. Had Agnes left her letter there so that Kitty and her son might one day meet? Was Harry her destiny? Who knew, but to unashamed romantic Kitty, when it came to love, anything was possible. After her father's death, she had been reborn in Harry's kisses. His love had been her salvation, his proposal, her future.

She glanced at the clock. Eleven o'clock. Stella had said the jury was due to go out this morning to begin their deliberations, after the counsels' closing speeches. Treacle's entire future rested in the hands of twelve perfect strangers.

She had told no one about Treacle's letter to her, received just two days ago and sent from behind bars. Instead, she had dutifully followed his request. As carefully as if she was handling lace, Kitty lifted the two packages from where she had kept them hidden in the secret compartment of the sewing machine. One to be given to Winnie in the event he walked free, the other to be given to her only should he be incarcerated. Closing her eyes, she muttered a fervent prayer and touched her lips to the package that signified freedom, before tucking them both in her satchel.

'There you are,' exclaimed Gladys, poking her head round the door. 'I thought you'd already locked up? Come on, gal, shake a leg, the jury might have gone out by now.'

'Coming,' Kitty replied, jumping up smartly. As she went round covering the machines in dust sheets, she couldn't help voicing her worst fears.

'Gladys, what if they don't believe that Treacle hit Tommy to stop him from killing Winnie? What if Tommy gets away with it all – his lies, his cheating? What if he comes after Winnie and her mum again, what if—'

'Hush now, child,' soothed Gladys. 'We have to stay strong, for Jeannie and Winnie's sake. One thing's for certain, it's a bloomin' good thing you unearthed that other woman of his and she backed up Treacle and Winnie's side of things.'

Gladys tutted, shook her head. 'Oh but didn't it turn you right over, listening to that poor soul. Losing her baby like that. Without her, I'd say Treacle was a dead man walking.'

She shook herself. 'Hark at me! I'm getting maudlin.

Now, before we go outside and meet Herbie, tell me this: have you and your Harry set a date yet?'

'Give us a chance, Gladys.' Kitty smiled as she unknotted her headscarf and raked her fingers through her long wavy hair. 'I haven't even formally accepted his proposal yet, which I'll be doing the minute he's back in the East End.'

'Well, I wouldn't dilly-dally too long if I was you, love,' Gladys remarked. 'Men and marriage are like wheelbarrows. You gotta push 'em to make 'em work!'

'Thanks, Gladys,' Kitty replied, rolling her eyes as she turned her back and fastened up the buttons of her coat. She bit her lip to stop herself asking how spinster Gladys might be privy to such information.

'In that case,' she said, turning back round. 'What about you and Herbie? You seem very close. Perhaps it might not just be my wedding we need to plan?' She raised one eyebrow teasingly.

'Oh, don't talk daft, girl,' said Gladys, flustered. 'At our age . . .'

'Come on,' Kitty grinned, holding open the door.

Her grin froze on her face the moment she stepped out onto Green Street. For standing next to Herbie, still dressed in his Merchant Navy uniform and clutching a bouquet of creamy white lilies, was Harry.

'Harry! You're back early!' she screamed, tearing into his arms with such force, petals cascaded onto the cobbles.

'Steady on, girl,' he chuckled, his green eyes shining with amusement. 'My ship docked a couple of days early, though I swear it was the longest voyage of my life . . . So . . .' he hesitated, his eyes searching her face nervously, 'I take it you saw my proposal in the paper. What's your—'

'Yes!' she shot back before he even had a chance to finish his sentence. 'Yes! Yes! Yes, of course I'll marry you, Harry, did you ever think I could say no?'

Harry started to laugh, took off his sailor's hat and plonked it on Kitty's head. Her blue eyes glowed with love as she gazed up at him beneath the brim. At that moment, it began to snow; fat fluffy flakes that spiralled from the white skies, speckling their faces.

'Oh, Harry,' she murmured, feeling heady from the scent of the lilies. 'I'm so happy, I only wish my father and your mother were here to share in all this.'

'But they are, Kitty,' he insisted, pulling her tighter into his arms. 'Don't you see? My mother is a part of *me*, your father is a part of *you*. The way I see it is, we came from them, so they'll always be with us.'

'I think I understand,' Kitty replied.

'And that's why I want you to have this.' He fished in his pocket and pulled out a velvet-covered box.

'Go on then, open it.'

Kitty did as she was told, her gaze softening as she took in the simple but perfect band dotted with tiny emeralds and diamonds.

'It's my mother's. I stopped in to see my dad on the way here, told him I had made you an offer of marriage. He was that pleased, said he can't wait to meet you again, and then he gave me this. Insisted that it's what Mum would've wanted.'

'And you, Harry, do you believe that?' Kitty asked, as he slipped the ring onto her finger.

'Yes. I really do,' he insisted. 'The way we met, don't you think my mum had a hand in that? We spent so many years apart because of my stupidity and her stubbornness.' He traced his finger tenderly over her top lip. 'I believe *you* are her gift to me.'

And then there were no more words to be said, as Harry touched his warm lips to hers and the world around them melted away.

'Come on, lovebirds,' Herbie chuckled, snapping them both back to the present. 'I hate to ruin the moment, but we've got to get up to the court.'

*

By the time they reached the Old Bailey, Kitty's euphoria had subsided. She felt sick as they clattered along the hushed corridors, Harry's hand gripping hers tightly, her satchel banging against her thigh. She was grateful for her fiancé's presence, but something about this walk was reminding her of the fateful day she'd walked into the hospital, only to find her father dead. Soon enough, they would all walk out of this building, their worlds irrevocably altered.

They rounded the corner and skidded to an abrupt halt. For there, sitting on the bench outside courtroom number 2, were Stella and Winnie, both their faces whiter than ash. Sandwiched between them, with her head slumped into her hands, was Jeannie. Her tiny, frail body shook with the force of her sobs. Winnie looked at them with unseeing eyes, and shook her head.

Gladys shrieked and covered her mouth with both hands.

The noise made Jeannie jump and she looked up.

'H-he's not guilty . . .' she wept, her voice echoing off the marble floor. 'He's not guilty.'

Kitty felt a little piece of her heart shrivel. Gladys burst into tears. Herbie held her as his face crumpled.

'Oh girls . . .' Kitty wept, falling to her knees in front of Jeannie and reaching either side to take Stella and Winnie's hands.

'We know he's not guilty! I–I'm so sorry . . . there must be something we can do, maybe an appeal?'

Winnie looked at her and, through her shock, her face flickered with confusion, and then slowly a light of understanding dawned, and she began to laugh.

'No . . . No, you don't understand, Kitty. What Mum means is, he's *not guilty*.' She repeated it, as if she hardly believed it herself. 'He's not guilty. The verdict just came back. Mum's crying out of relief. We're all sitting here, in a state of shock, waiting for Treacle to be released.'

'Oh my goodness!' Kitty trembled, not knowing whether to laugh or cry. 'You gave us such a fright . . .' And then the implications sunk in and she flung herself at Winnie, knitting her body tightly to hers.

'Oh, sweetheart,' Kitty gushed, her voice muffled in Winnie's dark hair. She felt Winnie's tears, hot and wet against her cheek, her body sagging in relief.

'It was a unanimous decision,' Winnie sobbed. 'The Judge even praised me and Ada, said we were brave to give evidence. I don't know about that, mind you. I think Treacle's the brave one.

'And you shan't believe this: Judge Askew asked that the police investigate an offence of bigamy against my father.'

*

They stayed that way for a long time, Kitty and Winnie hugging, with Stella's arms wrapped protectively around them both. Three friends who had weathered many storms: solid and unbreakable. In the centre of their embrace, Winnie had never felt so grateful for their love and, as her tears flowed freely, she realized, you may not be able to choose your family, but you sure as hell could choose your friends.

'I chose well,' she mused out loud.

Kitty drew back, puzzled, but suddenly the door to the courtroom opened. A tall figure emerged.

'Treacle . . .' Winnie whispered, feeling quite overcome with nerves.

He stood in the clothes he'd been arrested in that day at Herbie's hospital bedside and smiled shakily. A stone lighter, but twice as handsome, at least in Winnie's eyes. Because she realized with a breathtaking bolt of clarity, that she had never loved nor admired a man so much, nor so purely.

As he moved towards her, Harry, Gladys and Herbie parted to let him pass, Herbie patting him soundly on the back.

'Respect to you, sir,' he said admiringly. 'You're a true gentleman.'

When Treacle reached Winnie, he gently pulled her to her feet. In that moment, no words seemed adequate, not to convey the true strength of her feelings for the man who loved her so devotedly he was willing to go to prison for her. Instead, quite overcome, she rested her forehead against his wide chest. She could have stayed that way all day, except suddenly he was cupping her chin, lifting her gaze to meet his.

'I hope I've proved to you, Winnie, that some men *can* be relied on,' he breathed, his brown eyes burning as he took her hand and pressed his lips into the flesh of her palm. Overwhelmed with exhaustion and emotion, Winnie could only nod, then her eyes flickered shut.

When she opened them again, Kitty was taking something out of her satchel and handing it to Treacle.

He held it between his fingers, nodded gratefully at Kitty before folding it into Winnie's hand.

'W-what's this?' she stuttered.

'Read it,' he urged.

It was a love knot, its white ribbons perfectly stitched into graceful loops. Winnie had seen them countless times sewn into veils or on bridal headdresses, but this one was adorned with a message on each ribbon.

'The knot of love which has no end, to let you know my love is true,' Winnie read out loud. Puzzled, she turned the knot again.

'. . . and that to none alive but vow.'

Her heart picked up speed as she turned and read the final message, her breath catching in her throat.

'So be my wife and live with me as long as life shall granted be . . .'

Winnie broke off, her hand flying to her mouth as Treacle sank to one knee outside the courtroom.

'I've asked you this question before, but back then, I wasn't worthy of your love. This time, I hope I am.' He gazed up at her expectantly.

Winnie nodded furiously, tears spilling from her eyes.

'In that case, will you marry me, Winnie Docker?'

*

As the jubilant party spilled out onto the snowy steps of the courthouse, Stella was stunned to see half of Green Street waiting outside. Treacle's family and workmates, Auntie, Mickey, Miss Sugarman, and so many other familiar East End faces had been nervously awaiting the verdict.

Treacle paused on the top step, one arm around Jeannie, the other around Winnie. His breath billowed into the frosty air as he pumped one fist skywards, and the group descended on him in a rapturous hail of backslapping and enthusiastic handshaking. Treacle was one of their own, and his acquittal would be felt and celebrated by all in the East End.

'So when you gonna make an honest man of Treacle?' Auntie called out to Winnie. Nestled in the crook of his arm, she smiled, her face a mask of love and relief.

'Soon as he wants,' she replied. 'I think I've wasted enough time already, don't you?'

'Too right, love, no point hanging about,' Gladys piped up, looking pointedly at Kitty and Harry. 'You know the old saying: When December snows fall fast, marry and true love will last.'

'Oh, Gladys,' chuckled Herbie. 'Let's let the youngsters decide when they want to get married. Besides, I think you'll have enough on your plate as it is . . .'

'Oh yes and what do you mean by that, Mr T?'

He grinned enigmatically, his neat moustache twitching.

'Why, planning our wedding. If you'll have me, that is . . .' Herbie hesitated, fumbling for words. 'I . . . I always thought it was too late for me to find a companion again, someone to share my life with. The fire's made me realize, I was wrong.'

Stella watched, astonished. The colour rose up Gladys's

chest, right up to the tips of her ears and, for one dreadful moment, Stella thought she might keel over in front of the grand court.

'Herbie,' Gladys breathed, screwing her handkerchief into a ball in her pudgy fist and placing it over her heart. 'I-I don't know what to say.'

'That'll be a first then,' piped up Mickey.

'Watch it, you,' she grinned, poking him in the guts. 'I will, Mr Taylor. Oh, but of course I will. Ooh, but I'm all overcome.'

'Come on, folks, we better get this celebration back to the East End before this one splits her seams,' Herbie laughed, sliding one arm around Gladys's shoulders.

As the group moved off, all in need of a stiff drink, Stella hung back. Something made her turn. Slipping quietly out the door was Ada Elms, her diminutive figure clad in a dark coat, heels clicking as she hurried from the court.

A sad smile flickered over her face when she spotted Stella and she stopped.

'Join us for a celebration drink?' Stella asked, gesturing to the departing group.

'Thanks but no thanks. I've got to get back to Becontree. Mum and Dad'll be worrying about me.'

Stella nodded. 'I understand. Thank you, Ada. For everything that you've done, and I'm so sorry . . .' her voice faltered as she searched for the right words, '. . . for your loss.'

'It's me who ought to be thanking you,' Ada replied, hugging her arms around herself in the chill dusk. 'Looks like Tommy's finally going to get what's coming to him.'

'I expect the Crown takes a dim view of bigamy,' Stella

agreed. 'But at least it gives both you and Jeannie grounds to divorce him.'

'Divorce,' Ada murmured. 'I can scarcely believe it. I thought marriage existed until death did us part.'

'You could even remarry now, if you wanted . . .' Stella ventured, her voice trailing off awkwardly.

Ada shivered. 'Oh no. I shan't be going down that path again.'

Stella nodded, understanding perfectly.

'So long then,' Ada said.

'So long,' Stella replied.

Instinctively, the two women moved towards one another and hugged fiercely, their embrace conveying so much more than words ever could. And then Ada was gone, scurrying to catch a train that would take her back to the sprawling suburbs. Back to quietly try to repair her broken heart. How Stella prayed that Ada would find peace again, how all women who had suffered at the hands of a cruel man could find their way back to a life of safety.

Jeannie and Winnie's freedom from Tommy had been a hard-won fight, a little like the East End's fight for freedom in the Battle of Cable Street, as they were now calling it. But good had won out. Love – not hate – had won the day and there was much to be thankful for, much to look forward to. Three weddings, in fact! Three, to match the three Kings who had ruled over them this past year, Stella realized with a wry grin as she thought of the continuing hoo-ha over the King's abdication crisis.

There was no denying it, 1936 had certainly been an eventful year, Stella mused as she dug her freezing hands deep into her coat pockets and watched Ada's tram slide away. She would be glad to see the back of it, but if a housing protest, a riot, a fire and a court case hadn't finished them off, she doubted much would. In fact, if anything, their friendship seemed stronger than ever, with each of them aware of what they were truly capable of if they stuck together. Just as well, with all this talk of another bloody war brewing.

And what about her? Stella's fingers curled around the key she had picked up on her way to the court that morning and a satisfied grin stretched across her face. Stella Smee – the East End's newest portrait photographer, a business proprietress, no less, with a smart new studio to her name! Stella could still scarcely believe it, but deep down, she knew she had earned the right to her new beginning. All the Wedding Girls had, in fact! And with that wonderful realization, Stella pulled her coat tightly around her and hurried to catch up with her friends.

Epilogue

EAST LONDON ADVERTISER

Monday, 5 April 1937

The brilliant sunshine made a pretty scene last Thursday, 1 April, when the wedding was solemnized of Miss Kitty Moloney, daughter of the late George and Betty Moloney of Bethnal Green, to Mr Harry Richardson, son of William and Agnes Richardson of Poplar, at St John Church, Bethnal Green. The Rev. Reginald French officiated and during the touching service the congregation sung the hymn 'Love Divine'.

The bride, who was given away by Mr Herbert Taylor, former proprietor of Herbie Taylor & Sons, wore a most becoming dress of fitted lace with a sweeping fishtail train and a hand-embroidered ten-yard veil topped with a coronet of orange blossom, made for her by her former employer, renowned wedding dress seamstress, Gladys Taylor of Green Street, Bethnal Green. She carried a simple bouquet of tea roses and lily of the valley.

She was attended by five bridesmaids: two ladies-in-waiting, Miss Winifred Docker and Miss Stella Smee;

and three younger maids, Misses Sylvie, Betty and Bertha Docker. They formed an enchanting picture, in gowns of lilac silk, topped with large shady picture hats and bouquets of mauve tulips. Flowers supplied by Flora of Roman Road and wedding carriages by Messrs Jacobs & Sons of Mile End Road.

Bridal portraits were taken at Bethnal Green's newest photographic establishment, Herbie Taylor & Daughter, formerly of Green Street and now under new management, before the entire wedding party retired to the home of Mr and Mrs Taylor in Shipton Street, Bethnal Green. Many friends and local tradesmen were present and showered the couple with confetti as they later departed for their honeymoon, which is to be spent touring the West Country. The bride travelled in an oatmeal-coloured two-piece, trimmed with dark brown. There were summer ermine cuffs on a short swagger coat.

On their return, the newlyweds will take up residence in their new home on the Becontree Estate, Dagenham. The couple received many handsome gifts, including an eiderdown and an unusual Singer sewing machine, which was once owned by the groom's late mother.

*

Stella had prided herself on never shedding so much as a single sentimental tear at a wedding, but that was before her closest friend, Kitty, got married. Rarely had she seen a bride look so radiant or in love. Her simple lace gown fitted her willowy figure like a second skin, and her dewy complexion glowed. Watching her walk into Harry's arms in the church had filled Stella with an emotion that had surprised even herself, and now, as the wedding car slid to a halt outside her photographic studio, she didn't know how much longer she could hold her tears in.

'We're here,' she said brightly, squinting against the dazzling spring sunshine. 'Say! There's quite a turnout . . . looks like every bride you ever made a dress for is waiting.'

'Why, Stella Smee, is that a tear in your eye?' teased Winnie.

'Yeah, but don't tell no one,' she smiled, tweaking Kitty's chin. 'Or else we'll start this one off and I don't want the first bride I photograph to be a soggy mess.'

As the girls waited for the second automobile, carrying Herbie and the bridesmaids, they took a moment to compose themselves.

'Oh, Stella,' Kitty gushed, as she gazed out the car window at the crowded street outside. 'The studio looks smashing. You must've worked round the clock to get it finished for today. Are you quite sure you don't mind taking our photographs?'

'Yeah,' chipped in Harry. 'You don't hear of too many weddings where the bridesmaid ends up taking the wedding portrait!'

'Quite sure,' Stella insisted. 'Over my dead body am I letting a rival photographer take your wedding photographs. Besides, it's fitting, don'cha think, to have my oldest friend as my first sitter.'

With that they all stared out at the entrance to Herbie Taylor & Daughter, number 168 Bethnal Green Road. A horizontal band of glass wrapped the gleaming white facade, with the name proudly lit up in neon lights. It was definitely a case of out with the old and in with the new. Gone were the mahogany pillars, the fussy lace antimacassar and the heavy velvet drapes. Stella had whitewashed the interior, opting instead for a clean, uncluttered look with striking lighting to showcase brides to their absolute best. She had so many plans to drum up new business, her head was whirling with them all. A poster framed in the window announced an upcoming Bonny Baby show, alongside a search for Bethnal Green's Bride of the Year.

Above all, though, she wanted to be known for stylish weddings in a modern studio. She was determined to do things her way, to photograph women the way she knew they wanted to look. Just because she was located in the poorer quarter, didn't mean the working classes couldn't hold their heads up high. The East End had a long tradition of putting on the glamour, even if it was bought in weekly instalments, or paid for by a club, she thought with a wry smile.

'It's queer, isn't it?' Winnie remarked, pulling her back from her wonderings. 'That of all the people who were desperate to leave the East End this time last year, you should be the one to stay, Stell.'

'I suppose so,' she replied thoughtfully. 'But it was all the things we went through that made me realize: I belong here. The East End runs right through me, like a stick of rock.'

'You don't hate us for leaving, do you?' Kitty asked. 'You know I'll be back from Becontree to visit every weekend with my brood of ten nippers,' she added with a wink at Harry.

'Steady on, sweetheart,' Harry grinned, 'we only got spliced ten minutes ago.'

'How could I hate you?' Stella smiled, squeezing Kitty's hand reassuringly. 'Everything happens for a reason. You and Harry want to do better by your children when they start arriving, I get that.' She turned to Winnie.

'And you and Treacle deserve a fresh start after everything you've been through. When are you planning on leaving for Hampshire, anyhow?'

'Straight after the wedding next month,' Winnie replied. 'We've got heaps to arrange, not least new schools for the girls, but Mum's already lined herself up a job in a fish-and-chip shop. We'll probably be back pretty soon, mind you. Mum's got to sign her divorce papers and I want to make sure I'm there for my father's court case.'

'Both of them?' Kitty ventured.

Winnie nodded, checking her lipstick in a compact before snapping it shut.

'Yep. I want to make certain I'm there to see that man locked up and the key thrown in the Thames, with any luck.'

It was common knowledge that Tommy Docker had been arrested shortly after Treacle's trial on a charge of bigamy, for marrying Ada Elms when he was still married to Winnie's mum. What had come as more of a shock to Stella and the girls was his involvement in the fire.

It was Herbie's police inspector pal who had tipped them off that Tommy had also been charged in connection with the fire down Green Street the previous October. The same fire which had so nearly cost Stella and Herbie their lives, to say nothing of their livelihood. The police had picked up a man wanted in connection with the fire and, under

Interrogation, he had cracked and confessed, admitting that the man with him, the driver of the car that had clipped Stella, was none other than Tommy Docker. It had been so dark that night, and Tommy's face obscured with a scarf, but Stella could have kicked herself for not recognizing him.

'Why do you think he did it?' Kitty asked, her pale blue eyes darkening under her orange blossom headdress.

'Why does someone as disturbed as my father do anything?' Winnie shrugged.

'Probably under orders from the blackshirt mob, either to make it look like the BUF were victims, so that the anti-fascists got the blame, or an insurance job,' Harry remarked. 'It'll all come out at the trial, I'm sure.'

'Look here, girls, let's not ruin the moment with all this chat,' Stella scolded. '*This* is a happy day. *This* is the day our Kitty's waited for all her life.'

Kitty smiled wistfully and thought back privately to the vow she had made to herself outside a snowy Westminster church. She had come a long way from that knock-kneed fourteen-year-old, trembling in the crowds. She was a woman now. A wife.

'Stella's right,' Winnie declared. You are the most beautiful bride the East End has ever seen, so come on, let's let everyone take a look at you.'

'She's a pocket Venus,' agreed Harry, gazing at his wife like a man who couldn't believe his luck.

'Like something out of a Hollywood picture,' Winnie nodded. 'At least as lovely as our new Queen.'

'Behave,' Kitty said with a smile. 'I hardly think a few fish-paste sarnies and a knees-up at Gladys's is putting me in the same league as royalty.'

'Bet your wedding's going to be a whole lot more fun than their coronation, mind,' Stella shot back, thinking how at that precise moment there was nowhere on earth she would rather be than the East End.

''Alf a mo',' Winnie exclaimed, placing her hand on Kitty's arm as she moved to open the car door. 'I nearly forgot.'

She glanced over at Stella and gestured to the pale blue satin pouch in her lap.

'My days!' Stella gasped, clamping her hand to her mouth. 'Call ourselves the Wedding Girls, honestly.'

From out of the bag she pulled a silver threepenny bit and a gold brooch belonging to Gladys.

'Walk on sixpence,' Winnie said softly, as she removed the coin from the pouch and tucked it gently into Kitty's shoe.

'. . . dream on gold,' Stella murmured, picking up the old rhyme as she pressed the brooch into Kitty's hand.

'Two hearts together,' the girls chanted in unison, 'now your story unfolds.'

It was too much and Kitty's blue eyes brimmed over.

'Oh girls, I'll treasure both,' she wept, her hand finding Harry's and squeezing it tight. 'This does feel like the start of a whole new chapter.'

'Good,' Winnie beamed, throwing open the car door. 'Now can we celebrate?'

'They're here!' yelled a voice in the crowd, and out tore the figure of Gladys, no longer Tingle but Taylor, since her marriage the previous month to Herbie. The elderly matriarch was resplendent in a grey squirrel fur coat with an orchid pinned to the front, and was beaming proudly in a cloud of attar of roses.

'Stand back, everyone, let the bride through!' she ordered at the top of her voice.

And as Kitty and Harry weaved their way through the eager throng of well-wishers, amid clouds of confetti and cries of good luck, the tears that Stella had struggled to hold in finally broke free.

The Cable Street Girls

The Battle of Cable Street was a defining moment in the history of the East End. The tremendous turnout of ordinary men and women who prevented Oswald Mosley and his blackshirts from marching through their neighbourhoods was celebrated as a great victory for anti-fascism.

The sunny Sunday, where estimated crowds of up to 300,000 turned up at Gardiner's Corner and Cable Street to defend their streets with fierce chants of 'They Shall Not Pass!' dealt a crushing blow to the British Union of Fascists.

The battle was not with Mosley and his blackshirts that day, but between the people and the police, 7,000 of them, to be precise, including the entire mounted division, whose task it was to act as a protective shield and secure Mosley's passage through the East End.

The sights must have been extraordinary. Huge crowds singing and cheering, fierce fighting on the blockades, police on horseback charging at the crowds and, the sight which intrigued me most: women rolling up their sleeves and getting stuck in! In narrow Cable Street, housewives hurled the contents of their chamber pots down onto policemen's heads and helped to man the barricades. For that day only, men and women were on an equal footing.

The very next day, a humiliated Mosley left for Germany, where he married Diana Mitford at Goebbels' house with Hitler as a guest. Three months later, on 1 January 1937, the Public Order Act became law, banning the wearing of political uniforms and strengthening the law on marches, assemblies and the use of insulting language to provoke a breach of the peace.

When war broke out, Oswald and Diana Mosley were interned and they remained in prison, then under house arrest, for the remainder of it. Mosley's right-hand man, William Joyce, later became known to the world as the notorious Nazi propaganda broadcaster, Lord Haw-Haw.

History recounts their crimes, but back in 1936, in the teeming tenements of Whitechapel and Stepney, working-class folk had to fight the authorities in order to defend their streets against goose-stepping fascists!

Fast-forward eighty years and the lessons learnt that day seem as fresh and relevant now as they did back then. The story stands as a spine-tingling example of solidarity in the face of prejudice and hatred.

When I decided to feature the Battle of Cable Street in *The Wedding Girls*, I knew I could only bring that day to life by speaking to the women who turned out on the day. Archives and written accounts are all well and good, but where's the emotion, the colour and the small detail, which only a voice of wisdom can bring to the page?

Enquiries on East End Facebook groups brought interesting memories.

'My father-in-law Lew from Hackney got stuck in at the battle. He later became a staff sergeant in the British Army and fought all the way through to Germany's borders. Not bad for a boy who grew up with no shoes,' said Freddie.

Patricia proudly recalls her grandfather's reason for turning up to stop the blackshirts. 'Those men stood up for others as a matter of principle and belief. True Gentlemen. Working-class winners.'

Deborah's memories run even deeper. 'Granddad was a communist. He had a club foot, polio damage in both legs, and lost part of his chest in an operation to save him when he contracted anthrax from working at the docks. He was a boxer, a very successful one. During the Cable Street riots he helped to rescue some documents from the police station. According to my nan, he rescued his own file, stamped "Subversive". His name was John James Gentleman. His boxing name was "the Hackney Hammer". He is the only disabled boxer that I have ever known to fight as able-bodied. I am immensely proud of him.'

Just fascinating – how I would have loved to have interviewed the Hackney Hammer! But what of the *women* who were there on the day? When I asked around the East End, my questions were met with a lot of head-shaking and sucking in of breath.

'Unlikely you'll find any woman who could remember that day still alive,' remarked a librarian. Happily, I can report he was wrong. For when I visited a Jewish community centre in Stepney, I stumbled into a treasure trove of memories. The place was filled with indomitable women who were not only there on the day, but marched shoulder to shoulder alongside the men.

'My name's Marie,' grinned a woman with jet-black hair and bone-white teeth, her quick eyes gleaming. 'I can tell you a few stories about the East End. There's loads of women here who remember Stepney as it used to be. There's Beatrice and Millie, they're ninety-nine, I'm ninety-four – the young one,' she added with a playful wink, revealing a tenacious spirit. 'I work here, volunteering twice a week, and I still get up at half past six for my Saturday job.'

'Do you think you'll ever give up work?' I ventured.

'Give up work?' she scoffed. 'Why? I'm still young.'

With that, the nonagenarian bustled off and I scurried after her in hot pursuit. On our way to the 'memory room', a beautifully soothing room entirely furnished in 1930s style, complete with art deco mirrors and a wireless, we passed a dartboard with a photograph of Justin Bieber's face skewered to it.

I stopped and stared in disbelief. 'What, you think we sit around playing bridge all day?' said Marie with a gleeful cackle.

One hour later I was surrounded by women telling me the most remarkable, sad, funny and heart-wrenching stories, not just about the battle against fascism, but also about the grinding poverty of the Depression years, the hardships of which remained indelibly inked into their minds.

The memories laid down in childhood are so vivid, and in an uncertain world they remain a refuge to return to. The narrow East End streets these women roamed through in the 1930s may have been hard and brutal, but they also contained within them a golden world of community and camaraderie.

It is often the quiet voices of history that are the most revealing. These women and their unassuming thoughts and feelings tell us so much about how difficult, but also how rewarding it was to be a woman in pre-war Britain. Make no mistake: the East End, in common with all working-class communities, was a fiercely matriarchal society. Women in cross-over aprons and button-down boots were the beating heart of the East End. They were the ones who ruled the cobbles, kept the children fed, birthed the babies and laid out the dead. And those same women, as these stories go to prove, put the backbone into the Battle of Cable Street.

I came away from that visit on a high because, for me, history had just burst into life. The characters of Stella, Kitty, Winnie, Gladys and Auntie are inspired by these women and their ordinary, yet oh-so-extraordinary lives.

Beatrice, ninety-nine[*]

As a young woman living in the East End in the 1930s, I was no stranger to politics. I grew up watching the fascists marching and the street corner orators on their soapboxes. I was a lousy dancer, so I got involved in politics instead; it was real and raw to me.

At nineteen years of age, I wasn't allowed to vote, but I still had to defend myself against the fascist blackshirts.

'Go home, Jew,' they would shout. 'I am home,' I'd yell back. Then they would chase me, try and lash me with their big belt buckles. They never caught me, mind. I could run faster.

When the call came to stop Mosley and his blackshirts marching through the East End, did I turn out? Course I did. My mate Ginnie was charged through a plate-glass window at Gardiner's Corner by a mounted policeman. We

---

[*] All ages correct as of time of interview

got her bandaged up and then we returned to Cable Street to continue the battle.

I'll never forget the roar of the crowds or the celebration songs that went on long into the night when we learnt that we had forced Mosley and his thugs to turn back.

I also went to the Albert Hall when they [the BUF] had a meeting there and it was bloody murders. Unity Mitford was there and they was chased into Hyde Park by the anti-fascists. After that, I marched a lot and I held my head up high. I still do today.

Millie, ninety-eight

In the 1930s the Depression hit the East End hard. Men fighting down the docks for work, my mum having to ask for food on trust from shopkeepers, me sleeping four to a bed with my siblings. There was no peace anywhere. Unless you count the food that is – a little piece of this, a tiny piece of that!

We had it terrible: lived in one room, five of us at one time. You never got help like you do now. Never. I think we ended up with tickets, like bread tickets, that saved us from starvation some days, but we were always hand-to-mouth. My mum made cigarettes from home and my dad travelled to markets all round England looking for things to sell.

I left school at fourteen and went straight to work; which was a little better. I started with eight shillings a week, sweeping up in the factory, and my brother, God rest his soul, Friday afternoon, when we got paid, used to wait for me outside the factory to take the envelope back to my mother. My eight shillings a week bought the family food, and a little more time.

Against all this we had the blackshirts constantly causing trouble, beating up the young Jewish men and spreading lies that Jews were making all the money. What money? We never saw any!

Mari

I come from eight generations of proud Stepney women. My mum, Alice, was a butcher; tough, she was. She could butcher a lamb in under a minute. Growing up, we was never allowed to cry.

I was a saucy mare back then, always giving people lip. If the door went and someone was complaining about me:

'Your Mari hit my daughter, ain't you gonna hit her?'

'Not to please you I won't,' she'd reply.

The door would shut and she'd clump me!

She and my nan had strict morals, mind you. They taught me five things that have stayed with me all my life. Never borrow money. Work hard. Have a secret running-away fund. Speak the truth. And if you lose your way, never ask a copper or a priest the way, ask a tramp, and then give him a couple of bob for a cup of tea.

When I left school aged fourteen, I got a job as a machinist, working for Jewish firms in the East End. They treated me decent and paid me well. When my cousin, a famous boxer, joined the blackshirts, there were murders. Nan went mental. Ripped the shirt clean off his back.

I was told by Mum to stay indoors on the day of the Battle. Did I listen? Course not. You wouldn't believe the sights. Police and horses going into people, screaming and hollering. It was frightening and I didn't stick around for long.

My nan and mum loved the Jews. Good families with a strong work ethic. I've never been racist. I don't care if you're black, white, purple or green. I'll talk to anyone. The East End is made up of all colours and creeds, and I'm proud to still live in Stepney.

Marie, ninety-four

When the Battle of Cable Street broke out I was living in an old weavers' house down Folgate Street, in Bishopsgate, East London. I was fourteen years old and went along with my younger brother, Morry. That might seem young to some to get involved in a huge demonstration like that, but back then, fourteen wasn't considered young. I wasn't a girl, I was a woman, working 8 a.m. until 7 p.m. in a hat-making factory, and paying my way.

On the day it was thrilling, exciting, unreal, to hear the roars and screams of the crowd. I wasn't frightened, not even when I saw the police charging us with their horses. I was squashed up in the crowds and Morry scrambled up onto a window ledge to get a better view.

History was made that day and we knew we were witnessing something extraordinary. Mind you, it's the only riot I've participated in.

Want to hear something funny? That house I lived in

down Folgate Street is now a plush hotel where rooms cost £500 a night to stay in. My dad, who was a timber merchant, paid £1 a week in the 1930s, and even that was considered pricey back then. He'd be turning in his grave if he knew the price of his old house!

*

The following memories are reproduced with kind permission of the Cable Street Group and taken from *Battle of Cable Street 1936*:

Julie, deceased

The only thing I didn't approve of was when the police came down the street on their horses and they started throwing marbles underfoot. Perhaps I was stupid, perhaps I was wrong, but I didn't approve of that. The horses fell but they weren't hurt. When the police came down on horses, you see, we thought that Mosley was going to march after them, but they didn't.

People were throwing bedding, tables, chairs, everything out of the window to build the barricades. It was terrific to watch. Something you could never forget. I can remember the old girls with their aprons on and the men's caps that they used to wear in those days with shawls round their shoulders and glory on their faces. I'd like to be able to do a picture.

Joyce, deceased

On 4th October, I was twelve years old. It has been described as non-violent but I did not find it so. The violence was not coming from us. But for too many girls it was an absolute terror. The police first tried just to clear the roadway so that the traffic could get through. They were pushing us onto Gardiner's window. There were people going straight through plate glass windows. There were horses coming straight into the crowd, and the police were just hitting anyone indiscriminately. We never saw a fascist all that day. We were fighting the police. They were just hitting everyone, there were women going down under the horses' hooves. Absolute terror.

Wedding Traditions

Everyone loves a wedding-day tradition, but where do they come from?

Bread or cake has been part of celebration foods since medieval times – the bride and groom had to try to kiss over the pile of cakes to guarantee their future prosperity. But the traditional wedding cake as we now know it originated at the wedding of Prince Leopold, Duke of Albany, in 1882. And when Queen Victoria used white icing on her 1840 wedding cake, it gained a whole new title – royal icing.

The tradition of 'Best Man' originates from Anglo–Saxon England. Then, a groom would take along his most trusted and strongest friend to help him fight any resistance from the bride's family.

The popular expression 'Tying the knot' comes from the pagan tradition of Hand Fasting (a historical term for 'betrothal' or 'wedding'), in which the bride and groom

would have their hands tied with cord or ribbon for the ceremony to symbolize the union.

'Wedding ring finger' – the ancient Greeks believed that there was a vein that connected this finger directly to the heart. Technically, all veins lead to the heart, but it's a lovely thought and a worldwide tradition.

Brides in Roman times wore veils to ward off evil spirits. We have the Victorians to thank for heavy, long white ones; these came into vogue in the 1860s. The more ostentatious the veil, the bigger the status symbol.

When Queen Victoria married Prince Albert in 1840, she wore white because it was the colour of her favourite lace. Victoria set the trend for brides in the future, helped by the colour's association with purity – and the fact that white was a status symbol – only the wealthy could afford to have it washed!

'Something old, something new, something borrowed, some-thing blue and a silver sixpence in your shoe,' is a much-loved rhyme which dates back years, but brides still cherish today.

The 'Wedding Favour' was started by European nobility in the sixteenth century. They would hand out small boxes of

sugar — an expensive and rare delicacy at the time — as a show of wealth and to thank guests for attending. As sugar became more commonplace, it was succeeded by sugar-coated almonds (the traditional haul of five represents health, wealth, happiness, fertility and a long life).

The tradition of having bridesmaids started in Roman times, when brides would have ten witnesses dressed identically to them. The idea was that the bridesmaids would act as decoys to evil spirits trying to harm the bride. The lookalikes were also supposed to give the bride extra protection, should a rejected suitor try to kidnap her.

In Britain, throwing grains of rice at newlyweds goes back to pagan weddings, when it was seen as a symbol of fertility. It was the Victorians who first used shredded paper. And the word 'confetti' is an Italian word used for a type of sugared almond tossed into the air during special occasions.

It is traditional and thought to be good luck for the bride to throw her wedding bouquet backwards over her shoulder towards the guests when she leaves for the honeymoon. The one who catches it is supposed to be the next one married.

It is good luck for the groom not to see the dress before the wedding day and considered even luckier if he doesn't turn around as the bride walks down the aisle.

Wedding Traditions That Haven't Stood The Test Of Time . . .

It was always thought that the groom carrying the bride over the threshold protected her from any evil spirits lurking in their new home, but sadly this romantic tradition has all but died out.

If the bride stepped on the groom's feet, she was supposed to have the upper hand in the marriage; likewise, she would always be considered the dominant partner if she was the first one to make a purchase after the wedding.

Having a kiss from a chimney sweep might not be the number one priority for most brides leaving the church or registry office nowadays, but, believe it or not, it used to be considered extremely good luck to receive the Kiss of Luck from a sweep. Legend has it that when King George II's carriage horses bolted, the only person who attempted to stop them was a brave chimney sweep. By royal decree, the King proclaimed that all sweeps were bearers of good luck.

Traditionally, it was considered better for a couple to exchange vows as the clock's minute hand was ascending towards heaven, i.e. upwards, though this isn't strictly observed any longer.

Legend says single women will dream of their future husbands if they sleep with a slice of wedding cake under their pillows. Sounds a bit soggy, if you ask us!

The beautiful tradition of giving the newlyweds a piece of coal, so they might have warmth, a bar of soap, so that they may stay clean, and salt, so that they may always have food, has sadly fallen by the wayside.

The tradition of giving a wooden spoon dates back many years and was supposed to help the new bride in producing the best meals for her husband. A rolling pin is another alternative, although whether that's to help with baking, or keep the husband under control, we're not sure.

The tradition of throwing coins to crowds of children assembled outside the church – known as the 'wedding day scramble' – in order to share wealth and prosperity, is a lovely one, but not widely in use any longer.

Rebecca Lee-Wale of Daisy Chain Celebrants

If you've enjoyed *The Wedding Girls*, don't miss more books by Kate Thompson . . .

Secrets of the Singer Girls

1942. Sixteen-year-old Poppy Percival turns up at the gates of Trout's clothing factory in Bethnal Green with no idea what her new life might have in store. There to start work as a seamstress, and struggling to get to grips with the noise, dirt and devastation of East London, Poppy can't help but miss the quiet countryside of home. But Poppy harbours a dark secret – one that wrenched her away from all she knew and from which she is still suffering . . .

And Poppy's not the only one with a secret. Each of her new friends at the factory is hiding something painful. Vera Shadwell, the forelady, has had a hard life with scars both visible and concealed; her sister Daisy has romantic notions that could get her in trouble; and Sal Fowler, a hardworking mother who worries about her two evacuated boys for good reason. Bound by ties of friendship, loyalty and family, the devastating events of the war will throw each of their lives into turmoil, but also bring these women closer to each other than they could ever have imagined.

'A poignant and moving story of the friendship of women during wartime Britain' **Val Wood**

Secrets of the Sewing Bee

Orphan Flossy Brown arrives at Trout's garment factory in Bethnal Green amidst the uncertainty of the Second World War. In 1940s London, each cobbled street is strewn with ghosts of soldiers past, all struggling to make ends meet. For the women of the East End, their battles are on the home front.

Flossy is quickly embraced by the colourful mix of characters working at Trout's, who have turned their sewing expertise to vital war work. They fast become the family that Flossy has always longed for. Dolly Doolaney, darling of the East End, and infamous tea lady, gives her a particularly warm welcome and helps Flossy settle into wartime life.

Things aren't so easy for Peggy Piper, another new recruit at the factory. She's used to the high life working as a nippie in the West End, and is not best pleased to find herself bent over a sewing machine. But war has the ability to break down all sorts of class barriers, and soon Peggy finds the generosity and spirit of her fellow workers difficult to resist.

Dolly sets up a sewing circle and the ladies at Trout's play their part in defending the frontline as they arm themselves with their needles and set about stitching their way to victory. But as the full force of the Blitz hits London, the sewing bee are forced to shelter in the underground tube stations on a nightly basis.

In such close quarters, can Dolly manage to contain the secret that binds them all? And how will Peggy and Flossy cope as their lives are shaped and moved by forces outside of their control?

Acknowledgements

With grateful thanks to:

My agent Kate Burke at Diane Banks Literary Associates and Victoria Hughes-Williams – and the rest of the wonderful team at Pan Macmillan – for their unfailing enthusiasm, support and guidance. I consider myself very lucky to work with such a talented bunch of people.

Terri Coates, consultant midwife on *Call the Midwife*, for being such a stickler for period detail.

Max Levitas, 101-year-old veteran of the Battle of Cable Street, for bringing that day to life for me.

David Rosenberg for answering my many questions on the Battle of Cable Street and showing me where history was made.

Rachel Kolsky for taking me back in time to the 1930s with her tour of the Jewish East End.

Susan Prosser for her eagle eye and constant support.

Maggie Lee-Roberts for telling the oh-so-heart-wrenching story of her parents' wedding and allowing me to use it as inspiration for Joyce, Billy and Alan's story.

Edwina Ehrman, Curator of Textiles and Fashion at the Victoria and Albert Museum, for lending me books and allowing me to pick her brains.

Beatrice Behlen, Senior Curator of Fashion & Decorative Arts at the Museum of London, for showing me dress after beautiful wedding dress.

Martin Pel, Curator of Costume at The Royal Pavilion, Brighton Museum, for showing me Nancy Beaton's stunning wedding dress and sharing his knowledge of historical dress.

Marilyne from Halfpenny London for allowing me into the world of a seamstress.

Glennys Illand for sharing her stories of life as an East End seamstress.

John Lucarotti for his legal-eagle eye.

Professor Richard Hobbs for his eye-opening chat on East End crime and fascism.

Dr Robin Philpott, FRCPsych, Emeritus Consultant in Old Age Psychiatry, Liverpool, for helping me with the storyline of Kitty's father.

Colin Harding, Curator of Photographs & Photographic Technology at the National Media Museum, for sharing his knowledge of 1930s photography.

Sarah Ainslie for inviting me into her gem of a studio.

Hellen Martin for showing me her grandfather William Whiffin's photography and answering my many questions.

Michael Greisman for talking to me about his research for *Vintage Glamour in London's East End*. It was picking up this glorious book and reading about the life of Jewish photographer Boris Bennett and his influential role as a photographer in the East End that inspired me to think about setting a novel in a photographic portrait studio and the role of aspirational glamour in 1930s East End.

Dr Fiona Haughey, Archaeologist, for talking to me about

mudlarking (and making my son Ronnie's day by showing him a mammoth's tooth).

And last, but by no means least, to the following East End community centres for kindly allowing me to gatecrash their groups and speak with all the fabulous women who attend:

Carol and all at the East London Pension Club at St James the Less Parish Church in Bethnal Green.

Vince and all at the Stepney Jewish Community Centre.

Sister Christine Frost and all at the St Matthias Community Centre in Poplar.

Vicky and all at St Hilda's East Community Centre in Club Row.

*

Every photo tells a story, what's yours?
If you would like to share the story of a treasured
family wedding photo, please email:
katharinethompson82@gmail.com
or message me at
https://www.facebook.com/KateThompsonAuthor/

Further Reading

Books and sources I have found helpful:

Tower Hamlets Local History Library & Archives

The Imperial War Museum

Bishopsgate Institute

The Royal London Hospital, Bart's Hospital Trust Archives

Vintage Glamour in London's East End, curated by Michael Greisman, assisted by Frank Harris (Hoxton Mini Press, 2014)

Street of Tall People, Alan Gibbons (Five Leaves Publications, 2011)

Battle for the East End, David Rosenberg (Five Leaves Publications, 2011)

Battle of Cable Street 1936, The Cable Street Group (Five Leaves Publications, 2011)

Jew Boy, Simon Blumenfeld (Lawrence & Wishart, 1935)

The Thirties: An Intimate History, Juliet Gardiner (Harper Press, 2011)

1930s Britain, Robert Pearce (Shire Living Histories, 2012)

London Jews and British Communism 1935–1945, Henry Felix Srebrnik (Vallentine Mitchell & Co Ltd, 1995)

Becoming a Woman: And Other Essays in 19th and 20th Century Feminist History, Sally Alexander (Virago, 1994)

Metropolis: Histories and Representations of London Since 1800, David Feldman and Gareth Stedman Jones (Law Book Co of Australasia, 1989)

The London Look: Fashion from Street to Catwalk, Edwina Ehrman (Yale University Press in association with the Museum of London, 2004)

Married in the Movies, edited by Kyle Roderick (Collins Publishers, 1994)

Hollywood Gets Married, Sandy Schreier (Clarkson Potter, 2002)

A Dictionary of Catch Phrases from the Sixteenth Century to the Present Day, Eric Partridge, edited by Paul Beale (Routledge, 1985)